The Courtyard

Marcia Willett

Thomas Dunne Books

St. Martin's Griffin 〰 New York

THOMAS DUNNE BOOKS.
An imprint of St. Martin's Press.

www.thomasdunnebooks.com
www.stmartins.com

Library of Congress Cataloging-in-Publication Data

Willett, Marcia.
    The courtyard / Marcia Willett.—1st U.S. ed.
        p.   cm.
    ISBN-13: 978-0-312-30668-7
    ISBN-10: 0-312-30668-7
  1. Real estate development—England—Fiction.   2.
Recessions—Fiction.   3. Neighbors—Fiction.   4. Female
friendship—Fiction.   5. Nineteen eighties—Fiction.   6.
England—Fiction.   I. Title.
    PR6073.I4235C68   2007
    823'.914—dc22

                                            200702145

First published in Great Britain by Headline Book Publishing,
a division of Hodder Headline PLC

First U.S. Edition: October 2007

10 9 8 7 6 5 4 3 2 1

To Charles

One

1988

AUGUSTA MERTON ORDERED A pot of tea, refused cakes with a firm shake of the head and settled in her chair with the sensation that she was indulging in a great luxury. It was so long since she had allowed herself anything beyond absolute necessities that it seemed almost decadent to be sitting here in the quiet wood-panelled tea-room, with its comfortable Windsor chairs and pretty flowered china, watching the busy shoppers beyond the window hurrying along in the blowy golden April afternoon. She smiled at the waitress who unloaded the tea things onto the table, glanced a little anxiously at the bill which was tucked under the water jug and patted at her gingery grey hair which was twisted back into a wispy knot. Her eyes kept straying to her belongings and to one bag in particular and, succumbing at last to temptation, she picked up the plastic carrier and peeped inside before depositing it on the chair beside her with a sigh. She noticed with pleasure that there was a tea-strainer placed in a slop bowl – Gussie disliked tea bags – and, giving the contents of the pot a stir, she gazed about her as she waited for the tea to draw. At the next table a striking-looking young woman was drinking coffee. She had an exhausted, flattened look about her as if even the act of raising the cup to her lips were almost too much for her. She looked faintly familiar and, catching her eye, Gussie smiled encouragingly.

Nell Woodward was surprised out of her weariness by the quality of understanding in Gussie's smile. It seemed that this stranger had grasped the fact of her inability to deal with life at the moment and was offering both sympathy and strength. Well, she was certainly tired. As a naval wife of ten years' standing Nell had done her share of moving house but now she realised that it was even more difficult to cope when one's heart and head were absolutely set against the move. During those ten years she had trailed from Gosport to Faslane, from Faslane to Chatham and then back again to Gosport with only the minimum of fuss. It was to be expected if you married a naval man: it was all part of the job. You may not want to go, you might hate the married quarter but there would probably be old friends to meet up with and the framework of the Navy was in the background to support you. The move to Bristol had been something else again. John's decision to leave the Navy was, in Nell's opinion, nothing short of madness. What if he *had* been passed over? He'd still had a worthwhile job, with a good salary, amongst people he knew. Now they were living in a rented flat in Bristol with nearly all his gratuity used up to buy a partnership in a friend's estate agency. What did John know about selling houses? Nell felt the now familiar thrill of anxiety at the thought of their future. She drank some more coffee knowing that she must pull herself together and go back to finish the unpacking. The flat still looked like a furniture depository despite the fact that they had been in now for more than two weeks. Nevertheless Nell sat on, unable to find the energy or willpower to move.

Gussie began to pour tea. Her thoughts, distracted for a moment by Nell whom she simply couldn't place, returned to the contents of the plastic bag. Of course, paisley was always suitable and if the hem were to be let down . . . Her mind wandered a little as she sipped. How good it was of Henry to remember his elderly second cousin and invite her to his wedding. So kind. And an invitation to stay the weekend at Nethercombe. It would be wonderful to see the old place again. It must be years, oh at least fifteen, since she'd been there. Henry's mother, her cousin Louisa, had been alive then. Now, Louisa and her husband James were both gone and Henry had inherited

Nethercombe Court with its farmland and its famous Devon Red herds. And now he was to be married.

Gussie set her cup back in its saucer and her face fell into its usual pattern of worried lines: a furrow between the sandy brows, a gathering and puckering around the lips. It was becoming more and more difficult to live on her tiny pension and her small capital was nearly all gone. She had already moved from the large airy flat, near the Clifton Suspension Bridge and just a step from the Downs, to a smaller apartment in Tyndalls Park Road. Her heart gave a frightened bump and her hand shook a little as she poured her second cup of tea. Really, she shouldn't be here. A pot of tea or a cup of coffee in a café was such a luxury but the arrival of the invitation and the luck of finding the dress, combined with the idea of the wedding, had been so exciting that a little celebration seemed in order. The dress had been an extravagance, no doubt about it, but certain standards must be maintained and she couldn't go to dear Henry's wedding in her old blue. She mustn't let him down. If she had to make one or two sacrifices during the next few weeks it would be worth it.

'Soldier's daughter, soldier's sister,' she reminded herself, straightening her thin shoulders more firmly, and smiled again at Nell.

Something in the old lady's movement pierced the fog of Nell's exhaustion and touched her heart. She felt that some conversation was expected of her although she longed to remain cocooned within the peace of her isolation.

'Shopping's so tiring,' she said at random, too tired to think of an original remark. 'Unless, of course, one's buying something special.'

'Buying something new to wear is certainly a treat.' Gussie felt an overwhelming need to share her own excitement with another woman. 'I've been invited to my cousin's wedding and I've just bought myself a new dress.'

'How wonderful.' Nell responded instinctively to Gussie's barely repressed happiness. 'What sort of dress?'

'Well . . .' Gussie eyed the bag with a mixture of pleasure and anxiety. 'I think it's quite suitable, given my age. It's a paisley. Navy blue.'

'Sounds just the thing,' said Nell encouragingly, noticing that the bag bore no shop name and had a well-used look. She also noticed, without appearing to, Gussie's threadbare, if well-cared-for, appearance. 'May I see it?'

Flushed and a little embarrassed, Gussie shook the dress free and displayed it rather shyly.

'Not too fussy, you see. But smart.' She looked anxiously at Nell. 'Will it do, d'you think?'

'I think it's just right.' Nell's suspicion was confirmed. The dress was secondhand but it had been expensive once and its classic cut would stand the test of time. 'The colour will be very flattering on you. Shall you wear a hat?'

The worried look returned as Gussie carefully folded the dress and returned it to its bag.

'That's rather a problem,' she admitted. 'My felt's a little heavy for a May wedding but I'm afraid it will simply have to do.'

'I was just wondering,' Nell listened to her own voice in surprise, 'I've got a navy-blue straw. You'd be most welcome . . .'

It must be exhaustion, she thought. Getting involved and offering to lend a hat to a complete stranger! I'm going mad. Maybe she doesn't live round here . . .

But Gussie was looking at her in delight and gratitude and Nell found herself exchanging names and addresses and arranging for Gussie to come for coffee and a hat-trying session.

What have I done? she asked herself as she collected her things and headed for the door. What made me do such a stupid thing? And the flat's such a mess. Oh hell!

Gussie watched her go before squeezing a third cup of tea from the pot. She felt quite exhilarated by their exchange. She had made a new friend. And a really very beautiful one. Gussie wrinkled her brow a little. Nell's name hadn't been familiar but she certainly reminded her of someone. But whom? She sipped thoughtfully and happily: a new dress, a wedding to go to and an invitation to coffee. Life could still be very good.

BACK AT THE FLAT, Nell stared around her in despair. She simply couldn't shake off this terrible lassitude, this feeling that, in leaving the Navy, John had made a terrible mistake. Yet John himself was full of optimism and was happier than he'd been for months and months. It was tremendous luck that his old friend, Martin Amory, was prepared to take him into his business and at such a time. Ever since the stock market crash the year before, people had been putting their money into property and the estate agents were enjoying the boom. The fact that John had no qualifications in this field was, apparently, unimportant and Martin and John were quite sure that they would make their fortunes.

Nell set to work, the thought of Gussie arriving for coffee the next morning spurring her on. The flat, large and pleasant though it was, was a temporary measure until they could afford to buy. After all, John was in a prime position now to find a bargain and that must be their priority. It had been with only the greatest reluctance, and after some unpleasant scenes, that Nell had finally agreed that most of the gratuity should go into Martin's business to pay for John's partnership. She held out for one proviso. Enough must be kept back to pay the fees for the next year or two at Jack's preparatory school. Nell, who feared that their passage outside the Navy may well be a rough one, was determined that their eight-year-old son should have some stability in his life. He was already happily settled at his school in Somerset and she had no intention of disrupting him any further. Without the naval grant towards the fees, and without the generous salary, Jack's schooling might be at risk and she was adamant on this point. John, relieved that she was ready to capitulate, was only too happy to agree. Even with two years' fees set aside there would be enough left to buy his partnership, pay the advance rent for the flat and have a small sum left over.

By tea-time the flat was looking more like home. Never had Nell taken so long to get herself straight. Yet the place was no worse than some of the married quarters she had lived in. In fact the furnishings were a great deal better. The few pieces of furniture that Nell had collected lovingly over the years were in the tiny cottage at Porlock Weir that she and John had bought at the end of an idyllic leave on Exmoor. How Nell loved that little retreat! Often, when John had gone to sea for months on end, she and Jack would set off in a loaded car to this beloved spot where she was happiest. At all times, the knowledge of it was a warm refuge from the storms and upheavals of life. Even as she finished Jack's bedroom, sitting his soft toys on the ugly wardrobe and setting his model tanks on the bookcase shelves with his well-read books, she was wondering whether she could escape with him at half-term for a few days at the cottage.

She was well aware that part of her dismay at the idea of John coming outside was that much of her precious privacy, her closely guarded seclusion, must be lost. She was still getting used to having John there every day; seeing him off in the morning, welcoming him home in the evening with regular meals. Many naval wives hated the loneliness of their lives with husbands away at sea, nevertheless one became used to the independence and Nell knew that she would find it hard to give it up. She had never minded the separations; rather the contrary. It was relationships and other people that she found so wearing and demanding even to the extent that, once she knew she was pregnant, she had been afraid at the thought of the responsibility of a child. The idea of a tiny, helpless human being, absolutely dependent on her, filled her with terror. Yet when Jack was born and laid on her breast, the wide blue eyes gazing unwinkingly into her own, she had felt a great rush of identification with this scrap of humanity which stifled her fears. They had become friends at once; not just as mother and son, but real friends and, as he grew, this feeling strengthened. She saw into his heart and mind, divining his psychological needs with far more accuracy than she ever recognised his physical ones. He, in his turn, sensed her need for seclusion and was able to give her a companionship that still allowed her freedom. Neither of them really thought about their relationship, they simply acted on instinct and out of their love for each other. This became doubly precious to Nell after her parents emigrated to Canada to live with her younger sister who, after several miscarriages and a difficult birth, was a semi-invalid. Nell had felt hurt and resentful. After all, Pauline had chosen to marry a Canadian and live abroad yet, at the first cry for help, they had sold up and gone and Nell had learned to fend for herself and manage without them.

Nell glanced around the bedroom, shut the door behind her and went down the long passage to the kitchen. It was time to think about supper. Gone were the happy days of solitary meals with a book propped open on the table. Boiled eggs and cheese on toast were simply not sufficient for John at the end of a long day's work. Nell sighed and tried to bring her mind to bear on supper. She attempted, without success, to visualise the contents of the fridge. First, she decided, she would make herself some coffee and perhaps that would stimulate her culinary instincts. Whilst the kettle boiled she started to put away some books, left in a pile on the kitchen table, and paused with a volume of Browning in her hand. It opened at 'Pippa Passes' and she turned the pages and began to read a little. The kettle started to sing. Presently she sank down into a chair, still reading. The kettle boiled and switched itself off. The bright spring afternoon lengthened into evening but Nell sat on, still reading.

' . . . SO I WENT STRAIGHT home,' said Gussie, 'and took down my art encyclopaedia and there you were. Dante Gabriel Rossetti's *Sibylla Palmifera*. The likeness is quite startling. Has no one ever mentioned it before? Your hair is much darker but it really is quite uncanny. I understand that he often used his wife as a model.'

'I like his sister's poetry.' Nell poured tea and ignored the pain in her heart, hoping that Gussie would be distracted and not hurt by the indirect change of subject. One other person had likened her to Rossetti's painting.

'*Goblin Market,*' mused Gussie, taking her cup. 'It's some years since I read it but I learned it at school. "For there is no friend like a sister, In calm or stormy weather." I never had a sister. I had a brother who was killed in the war. He was in the Army. A regular. So was my father. He was too old to fight in the second war but he was at the War Office in London. He and my mother were killed in the Blitz.' She sipped at her tea. 'I lost them all within a year. I was out in France driving an ambulance.'

She shook her head, more in surprise at her sudden burst of confidence than at the tragedy that she described. She wasn't given to making people a present of her history. She disapproved of self-indulgence and emotional outbursts. So did Nell who stared at her in dismay.

'I'm so sorry,' she began. And stopped not knowing what to say.

'My dear, it was forty-five years ago. I can't imagine why I should have mentioned it. This is delicious tea. Dear old Earl Grey. How amazing that your hat should fit me so well and should match with the dress. I do call that a splendid piece of luck. It really is very kind of you. I shall take great care of it.'

Nell accepted the change of subject with relief and agreed that the whole thing was providential. They talked about the coming wedding, the relative merits of flats – with and without gardens – and Nell, voluntarily, explained her naval background and John's new venture. When they finally separated, both women were surprised at how far the friendship had developed given that they each had a natural tendency to reticence. Neither felt her privacy had been violated and both felt a little glow of kinship. Nell saw the thin, angular figure out to the gate, promised to go for coffee the following week, and went back to clear up the tea things.

'My little Pre-Raphaelite . . . how's Sibylla today?'

Rupert's voice, tender and teasing, echoed in her thoughts; a ghost raised by Gussie's acute observation. Nell put the cups into the sink and wrapped her arms across her breast. Rupert: whom she had loved since she was a little girl, whose younger brother she had married when she knew Rupert would never take her seriously. Rupert: who had been her idol and who had been blown to pieces in the Falklands War. By the time he had realised that she had grown up, it had been too late. She was his brother's wife. John was so like him physically. They had been difficult to tell apart except that Rupert had all the fire, all the charm, and John was so quiet, so reserved. Was it cheating to pretend quite so often as she did that he was Rupert?

Of course it was. Nell pushed back the heavy mass of dark red hair and ran water into the sink. But John would never know that she did it. Rupert had been the clever one: brilliant at school, honours at Sandhurst, a crack regiment, knee-deep in pretty women. John had plodded behind, never quite achieving a similar standard: failing Perisher – the submariners' Commanding Officers' Qualifying Course – and then being passed over. Only Nell knew how bitter he was, how determined to redress the balance. Nell had helped to do that. To capture such beauty had been a tremendous feather in his cap. Nell felt it was a poor return for the deception that she often practised in her heart. She began to wash up, trying to still the ghosts that Gussie had raised, trying not to think of Rupert, dead. She thought of other lines written by Christina Rossetti: 'Remember me when I am gone away, Gone far away into the silent land.'

It was six years now, since he had gone into the silent land, but he still lived on in her memory and in John. And in Jack.

Nell dried the cups and saucers and put them away. John would be home soon and tonight she really must make an effort about food.

Two

HENRY MORLEY, SITTING AT his paper-strewn desk and wrestling half-heartedly with some accounts, was marvelling at the good fortune which had brought him Gillian who, by this time tomorrow, would be his wife. Although Henry loved Nethercombe, gave his every waking thought to its well-being and spent all his income on its upkeep, he couldn't believe that she was marrying him for his worldly goods. Even he, blinded by love and familiarity, could see that the gracious Georgian house needed vast sums to put it in order and the grounds needed much more time than he and Mr Ridley – his handyman and general factotum – could give to it. Yet Henry loved Nethercombe with all his heart and his whole will was bent on keeping it running as an estate, if now a very small one, and holding what was left of it intact – if dilapidated.

So what did she see in him? Running his hands through his thick brown hair, Henry shook his head, grimaced ruefully and glanced around the small, rather dark study where he dealt with the paper-work and business of the estate, trying to see it through Gillian's eyes. For himself, he wasn't too bothered about things like damp or mice. The drawing room was still fairly respectable – although Henry tended to live in the library, a cosy, panelled room, comfortably furnished – and he ate in the cheerful little breakfast room which had windows looking east and French doors that opened on to the terrace. His bedroom was so austere, cold in summer and winter alike, that Mrs Ridley had prepared the big double chamber his parents had once occupied for the young couple's return from honeymoon.

The Ridleys lived rent-free in the Lodge at the end of the avenue and Mrs Ridley cooked and cleaned and cared for Henry and the house generally. Henry paid them as much as he could and the three of them lived very happily and undemandingly together. If the Ridleys were concerned at the thought of a new mistress they were keeping it to themselves.

Henry gulped at a cup of lukewarm tea, placed by Mrs Ridley on his desk some time earlier, pushed back his chair and wandered over to the window. Digging his hands into the pockets of his disreputable old moleskin trousers he gazed out at the side lawns and the rhododendron bushes, now in full, magnificent flower.

It had been a strange courtship. He'd first met Gillian in a friend's house at a party to which he went hoping to meet a young architect called Simon Spaders. Simon lived and had his practice in Exeter but his reputation was beginning to be widely known and Henry wanted to meet him. The small, slender, blonde girl with Simon had a lively mind and a witty tongue and Henry was rather taken with her. He talked to them about his dream of developing some of his old stable buildings set round a courtyard and she made some very sensible observations. Simon agreed to come and have a look. Rather shyly Henry suggested that Gillian, for this was her name, might like to come along too. It had been a lovely afternoon and Henry enjoyed showing them both round and telling them his hopes and plans. Mrs Ridley brought them tea on the terrace and they sat in the warm September sunshine, looking out across the roofs of the stables below them to the stream and the woodland that bordered Nethercombe to the south.

'Must be worth a fortune,' remarked Simon as he and Gillian drove away. 'On paper, anyway. He ought to sell the whole lot. It's a property developer's dream. Old Henry would be a millionaire overnight. Just needs the right person to give him a push.'

Henry was surprised and flattered to receive a telephone call from Gillian a few weeks later asking him if he would accompany her to a charity ball. Henry was charmed and enjoyed the evening enormously.

During the next few months, encouraged unobtrusively by Gillian, he found himself taking the initiative, asking her out, accompanying her to parties, even taking her to the theatre in Plymouth. Never had Henry been so social. Even now, he thought, as Mr Ridley – seated on the lawn mower – passed across his line of vision, even now he could not quite remember how the proposal had taken place. Somehow something had been said, certainly not planned or intended, and Gillian, to his surprise, had thrown her arms around him and kissed him and accepted what she had taken to be an offer of marriage. He had been too delighted, too taken aback by his good fortune, to disillusion her. It would have taken him years to work himself up to a formal proposal. And instead, not much more than seven months after meeting her, here he was about to be married to her. Henry shook his head, glanced at his watch and gave a low cry of dismay. Swallowing the last of the now cold tea, he seized his car keys from the untidy desk and hurried out. He'd been day-dreaming and now he would have to hurry to be in time for the train.

GILLIAN STOOD AT THE bedroom window and watched her mother and godmother walking on the lawn. She was grateful to her godmother for letting her be married from her home and for footing the bill. It was many years now since Gillian's father had left her mother and set up another home and a whole new family. Her improvident, extravagant mother – who had never saved in her life and refused to contemplate the thought of working to supplement the allowance her ex-husband made her – was quite unable to meet the bills for the sort of wedding Gillian had in mind. Her father, who had suffered too long Gillian's outspoken animadversions on his character and behaviour, ignored his daughter's rather curt suggestion that it was his duty to pay, informed her that he would be out of the country for the wedding and sent her a cheque for two hundred pounds. Gillian paid the cheque into her account and allowed her father's character to be blackened further by letting it be known that he had not only refused to attend his daughter's wedding but would not assist in any way financially. Her mother had immediately telephoned her oldest friend and plaintively poured out her problems. How, asked Lydia, could Angus be so unfatherly as to refuse to give his daughter away and how could she do anything from a small flat in Exeter and on the pitiful pittance that Angus allowed her? If only to cut short the well-worn recital of the prodigal and unnecessary amounts of money his new wife and progeny spent, Elizabeth Merrick took the whole responsibility to herself and privately cursed the day, twenty-three years before, when she had stood in the church with the baby Gillian in her arms and had neglected to seize the opportunity of drowning the infant in the stone bowl of the font. This, now, was to be her last act of duty and she intended to do it generously and with style, even going to the lengths of persuading her old friend and accountant, who had known Gillian all her life, to perform Angus's role at the ceremony.

Gillian turned back into the room and returned to the pleasurable task of looking over her new wardrobe, a small part of it by courtesy of her father's cheque. She had given up her job at the wine bar, vacated the room in the flat she shared with two other girls and, having deposited her very few belongings at Nethercombe, she and Lydia had come to stay with Elizabeth for the last two weeks of her single state. She was enjoying herself. Whilst she would have been perfectly happy to have moved in with Henry before marrying him – it had never occurred to Henry to suggest it – she was delighted to have this big send-off for which no expense had been spared. She felt that Nethercombe deserved it and that none of Henry's friends would be able to say that she was marrying him for his money or his land. For, in this instance, Henry was quite wrong. Gillian was one of those people who, despite outward and visible evidence to the contrary, believed that anyone who lived on an estate like Nethercombe must, *ipso facto,* have money hidden away somewhere. Simon's remarks had been more than enough to make her feel that Henry was well worth cultivating and, though she had sometimes despaired of ever bringing him to the point, she felt as though her hands were at last on the ropes and the things that she had longed for were within her grasp. She didn't love Henry and was quite shrewd enough not to mistake his feelings for her as the authentic fire. Henry was not at all the sort of man to be the victim of a grand passion but he would be affectionate, caring, loyal – and he owned Nethercombe. Gillian was quite happy to settle for this and knew that she was experienced enough for Henry never to suspect that she didn't love him. She intended to play fair according to her own rules.

Her mother's voice could be heard calling her down to tea and, with a little satisfied nod at her lovely new clothes, Gillian went out and shut the door behind her.

GUSSIE, STEPPING CAREFULLY FROM the train, saw Henry before he saw her. She smiled as she watched him anxiously scanning the opening doors and decided, as she always did, that he looked exactly like his father had at that age: stocky, broad-shouldered, with his straight hair flopping. She was almost up to him before he turned and his brown face creased into a delighted smile of welcome and relief. He took her case and she had to stoop a little – for Gussie was a tall woman and Henry was only of average height – to exchange a formal kiss.

'Henry dear. This is so exciting. I'm so looking forward to meeting Gillian. Many congratulations.'

She followed him out to the battered Peugeot estate car, whose back seats were all folded down so as to accommodate various agricultural requirements, and he opened the door for her.

'So glad you could come,' he told her, when he was settled behind the wheel. 'I shall like to feel that you're there behind me. In the church. Not many of the family left now, you know.'

They exchanged news as he drove out of Totnes station, waited for the traffic lights to change and turned left up the hill.

'It's lovely to be back,' said Gussie looking up at the castle and noticing some new buildings on the edge of the town. 'I'm so looking forward to seeing Nethercombe.'

Henry gave her an anxious sideways glance. Her tone had been particularly heartfelt and she looked rather thinner and more fine-drawn since he had seen her last. Of course, she was getting older . . . Henry felt a pang of guilt. He ought to ask her down much more often than he did. He remembered that Gussie had always loved Nethercombe and his heart warmed to her anew. She should come and stay now that he would have a wife to make the place more comfortable. He would invite her for holidays. Perhaps for Christmas . . .

Gussie, unaware of Henry's plans for her, gave a sigh of pleasure and settled back to watch the familiar countryside. It was wonderful to be back in the country again and the weekend stretched deliciously ahead. As they drove through Avonwick and crossed the A38, Gussie could see the high tors of Dartmoor in the distance. Nethercombe was set just within the National Park and its fields, farmed by Henry's two tenant farmers, led up on to the foothills of the moor. The house itself, however, was sheltered within its wooded valley and Gussie sat up as they turned into the narrow lane from which the drive led. Henry no longer used the main avenue to the house but drove in, past the stables which he hoped to develop, up between the stretches of lawn and rhododendrons, and round beside the house. He switched off the engine and smiled at her.

'Home,' he said. 'Welcome back.'

THE MORNING OF THE wedding dawned dry and mild, if overcast, and Gussie and Henry drove to the church together with the Ridleys sitting rather shyly – but very proudly – in the back of the newly polished hatchback which Mr Ridley would drive back to Nethercombe when Henry and Gillian were taken to the airport by the best man. Gussie smoothed the paisley skirt, adjusted Nell's straw hat and cast sideways glances at Henry who hummed 'Time was when Love and I were well acquainted' in an attempt to calm his nerves.

The small granite church was dim and cool, the flowers making bright soft pools of colour. The Ridleys slipped determinedly into the very back pew but Gussie, chin high, shoulders back – 'soldier's daughter, soldier's sister' – followed the usher to the pew behind the one in which Henry and his best man would sit when they'd finished being photographed in the porch. Henry had told her that he would like to know that she was there behind him in the church and that was where she intended to be. She gave a little nod – a nice blend of regal friendliness – to the bride's family and slipped forward on to her knees to pray, aware of the rustlings and excitement all around her.

'*DEARLY BELOVED, WE ARE gathered together here in the sight of God . . .*'

She's made it! thought Simon Spaders, who had decided to count himself a friend of the bridegroom now that Henry had approached him to draw up plans for his courtyard development. He looked at Henry's firm chin, etched against the white of the vicar's surplice, and wondered whether things were going to be quite as easy as Gillian imagined. He pursed his lips thoughtfully and let his gaze wander over the two grown-up bridesmaids. Lucy's looking very serious. That strange greeny-blue colour suits her. I could fancy Lucy. Perhaps with Gillian otherwise engaged . . .

'. . . *to satisfy men's carnal lusts and appetites . . .*'

Doesn't sound much like Henry, thought Lydia, who had become very fond of her future son-in-law over the past weeks. He's not that type at all. I think Gillian's going to be rather disappointed in that direction. I do hope that she knows what she's doing. Oh dear . . . Her thoughts roamed distractedly and she eyed Elizabeth's beautifully cut outfit enviously. Perhaps I should have worn the blue silk . . .

'. . . *First, It was ordained for the procreation of children . . .*'

Yes, well he can forget all about that, thought Gillian, keeping an expression of gentle sweetness on her face which was turned up to the vicar, and thanking God for the pill. Damned if I'm going to tie myself down . . .

'. . . *for the mutual society, help, and comfort, that the one ought to have of the other, both in prosperity . . .*'

How nice that sounds, thought Henry. How wonderful to have someone to share Nethercombe. He imagined he and Gillian tucked up in the library on a winter's evening, listening to his Gilbert and Sullivan recordings and talking over the business of the day. He slipped a glance sideways and was struck by the radiant expression on his bride's face . . .

'. . . *Therefore if any man can shew any just cause* . . .'

And the trouble is, Lord, thought Gussie, who frequently had informal chats with the Almighty upon whom she looked as an ever-present spiritual friend and advisor, if I were to stand forward now and say, 'This is all wrong,' no one would understand. But it is all wrong, just as much as if Henry were a Mr Rochester and had a wife locked in the attic at Nethercombe. I can't put my finger on it but it's all simply wrong . . .

'. . . *I Henry, take thee Gillian* . . .'

But will you be able to keep her? wondered Elizabeth, looking at the slim straight back of her goddaughter. Gillian's never stuck to anything yet and, frankly, I can't see her as a landowner's wife. Well, it's simply not my problem. As Lydia took out a delicate lace-edged handkerchief and began to exhibit signs of motherly emotion, Elizabeth stiffened a little and exchanged a tiny smile with the tall distinguished man who stood on her right. How kind of Richard to agree to give her away. I'm glad he's coming back with the others to the reception. How beautiful the flowers are . . .

'*With this Ring I thee wed* . . .'

And good luck to her, thought Lucy, the chief bridesmaid, Gillian's old schoolfriend and erstwhile flatmate. And now she can jolly well cough up that back rent she owes. He's rather sweet really in a brotherly sort of way. Not Gilly's sort at all, even with that big house. I should have thought that Simon was much more her type and she was so keen on him. The best man looks rather fun . . .

'. . . *I pronounce that they be Man and Wife together* . . .'

Three

NELL PUT DOWN HER book, glanced at the clock and went to put the fish pie in the oven. She was very proud of her fish pie. Gussie had given her the recipe, stood over her whilst she prepared it, and had been delighted to hear that John had enjoyed it enormously. Nell, amazed at her ability to provide something that John really liked to eat, had served it up at regular intervals thereafter and if John was heartily sick of fish pie he hadn't said so. To be honest, Nell wondered if John noticed what he was eating. During the summer he had been so excited by the success of his partnership with Martin that everything else had paled into insignificance. At last things were going right for him and Nell had agreed that it seemed as if his luck had turned. People were still putting their money into property and, since he had joined with Martin, house prices had increased by thirty per cent.

John was jubilant and Nell was beginning to believe that perhaps he had been right to leave the Navy and start a new career. Soon, he promised her, they would be able to buy a home of their own. Nell hoped so. Roomy though the flat was, it had seemed small with Jack home for the summer holidays. She had taken him to the zoo and for walks over the Downs but the high spot was the visit to Porlock Weir and the cottage. John was too busy to go with them but Nell was used to doing the trip without him and it was wonderful to be out of the city, to be surrounded instead by the smells and noises of the countryside and to watch the sea breaking against the North Somerset shore. John hurried down for a long weekend and urged her to stay for as long as she wanted. Despite the evidence that their future looked secure, John still felt guilty that his decision to come outside had meant a reduced standard of living for Nell and guessed that she found the flat restrictive. He knew of her need for solitude and peace and how much the little cottage meant to her. Although he missed her, it soothed his conscience to know that she was happy there with Jack and, after all, he really was very busy. Martin was always ready to have a pint with him in the evening or to share a Chinese takeaway back at the flat. He was estranged from his wife and small daughter, both of whom he missed quite desperately, and was only too pleased to help John pass a lonely evening. Generally, however, they worked until quite late and through most weekends and the summer passed quickly.

It passed too quickly for Nell. All too soon September arrived and Jack went back to school, looking forward to the rugby season, firework night and all the excitement of Christmas at the end of the term. Perhaps, thought Nell, Christmas might be quite fun in a big city with all the shops and lights and decorations. She was planning to book tickets for the pantomine at the Hippodrome and hoped to go to the Festival of Christmas Carols and Music at the Cathedral. She was still wondering whether that might be rather too much for Jack, who was not particularly musical, when she heard John's key in the lock and his usual shout of greeting. She went out to meet him in the hall and he hugged her.

'We've had a wonderful day,' he said as he followed her through to the kitchen. 'We exchanged contracts on the house at Sneyd Park. And we've taken on two new properties. I said we'd meet Martin later for a drink. Poor old boy. It seemed a bit mean to leave him all on his own. It'll be awfully flat for him after all the excitement. You don't mind, do you darling? I'm starving. How soon can we eat?'

Nell poured him a drink, reflecting on how much more confident he was now that things were going so well. It was good to see him so ebullient and happy and she smiled at him as she gave him his glass.

'Congratulations,' she said. 'Let's drink to it. You should have brought Martin back with you. He's become quite partial to my fish pie.'

'So have I!' declared John enthusiastically, pulling her close with his free arm and nuzzling into her neck.

His happiness and his relief that he was making a go of things was so overwhelming that it embraced even the fish pie. For the first time since those early days at Britannia Royal Naval College, when he had been so determined to succeed as well as Rupert had at Sandhurst, he felt in control of his life and his future. He looked at Nell and his heart overflowed with all sorts of mixed emotions – gratitude, love, amazement – as he beheld her beauty. His wish that Rupert could see him now was diluted with the instinctive wave of relief that he was dead and that the lifelong contest was over. He was ashamed of that relief, knowing that the contest had only ever been on his side, never on Rupert's. Rupert had been far too confident, successful, loved, ever to have felt the need to compete with anyone. Everything had come so easily to him. Their mother had adored Rupert whilst worrying over John. How humiliating, how crushing that worrying had been, made even more obvious by her confidence in Rupert and her reliance on him when their father died. How relieved John had been to pass the Admiralty Board and escape from beneath that canopy of care that made him feel like a child and sapped his confidence. The Navy and Nell between them had provided the passport to manhood and he had seized it gratefully. The honours at Dartmouth had eluded him but at least he had a son – Rupert hadn't married – and then, quite suddenly, it was all over and Rupert was dead. His widowed mother was devastated by grief and John, confused and ashamed that his overwhelming emotion was relief that Rupert would not now know that he had failed Perisher, attempted to comfort her. Surely now, with both Rupert and his father dead, he would at last come into his own. He would be head of the family and his mother could turn to him for guidance and comfort as she had turned to his father and later to Rupert.

'Oh, John,' she'd said, her eyelids swollen, her face sodden and shapeless with tears, 'what shall we do without him?' And she wept again. Presently she pulled herself together a little and patted his hand. 'Never mind,' she said, as one who was making the best of a bad job but intending to be brave about it, 'I've still got you.' But her eyes wandered to Rupert's photograph and, unconsciously, she sighed and John was aware of his inadequacy and knew that his desire to be recognised on equal terms with his brother was to remain unfulfilled.

Now, six years later, John dragged his thoughts away from the past, finished his drink abruptly and smiled at Nell.

'Let's eat,' he said.

GUSSIE WAS SURPRISED AND thrilled to receive an invitation to Nethercombe for Christmas. She couldn't believe her luck. Now that the last of her friends had been installed in a residential home too far away to be visited, Gussie was beginning to feel the loneliness of old age creeping up on her. There were simply too many hours in the day in which to keep happily employed since she had retired from the university library. Her friendship with Nell was a blessing but she could hardly expect to spend Christmas with her and, even should Nell offer, she would have too much pride to accept the invitation. Nethercombe was different. Nethercombe was, in a way, her home and Henry her cousin. To Gussie the ties of blood were strong and contained obligations and she would not feel that she would be intruding at Nethercombe, grateful though she was at Henry's thinking of her.

His letter was typical of the sort of communication that she had received from him during the years: short, somewhat haphazard, tending to go off at tangents. He wrote as he thought and as he spoke and his letters always recalled him very vividly to her mind. At least it sounded as though he found married life satisfactory but Gussie was not convinced. Her first impressions were usually reliable and it was very early days. She was looking forward to being able to observe for herself exactly what sort of fist Gillian was making of her position as mistress of Nethercombe and wondered how she had reacted to Henry's suggestion – not for a second did Gussie think that the idea had come from Gillian – that Gussie should spend Christmas with them. How dear it was of him to think of her. She sat down at once to reply to the letter promising herself that, when it was done, she would allow herself the luxury of a telephone call to Nell to tell her the good news.

GILLIAN, WHO WAS PLANNING to fill Nethercombe with as many friends as she could for Christmas, was surprised though not particularly put out when Henry told her that Gussie had accepted his invitation. She raised her eyebrows at him.

'Won't she feel rather out of it?' she asked. 'I mean she's a bit old, isn't she? To fit in with our friends?'

'Gussie's a friend too,' said Henry, who was wondering who all these friends might be. 'I'm very fond of Gussie. Always remembered to have a present waiting for me when I went back to school. Good presents, too.'

'Lovely for you.' Gillian gave a mental shrug and rolled her eyes a little. Touching excursions to the past were not her forte but she had decided to be tolerant about Henry's passion for anything ancient and decaying, even when it extended to his relatives.

'Well, it was,' said Henry, eyes turned inwards to dormitories, first nights back, the misery of being away from Nethercombe. 'Those are the things that make all the difference. People remembering you.'

'If you say so.' Gillian spread marmalade with a lavish hand and crunched toast.

Henry, brought back to the present by the crunching, smiled at his wife.

'There was a green woodpecker on the bird table this morning,' he said. 'Wonderful birds. And a nuthatch. The cold weather brings them in.'

Gillian swallowed her toast and poured some coffee. If it wasn't antiquities or Gilbert and Sullivan, it was the Natural World. She sighed and stirred in sugar, wondering if she might persuade Lucy to meet her for lunch in Exeter. Life at Nethercombe wasn't as exciting as she'd hoped. Henry had a small circle of friends, mostly other landowners, who weren't her sort at all and, apart from occasional dinners with this little group, he never seemed to go anywhere or do anything. He worked hard on the estate, she was prepared to concede that, but he was perfectly content to spend the evenings reading or watching television or listening to music. Gillian was biding her time. She had great schemes for the redecoration of the house and then she planned to entertain on a grand scale: no point in having a house the size of Nethercombe if you didn't use it. In the summer she would have parties round the pool that was built on a little natural plateau of ground below the house. Backed on three sides by towering rhododendron bushes and falling away to the meadow on the fourth it was an enchanting spot. It only needed a few things done to it to make it perfect for parties. So far, her suggestions had fallen on deaf ears but it was just a question of time. She was much too clever to try to rush him. Now, as he finished his eulogy on the family of long-tailed tits he'd seen up in the beech walk, she smiled at him and pushed back her chair.

'I've got to dash up to Exeter,' she told him. 'Really boring. Poor old Lucy's got some sort of drama going on and she's asked me to meet her. Can't let her down. So I shan't be here for lunch.'

'Right.' Henry stood up too. 'Poor Lucy. Give her my regards. Drive carefully.'

She gave him a quick kiss and he watched her go, still dazzled with the speed with which she did everything, darting hither and thither, laughing at things which her friends said that were outside his comprehension, making him feel slow and stolid beside her. It didn't worry him at all. Henry didn't waste time on introspection or expend mental energy worrying about talents he didn't have. All sorts were needed to make a balance and he could see no reason why he and Gillian shouldn't be very happy. He felt that each of them was adjusting very well to the other's way of life and that, given time, they would settle down comfortably together.

Henry smiled to himself as he went to tell Mrs Ridley that Gillian wouldn't be in to lunch. He was remembering Gussie's letter: precise, informative, to the point. It was exactly like all the other letters he had received from her over the years and as such was comforting. She had been delighted by the invitation and he had been delighted by her acceptance of it. Christmas was a family time, underlining the sense of continuity and, now that he was married and the festivities would be properly observed, he felt that she would have as happy a time at Nethercombe as she would with her friends in Bristol. Henry had no idea of Gussie's lonely existence or financial restraints and not for a moment would she have let him suspect that all was not very well with her. To him it was all quite simple. Gussie loved Nethercombe and now that he was no longer a bachelor living in a cosy, untidy old muddle, it would be very nice to invite her down more often. She loved to walk in the grounds and had as great a passion for the natural world as Henry himself.

Henry hummed a line from *Princess Ida* as he went down the long passage that led to the kitchen.

GILLIAN, HAVING NO SUCCESS in rousing her friend, descended on her mother's flat in Southernhay and invited her out to lunch. Lydia, undeceived by this gesture of filial generosity, took it at its real value but accepted nonetheless. A free lunch is a free lunch.

'Have you seen Elizabeth lately?' she asked as she went to get ready for this treat.

Gillian prowled restlessly, suspecting censure if her answer were to be in the negative.

'I've telephoned once or twice but she's always so busy,' she said mendaciously, hoping to deflect criticism.

'Oh, busy!' sniffed Lydia, distracted as Gillian had hoped she would be. 'She has absolutely no need to work. Her parents left her that lovely little house and a perfectly adequate income. Interior design! It's her way of feeling superior.'

'She's good at it though.' Gillian fanned the flames of jealousy and discontent a little higher. 'She says she only works for New Money these days. Does their Georgian houses up for them and then goes round all the antique shops buying them a past. That's what she calls it.'

'I think it's patronising,' said Lydia, remembering anew her failure to charm the tall good-looking Richard away from Elizabeth at the wedding reception.

'I can't imagine why she never got married,' mused Gillian, looking through her mother's wardrobe to see if she'd bought anything new and if so whether it might be borrowable. 'She's really stunning. And that dishy Richard is obviously mad about her.'

Lydia zipped up her skirt with a vicious whisk.

'She always says that she's never met a man for whom it would be worth the irritation of waiting to use the bathroom. More affectation. Anyway, she's got two bathrooms.'

Gillian grinned into the wardrobe.

'Of course, she was wonderful about the wedding . . .'

'She's your godmother, after all.' Lydia drew her stomach in and peered at herself sideways in the mirror. 'And she can certainly afford it.'

'Still. You're quite right. I simply must get in touch with her . . .'

'Oh well. She's not going anywhere. You sent your bread and butter afterwards?'

'Of course I did.' Gillian, following her mother down the stairs, allowed a self-righteous note to creep into her voice. 'I wrote while I was on honeymoon. Honestly, Mum!'

'Sorry, darling. Let's forget about Elizabeth, shall we? Where are we going?'

'Coolings, I thought. And I want to have a look in Russell and Bromley.'

Several hours later, back in her flat alone, Lydia sank down on the sofa with a cup of tea and wondered how Gillian had managed to inveigle the rather expensive pair of loafers out of her. From a tiny child her only daughter had been able to wind her round her little finger, wheedle things out of her, and when Angus had left them Lydia had been even more tempted to spoil her in her anxiety to keep the child's affection. She felt rather guilty when she remembered how she hadn't hesitated to pour out her resentments and hurts to Gillian, knowing that this had influenced her against her father.

Lydia made a face. After all, Angus had another family now and didn't need Gillian as she did. A mother and a daughter could be friends and she and Gillian were so close. Look how she came up to Exeter so often and took her out shopping with her and bought her lunches and cups of coffee! Of course, she did find herself occasionally talked into forking out on little treats — such as the shoes today — and, as Lydia sipped her tea and brooded on her gullibility, a saying she had heard lately slipped into her mind.

'There's no such thing as a free lunch.'

four

GUSSIE CAME BACK FROM Nethercombe full of Henry's plans for his courtyard development. When it came to Gillian, however, Nell was aware of a certain lack of enthusiasm on Gussie's part that made itself apparent more in her reluctance to speak about her than in anything that she actually said. Nell was not aware how difficult Gussie found the return to her cramped flat and restrictive economies after the space of Nethercombe, nor how painful the decisions to accept or refuse Nell's uncalculated generosity. Since Jack was away at school and Nell was not at all the sort of person to join clubs or societies, she found herself in none of the situations where acquaintances were struck up or friendships flourished. This didn't particularly bother her for Nell had an inner life of reading and imagination to sustain her. Nevertheless, she enjoyed Gussie's company and they had fallen into a habit of meeting most weeks for coffee or tea. Nell discovered early on that Gussie was not a dropper-in. She disliked being taken unawares, too, and Nell respected her feelings. She was like it herself although perhaps not quite to the same extent. They were both private people but Gussie had more to hide. She could no longer afford the small luxuries of life and if Nell had arrived unexpectedly to discover her wrapped in layers of clothing because she couldn't afford to heat the flat, or to find that there was no biscuit with her coffee or piece of sponge with her tea, Gussie would have been humiliated.

Nell did her best to protect Gussie's pride. When she discovered that Gussie loved Shakespeare she bought tickets for the Old Vic and then told Gussie that John was working and that it was a pity to waste the ticket. There were limits of course and even she had no idea of the sacrifices Gussie made when, in an effort to repay Nell's kindnesses, she took Nell out to lunch or bought tickets for the ballet or insisted on paying for tea when they went on little trips in Nell's car. Gussie, shivering by her unlit fire and trying to ignore the pangs of hunger, wondered how long she could continue to afford the luxury of a telephone and planned to sell the last few valuable pieces that she had inherited from her mother.

Nell, meanwhile, was watching John even more closely than she was observing Gussie. At some point, as 1989 drew on, she sensed that his ebullience was becoming more of a bluster, that he was attempting to convince himself as much as her. Of course, he said, nobody had expected that the housing boom could continue at such a pace: naturally it would level out but things were still good. However, Nell noticed that talk of buying their own home was no longer a regular topic of discussion and her old fears began to creep back.

GILLIAN, TOO, WAS BEGINNING to realise that her dream of a refurbished Nethercombe was destined to remain unreality. Having obtained Planning Permission from the National Park for the conversion of his stables, Henry's whole concentration and every spare penny were devoted to the project. She was also beginning to learn that Henry was by no means the simple, quiet pushover she had taken him to be. With anything relating to the estate he was immovable.

'For heaven's sake!' she stormed at him, when her frustration at being baulked was too great. 'If you never spend any money on the place it'll fall down. What's the point of building a whole lot of new cottages if you let this house crumble?'

Henry smiled at her. He knew perfectly well that Gillian's idea of spending money on Nethercombe meant new furnishings and hangings and had nothing to do with the structure of the building.

'Been standing for over two hundred years,' he said comfortably. 'Shouldn't think it'll fall down yet.'

Gillian ground her teeth and wondered whether to dilute his complacency with the contents of her wine glass.

'It's a wonder you're not ashamed to invite your friends here,' she said but her tone lacked confidence. All Henry's friends seemed to live in similar conditions of decaying grandeur. 'At least you ought to think about central heating. It's so humiliating when you invite your friends to dinner and they're afraid to take their coats off.'

'I've been thinking about it,' Henry said surprisingly. 'I've been discussing it with Simon. Have to be careful, of course, in a house of this age. We'll see what profits we make out of the Courtyard. We might manage to run heating to some of the rooms. Not all, of course. The drawing room and the library perhaps. And our bedroom.'

Gillian breathed heavily through her nose. 'How exciting,' she said bitingly. 'I can hardly wait.'

Henry went to her and put his arm round her. 'Poor Gillian,' he said. 'The thing is that I'm used to it, I suppose. I know it's shabby but it's been like this ever since I can remember and it's . . . well, it's home.'

'But it's my home too, now,' cried Gillian, moving away from him. 'You make me feel like a permanent guest with no rights or say in how it should look or be run. How can I feel that it's my home when you and Mrs Ridley have the last word about everything?'

Henry looked at her in consternation. He hadn't realised that she felt so strongly.

'I'm sure that Mrs Ridley would be more than happy for you to take over some of the running of the house,' he said, unerringly picking the one aspect of Gillian's complaint which had no truth in it. 'It's such a big place and she's not as young as she was.'

Gillian bit her lip and turned swiftly back to him. 'Honestly, Henry. You haven't got a clue. She'd hate it if I interfered. She's been in charge all these years and she'd loathe it if I muscled in and started to tell her how to do things. A bit like you not wanting to change how it all looks. It's not my fault if I feel left out in the cold.'

Henry stood, irresolute. It was perfectly possible that Mrs Ridley may not care for interference on Gillian's part and, to be perfectly honest, he couldn't seriously imagine Gillian wanting to take over the responsibilities of housekeeping, nevertheless . . .

Gillian watched him. 'I just want to feel it's my home, too,' she said, with just the right amount of pathos in her voice. 'You know, a few things of my own, as well as all the lovely things that belonged to your family.' She shrugged. 'It's not that I'm asking for much, after all. Some new curtains in the bedroom . . .' Her voice trailed away. Her smooth blonde head drooped a little.

'Oh, darling.' Henry went to her and took her in his arms. 'I'm sure we could afford some new curtains.' Could they? Still, it was a bit unfair on her. 'Tell you what. Suppose you go to Exeter and price a few things. Get an idea of the things that would make you feel more at home. I want you to be happy.' He stared down at her anxiously.

'Oh, Henry.' She smiled mistily up at him. 'How sweet of you. It would make such a difference.' She slipped her arms around him and he bent his head to hers.

'Dinner's in! Gettin' cold!' Mrs Ridley stood at the door watching them.

'Coming, Mrs Ridley.' Gillian held firmly on to Henry as he attempted to break away from her.

The two women's eyes met and looked for a moment and then Mrs Ridley whisked out. Gillian gave Henry another kiss and they went into the breakfast room together, arm in arm.

JOHN SAT IN THE corner of the bar, his pint barely touched on the table before him. Despite Martin's assurances that there was no need to panic, John could feel his newly found confidence ebbing gently away from him. The boom was over, the winds of change were blowing and, outside the comforting structure of the Navy, John felt vulnerable. Even within the safety of his partnership with Martin, in the middle of the excitement of rising prices and big profits, he had seen that life outside was very different to everything he'd known. Going straight from school to Dartmouth he had merely exchanged one establishment's set of rules and regulations for another's and civilian life ran on very different lines. John no longer had the rings on his sleeve to show people at a glance where he belonged and what attitude they should adopt towards him. Nor could he read the signals in reverse. Categorising people into upper and lower deck, junior or senior officers had got him into a lot of trouble. Had he not been able to go straight into a partnership with Martin it was doubtful that he would actually ever have left the Navy. Once outside he realised that a partnership wasn't like being the captain of a submarine. Nobody was terribly impressed: the most unlikely people seemed to own companies, run enterprises. The glory that had eluded him within the service seemed still beyond his grasp in civilian life and John missed the privileges of rank, the shared language, the feeling of camaraderie. He was good with the clients but, apart from Martin, found it difficult to make friends. None of this would have mattered if business had stayed at the same level, fast, exciting, profitable.

But supposing things went wrong? John took a long swallow at his beer and summoned his common sense. Because the boom was over didn't mean that they couldn't make a perfectly adequate living. Perhaps they had been unwise to move the office to larger more expensive premises. The purchase of the lease had taken every penny but there seemed to be plenty more to come. Supposing . . . ? John finished his drink and stood up. He mustn't brood; that way madness lay. He must get home to Nell.

Nell. At the mere thought of her his heart sank again. She had been so against it all and now it seemed unlikely that they would be able to buy their own place. Not that she ever mentioned it. As long as she had the cottage at Porlock Weir she seemed happy enough, although the holidays were difficult. Jack was growing fast. He had needed new uniform this term and next year the fees would have to be found. The fund that Nell had insisted on for the two years would be finished. John felt his stomach tighten. Supposing . . . ? He picked up his glass and went to the bar.

'Same again, please.'

GUSSIE WATCHED THE APPROACH of autumn with fear in her heart. Her mind turned this way and that, seeking new ways of making economies, of keeping warm, of paying the rent. The money simply wouldn't stretch. The summer visit to Nethercombe had been a mad extravagance, paid for by the sale of her last remaining pieces. The trouble was that buyers recognised the look and smell of poverty and she knew that she should have got much more. In the end she was grateful for what they gave her. It bought her a return ticket to Totnes and left her a tiny sum against the depredations of winter. Perhaps now was the time to leave her flat and move to a bedsit. Gussie put her thin, age-mottled hands over her eyes and shook her head. Whilst she could move from her bedroom to this sitting room, tiny though it was, and have a separate kitchen and bathroom, life still held a shred of dignity. But to live, eat, cook, sleep all in one room . . . Gussie took her hands from her eyes and straightened her thin shoulders. 'Soldier's daughter, soldier's sister,' she murmured but the mantra was beginning to lose a little of its power and she turned to a more reliable and infinite source of support.

'The thing is, Lord,' she sighed, getting to her feet and wondering whether a mid-morning cup of coffee was too much of a luxury to be considered, 'where one lives really shouldn't matter, I know that. But it does. Pride's a terrible thing but it does help to keep one going, but I know that You, Lord, will help me to bear whatever may come. And I have dear Nell who is such a comfort.' She opened the fridge door and stared bleakly at the small quantity of milk in the bottle. Her experienced eye assessed it: two more cups of tea or coffee, three at the most. One after lunch and one at tea-time and just enough for an early morning cup before the milkman arrived. She could only afford one pint every other day. Or she could have a late night cup of tea, so comforting and warming at bedtime, and hope that she didn't wake too early . . .

'I'm afraid not this morning,' she said, turning from the emptiness of the fridge. 'Why is it, dear Lord, that we always crave most for what we can't have? We all drink far too much tea and coffee. All the same –'

The telephone's cry interrupted her communication with the Almighty and she hastened to lift the receiver.

'Gussie?' Nell's voice was clear and cheerful. 'How are you?'

'Nell, my dear. Very well. And you?'

'Fine. We're all fine. Listen. Jack and I want to take you out to lunch. No. No excuses. He's off to school next week and he wants to say goodbye to you. And it's to thank you for babysitting. All right, Jack.' Gussie could hear Jack's voice in the background, uplifted in protest. 'I know you're not a baby. OK. For Jack-sitting, then. Sorry, Gussie. Please come. How about today? It's such a perfect day. We thought that we'd head out into the country. Are you busy?'

'No.' Gussie felt an unusual and unwelcome suspicion of moisture about her eyes. 'No. Not busy at all. I should like to very much.'

'That's wonderful. We'll pick you up in about half an hour. Oh, hang on, Jack's saying something about a book. You were going to write down the title and author for him. Something about the Romans?'

'Oh yes. I did promise him. He's doing it in History next term. But I wasn't certain if he really wanted it.'

'He certainly does. He's nodding madly. If you could then. We'll have some coffee somewhere on the way. See you soon.'

The line went dead and Gussie replaced the receiver. Her lips trembled a little and she swallowed once or twice. Nell and Jack made her feel needed, important to their well-being. Loved even? She shook her head fiercely.

'What a fool I am, Lord,' she muttered. 'But thank you. Now. Where did I put that piece of paper?'

Five

GILLIAN TORE OPEN THE envelope containing her Barclaycard statement, stared with dismay at the amount required for the minimum payment and opened her eyes even wider in disbelief at the balance owing. Surely there must be some mistake? It had been rather exciting to find that, when she received her new card in her married name, the credit limit had been raised quite substantially but surely she couldn't have used it all up and even exceeded it? She checked the list of names: Dingles, Russell and Bromley, Laura Ashley. Gillian groaned and, picking up the rest of her post, hurried out of the breakfast room and up the stairs.

Mrs Ridley, coming through from the kitchen with a tray, watched her go. Gillian made no effort to help with the running of the house and it was only Mrs Ridley's affection for Henry and her loyalty to him that prevented her from making Gillian's life at Nethercombe a great deal more uncomfortable than she found it already. In her opinion, Henry had been taken in. Of course, Mr Ridley was all for making allowances, thought that his wife's judgements were a bit harsh, but then he was hardly ever in the front of the house and Gillian was young and pretty. Mrs Ridley sniffed contemptuously, waddled across the hall and went into the breakfast room. Her stout short figure was wrapped in an overall which was tied firmly round her middle, giving her the appearance of an untidily packed parcel. She put the tray on the table and started to clear away the breakfast things.

Upstairs Gillian gazed out of her bedroom window, across the roofs of the Courtyard to the woods beyond, where the first tender haze of green was beginning to show. The early spring sunshine, the thin, pale, washed-out blue of the sky, heralded a break at last from the long wet winter months but Gillian barely saw the glory of the day. Hands clenched into fists, arms folded beneath her breasts, her view was inward. How on earth was she to pay? Henry had made it quite clear that he couldn't afford any more at present. She had completely done over their bedroom and the paying of the bills had left him rather quiet. When they got married he'd opened a joint bank account and given her a cheque book along with a clear idea of the sum usually at their disposal. Gillian also kept her own account, unknown to Henry, into which she siphoned small amounts of money against a personal emergency. Well, this was a personal emergency but she knew very well that her own account was overdrawn and she'd been politely but firmly warned that no further cheques would be honoured until funds had been paid in. If she paid her Barclaycard out of the joint account, Henry would know. He always checked the statements when they arrived and Gillian was only too aware that Henry didn't approve of credit cards. He was quite gullible enough to believe that her new clothes and shoes were merely ones he hadn't seen before but he would certainly want to know what such a large cheque had been spent on and then he would probably want to see the Barclaycard account.

Gillian's heart gave a little tock of fear. There was nothing menacing or chauvinistic about Henry. He simply had a strong sense of right and wrong. She knew very well that he couldn't afford the amount she'd spent on the bedroom but he gave it generously, was delighted with the result – Gillian had a remarkably sensitive eye for period and quality – and made it fairly clear that this must be all for the time being. She'd agreed quite willingly whilst taken up by the excitement of the choosing and buying and rearranging but the novelty had quickly worn off and other temptations presented themselves. And it was so easy with credit cards; not like using real money at all. Not until it came to paying the bill. That was real money all right! And where on earth was she going to get it? She considered and rejected several possibilities and then, tucking the statement into her shoulder bag, ran downstairs and into the study. She dialled quickly and then spoke.

'Hello, Elizabeth. It's Gillian . . . Yes, it is isn't it? I seem to keep missing you . . . Oh, are you? Just bad timing then. I was wondering if I were to pop in later this morning you'd be around? . . . Great . . . Yes. Lunch would be super . . . OK then. About half an hour.'

She replaced the receiver, went to get her things together and presently put her head round the kitchen door.

'I'm off out, Mrs Ridley. I'm having lunch with my godmother. Could you tell Mr Morley?'

'Dare say I c'n manage that.'

Mrs Ridley didn't look round from the washing up and, after a moment, Gillian pulled a face at the unresponsive back and went out. A little later, her small car was turning into the drive of her godmother's grounds. The delightful Georgian house, a miniature gentleman's residence, looked well cared for and welcoming and Gillian, switching off the engine, wondered if Elizabeth was going to leave it to her in her will. After all, she had no other living relative. As she gazed, her godmother opened the front door and stood looking at her.

'Hello there!' Gillian had the horrid feeling that Elizabeth knew exactly what she was thinking. She scrambled out of the car, seizing the bunch of early daffodils that she had bought in Ashburton en route. 'How are you? Looking glamorous as ever. How on earth do you do it?'

Elizabeth raised her eyebrows as she bent to receive the kiss and the flowers.

'The best butter,' she murmured and drew back.

'Not a bit,' protested Gillian. 'Simply the truth. You look younger all the time. Drives Mum mad.'

'Well, it'll certainly get you a drink. Let me just put these into some water. I'll arrange them later. How pretty they are.' In the spotless kitchen she filled a bowl and put the daffodils' feet in it. 'There. That will do for now.' Elizabeth led the way into her small, perfect drawing room. She disliked spending time in the kitchen unless it was in the preparation of food. 'What would you like? Gin and tonic? Some wine?'

'I'll stick with wine since I'm driving.' Gillian sat down in a deep, squashy armchair and stretched her legs to the bright log fire. 'How lovely this room is. It seems so, well, so organised, after Nethercombe.'

Elizabeth frowned a little as she poured the cold dry wine. 'Organised?'

'Yes. You know. The paint's all sparkling instead of peeling and the chair covers don't look as if they've been dogs' beds for centuries.'

Elizabeth chuckled a little. 'Nethercombe's not that bad. Just needs a bit of a face-lift. I must admit I wish I could get my hands on it.'

'I wish you could, too,' said Gillian feelingly. 'It's just so sad. It's such a wonderful old place. Actually . . .' She paused, staring into the flames.

Elizabeth stood quite still, looking down at her goddaughter's blonde head. Her eyes were narrowed a little, as if she waited for something. Gillian gave a quick sigh and glanced round and Elizabeth gave her the glass and sat down opposite. She crossed her long elegant legs and laced her fingers round the bowl of her own glass.

'Actually what?'

Gillian gave her a little look of well-simulated surprise. What? Oh. Yes. Well, it's got me into a bit of trouble actually.' She gave a little grimace, hoping that Elizabeth would help her along, ask her what she meant. But Elizabeth sat quite still, watching her, her face thoughtful. Gillian gave a self-deprecating little laugh. 'I felt I simply must do one or two things. Not much. The poor old place needs so much attention. I know you'll sympathise. But the thing is, you see, although Henry gave me some idea as to what to spend I think we got our wires crossed a bit. Anyway,' she made another face, 'I put some of it on my credit card and I haven't got enough to pay the bill.' She glanced quickly at Elizabeth and took a sip of her wine.

'What does Henry say?'

'Well.' Gillian swallowed and smiled. 'I haven't told him. You see, he simply hasn't any idea what these things cost and when I realised the sum he had in mind . . .' Gillian shook her head. 'Honestly. It's ridiculous really.' She shrugged. 'It's on my mind a bit, that's all. Sorry. Didn't mean to bore you with it.'

Gillian gave Elizabeth another quick glance and saw that she was smiling a little. It wasn't a very comforting smile.

'How much?'

Gillian wondered whether to pretend not to understand but abruptly abandoned subterfuge. 'Sixty-three pounds.'

'That's the total amount owing?'

Gillian hesitated.

'Oh, come on,' said Elizabeth impatiently. 'No lies. What is the amount outstanding?'

Gillian told her. Elizabeth closed her eyes for a moment and Gillian took another hasty gulp at her wine.

'You spent all that on furnishings?'

'Yes.' Gillian stared her godmother straight in the eye, praying that she wouldn't ask to see the account. 'You of all people must know that it goes nowhere.'

'I shall look forward to seeing the results,' said Elizabeth drily. 'I hope you got your money's worth.'

Gillian shrugged. 'So do I. I got a bit carried away, I suppose. And in a house the size of Nethercombe it's just a drop in the ocean.' She crossed her fingers under her thigh. 'You must come and give me your opinion.'

Elizabeth got up and went to her bureau. She took her cheque book out of a pigeonhole and unscrewed her fountain pen.

'To whom shall I make it payable? Which credit card do you have?'

she asked, and when Gillian – who had hoped to use some of it to clear her overdraft – told her, Elizabeth sat down and began to write.

Gillian took a deep, deep breath and relaxed back into the cushiony chair. The room seemed to gather itself round her as though, in the last few minutes, it had withdrawn, holding its breath, waiting. Now, time moved on again, life flowed back. The tick of the clock was suddenly loud as the fountain pen whispered over the paper, the flames burned and crackled merrily in the shining grate and the strident voices of the rooks, quarrelling vociferously in the tall trees beyond the long sash windows, impinged upon her consciousness. She realised that she had been tense, watchful, waiting for opportunities, calculating her replies, and she drank deeply from her glass.

Elizabeth tore the cheque from the book and stood up.

'This is the last, the very last time, Gillian, that I intend to bail you out. Do you understand? I'd decided that your wedding was to be my last contribution, as I told you at the time, but I'll give you one last chance to grow up and start taking responsibility seriously. You can look on it as your Christmas and birthday presents for the next ten years.' She dangled the cheque in her fingers, inches from her goddaughter's head and, after a moment, Gillian took it. Her face was sulky and she muttered her thanks with a very bad grace. She glanced at the figure and her eyes widened. When she looked up at Elizabeth, her expression was genuinely grateful.

'That's . . . that's really good of you, Elizabeth. Thanks. Honestly.'

'Last time, Gillian. Believe it. Now. Let's have another drink to take the taste away and you can tell me how Lydia is. I haven't seen her for months.'

NELL SAW JOHN'S BARCLAYCARD statement quite by mistake. In a rare moment of zeal, she decided to turn out the spare bedroom which he used as a small study. She tidied the top of his desk, trying to leave things as undisturbed as possible and, as she carefully lifted the pile of papers to dust beneath them, the statement fell out from between the pages. Nell, bending to pick it up, was arrested in the act, staring in disbelief at the amount owing. She straightened slowly, still staring at the sheet, noting that things for which she assumed they were paying cash were being put on the account. It seemed that very little had been paid for by cash for a long time. Nell's heartbeat seemed to hurry a little. Only the minimum payment had been paid last time and John was over his credit limit. Nell put the paper back and went out, down the passage and into the kitchen. She filled a tumbler from the wine box that John had brought home from the supermarket – and paid for on his credit card, no doubt – and sipped thoughtfully.

Knowing John's sense of inadequacy, his readiness to believe himself a failure, Nell was always careful how she approached him with anything that might resemble a problem for which he could be held in any way responsible. His reactions tended to be defensive and she tried to avoid aggressive confrontations. She knew that things were not going so well now but Martin had assured her that, if they didn't lose their heads, there shouldn't be any difficulty. Nell guessed that John had asked Martin to talk to her, hoping to fend off any questions.

Well, she'd believed him. She took another sip and set down her glass. Raising her arms, she deftly twisted up the long hair into a more secure knot and, dropping her head back, tried to relax her neck muscles. What was going on? A thought struck her and she went back to the study. It didn't take her long to find the bank statement and when she looked at it she drew in her breath in horror. It simply couldn't be that bad! Nothing had been paid into the account for weeks and it was well overdrawn. When they'd moved to Bristol, John had taken over the financial side of life and Nell, anxious to show that she trusted and supported him, had let him do it. Now she was really worried. Years of large mess bills and unrealistic budgeting had shown her that John was useless with money but she'd taken charge of it whilst he was at sea and kept their financial dealings more or less under control. With him at home full time there was no longer any excuse for her to hold the reins and she'd passed them over and hoped for the best.

Nell replaced the bank statement and went back to the kitchen. She realised the time had come to talk about things, but how should she approach it? She would have to tell him what she knew or he would palm her off with verbal placebos. As her imagination got to work and she began to feel the familiar sensations of anxiety, she tried to keep her fear under control. There was no point in getting worked up until she knew the exact situation. But would John *tell* her the exact situation? She knew very well that his hopes and desires often got mixed in with his perception of reality and, if she stripped away his illusions, he might not be able to confront the bare truth without a massive loss of confidence. Perhaps now was the time to try to find a job herself and make some contribution towards the household expenses. When this subject had been raised in the past John had protested loudly against it; he was perfectly able to support his wife, he told her. She suspected that if she were to suggest it now it would merely underline the fact that his ability to provide was in question. Nell rubbed her hands over her face, picked up her glass and went to refill it. Even as she raised it to her lips, she heard John's key in the lock and his step in the hall. He put his head round the door.

'So there you are.' The smile, the thick fair hair, the blue eyes, were Rupert's. And Jack's. Her heart contracted with love. 'I've got to meet a client at a property just round the corner so I thought I'd pop in for a quick cup of coffee,' he said. His eye fell on her glass. 'Goodness!' His eyebrows shot up and the corners of his mouth down. 'Bar's open early, I see.'

'Oh, John.' She stood the glass down and went to him. Thoughts struggled together in her head. Should she tell him now? Was there time to work through it all before he went to meet his client? Although she knew the unwisdom of it, her anxieties were so great that the words were out before she could stop them. 'John, I saw the

Barclaycard statement. I didn't mean to. I was tidying up and it fell on the floor. Oh, John, I didn't realise things were so bad.'

The smile died away as she spoke and a hastily assumed expression of surprise and amusement took its place. Nell recognised it and her heart sank.

'Poor Nell. That'll teach you to go poking around in my study. Nothing to worry about. All under control. Bit of a cockup last month but everything will be sorted out in a day or two. Now what about some coffee? I haven't got long.'

Nell stared up at him, longing to believe him, wondering whether she dared mention the bank statement.

'But what went wrong? Are we . . . ?' She hesitated. 'Are we OK at the bank?'

She waited. Her peace of mind hung on the manner in which he answered the question.

'The bank?' His little frown of amazement, his chuckle which ridiculed the suggestion, struck fear into Nell's heart. 'Of course we are. Why ever not? You really mustn't panic so easily, my darling. Martin told you that everything was fine as long as we don't panic, didn't he? You must just leave it all to us.'

'But, John.' She couldn't leave it alone and his face grew bleak. 'Your Barclaycard's right over its limit. If we're OK at the bank, why have you let it go so far?'

'Nell, please!' It was a plea and the compressed lips showed that he only just had himself in hand.

'I'm sorry,' she cried, 'it was a shock! I simply can't see why it should be so bad.' She took his hands. 'John, you must tell me if there's a problem. Please! Let me share things with you.'

'Why does there have to be a problem?' he demanded and his voice was high and full of fear and resentment. He pulled his hands from her clasp. 'Why must you always assume that I've got it wrong?'

'Oh, darling, I don't. I don't I'm sorry. Look, let me make you some coffee.' She turned away from him and went to the kettle.

'It's too late now.' His voice was still charged with emotion and she feared that he might burst into tears. 'I've got to see this man. Oh Christ!'

He ran out, his footsteps hurrying across the hall. Nell stood, clutching the kettle, unable to move. The front door slammed and there was silence.

Six

GUSSIE WOULD NOT HAVE been able to accept Henry's invitation to Nethercombe that summer if it hadn't been for Nell who, in addition to her anxiety about John, was becoming more and more aware of Gussie's stringent economies. When Gussie told her that she had decided not to go, as she didn't feel quite up to the train journey, Nell put two and two together and made the total the price of a return ticket. A solution presented itself almost at once but Nell offered it to Gussie rather casually lest she should suspect and reject it on the grounds of charity. It was quite simple. Nell had decided to go down to the cottage for a week or so. On her way to Porlock Weir she would drop Gussie at Nethercombe and collect her on the return trip. When Nell suggested it, Gussie felt her heart give a little throb of hope.

'But are you sure that you'll want to be going then?' she asked. 'Henry knows that I love to go when all the rhododendrons are in flower. But isn't that rather early for your summer holiday?'

'Oh, I like to do a trip to the cottage about then,' said Nell, stirring her tea and avoiding Gussie's penetrating gaze. 'There's hardly anybody about and I enjoy having the place to myself. I can be totally selfish and do as I please. We'll all have a proper holiday together later on, of course. And you'll be company for me on the journeys to and fro.'

'But surely you don't go that far down?' Gussie looked anxious. 'Nethercombe is beyond Ashburton. Don't you turn off near Tiverton?'

'It's hardly any distance,' said Nell firmly. 'And I'd love to see

Nethercombe after all you've told me about it. And I'd like to meet Henry. And Gillian, of course. Unless you'd rather I didn't?'

'Of course I should love to show you Nethercombe,' said Gussie, distressed that her protests may have been misunderstood and swallowing the bait whole as Nell intended. 'And Henry would be delighted to meet you. You know it's not that, my dear.'

'That's splendid, then,' said Nell, before Gussie could reiterate her anxieties. 'We'll make an early start. And I can pick you up again on my way back.'

Gussie was overjoyed: to be taking a friend to Nethercombe, to show Nell the dear old place and introduce her to Henry. She could hardly believe it. She had been schooling herself to overcome the disappointment of refusing, willing herself to write the letter that put an end to all her hopes, and Nell's offer, coming suddenly out of the blue, had the same effect as sunshine after rain. The whole world looked different: shining with possibilities, sparkling with joyous prospects. Even Henry rose to the occasion and wrote to Gussie inviting Nell to lunch if she could stay. It was the icing on the cake.

'And You know that it's not really pride, Lord,' Gussie said as she packed her case. 'Not really. It's simply that it makes me feel as though I still belong. That I have a tiny share in Nethercombe and that I can make Nell welcome there as though it were my own home. How good You are, Lord. Just when I thought that my visits to Nethercombe were over. How blessed I am. I think I'll put the paisley in, just in case . . .'

Gillian was on the terrace when they arrived. She strolled towards them, smartly casual in expensive cords and a cashmere jersey and obviously curious to see Nell. Her eyes narrowed a little as Nell emerged from the driving seat and Gussie watched with satisfaction as Gillian took in Nell's striking beauty.

'Hello.' Nell took Gillian's outstretched hand. 'You must be Gillian.'

'Must I?' Gillian smiled blindingly and turned as Henry came hurrying out of the house. 'Look what Gussie's brought us, Henry,' she said.

'I told you she was beautiful,' said Gussie, smiling a little at Henry's reaction.

'So you did,' said Gillian, taking Henry's arm. 'Over and over again.'

Henry released Nell's hand reluctantly. Her beauty overwhelmed him.

'You see what I mean, Henry? About *Sibylla Palmifera?*'

'Please, Gussie!' cried Nell involuntarily. She blushed painfully and smiled quickly at Henry. 'What a lovely place this is. The rhododendrons are magnificent. I quite see what Gussie means.'

'Well, of course, I'm prejudiced.' Henry, sensing Nell's embarrassment, tried to help her overcome it. 'You must come and see my new development. We're converting some old barns.'

'Gussie's been telling me about it,' said Nell, accepting the change of direction gladly and ignoring Gillian's expressions of bored impatience. 'It sounds very exciting. I should love to see it.'

'But she'd like some coffee first,' said Gillian, seeing that Henry was about to take Nell at her word and rush her down the drive. 'And Gussie, too. They've come a long way. I'll go and tell Mrs Ridley.'

'And I'll take my suitcase in.' Gussie opened the car door. 'No, no, Henry. I can manage it perfectly well. You stay and talk to Nell.'

Nell leaned her arms on the stone balustrade and gazed out over the countryside and Henry was able to stare at her in wonder and admiration. Her pale profile was cameo-clear, the heavy hair was thickly braided although tendrils escaped to curl about her face, and her tall slender figure was flattered by the black high-necked jersey, tucked into a long skirt of soft corduroy the colour of pine needles. Henry pulled himself together and cleared his throat.

'It was very good of you to bring Gussie down.'

'Not a bit. It was nice for me to have some company.' Nell continued to stare out, feeling his eyes on her. 'Is that the Courtyard? Down in the trees there?'

'Yes. Yes, it is.' Henry was distracted as she'd hoped he would be.

'We've finished the first cottage. Hoping to sell it so as to get the money to do the second one.'

'My husband sells houses,' said Nell lightly. 'The market's not too good at the moment, is it?'

'No,' said Henry flatly. 'It isn't. Simon says we may have missed the boat.'

'Simon?'

'Simon Spaders is the architect. He's made a really good job. You'll see.'

'Coffee!' called Gillian. 'Too cold outside. Mrs Ridley's put it in the study.' She smiled at Nell as they came inside. 'Want to come upstairs first?'

'Oh, yes please,' said Nell gratefully.

'You start pouring, Henry.' Gillian headed for the stairs, Nell in tow. 'We shan't be long.'

Gillian was nowhere in sight when Nell came out into the corridor again. A little further along a door stood ajar and Nell could hear someone within. She could just see Gillian inside, moving to and fro, humming to herself. Tentatively she pushed the door a little wider and Gillian nodded to her to come in.

'Want to tidy up a bit?' she asked and Nell, who had left her bag in the car, indicated her empty hands. 'Oh, you can use my stuff,' said Gillian carelessly. She watched as Nell approached the dressing table and made a show of tidying her hair. 'Why don't you stay on for a day or two? Do you have to rush away?'

Nell stared at her in surprise through the glass. 'Stay on?'

'Why not? It would be fun to have you here. We could get up a bit of a party.'

'Well . . .' Nell was nonplussed.

'Why not?' asked Gillian again. 'Gussie would be pleased. She could do her Lady Bountiful thing. You know. Pretending Nethercombe is hers. And the way that Henry was looking at you, I can see he'd be only too pleased.'

Nell turned from the glass. She felt uncomfortable. 'It's very kind of you but I don't think I could. I've made arrangements with the girl who keeps an eye on the cottage for us. She's expecting me.'

Gillian shrugged. She looked disappointed. 'Couldn't you telephone her?'

Nell was surprised at her insistence. 'It would be too difficult, I'm afraid. She'll have got milk and things in for me and probably lit a fire. Perhaps on the way back . . .'

'Oh yes.' Gillian seized on the idea, recovering her good humour. Things had been very dull of late, money being rather tight, and it was simply too good an opportunity to miss. After all, Henry could hardly refuse if she made the suggestion in front of Nell. 'Brilliant. Gives me time to plan. You could stay for a few nights and we'll have a bit of a shindig. I'll get some friends over. Great! Now, when would that be? Let's fix it before we go down, shall we?'

Nell drove away from Nethercombe feeling confused and anxious. When they had got back to the study, Gillian announced that Nell would be staying on the way back and that they had planned to have a party. Nell noticed that Henry's first reaction was one of dismay, although his good manners had instantly covered his lapse and he made it clear that he would be delighted to see Nell again for a longer time. Gussie was obviously thrilled, Gillian looked very pleased with herself and the rest of the visit had gone smoothly and pleasantly. Nell, however, felt as though she'd been manipulated although she couldn't quite see how. Presently she shook her head. It was no use worrying about it now. She turned on to the A38, pushed her foot down on the accelerator and headed back the way she had come.

JOHN PUT DOWN THE telephone receiver and let out an exclamation of despair.

'What now?' Martin coming through from the kitchen with two mugs of coffee looked resigned.

'That was Mrs Morrison. They won't be able to proceed with the purchase of the house in Lansdowne Terrace. Their own sale has just fallen through.' He put his elbows on the desk and buried his head in his hands. 'Oh Christ!'

'That's a bit of a bummer.' Martin stood a mug on John's desk.

He was getting used to John's explosive outbursts, his plunges into despair, and deliberately maintained a placid exterior in the hope of keeping him calm. It was both touching and terrifying to see how readily John turned to him for comfort, clinging to Martin's optimism and positive thinking as a drowning man clings to the wreckage.

'That's a bit of an understatement, isn't it?' John stared up at him. 'We needed that commission to pay the rent. And what about the telephone bill?'

'I know, I know.' Martin's tone was deliberately soothing. 'We'll just have to stall them a bit longer, that's all. You can't lay your hands on anything, I suppose?'

'You know I can't.' John's face was strained and his jaw moved as though he were chewing something. 'I've told you. We're broke.'

'OK.'

Martin looked away from the desperation in John's face and wandered over to the window. He stood looking out into the busy street. It had been a mistake to take John into partnership. He had neither the cool head nor the ready wits that were necessary in business when the chips were down. Martin, sipping at his coffee, stuck his free hand in his pocket and jingled his loose change. They shouldn't have taken over the new premises; that had been a serious error of judgement. The timing was all wrong and things were getting uncomfortable. The bank, the company who leased the photocopier, the landlord, British Telecom, all of them were on his back. He whistled a little tune between his teeth.

'What are we going to do?'

John was at his shoulder. Martin smiled at him, considering and rejecting various responses. It was no good panicking him, he'd learned that much.

'Telephone's priority. Got to keep them sweet. No phone, no business. Why don't you pop out for a quick bite while I make a few phone calls? Sort something out?'

He could see John willing himself to believe that things could be sorted out and continued to smile at him reassuringly.

'I'll drink my coffee first.' John turned back to his desk and Martin allowed his face muscles to relax. 'Can't afford any lunch anyway. Our own rent's due. God knows what I'm going to do.'

'Could Nell help?'

'Help? How?' John stared at him. 'Nell hasn't got any money.'

'No. I just meant . . . Well, perhaps she could get a job or something?'

John slumped down in his chair. 'She's suggested it but she's not really qualified to do anything and jobs are thin on the ground at the moment. I've always been against it, to be honest. I like to think that I can support my own wife and she doesn't know how desperate things are. I simply can't tell her. You know she didn't want me to come outside?'

'You told me.' Martin rose on his toes and dropped back on his heels once or twice. His face was thoughtful, his mind busy. 'What about that cottage of yours? On Exmoor, isn't it? Would you get much for that? Assuming that you could find a buyer.'

'What? You mean sell it?'

'Why not? Help to keep us going till the tide turns.'

'It's out of the question!' John stared at Martin. 'Not on! Nell would kill me. It's all we've got left.'

'Oh well,' said Martin lightly, after a moment, 'at least you'll have a roof if things go wrong.'

'Wrong? What d'you mean? Wrong?'

'Nothing.' Martin cursed himself and achieved an amused laugh. 'You really must stop panicking. The trouble with you service chaps is that you're no good without your book of rules. Out here in the cold world we have to make our own up as we go along. Go on. Go and have a pint while I make some phone calls.'

John swallowed his coffee, put the mug on his desk and stood up. 'I'll go and have a stroll round,' he said. 'Clear my head a bit. I can't afford to go to the pub.'

'For heaven's sake!' Martin dug in his back pocket and brought out his notecase. He riffled through it and gave a short laugh at its paucity of substance. 'Here! Take this and get yourself something. Bring me back a sandwich. Go on. Take it.'

'Is it all you've got?' John stared at the proffered note.

'Take it!' Martin shook it impatiently. 'I was going to put it in the petty cash. But we should last out and we don't need any stamps. Get yourself a drink and unwind a bit. We'll manage, you'll see.'

'Yes.' John hesitated for a moment and then took the note. 'We will, won't we?'

'Course we will.' Martin gave him a little wink. 'Go on. See you later.'

John managed a smile, picked up his jacket and went out. Martin stood for some moments after he'd gone and then, going into the inner office, he picked up the telephone receiver and dialled his estranged wife's number.

Seven

IN THE AUTUMN, HENRY sold the first of the Courtyard cottages. The buyers were a middle-aged couple from upcountry who wanted it for holidays and eventually for their retirement. Since they had heard of the cottage through Simon Spaders, Henry felt it incumbent upon him to give him a commission on the sale. Simon, who had already made quite a tidy sum out of Henry, accepted the commission and used it to pay for a week's holiday in Tenerife. Gillian went with him.

'You really are the most unprincipled person I've ever met,' chuckled Simon as they lay on their bed, worn out with too much sun, too much food and too much sex. 'Even I think it's a bit much that your husband is paying for all this debauchery.'

'No you don't.' Gillian rolled over lazily to reach for her wine-glass. She propped herself against the mound of pillows and sipped. 'Stupid people deserve what they get.'

'Is it stupid to trust your wife?' mused Simon, folding his hands behind his head and watching the patterns of evening sunlight on the carpet. 'An awful lot of men do it.'

'Which only goes to reinforce my opinion of the average man.' Gillian giggled suddenly. 'You have to laugh though, don't you? He thinks I'm with Lucy. A week with Lucy in the sun was my little present out of the proceeds. He simply couldn't imagine that I'd want a holiday. To him, Nethercombe is paradise. Do you know he hasn't had a holiday for years? Since he was a kid.' She shook her head. 'Amazing.'

'I still don't agree that he's stupid,' protested Simon. 'Gullible, trusting, generous —' Gillian snorted — 'kind . . .'

'Oh, for goodness' sake! You make him sound like an ad in a lonely hearts column. "Kind, gentle, trusting landowner . . . "' She burst out laughing and finished her wine. 'Anyway, anyone who prefers cold wet windy Devon to all this is definitely stupid.' She lifted the bottle and tilted it. 'The wine's all gone.'

'Too bad,' said Simon.

Gillian ran her finger over his bare skin and started to giggle again. 'Honestly,' she said. 'Henry in bed. He hasn't got a clue . . .'

'Oh, shut up, Gillian.' Simon pushed her hand away and got off the bed. He felt a sudden sense of revulsion at using Henry's money to cuckold him and he had no intention of adding to it by discussing his prowess — or lack of it — between the sheets. 'It must be dinner time. I'm going to have a shower.'

Gillian made a face at his departing back and turned over, burying her head in the pillow. In moments she was fast asleep.

NELL, CURLED UP IN the corner of the sofa, was only pretending to read her book. Her head bent, she was watching John who sat in the chair opposite. He, unconscious of her scrutiny, stared unseeingly at the fire and made no pretence of reading the paper which had fallen on to his lap. He felt himself to be living in a nightmare from which there was no waking and even Martin's confidence and optimism could no longer buoy up his spirits or disguise the truth.

It was two years since he had joined Martin and now, with every day that passed, he wished that he'd followed Nell's advice and stayed in the Navy. A few weeks before, he'd made the terrible mistake of going to a submariners' reunion dinner and the sight of all the old faces, the jargon, the jokes, had undone him even more than the day-to-day terror of wondering how they were going to survive. Why, oh why hadn't he listened to Nell? The Navy was his place, where he belonged. What on earth had made him think that he'd want to be outside where people talked another language and life was played with a different set of rules?

He'd stopped off to see his mother in Bournemouth on his way back from Gosport and wheedled enough money out of her to pay the rent on the flat and to keep his bank manager quiet for a while. If she had been disappointed it might have been easier to bear but her resignation merely indicated, as it had all down the years, that it was no more than she expected from him. He ground his teeth in humiliation at the memory of it and Nell's hands clenched involuntarily on her book.

'You look terribly tired. What about a hot bath and an early night?' she asked. Anything to break the train of thought that brought him such obvious misery.

The gentle question was more than he could bear.

'Don't speak to me as if I were a child!' he cried, hearing in her voice the same quality of pity that he'd seen on his mother's face. 'I'm not Jack! Don't patronise me!'

'John.' She stared at him in surprise. 'I'm not. Oh John, please talk to me. I can see something's wrong.'

'Oh, of course you can.' His fear was translating into rage and it was a relief to let it erupt and get it out of his system. 'You can always see everything, can't you? You're so bloody clever. You're always right and I'm always wrong.'

'That's not true—'

'Oh yes it is. It's always been true. My parents, Rupert, you. Always right! And I'm sick of it. Oh God!'

He buried his face in his hands while Nell watched him in horror. She cast around for something that she might say that wouldn't be misunderstood. In the end she could only think of one thing.

'I love you,' she said. 'I love you, John.' She moved to sit beside him and tentatively put her hand on his arm.

'No you don't.' John lifted his head and stared in front of him. His face was bleak and Nell felt frightened. 'Nobody ever has. Nobody could. It's just not possible.'

'John—'

'No!' He threw off her hand and got up. 'Leave me alone. And for God's sake stop looking like that. Oh Christ! I'm going out!'

The door slammed behind him and Nell pressed her hands tight together to stop them trembling. Her hopes that things might not be as bad as she feared completely vanished away. She had been waiting for a moment to talk to him, to ask how things were, without it seeming like a confrontation but the moment never arose. He accused her, before she'd hardly started, of mistrusting him, of having no confidence in him and he managed to create a situation which made it impossible to ask him anything without it looking exactly as he said.

Nell drew up her legs and folded them under her. She had started to scan the newspapers for jobs that she might be able to apply for on the grounds that they sounded like fun or offered a challenge so that he might think that she was in no way criticising him or posing a threat. So far nothing in this category had appeared. All the time that they weren't evicted, had enough for the housekeeping, paid the bills, she had nothing of which to complain, nothing to question. And somehow, he was still managing to achieve these things – as far as she knew. He was careful now to keep all his correspondence hidden away – probably at the office – but the time was coming when one particular issue had to be discussed.

The fund that Nell had insisted on setting aside for Jack's School fees was nearly finished. Soon she was going to have to ask where the rest of the fees would be coming from and she had no intention of being ignored or distracted from it. This was the one thing that she wouldn't let pass and, as her own world seemed to be crumbling round her, she was adamant that Jack should have a stable education. John was already making noises about finding a cheaper flat and the small luxuries that she'd once taken for granted were no longer forthcoming. She didn't mind that too much. For herself, she could cope. But Jack must have the best that she could do for him. He loved school; enjoying the companionship of other boys, excelling at his lessons, revelling in the outdoor life and the sport that the school offered. He was asked out to his friends' homes on Sundays and invited on holidays with them and Nell knew that he was building up a network that would be there for him all his life. It was the best she could do for him and nothing would prevent her. There was talk of a scholarship to Sherborne or even Winchester and after that it was up to Jack himself. Until then every sacrifice must be made.

Nell shivered. The fire had died down and the room was cold. Before she could move, the door opened and John stood looking at her.

'I'm sorry, Nell.' He looked at her beseechingly and his mouth twitched pitifully. 'I don't know what came over me. I'm really sorry. I love you, Nell.'

He stayed just inside the door, watching her, attempting to gauge her reaction and Nell was too relieved to see that his anger was past to risk any further eruptions.

'Oh, John.' She smiled at him. 'I love you, too.'

And, praying that her expression was not one of pity, she held out her arms to him and gathered him to her breast.

NELL MANAGED TO GET Gussie to Nethercombe for Christmas by the simple expedient of insisting on spending the holiday at Porlock Weir and offering Gussie a lift both ways. John, whose temper was now on a very short fuse, was only too grateful to be able to grant Nell's wish. It was little enough that he could do for her at the moment and he knew that it was better for Jack at the cottage. Nell was relieved at his ready acquiescence. She hoped that John's worries would recede a little once he was away from the office, along with the perpetual feeling that she was living on the edge of a volcano. She felt that, at the cottage, Jack might be less likely to notice the atmosphere of tension and anxiety or provoke John's ready temper. It was becoming apparent that the ten-year-old Jack was more like his Uncle Rupert in terms of achievement and not only in study and sport. He had an easy outgoing temperament which attracted people of all ages to him.

The friends that he brought home on exeats were obviously very attached to him and even the staff had a tolerant eye for his boisterous, good-natured enthusiasms.

So it was decided. They started very early on Christmas Eve so as to have lunch with Gillian and Henry before the Woodwards continued their journey. Nethercombe was looking very festive and Mrs Ridley produced an excellent lunch. Henry was obviously delighted to see Nell, and Gillian watched John from the corners of her eyes whilst carrying on a flirtation with Jack who thought her frightfully amusing and was enormously taken with her. Once again she saw the opportunity for another party which Henry could hardly refuse.

'Why don't you all stay?' she asked, as lunch drew to an end and Mrs Ridley was bringing in the coffee. 'It would be such fun, wouldn't it, Henry? Just what Nethercombe needs at Christmas. Lots of people to fill it up. Give it a bit of life. What do you say?'

She widened her eyes questioningly at John and then smiled at Jack who was working his way through a third helping of pudding. Mrs Ridley's glance met Gussie's above Gillian's head and Gussie spoke into the rather startled silence.

'It's a lovely idea but isn't it rather short notice for everybody? I know that Nell's made her own plans which would be rather difficult to change.'

'I'm afraid so.' Nell looked with relief at Gussie. 'And poor Mrs Ridley! Having to cater for three extra people. Well, half a dozen seeing that Jack eats for three!'

Mrs Ridley allowed her features to soften a little. Jack had already found his way to the kitchen and told her all about school food while the others were having a drink before lunch.

' 'Tis always a treat to feed someone who appreciates good cookin',' she said shortly.

Gussie could see that Henry was looking disappointed and, whilst she was overjoyed that he had taken to her friends so readily, she felt sorry that she was the one to dash his hopes. Gillian was fiddling with her coffee spoon and Gussie knew that she was busy trying to think of a way through the problems. For once Henry got in first.

'I can see that it might be difficult,' he said diffidently. 'But Gillian's quite right. It would be lovely to have you all to stay. Got an idea. What about stopping over for the New Year? On your way back? Just for a few nights. What d'you think?'

'Darling!' exclaimed Gillian, who never called Henry 'darling.' Well, well! This was a turn up for the book! She shot Nell a calculating look. Dear old Henry was quite smitten with her. Well, why not? It would all add spice to the gathering and John looked as if he could be fun with a little encouragement! 'What a splendid idea. And that will give Mrs Ridley time to get herself organised.'

Her glance drifted round to John who caught her eye and coloured a little.

He looked at Nell. 'Suits me,' he said. He raised his eyebrows interrogatively and after a moment she smiled at him.

'Sounds wonderful,' she said and felt warmed by Gussie's obvious delight and Henry's beam of pleasure. Her visits to Nethercombe thus far had given rise to varying sensations. She always loved to be with Gussie and Henry's old-world gallantry was charming but she suspected that, as far as Gillian was concerned, she was merely a pawn to be used in the pursuit of pleasure and as an alleviation from the boredom of country life.

'We'll have a lovely party,' said Gillian, pouring coffee. 'Won't we, Jack?'

'Oh yes!' said the boy, putting down his spoon and beaming at Mrs Ridley, who was going out with a loaded tray. 'That was smashing! May I stay up to see the New Year in?'

'No,' said John.

'Yes,' said Gillian simultaneously and they both burst out laughing.

'Please,' begged Jack, sensing Gillian's partisanship. 'I never have been allowed to. All my friends do.'

'House rules,' said Nell firmly, unwilling to let Jack be the pawn in a game between Gillian and John. 'When you're a guest you obey the rules of the house. You'll have to ask Mr Morley.'

Jack leaned forward to look at Henry who had just got up to open the door for Mrs Ridley and seemed rather nonplussed by the powers suddenly attributed to him. He recalled the days of his youth and decided to compromise.

'Bed as usual. Then you can get up just before midnight for a glass of champagne and to see the New Year in. How's that?'

He looked at Nell anxiously, hoping that he hadn't rocked any domestic boats and saw that she was smiling. So was John.

'You'll sleep right through it,' he said to Jack.

'I shall wake him up,' said Gillian over Jack's protestations to the contrary and with a provocative smile at John. 'Don't worry, Jack. You shall have your champagne.'

'Gillian's nice,' said Jack, waving furiously through the back window as they drove away. 'I like her. You like her too, don't you, Dad? I could tell.'

'Yes,' said John, after a moment. He slipped a glance at Nell who was staring ahead. 'Yes, I like her. I like them all.'

'I'm glad we're staying on the way back.' Jack settled into the small space left for him in the loaded car. He opened the paper napkin that Gillian had slipped him and saw with pleasure several of the chocolates that had been put on the table with the coffee. He slipped one into his mouth and sucked contentedly. 'I like them all, too. But I like Gillian best.'

John slipped another glance sideways. He took his left hand from the steering wheel and laid it over Nell's clasped ones.

'I like Mum best,' he said.

'Oh well.' Jack's voice sounded rather sleepy and he nestled into his quilt that Nell had tucked into his corner to make it as comfortable for him as she could. 'That's different, isn't it? I don't count Mum.'

Eight

THE PARTY AT NETHERCOMBE set the New Year off to a good start. Henry sold a second cottage, albeit one of the smallest ones, in the Courtyard and John and Martin sold two properties which enabled them to pay some of their creditors and earned them a breathing space. John's volatile spirits rose and he was able to believe that things were going to pick up at last.

Nell, relieved by this improvement, now started to worry very seriously about Gussie. There could be no doubt that she was going without things that were important to her health and she looked thin and haggard. When she mentioned, quite casually, that she'd been looking at smaller flats, Nell took fright. She could guess how much Gussie would hate living in quarters even more cramped than those she presently occupied and realised that her fears were quite justified. But what to do about it? She knew quite well that, even if she and John were in a position to do anything substantial to help, Gussie would refuse it. As she pursued her daily round, Nell's thoughts were busy with this problem and, when Gussie fell ill with flu, Nell finally took matters into her own hands and telephoned Henry.

'Nell. How nice.' His voice was so warm and friendly that Nell felt her courage rising. 'Are you all well?'

'Well, we are, Henry. But Gussie isn't. She's got flu.' His expressions of distress encouraged her and she hurried on. 'Oh, Henry, I'm so worried about her. Oh dear. This is so difficult to say but . . . the thing is, I don't think she's managing very well. You know? Financially.

She's going without things. Food. And heat. And now she's talking of moving into a bedsit. Just one room and a shared bathroom. She'll hate it so much. And now she's ill and there's no food in the place and it's freezing. I put the heat on when I'm there but I know that, after I've gone, she drags herself out of bed and turns it off.'

Nell stopped and took a deep breath. Her voice seemed to echo on and on in the silence but at least she'd managed to say it all. She waited for Henry's reaction.

'Nell, this is dreadful,' he said at last. He was obviously quite shocked. 'I knew nothing about it. Somehow I just assumed that she was perfectly all right. How ill is she? Not in any danger?'

'Not if she keeps warm and eats properly. I wanted to move her in with us but she wouldn't hear of it. The doctor goes in every day.'

There was a pause. Nell held her breath.

'If I were to drive up to Bristol tomorrow, would she be well enough to travel back to Nethercombe with me?'

Nell closed her eyes with relief, thanking God that it hadn't been necessary to suggest it herself.

'If she's wrapped up cosily and there's a warm bedroom waiting for her.' Knowing Nethercombe it was essential that this must be emphasised. 'She mustn't have temperature changes. Straight out of the car and into bed and I should think she'd be OK. I could check with the doctor. Anything must be better than that freezing little flat.'

'Then that's what I'll do. I'll ask Mrs Ridley to get the bedroom sorted out. Don't worry. We'll look after her between us.'

'Oh, Henry, that's wonderful. I've been out of my head worrying about her.'

'I should have thought about it myself.' Henry's tone indicated that he was put out with himself. 'I've been so taken up with things, the Courtyard and so on. I feel very ashamed. May I come to you first to-morrow and perhaps we could go round to see her together?'

'That's a good idea.' He was making it very easy for her to protect Gussie's independence. 'She's given me a spare key so that she doesn't have to keep getting out of bed and I'm doing her shopping and cooking for her.'

'That's incredibly kind of you.'

Nell laughed. 'You haven't tasted my cooking. And, Henry, don't tell her that I phoned you. Listen. I shall go round to see her in a minute. I go in every morning and then again in the afternoon. Telephone whilst I'm there. As if you were phoning her just out of the blue. Then she can think it's all your idea and won't think I've been interfering or telling tales.'

'That's very thoughtful.' Henry still sounded rather chastened.

'Rubbish. I'm very fond of Gussie. And what about this bedsit business?' Nell grimaced to herself. He would think her an interfering cow. 'Sorry, Henry. I really don't mean to nag. I'm just so worried about her.'

'Well, stop worrying,' said Henry firmly. He was quite confident now. 'I shall do what I should have done ages ago. I shall ask Gussie to make her home at Nethercombe. She loves it here and there's plenty for her to do, to keep her happy. Mrs Ridley will be delighted to have her here.'

'But will Gillian?' The words were out before Nell could stop them and she gave a tiny horrified gasp. 'Sorry, Henry. It simply isn't my business. I think it's the most wonderful thing that could happen to Gussie. Although I shall miss her terribly.'

'Well, you'll have to come and see her very often. We should all be delighted to have you here.'

There was a genuine note of welcome in Henry's voice and Nell smiled to herself. What a dear he was.

'That would be lovely. Now, if you've got a pencil I'll tell you how to find me.'

She gave him directions, told him to give her half an hour to get

round to Gussie's and, replacing the receiver, gathered up her belongings and hurried out.

A FEW WEEKS LATER, Martin dropped his bombshell.

'Getting out?' John stared at him in disbelief. 'How do you mean?
You can't just give it all up.' His voice rose a decibel or two. 'What
about me?'

'Listen, John.' Martin had been preparing himself for this moment. 'The writing's on the wall, I'm afraid. I thought that things
might straighten out this year but it's not going to happen. We're too
small to survive. Perhaps if we were in a country town and had rented
properties on our books, or if we'd been established for years and
owned this property, it might be different. But we jumped on the
bandwagon at the last moment and I'm afraid it's a question of last
on, first off. There's no shame in it. A lot of offices bigger than ours
have had to shut their doors.'

'Wait a minute.' John looked dazed. He passed a hand over his
face. 'Do you mean that you're just going to walk out? What about all
the bills?'

Martin shrugged. 'What about them?' he asked easily. 'Can't get
blood out of a stone, can they? I haven't got anything. Neither have you.'

'I've got the cottage at Porlock Weir.'

'Ah yes.' Martin turned away. He pursed his lips and whistled tune-
lessly. 'Well, I'm afraid that it may have to go, old boy.'

'But it can't! I told you that before. It's Nell's as well as mine. You
know that. You can't do this!'

'It's not me, John. It'll be the creditors. If we close the doors
they'll be on us like a ton of bricks. I know we never had a formal
partnership agreement but we're both responsible, jointly and sever-
ally. Now, since I've got nothing, they'll come to you. Nothing you
can do about it. Not unless you keep the business running, of course.'

'But how can I?' John thrust back his chair and got up. 'How can I
do it on my own?'

'Why not? It's not as if either of us is qualified. During the boom that didn't seem to matter and I don't see that it'll make any difference now. If I leave, you're no worse off and it means that you've got more of the profits to yourself, doesn't it? The business will only have to support one of us instead of two.'

John stared at him. A muscle twitched in his cheek and his hands flexed, indicating his internal tension. Martin looked away from him.

'I'm really sorry it hasn't worked out. If you don't think that you can carry on by yourself, then the only thing to do is to chalk it up to experience and try something else.'

'Oh great! And that's it, is it? Chuck my gratuity down the drain, borrow from my mother, lose everything we've got and then chalk it up to experience.' John was shouting now. 'Quite simple. No problem. And what's Nell going to say? And what the hell am I supposed to do next?' A thought struck him and he paused. 'What are *you* going to do?' he asked. He stared at Martin. 'What's *your* next venture going to be?'

'Well.' Martin paused. After all, John had to know sooner or later. May as well come clean. He cleared his throat a little. 'The thing is, I've had a stroke of luck.' He glanced quickly at John and away again. 'You know that Janie and I have been having a bit of a reconciliation? Well, her father runs a very posh pub with a restaurant that's almost famous. Janie and little Alex have been living there ever since we broke up. She works in the office. Well, her father's lost his manager and, times being so hard and all that, he's decided to give me a go at it. It means Janie and I can make another start. There's no money in it but it's a roof over our heads and so on. There may be a chance later to take over the whole thing. After all, I suppose any fool can run a pub.'

'That's what you said about estate agency. "Any fool can sell houses." That's what you said to me when you suggested that we become partners.' John thrust his hands deep into his pockets, so great was the temptation to lash out. Martin was simply going to turn his back on him and walk out, leaving him to carry the can. 'So you're all right, then? You can walk straight into another job.'

'Look, John, I'm really sorry. But it's not my fault. I couldn't possibly have foreseen this slump. There's never been anything like it. Everyone's been caught out. If you had my chance, wouldn't you take it? Be fair.'

They stared at one another.

'Yes,' said John at last. 'Yes. I'd take it.'

Martin relaxed a little. 'It's a condition really. The job goes with getting my wife and kid back. I've got no option.'

'Yes. I can see that.'

John turned away and Martin sucked in a deep breath and rolled his eyes. It had gone more easily than he had dared to hope. He looked at John's sagging shoulders, his bowed head and remorse struck at him. Poor chap! He hadn't got a hope in hell.

'I really think that you should carry on, you know,' he said. 'Tell you what. Just had a thought. Janie's dad's loaded. I'll tell him that there's a few debts to be cleared up before I can get out. He wouldn't want to think I was leaving a mess behind. I'll see what I can do. Perhaps I could pay off the telephone bill and get the rent up to date. How about that?'

John was looking at him with hope struggling in his face. 'D'you think that's likely?'

'Sure of it.' Martin laid an arm along his shoulders. 'Get you straightened up so you can start fresh. I think you might do quite well on your own. Think what it would be like to have all the commissions to yourself instead of splitting them in half. And you always say I'm on the phone too much. You'll probably find the bill's half the usual amount when I'm gone.' He gave him a little shake. 'I really think it might work.'

'Honestly?'

The hope was still in John's eyes and Martin had to will himself to stare into them and smile at him.

'Sure of it. Tell you what. Let's shut up shop and go down to the pub. My treat. We both need a drink.'

I certainly do even if you don't, he thought, watching John switch on the answering machine and pick up his coat. Poor sod! I give him six months at the most.

Martin smiled confidently as John turned and came towards him. He opened the door and stood aside to let John go first. He'd been let right off the hook and he was grateful. The least he could do was buy the poor chap a drink.

LYDIA WATCHED ANXIOUSLY AS Gillian pushed her cream cake listlessly around her plate.

'I'm really sorry, darling,' she said. 'I couldn't sympathise more. But I simply can't. I haven't got a bean till the end of the month. I could squeeze a fiver.'

'Oh honestly, Mum,' said Gillian despondently. 'I need a hundred pounds. What use is a fiver?'

Lydia, who could remember what it was to have secrets from one's husband, knew better than to mention Henry's name.

'What about Elizabeth?' she asked. 'Perhaps she could help you.'

'No chance.' Gillian gave a mirthless laugh and sat back in her chair. 'I've been warned. No more. The wedding was the last.' She sipped her coffee and glanced round. Butlers was quite full this morning but there was no one Gillian knew. 'She's made it perfectly clear. The wedding's to be my birthday and Christmas presents for the next ten years. Those were her very words.'

'Oh dear.' Lydia clicked her tongue sympathetically. 'Still. It was very generous of her—'

'Don't go on, Mum. I was suitably grateful. Anyway, she won't help. Let's forget it. I'll think of something.'

'Aren't Henry's barns selling?'

'He's sold two of them. The money all goes into doing up the remaining ones so there's nothing spare.'

'Well, I expect at the end . . .'

'Oh yes, I expect so.' Gillian sighed. 'It's now that I need it, though. Not next year.'

'Perhaps your father—'

'You must be joking. Look, just leave it, Mum, OK? Anything special you want to do? I'm meeting Simon at midday. He's treating me to lunch.'

'Oh.'

Lydia looked at her daughter and Gillian looked back. A signal passed and Gillian shrugged.

'Never know your luck, do you?'

'And after all,' said Lydia obscurely, 'Henry's put a lot of business his way.'

'That's what I thought,' said Gillian.

When she pushed open the door of Coolings wine bar an hour later, she saw that Simon was not alone. Cursing under her breath she approached the table.

'Hello, Simon,' she said and smiled at his companion as both men got to their feet.

'Gillian,' said Simon, 'meet an old school chum. This is Sam Whittaker. This is the love of my life, Sam. Gillian Morley.'

Gillian shook hands with Sam and slid into the seat beside Simon. Sam remained standing.

'What can I get you?' he asked, picking up Simon's empty glass.

'Oh, a glass of house red, please.' She watched him make his way to the bar, a tall, heavily built man but light on his feet, and then glanced at Simon. 'I need some money,' she said without preamble. 'I'm really stuck.'

'Oh not again, Gillian!' Simon shook his head. 'This is becoming a habit. Your old man didn't pay me that much, you know.'

'Yes, but you got a lot of recommends out of him, didn't you? From his farmer friends who wanted barns developed? Come on, Simon. I'm really desperate.'

'How much?' Simon looked annoyed but resigned.

'A hundred.' Gillian raised her chin a little as Sam turned to look at her from across the crowded floor. She met his gaze without expression and he smiled a little before turning back to the bar.

'Bloody hell!' Simon shook his head in despair. 'What do you do with it? Eat it? Have you ever thought of staying quietly at home?'

'Not since Henry brought that old bat to live at Nethercombe. Honestly! It was bad enough before—' She broke off as Sam came back with the drinks, relaxing back in her chair and arranging her features in a faint smile, eyes narrowed a little, enigmatically. She felt for Simon's leg and pinched it.

'Ouch! OK, OK,' he muttered. 'Just this once. Thanks,' he said to Sam, who was passing round the drinks. 'Listen. I've just had an idea about what you were telling me, Sam, before Gillian turned up. I've thought of a way that she can help you and earn some money at the same time. She's just the girl you need.'

'Really?' Sam sat down. His glance slid over Gillian and came to rest on her face. He raised his eyebrows. 'Sounds promising so far.'

'Hang on,' protested Gillian. 'I'm a drone, remember. I hate work.'

'In that case we speak the same language, lady.' Sam nodded at her and she gave him a tiny intimate smile.

'That's why it's a brilliant idea,' argued Simon. 'All you need is the right person and you'll both make some money.'

Sam and Gillian looked at one another. He sent her an almost imperceptible wink.

'You have our attention,' said Gillian, raising her glass. 'I wouldn't like to miss out on a new experience. OK, Simon. Spit it out!'

Nine

GUSSIE LEANED HER ARMS on the stone balustrade and gazed out over the countryside: the Courtyard, Nethercombe woods, the little stream bordering Nethercombe's fields where their own herds browsed contentedly. Home! Even after a few weeks her heart still swelled and throbbed at the word.

She had been amazed to find Henry at her bedside at the flat, protested feebly when he talked of carrying her off to Devon and had sunk luxuriously into being nursed back to health by Mrs Ridley. It had taken longer than she could possibly have imagined. Weakened by her poor diet during the long winter, she had no strength left to fight the infection and even now in early May, with the rhododendrons just coming into flower, she still felt weak but it was a weakness that was purely physical. The fears and doubts of living alone, of making ends meet, of simply existing had vanished away. Henry made it quite clear that her pensions were her own but Gussie's pride insisted that she pay a small sum for her keep and Henry, realising that she would feel happier if she did, accepted it. Even so, it left Gussie feeling relatively wealthy and she had many happy moments imagining how she would spend her money, once it had accumulated, to the benefit of Nethercombe.

Now, for the first time for more than forty years, Gussie felt that she was not alone. Looking back, she knew that she had never felt as much at home anywhere as she did here; not in the army quarters as a child nor in her flats in Bristol, and she knew that the medicine which had done her most good was the news that she was to live permanently at Nethercombe. She could hardly believe it and, when Henry had assured her that it had been in his mind for some while but he'd feared she might not want to give up her independence or leave her friends in Bristol, tears slid weakly down from beneath her closed eyelids. He wanted her, it seemed; needed her. Even loved her? She had been given two rooms on the corner of the east wing with a bathroom adjoining but Henry made it clear that she was to look upon the rest of the house — apart from the set of rooms upstairs that he and Gillian used — as her home too.

Her first thought, when she was stronger and her mind was clear again, was how on earth Gillian had taken the news. There certainly seemed to be no change in her behaviour which was still casual, easygoing, natural. She often spoke to Henry in a way that made Gussie wince, making no effort to dissemble or hide her feelings in any way and, after a while, Gussie managed to harden herself to it. It didn't take long for Gussie to discover that Gillian was rarely around during the daytime and often not in the evening either but she tried to keep out of their way as much as she could, spending time in her own rooms, in the grounds and in the kitchen with Mrs Ridley. Here a real alliance had sprung up, neither of them saying much but both definitely on the same side. Sometimes Gillian spent the night with her friend Lucy in Exeter and, whenever she appeared in the kitchen with this particular piece of information, the two women would stiffen at their tasks and when she'd gone their eyes would meet and exchange a look of understanding.

'Real fond o' that Lucy,' Mrs Ridley would say, kneading dough with a rhythmic twist of the wrist.

'I never think of Gillian as a girl who gets on particularly well with her own sex,' Gussie would say thoughtfully, polishing the silver.

'Which is quite wrong of me, Lord,' said Gussie now, looking out over the woods. 'Encouraging Mrs Ridley to gossip and undermining her employer's wife. Not to mention making judgements. "Judge not, lest ye be likewise judged." But I know quite well that she is deceiving Henry and it's a terrible thing to have to stand by and do nothing. I know that You will deal with her accordingly. "Vengeance is mine; I will repay, saith the Lord." But it's hard. You've got to admit.' She paused, wondering why it was so hard, and discovered a tiny unpalatable truth lurking in a dark corner of her mind. She hauled it out into the light and had a good look at it. Presently she sighed. 'You're quite right of course, Lord. Always the dear self. The truth of the matter is that I find it very hard to let her go on believing I'm such a stupid old woman that I can't see what she's up to.'

She leaned forward to watch Mr Ridley cutting the lawns which ran down to the Courtyard. She knew that he loved his mowing, seated on the machine, driving to and fro across the grass: his cap was perched at an angle and even the set of his shoulders looked jaunty. Gussie smiled and then looked serious again. Her second thought, after her arrival, had been for Nell. She missed her so much and was eternally grateful for all she had done for her during the last three years. She knew now that she would never have managed without her, especially during the last year. Nell may not have offered her a home but she too had made her feel needed. Despite the age difference she was the best and dearest friend Gussie had ever had and the one fly in the ointment was leaving Nell behind. She told them this one evening during supper and Henry insisted Nell should come to stay whenever she was able to and Gillian smiled at him oddly and said she certainly must, and John and Jack, too. Henry had blinked a little and said that, naturally, they were all welcome. Gussie remembered this little scene now, with the sun warm on her back and the swallows wheeling above her, and she frowned a little. There had been something in Gillian's voice . . .

' "The flowers that bloom in the spring, tra-la . . . " '

She turned in surprise as Henry came out on to the terrace behind her. She'd assumed that he was helping with the silage at Higher Nethercombe since the tenant farmer had broken his ankle. Henry was always ready to muck in and lend a hand wherever it might be needed.

'Wonderful day!' he said. 'Watching the swallows? Mrs Ridley says is it warm enough to have coffee out here?'

He was tilting back the wrought-iron chairs which always stood on the terrace and Gussie's heart filled and overflowed with love and gratitude.

'Oh, I think it is, Henry, my dear,' she said. 'I'll go and help her carry.'

Henry strolled to the balustrade and he, too, looked down at Mr Ridley and beyond him to the Courtyard. It was doing very well and Henry allowed himself a moment of self-congratulation. It had been a quite terrifying project for one of his temperament and yet, despite the recession and the slump in the housing market, the Courtyard development was gradually working, the cottages selling. Henry blew out his lips in grateful recognition of what a disaster it might so easily have been. The Beresfords, who had bought the very first conversion, had spent Easter in their cottage and the new young man in his mid-twenties who had bought the smallest cottage was settling in happily. Henry frowned a little, cudgelling his memory. Guy. That was it. Guy Webster. He ran a yacht brokerage in Dartmouth and was often away, moving boats to and fro. He wanted somewhere in the country, he told Henry, but where there would be somebody around to keep an eye on things during his absences. The Courtyard was perfect, he said, although Henry suspected that Guy had a reservation that it might be a little too friendly. He looked like someone who kept himself to himself. Henry had bent to stroke the golden retriever which was always at Guy's heels.

'Nice dog,' he said. 'Bertie, is it?'

'That's right.' They both looked at Bertie who looked back, unused to this concentrated interest. He wagged his tail a little and looked at Guy. 'My mother breeds them,' he said, almost reluctantly, and Henry knew that he was right and that this was a very reticent young man who resented parting with any information about his private life.

'Well, you know where we are,' he said lightly. 'Don't be lonely. You're all on your own down there at the moment. The Beresfords only use their cottage for holidays. Let us know if you've got a problem. When you've settled in you must come up for a drink and meet my wife and my cousin. And Mr and Mrs Ridley.'

They parted and although a week or two had passed, Guy had not yet been up for his drink.

Plenty of time, thought Henry. And now there was another prospective buyer coming to look at one of the two remaining cottages. Usually his agent showed people round but this morning there had been a hitch and Henry agreed to meet the client at eleven thirty down in the Courtyard. As he heard the coffee arriving behind him, he had an idea.

'Got a woman coming to view,' he told Gussie, strolling over to the table where she was assembling cups and saucers. 'Mr Ellison can't make it. Like to show her round?'

Gussie stared at him, arrested in the act of pouring. 'I?' she said, round-eyed. 'Oh . . .'

'Why not?' Henry sat down. 'You know the setup as well as I do now. You'll do it much better. Get myself tied up in knots.'

'Oh, Henry!' Gussie passed him his cup, a spot of colour burning in each cheek. 'I should love to, of course . . .'

'That's settled then,' said Henry comfortably. 'It's a Mrs Henderson. Now I can have my coffee in peace and get back up to Higher Nethercombe. I don't think this weather will hold much longer.'

He stole a glance at the silent Gussie who was now sitting bolt upright in her chair, gazing in front of her. Her lips moved silently and he wondered if she was having one of her frequent conversations with the Almighty or rehearsing the details of the cottage.

Henry smiled to himself and sipped his coffee. It had been a good day when Nell telephoned from Bristol and he'd decided to offer

Gussie a home. Nell. At the thought of her the smile softened on his lips and his eyes grew dreamy. How beautiful she was and how kind she'd been to Gussie! He remembered her cry, 'But will Gillian?' and his smile faded.

Gillian had behaved very well; much better than he'd dared to hope. She made no demur at the idea of Gussie coming to live at Nethercombe. Rather to the contrary, she'd seemed to welcome it. Henry was deeply relieved, touched by her generosity and suggested that now might be the time for thinking of redecorating their private sitting room upstairs. Gillian opened her eyes at him and he felt as though he were treating her as he might a child or offering her bribes.

'Lovely idea,' she said. 'Come into some money, have we? That's a lucky coincidence, isn't it? Just as Gussie's arrived.' She laughed at his confusion. 'I'll look around. Get some ideas together.'

He had begun to notice, however, since Gussie's arrival she was at home even less than she'd been before and he wondered if she had seen Gussie's presence in the house as a possible cloak for her own activities. Henry sighed and stirred. Gussie was getting to her feet.

'I must go and keep my appointment, my dear,' she said, her voice vibrant with pride.

Henry smiled up at her. 'Good luck,' he said. 'Bring me back a sale.'

'I shall do my best, Henry.' She smoothed down her tweed skirt and patted her hair. Henry watched affectionately.

' "She may very well pass for forty-three," ' he sang, ' "In the dusk with a light behind her!" '

He grinned at her and she made a shocked face at him. At the end of the terrace she turned.

'Henry?' she said. He raised his eyebrows, still grinning. 'Drink your coffee! It's getting cold!'

JOHN SAT IN THE little study with his head in his hands. Never before had he felt so alone as he did now. He could never have imagined how much he would miss Martin; how desperately he longed to have someone to talk with who knew exactly what was going on, from whom nothing need be hidden. Friendship and camaraderie were what had carried him through in the Navy. Now, without Martin's cheerful optimism, problems were almost too difficult to bear. John didn't have his easy way with people, his ability to lie his way out of trouble, his instinct to make light of disasters. But it was more than that. It was just the fact of Martin himself, there, bustling about, jollying him along: coming in with a bar of chocolate or a sandwich for him, taking him to the pub at lunch time for a pint, slapping him on the back with relief when they solved a problem, calmly talking things through when life was getting too much for him. Nothing ever seemed quite impossible to cope with when Martin was around. And now John was alone.

He groaned aloud. The sheer emptiness of the office, the silence, almost defeated him before he got through the door each morning. While Martin was with him, encouraging him, showing him the advantages, he'd believed that he could do it alone. He'd come home to Nell and told her, his heart still high with hope, boosted by Martin's assertions that he would succeed. Nell stared at him, anxiety plain on her face.

'But how will you manage alone?' she asked. 'If Martin doesn't think there's any point in carrying on, is it sensible?'

He told her that Martin was under pressure to go back to his wife and he put forward Martin's theories about how he might do even better alone. Nell, however, was not convinced and John could feel his hard-won confidence seeping away. As usual, he masked his fear with anger.

'Why shouldn't I manage?' he asked, his voice loud. 'Why can't you ever support me?'

'I have supported you,' she replied. 'Be fair. You know I have.'

But he didn't want to be fair. She had roused his demons of insecurity and fear and they would not be quieted without a scene. He'd lost his temper and then had flung out and gone down to the pub. He returned, as usual, repentant and in desperate need of her love and she'd given it. But for how long could their relationship bear the strain?

Martin kept his word and provided enough money to keep all the creditors quiet, if not paid off, and two weeks later John sold a very large property to a company which was sending one of their employees to work in the area. The deal went through quickly and John's spirits flew up on wings of hope. Nell, who was learning lessons, didn't point out that it was probably just an enormous stroke of luck but enthused with him, agreed that the tide was turning and that things were going to be all right. For three days he lived on cloud nine, buying her flowers and taking her to the theatre. He booked a table at their favourite restaurant and took her out to dinner and it was so wonderful to see him relaxed, happy, talkative, that Nell threw all her caution away and laughed with him. Euphoric, delighted with themselves and the evening, they staggered home and made wonderful, satisfying, ecstatic love for the first time in months.

Now, John shook his head and felt like weeping. Why did life have to be so cruel? So relentless? The money had gone so quickly; there were so many expenses and, unlike Martin, John panicked at the final demands, the threats of court action. He seemed unable to hold creditors off with a placating telephone call or lies about imminent sales. His own bank manager was continually on his back and now this letter from the building society was the last straw. It had been impossible to keep up with the mortgage payments on the cottage at Porlock Weir and John had been keeping his fingers crossed that a miracle would happen and he would be able to pay it all back in a lump sum. Unfortunately, the quarterly payment for their own rent had also fallen due when he'd been in funds and, what with one thing and another, the mortgage payment had been put aside yet again. But to foreclose! John beat his forehead against his clenched fists and gave a dry sob. How on earth had it mounted up so quickly? Six months' back payments were due and the society had had enough. He'd arranged that all communications should be sent to the office, thus preventing Nell from seeing and opening the letters, but lately he'd been putting the familiar envelopes unopened into the bottom drawer of his desk. He simply couldn't face them. He remembered, too late, Martin's advice.

'Keep talking to people. Let them know you know the problem and are trying to deal with it. Never ignore people you owe money to!'

But how was he to tell Nell? He couldn't go to his mother for help. He knew that she simply didn't have that sort of money tucked away and was finding it difficult enough to live on the widow's allowance of his father's army pension. She'd already helped him out and now, anyway, she was in hospital. John raised his head and stared ahead. The cottage would have to go. With the mortgage paid off there should be enough spare to pay Jack's school fees for the next year at the very least and the rest would straighten up their own financial muddle; the bank, Barclaycard, the usual bills. It would have to be sold. He imagined Nell's face and put his head back in his hands. He couldn't do it. He simply couldn't face her. Perhaps something would turn up. He opened the drawer in his little desk and took out a miniature bottle of whisky. He needed something to keep him going. Putting the bottle to his lips, he gulped back a mouthful of the strong golden liquid. He swallowed, rubbed his lips and fetched a great sigh. After all, another day or two might just turn the tide. He took another swig. It would be foolish to act precipitately; he needed time to think. And he was so tired. John sighed again and took another smaller sip. The whisky warmed and soothed, dulling his fears, making light of his terrors. He seemed to hear Martin's voice in his ear.

'Don't let the buggers get you down.'

He smiled a little and his eyelids grew heavy. He was so damned tired. No, he simply mustn't panic; anything could happen. Anything . . . John's head drooped forward and presently, with his forehead on his arms, he slept.

Ten

GILLIAN SAT IN COOLINGS waiting for Sam. Although they'd met several times since that first occasion with Simon, this was the first time she'd agreed to see him alone. To her surprise she was nervous. Ostensibly, this was a business meeting but Gillian knew that for both of them it was more than that. Hitherto, Simon had been there, keeping the situation under control, and Gillian's heartbeat hurried a little as she thought of being alone with Sam. Simon had seen none of the signals that passed between them. He was too absorbed in their new project, or rather, Sam's project.

Sam was the owner of some derelict barns, very like the ones at Nethercombe, but the friend who was to put up the funds to develop the site had lost his money and Sam was looking for an equity partner with whom he could proceed. Both he and Simon felt that he may have missed the boat. After all, no one was likely to invest in property development with the market so low. The site, however, was in a prime spot in a valley overlooking the sea just outside Dartmouth and Sam claimed that he had buyers for all three conversions if only he could build them. Simon's thought, first and foremost, was that he would get the job as architect. Sam was only too willing to agree.

'Find me someone who will fork out the money, old son,' he said, as they sat in Coolings waiting for Gillian on that first occasion, 'and the job's yours.'

Simon was thoughtful. There wasn't too much work around at the moment and it would be a godsend. It was then that it occurred to him that Gillian might have someone amongst her acquaintances who could be interested in it if the scheme was presented in the right way.

And who better, he thought bitterly, to detach some unsuspecting mug from their hard-earned cash than Gillian!

She had listened carefully, driven a hard bargain for the commission she would receive should she find an investor and had immediately drawn up a list of names of people that it might be worth approaching.

Sam raised his eyebrows at her businesslike attitude and bought her another drink. He agreed to let Simon have the plans and one afternoon they drove out to see the site. It was like Nethercombe all over again except that Sam had bought the barns from a farmer and the stone farmhouse was already occupied.

'Henry's places are selling,' said Gillian, shielding her eyes to look out over the sea to the lighthouse at Start Point. 'And this really is a magnificent site.'

'Well, I've drawn a blank,' shrugged Sam. 'People are afraid to take risks at the moment. And who can blame them?'

Simon was examining the buildings and, after a moment, Sam drew nearer to Gillian.

'Your husband must be a very trusting man,' he said lightly. 'Letting you loose with two unprincipled chaps like me and Sy.'

'Simon's not unprincipled,' protested Gillian, still staring out to sea. 'What makes you say that?'

'I was at school with him,' returned Sam. 'Share a dormitory and then a study with a guy for five years and there's not much you don't learn about him.'

Gillian glanced at him. 'If you say so,' she said coolly. 'Of course, I've only shared his bed but I think I've learned a few things.'

Sam gave a shout of laughter. 'Not as much as he has, I'll bet,' he said and Gillian began to laugh too.

'What's so funny?' asked Simon, returning from his prowling.

'You,' said Gillian, taking his arm. 'Sam's just been telling me all about your schooldays.'

'And about all that trouble he got me into?' asked Simon, leading the way back to the car. 'Don't trust this man an inch, Gillian. I warn you.'

Gillian remembered this conversation as she sat watching Sam threading his way between the crowded tables. He was wearing flannels and a blazer and Gillian grimaced at him.

'You're looking very smart,' she said, determined to keep things under control. 'Meeting someone important?'

'I'm meeting you,' he said. 'I thought we were having lunch? I was brought up to believe that if one takes a lady out to lunch one dresses accordingly.'

'One certainly does,' mocked Gillian.

'Well then.' He remained standing, looking down at her.

He was very tall and very good-looking and Gillian shivered suddenly. His eyes narrowed a little.

'Drink?'

'Thanks. The same will be fine.' She passed him her empty glass.

'House red, I believe?'

She nodded, refusing to remark on the fact that he had remembered, and he turned away. She watched him go, her feelings all in a tumult, and wondered if she might be getting out of her depth. Hitherto, she had concentrated on men whom she could wheedle and bully, who found it worth putting up with her moods and expensive tastes for the physical pleasures she bestowed upon them. Sam didn't look that sort. Up at the bar, he ordered the drinks and, lazily leaning on one elbow, he stared at her unsmilingly. Unnerved but determined not to show it, Gillian stared back. Quite suddenly he smiled and it was as though he had asked her a question. After a moment, she smiled back and he gave a little nod and Gillian knew that from now on there could be no more pretence and, for her at least, no turning back.

NELL LET HERSELF INTO the flat, went into the sitting room and sat down at the end of the sofa, too shocked to do anything else. The news which she had just received made her feel quite desperate. She thought of John and a spasm of fear shook her. He was behaving so oddly. Not long ago he'd been euphoric; now he was almost suicidal. She never knew where she was with him. It was as though she were walking a tightrope; an unconsidered remark, a thoughtless observation, and he would be shouting and raging about her inability to support him and her tendency to think only of herself. He accused her of destroying his self-confidence, of sapping his ability to achieve. It had always been the same, he cried: first his mother, then Rupert and now her. None of them had ever believed in him or wanted him to succeed.

Nell sighed and leaned her head back against the cushions. Apparently, it was to be everyone's fault but his if things went wrong. If! She gave a mirthless little laugh. Things were already definitely wrong. Ever since the sale of that house just after Martin left, things had been gradually deteriorating again. John spent longer at the office and, when he did come home, shut himself in his little study. Several times she'd smelled spirits on his breath. One morning, she'd even descended to the level of searching the study. Nell gave an instinctive grimace of distaste at her action. She was simply so worried that she didn't know what else to do. All private papers and letters had been removed and Nell guessed that he had them at the office. If only he would talk to her! Every time she attempted to find out what was going on, he met her tentative approaches with aggression and generally worked himself into starting a row which gave him the excuse to storm out. Sadly, their reconciliations were happening with less and less understanding and generosity on Nell's side. She began to dread the crumpling into disintegration that inevitably took place on his return. She was barely able to prevent herself from despising him. Each time she had to summon all her love and loyalty and each time it grew harder and harder. She felt that his behaviour was a form of cheating. He was using weapons to hold her at bay, to prevent her from discovering the truth.

It was her life too and she had the right to know what he was doing with it.

And now this. Nell pulled herself forward but as she prepared to stand up, she heard the front door open and she was still sitting on the edge of the seat when John appeared. He looked white and strained and Nell gazed at him in terror. What now? That muscle was twitching in his cheek again and she could smell the whisky on his breath.

'You're early,' she said and her voice shook a little. 'How nice. I've got something to tell you.'

'And I've got something to tell you,' he said, before she could go on. 'Bad news, I'm afraid.' He looked away from her. 'I've just heard that the cottage is going to be repossessed. The mortgage hasn't been paid and they won't wait any longer. It'll have to be sold.'

Nell's hands clasped convulsively and she stared up at him in horror.

'But why?' she whispered and cleared her throat. 'Why?' she asked more strongly. 'You never said anything about it. What's been happening? They don't repossess just because you miss a payment or two.'

'It's not just one payment. Or two. It's six. There's nothing we can do about it.'

'*Six?*' Nell was silenced.

'There was just too much.' John's tone implied that only she would have expected it of him. 'The rent here, the mortgage, the business. The money simply won't stretch. If we sell, at least we'll be able to pay Jack's school fees.'

'Wait a minute.' Nell was on her feet. 'You said that you'd put those aside out of the money you got from that sale just after Martin left. You said you'd put a year's fees to one side.'

'Well, I didn't.' John faced her at last. He looked defiant and something else. It occurred to Nell that he was completely unconcerned by it all, indifferent to the pain he must know that this would cause her. The cottage could go and good riddance to it and the proceeds from the sale would be just that bit more for him to throw away. 'In the end there wasn't enough to go round. It's no good, Nell.' His voice was louder now; prepared to shout down anything she may have to say. 'This recession has ruined lots of people. At least we've got the business and a home here. And we can pay Jack's fees. I know how much that means to you.'

There was a change in his tone then, as if the money for the school fees was a special dispensation for which she should be grateful, which should buy her gratitude and forgiveness.

'I should have thought that Jack's education was important to you, too.' She looked proud and cold and John's heart beat fast with fear. 'He's your son, too.'

'With you spending every waking thought and every penny we've got on him,' he said spitefully, 'there's no need for me to worry, too.' Her look of contempt struck to his very soul and he gave a cry and dragged her to him. She stood stiffly in his arms, fighting back tears, trying not to hate him.

'I'm sorry, Nell,' he cried. 'Oh God! I'm sorry. You know I didn't mean it. I'm as upset as you are. It's just been such hell getting up the courage to tell you. Please understand. I'm really sorry, Nell. I know how much the cottage means to you. Please try to forgive me.'

Slowly Nell relaxed. With a tremendous effort she put her arms round him and held him while he cried, staring all the while beyond his shoulder and trying to come to terms with the idea of losing the cottage.

Presently he pulled himself together, feeling for his handkerchief, mumbling apologies. Nell patted his shoulder lest he should sense her urgency to be apart from him. She moved slowly away. His face was a pitiful sight and she was touched in spite of herself. He mopped his face.

'Oh, what was your news? Sorry. I rather had to get that off my chest.'

'Yes.' Nell paused, wondering if she should tell him. Well, why the hell not? Terror and rage surged anew in her and she raised her head and looked at him. 'It seems that we've achieved the impossible. After eleven years I'm pregnant again.'

John's head snapped round and the horror in his eyes confirmed Nell's fears of how he would react to the news.

'Oh Christ,' he whispered.

Something clicked inside Nell's head.

'I thought you'd be pleased,' she said, bitter sarcasm hiding her hurt. 'You're always telling me what a failure everyone thinks you are. Well! At least you've managed to achieve something!'

His face was suffused with a dusky, ugly red as the blood surged under the skin and he stared at her as though he hated her.

'You bitch!' he whispered and ran out into the hall.

Nell stood quite still as the front door slammed. Presently she covered her face with her hands and, sinking back on to the sofa, burst into tears.

'LETTER FROM NELL?' ASKED Henry as they sat at breakfast.

'It is indeed,' replied Gussie with pleasure, neglecting her toast. 'It's good of her to write as often as she does.' She turned a page, whilst Henry watched her progress, waiting for news. Gussie always shared parts of Nell's letters with him. 'Oh . . .'

'Something wrong?'

'Oh dear. Poor Nell. Yes indeed. They've had to sell their cottage. Oh how very sad. Nell must be heartbroken. It sounds as if she's being very brave but I know how she loved it.' Gussie turned another page.

'But did they have to sell?' Henry looked distressed. 'They don't own the flat in Bristol, do they? The cottage was the only home they had.'

'Sorry, my dear?' Gussie glanced up at him. 'Oh yes, yes, I'm afraid that's so. Nell doesn't say much but it seems there were school fees and other expenses. And John's mother is ill in hospital.' She shook her head. 'Troubles never come singly.'

'I must say that I wouldn't want to earn my living by selling houses at the moment,' said Henry. He looked troubled. 'Have they actually sold it?'

'Yes.' Gussie turned back a sheet or two. 'Apparently a naval friend had always coveted it and gave them a good price. Nell's going down next week to move the furniture out. She says that they'll have to sell that, too. There's no room at the flat for it all.' Gussie looked sombre. 'It must be a frightful blow for her.'

'She mustn't sell the furniture,' declared Henry. 'Write to her, Gussie. Better still, telephone her. Tell her to have the stuff brought here. We've masses of space to store it for her. She may want it later on when they get another home. She mustn't lose everything.'

Gussie looked at him with great affection. 'That is a very kind of-fer, Henry dear. Nell will appreciate it, I know. She had all her special things there. It was her little retreat. Poor child. I do wonder if they're not getting into difficulties.' She sighed. 'Nell's a very private person and it's not easy to know exactly what is happening. It must have been something very serious for her to sell her little cottage.'

'It must be dreadful to lose your home.' Henry looked quite shocked. 'Ask her if there's anything we can do.'

'I will, of course.' Gussie folded the sheets and put them by her plate. 'Poor Nell. She used to so look forward to her little holidays there. And Jack will be very upset. Which will make it even worse for her, of course. She'll have nowhere to take him now.'

'They must come here,' said Henry at once. 'Tell her that too when you speak to her. There's plenty of room for all of them and plenty to do. They'll be welcome any time they wish to come.'

'Oh, Henry.' Gussie rarely let her emotions have a free rein but her eyes felt rather prickly and she blinked a little. She cleared her throat. 'That is extremely generous. I know that Nell will be very touched. You know, she was so very good to me . . .'

Gussie fished her handkerchief out of her sleeve and blew her nose loudly. Henry, who knew just how good Nell had been, smiled at her.

'I shall love it,' he said. 'Nethercombe was made to have lots of people in it.'

'Just what I always say myself.' Gillian strolled in and smiled sleepily at them. 'Good morning. Are you thinking of having a party, Henry?'

'Well, actually, I think I might be.' Henry beamed at her. 'It's time we had the people up from the Courtyard. You haven't met Guy yet, have you, Gillian? And the Beresfords are down next week for their holiday. It's time we all got together. We may even have Nell here.'

'Oh?' Gillian sounded unenthusiastic. 'Why?'

'She's on her way back from somewhere,' he said blandly while Gussie looked at him in surprised admiration. 'And we may have something to celebrate.' He picked up one of his letters. 'It looks as if Gussie may have sold another cottage for us!'

'Henry!' Gussie sat bolt upright in her chair. 'Oh! How wonderful! Mrs Henderson?'

'That's right. Pretty good, isn't it? I'm going in to see Mr Ellison this morning. Want to discuss the offer with him. Better get on.'

'Wonders will never cease.' Gillian yawned and poured herself some coffee as Henry pushed back his chair and went out. 'I'm beginning to hope he might be human after all.'

Gussie opened her mouth to speak, thought better of it and shut it again.

'I must make a telephone call,' she said. 'You'll have to excuse me.' She gathered up Nell's letter and disappeared into the hall.

'Only too willingly,' muttered Gillian, gazing with distaste at what remained of breakfast.

She drank her coffee and thought about the proposed party. She'd need something new to wear, especially if Nell were coming. It occurred to her that John might be coming too and her eyes narrowed a little and a tiny smile played around her lips. Definitely, something new would be required. She'd telephone Lydia and scrounge some lunch and have a potter round the shops.

'Finished then?' Mrs Ridley stood in the doorway.

Gillian's smile widened. 'Haven't even started,' she said. 'Nothing worth eating. Never mind. Don't let me hold you up.'

She got up, taking her coffee cup with her, and, bowing ironically as Mrs Ridley stood aside for her, she passed through the hall and went back upstairs.

Eleven

IN THE END, AT Gillian's insistence and in the face of
Henry's protests, it turned out to be a pool party. With the aid of Mr
Ridley and Bill Beresford, Gillian transformed the dilapidated if spa-
cious summerhouse tucked away beside the swimming pool. They
painted and creosoted, cleaned the windows, refelted the roof, laid
new rush matting on the floor and installed comfortable Lloyd Loom
chairs that Gillian found in various unused bedrooms. When she was
satisfied with it, she went off in her car and returned with a barbecue.
Bill Beresford assembled and erected it whilst Mr Ridley strung fairy
lights in the branches of the rhododendron bushes and by the time
everything was ready the whole setting looked delightful. Even
Henry decided that it might be quite fun after all.

Late in the afternoon of the day before the party, Nell had arrived,
to be followed, in due course, by a removal van, and Gussie showed
her upstairs where the furniture was to be put.

'But these are bedrooms, Gussie,' said Nell anxiously. 'Won't
Henry want to use them? Not that I mind if he uses our furniture but
even so . . .'

'Henry wants to feel that you can come and stay with all your
things round you,' said Gussie. 'Now please don't worry,' she added
quickly, seeing a variety of emotions struggling on Nell's face. 'Good
heavens! There are so many empty rooms that it won't make any difference at all. We thought this bedroom for you and John, you see,

because it's got a dressing room off it which could be used as a little sitting room. And there's another room next door for Jack.'

'Wait a minute, Gussie.' Nell shook her head. 'What do you mean? You make it sound as if we're about to move in with you.'

'No, no, dear. Of course not. I explained to you when we spoke on the telephone. Henry hopes very much that you'll spend your holidays here now that you can't go to the cottage. And he wants you to be comfortable and feel at home. He thought having your own things would help.' She peered at Nell, praying that she wouldn't be too proud to accept the offer. 'We'd be so happy, Nell,' she pleaded, 'if you thought you could come. I've missed you so much and Henry was so taken with Jack. It's a wonderful place for a child.'

'Oh, Gussie.' Nell looked quite desperate. 'It's amazingly kind of him, of all of you, but honestly, I can't just use Nethercombe as a hotel. It's terribly good of Henry to store my furniture. I would have hated to sell it. But I wasn't angling for a private suite . . .' She swallowed and walked over to the window.

Gussie watched her. She guessed very accurately at the loss of pride as well as the pain that Nell must be suffering and made no attempt to insult her by attempting to belittle it or gloss over it.

'It was selfish of us,' she said quietly to Nell's back. 'I realise that. We were so delighted at the thought of seeing more of you that we didn't really think about how you might see it. I hope you'll forgive us. You must do whatever is right for you.'

'I'm sorry.' Nell turned back. She looked exhausted. 'I'm being quite unreasonable and very ungrateful. It's been rather dreadful, packing everything up and leaving the cottage.' Gussie nodded understandingly, privately shocked that John had allowed her to make this particular trip alone, but she said nothing and Nell attempted a smile. 'I should love to think that we could come to Nethercombe and I know Jack would be quite beside himself. It's so generous of you all.'

'No more generous,' said Gussie, 'than you were to me in Bristol. Oh yes,' she said firmly, as Nell made as though to speak, 'I know that

I couldn't have managed without you. So please, my dear, shall we just look upon it as a kind of *quid pro quo*? Could you do that? Just until things improve again for you? It would give me so much happiness.'

'Put like that, how can I possibly refuse? Thank you. It will be wonderful to think that we can come and see you all.'

'Then that's settled.' Gussie's relief was palpable. 'Now you're going to have something to eat and when the van arrives I'll see to it. There's to be a little party tomorrow beside the pool so Gillian's busy getting things ready and Henry's off somewhere but you'll see them both later.'

Nell, following Gussie downstairs, was too tired to make any more objections. The thought of a party was too horrific for words but she felt that it would be churlish to make any more protests. Perhaps tomorrow she would feel more up to it.

In fact, she almost enjoyed it. Although it was now September the weather was very warm and several guests swam while Bill Beresford instructed Henry in the art of barbecuing. Nell sat in the dim interior of the summerhouse, her mind pleasantly dulled by fatigue and wine, and made no attempt to be anything but an onlooker. She met people whose names she almost immediately forgot and wished she could spend the rest of her life sitting in this comfortable chair, watching the twilight gather in the rosy sky, whilst the murmuring of voices and clinking of glasses surged and ebbed around her. Bats darted among the shadowy branches of the trees and presently a slender silver arc of moon appeared above the roofs of the Courtyard cottages. The fairy lights twinkled like multicoloured stars, casting their reflection in the water below, and people moved to and fro like actors in a play.

The strain of the last two years, culminating in the shock of having to sell the cottage and finding herself pregnant, had left Nell feeling quite light-headed in this magic setting. Reality had drawn off from her and she wondered if she might wake tomorrow and find that none of these dreadful things had happened. She was aware that someone had come into the summerhouse and she saw now that it was the young man to whom Gillian had been speaking earlier beside the pool. He was tall and dark with an unsmiling countenance and cool grey eyes. Nell was almost too relaxed to acknowledge his presence but she roused herself enough to smile and he took the chair that stood next to hers.

'I don't think we've been introduced,' he said and his voice was warmer and more flexible than she had expected. 'I'm Guy Webster. I live down in the Courtyard.'

'I'm Nell Woodward.' Even as she spoke, she felt again the sense of unreality and gave a little chuckle. Guy looked more closely at her. 'I'm sorry,' she said, still chuckling a little, 'I feel as if I've stumbled on an enchanted scene. You know. Like Bottom and Titania.'

'Well, I've certainly been called an ass often enough . . .' began Guy cautiously and Nell burst out laughing.

'No, no,' she protested. 'It's nothing personal. Don't take any notice of me.' She made an attempt to be social. 'Are you happy in the Courtyard?'

'Oh, I think so.' She was aware of his eyes studying her in the shadows. 'Have you bought one of the cottages, by any chance?'

'Good heavens, no.' Nell shook her head. 'In fact, I've just been selling my cottage. I moved out yesterday.'

She fell silent, unwilling to be drawn back into the present. Guy simply couldn't stop looking at her. He was mesmerised by her unearthly beauty and they sat without movement or speech for some time. Presently Nell stirred and, as if a spell had been broken, Guy leaned towards her.

'Another drink?'

'I'm not sure that I should have any more,' said Nell reflectively. 'It seems to be having a very strange effect on me. I feel most peculiar.'

'Maybe you're tired,' suggested Guy. 'If you moved house yesterday you must be feeling the effect today. Do you live round here?'

'I live in Bristol,' answered Nell reluctantly. The magic was beginning to fade and the familiar sensations of weariness and fear were hovering close at hand. 'Perhaps I will have another drink after all.'

Guy stood up and took her glass. He hesitated for a moment but, before he could speak, Gillian appeared in the doorway. She was dressed in a long black sinuous garment that clung to her slender figure and accentuated her fair hair.

'It looks as if we're going to be able to eat at last,' she said, her glance flitting between the two of them. 'Burnt offerings all round! Coming, Guy?'

'Oh, yes. Right.' Guy paused and looked at Nell. 'Are you . . . ?'

'I'll be there in a minute. You carry on.' Nell nodded, encouraging him to go, feeling an almost desperate longing to be alone again, to recapture that glorious feeling of light-headed peace. 'Honestly. I'm not terribly hungry. And don't bother with that drink. Like you said, I'm very tired.'

'Suit yourself,' said Gillian easily. 'Plenty of time.'

Guy followed her with a backward glance at Nell who tried to relax back into her former state of mind. It eluded her. All she could think of now was the cottage: empty, abandoned, no longer her refuge; of John: sullen, silent, wary and unapproachable; of Jack: in Tuscany somewhere with friends, not knowing that he was to have a sibling. Finally she thought of herself, the child she was carrying and how she would deal with all these separate problems.

There was a burst of laughter and a black, feathery cloud, silver edged, hid the moon from sight. Nell stood up and slipped away, passing through the little wrought-iron gate on to the path which led up to the house. In the hall, she paused for a moment. Mrs Ridley, who was putting out coffee cups in the drawing room, saw her and came out to her.

'I'm going up to bed, Mrs Ridley. I feel very tired all of a sudden. Goodnight.'

'Yew'll want a bottle.' It was a statement. 'An' a nice 'ot drink, p'raps.'

'Oh, no, no. It's really kind but I'm perfectly OK.'

'Hmm.' Mrs Ridley gave a disbelieving snort. ' 'Tisn't no trouble to do a bottle. An' there's a pan o' milk on the stove, ready for the coffee. They'll all be in, wantin' somethin' to warm 'em up. Seems daft to me, sittin' out there in the dark, bein' bit to death by midges. Go on up. I'll be there direckly.'

Nell had no energy to protest. She climbed the stairs, visited the bathroom and went into her bedroom. How odd it looked, this high, large room with her cottagey furniture in it! Nevertheless she was glad to see her old friends placed around the room and her heart lifted a fraction. She was standing at the window, gazing out at the fields and woods, shadowy and mysterious, when Mrs Ridley arrived, a hot-water bottle under one stout arm and a mug of hot milk in her hand.

'There d'be nuthin' like a bit o' warmth when yew'm breedin',' she said comfortably, putting the bottle into the bed. She brought the mug to where Nell stood. 'Drink it 'ot, now.'

'Breeding?' Nell faltered a little over the word as she took the milk obediently.

Mrs Ridley gave her a quick glance up and down. 'Three months?' she hazarded. 'Not more 'n four.'

'Three. But nobody knows yet, Mrs Ridley. Please don't say anything. I can't imagine how you guessed. I don't want anyone to know just yet.'

Mrs Ridley's mouth relaxed into what, for her, passed as a smile.

'I shan't say nuthin'. Yew get to bed now an' rest. 'Tis a tricky ol' time, the third month. Movin' 'ouse 'n I don't know what all!'

Clicking her tongue disapprovingly, Mrs Ridley passed from the room and Nell undressed quickly and climbed between the warm sheets. She lay propped against the pillows, sipping the slightly odd-tasting milk and listening to an owl in the woods. It was only after she'd set down the mug and was almost asleep that it occurred to her that Mrs Ridley had laced the milk with brandy.

HENRY SAW NELL GO and caught Gussie's eye questioningly. Gussie shook her head. She guessed that Nell needed to be alone and she intended to see that her privacy was respected. Gussie was enjoying herself enormously. The guests treated her as though she were almost part owner of Nethercombe with Henry and she revelled in this wonderful feeling of belonging. She'd needed her mantra less and less since she'd been here, although her gratitude to the Almighty had increased more and more as her blessings pressed in upon her. Truly her cup was running over. She moved among their friends and her heart was full of happiness. Only Nell was a cause for concern. Even Gillian seemed quieter just lately, less provocative, readier to adapt. Perhaps her first instinct had been wrong and all Gillian needed was time. She shivered a little in the cool night air and wondered if the moment had come to shepherd everyone indoors.

The same idea had already occurred to Gillian, whose dress was not designed for warmth, and she was already encouraging people up towards the house. The party had been a great success and Gillian was puzzled that her enjoyment of it had been rather muted. She was not even particularly disappointed at her singular lack of success with Guy or annoyed at his obvious interest in Nell. She had felt this strange listlessness ever since her lunch with Sam Whittaker; she simply couldn't get him out of her mind. She was beginning to realise that her first sensations of nervousness should have warned her that this relationship was going to be unlike anything she'd known before. She imagined that it would take the usual course but Sam seemed to be in no hurry to get her into bed and she was confused. They'd met several times now but Sam seemed much more interested in their project than in seriously pursuing her and Gillian began to wonder if she were mistaken in his intentions. She found him immensely attractive and this tendency to hold her at arm's length only fascinated and excited her more. During their discussions, she would catch an expression in his eye or he would run his finger across the back of her hand and she would know, without doubt, that he felt exactly as she did. But as the days passed and he made no move, doubt would creep back and she felt uncertain and off balance. Her ambition to find an investor for his scheme grew strong and she was determined to achieve it, and not just because of the handsome commission he'd promised her.

Up in the drawing room she took Henry his coffee, pausing to kiss him lightly on the cheek. Hitherto, she'd been careless of his feelings and suspicions. It was different now. This was far too important to jeopardise. She knew instinctively that Sam was not the sort of man who would want a messy relationship. He would be up and away at the least sign of an angry husband or a badly conducted liaison. Gillian smiled at the surprised Henry but bit her lip as she turned away. If only she could find someone with some money to spare, someone who could recognise a good deal. Sam was prepared to be very generous to whoever helped to get his scheme off the ground. Suddenly she thought of Elizabeth. After all, this was quite different from borrowing money. Elizabeth might welcome the opportunity of such an investment. Gillian took a deep breath and turned a blinding smile upon Joan Beresford who was congratulating her on such a lovely party. Tomorrow she would speak to Elizabeth. Her thoughts flew ahead, imagining herself telling Sam that she had found his investor, accepting his praise and her rewards, and her heart beat hard and fast.

Henry looked about for Nell and guessed that she'd slipped away to bed. He'd been concerned to see her looking so pale and drawn and thinner, too. In some ways it suited her particular sort of beauty but he was anxious for her as he might be for some mistreated rare and lovely work of art. Like Gussie, he was shocked that John had left her to make the last painful journey to the cottage alone and his chivalrous nature longed to cherish and protect her as much as he was able, but his feelings for her were all emotional. No physical desire stirred to distress him. He smiled at Gillian's kiss and beamed at Gussie's evident happiness and felt content. He accepted the limitations of his marriage philosophically and immersed himself, as he had always done, in the continuation and preservation of Nethercombe.

Upstairs, Nell slept fitfully as nightmares and strange presentiments disturbed her rest and she tossed and muttered until, finally towards dawn, she fell into a heavy dreamless slumber.

Twelve

TO NELL'S OVERWHELMING RELIEF, Jack's sorrow at the news of the cottage being sold was quite overshadowed by his delight when he heard about the new baby. Along with the relief, Nell felt surprise at his excitement. Far from suspecting that he had longed for a brother or sister, she feared that he might be horrified by the news. She imagined that he would find the whole thing embarrassing and, knowing eleven-year-old boys, wondered how he would deal with it at school. As usual, Jack's confidence was quite equal to it and he was hardly out of the car on the first day back before he was telling the glad tidings to his friends. There were no sniggerings or pitying glances and Nell felt, such was Jack's charisma, that his friends' mothers would soon be besieged with requests for babies. She felt quite weak with gratitude and drove back to Bristol with a lighter heart. The proceeds from the sale of the cottage had eased the burden a little, lightening John's spirits and, encouraged by Jack's love and optimism, Nell was determined that she and John must face any new troubles together rather than allow problems to drive them apart.

For a few weeks Nell held to the belief that this could be achieved but the financial situation was already beginning to deteriorate again when John's mother died. The half-term trip to Nethercombe had to be postponed because of her funeral and John felt a new guilt. He should have spent more time with her, visited her more often but, even as he thought it, he knew he was glad that he need never again suffer the humiliation of being weighed in the balance and found wanting or judged and criticised when things went wrong. He remembered a similar reaction when Rupert died and he made haste to justify it by reminding himself of all his old grievances against his mother and brother. Also, of course, there was the house. His mother had very little to leave in the way of money or valuables, she didn't even run a car, but she owned outright the large family house and this she left to John.

Nell's first idea was that they should move into it, close the business and manage on John's pension until he could find a job. It was wonderful to know that, once again, they could have their own home and she began to dare to believe that things were really beginning to take a turn for the better. She was shocked at herself that this relief was a more strongly felt emotion than grief at her mother-in-law's death but Nell was beginning to understand the meaning of the word 'survival' and the security of her own family must come first. She'd never had a particularly close relationship with John's mother, nevertheless she knew she was being specious when she told herself that, since Rupert's death, John's mother had lost all her zest for life — after all, surely no one would prefer death to life — but it made her feel less ashamed of her relief.

Jack was the most affected by his grandmother's death. He genuinely mourned the kind old lady who had seen in him a reincarnation of Rupert and had always shown him great affection and never failed to exhibit pride in all his achievements. He insisted on going to the funeral in his Sunday suit and felt quite comfortable about the fact that she was now with his grandfather and Uncle Rupert in some celestial mansion, which was a great deal better for her, in his opinion, than living on her own in Bournemouth. Since she'd always evinced such pleasure in his company he felt regretful that she hadn't been allowed to see more of him but he was prepared to be philosophical about it. Nor was it his fault, since the rarity of his trips to see her was mainly due to the fact that her obvious adoration of Jack exacerbated all John's resentments and insecurities and visits took place mostly when Jack was at school.

John continued to soothe his conscience by convincing himself that she'd never loved him anyway and wondered how he could borrow money against the house. He knew he couldn't give up and, having put so much into the business, he must make a go of it. He simply couldn't bear the idea of another failure and was quite certain he would never get a job. Everywhere he looked he saw the casualties of the recession: unemployment, redundancies, bankruptcies. All the time he could go daily to his office, keep his head above water, have something of his own, he could cope. He suspected that sitting day after day in the house which had been witness to so many of his failures and Rupert's successes, writing for jobs that would never be forthcoming, would be his undoing. When he told Nell that he wanted to carry on as they were in Bristol she was troubled.

'Is it wise?' she asked tentatively. 'Isn't it sensible, sometimes, to cut your losses and get out?'

'I think the recession's bottoming out,' he said confidently. He'd heard someone say that in the pub only yesterday. 'It would be crazy to lose everything we've put in now. And the house is there if we need it.'

It was that comforting fact that made Nell feel she must agree with him.

'But we won't sell it, will we?' she asked anxiously. She knew now that, if they were to sell, the money would disappear as all the rest had. 'We'll keep the house, just in case. We could rent it out. It would help pay the rent here.'

'Not a bad idea. I'll look into it,' said John who had no intention of letting the house. He needed money and the house was his only hope. 'Don't worry. Things will be OK now.'

Hope born of desperation encouraged her to believe him and, with the fees paid for the whole of Jack's final year at prep school, Nell felt she could afford to relax.

SAM WHITTAKER STOOD STARING out over the rooftops of Exeter wondering how long he could go on preventing the bank from foreclosing on his site. The interest had been rolling steadily on the fifty thousand pounds he'd borrowed – half the purchase money required – and now stood at more than twelve thousand pounds. He needed an input of at least fifty-six thousand pounds to satisfy the bank and start work and who was going to risk that in the present market? He had great hopes of Gillian but, as yet, nothing had come of her attempts to raise the money from amongst her friends. Sam turned away from the window and lit a cigarette. It had been a great stroke of luck that his old chum Jeremy had to go off to the Middle East and was letting him caretake the flat. He had nowhere else to go except for his tiny cottage tucked away in Provence. He'd sold everything else to put in the other fifty thousand that the bank had demanded for the purchase of the site near Dartmouth and when his partner had drawn out he hadn't known where to turn. If only he could sell the site and get out!

Sam inhaled deeply on his cigarette and thought about Gillian. Some instinct told him that, all the time he held her off physically, her will to succeed for him would be greater. He sensed that, with her sexual needs satisfied, she might lose her edge and he had a strong intuition that she was going to help him get what he needed. He gave her just enough of himself to keep her off balance, wanting more, eager to please and, although he would have liked to satisfy both their needs, that same instinct warned him to wait. She was certainly doing her best and he encouraged her with drinks, lunches, caresses, and wondered from whom he could borrow more money.

Sam glanced at his watch. This waiting was driving him mad: the days seemed endless. He'd arranged to meet Gillian at lunch time to discover whether she'd had any success with her godmother. He toyed with the idea of inviting Gillian back to the flat and rejected it almost immediately. He must be patient a little longer. Sam finished his cigarette and went to have a shower, praying that this time she would have good news for him.

THE NEWS THAT ELIZABETH had just left the country for a month's holiday acted as a cold shower on Gillian's plans and hopes. She now felt all the emotions for Sam that had been so obviously missing

in her feelings for Henry and more and more often, as she paced her
bedroom floor and attempted to control her frustration, she found herself visualising how life with Sam might be should she throw her lot in
with him. He'd told her about his little cottage in France, extolling the
virtues of the Provence countryside and climate, and hinted at great ex-
pectations from an ageing uncle, and Gillian was beginning to build up a
very attractive picture of the future. For the first time in her life she was
experiencing that heavy, overpowering sexual enthraldom that drugs the
senses and clouds judgement. Even now she did not suspect that Sam was
withholding sexual favours deliberately: he was far too clever. He implied
that he found her desirable but, for unnamed reasons, there was nothing
he could do about it. Gillian pondered what those reasons might be. Was
it because she was married? Surely not. She'd been quite open about
her affair with Simon. Perhaps she hadn't made it obvious to him that
she was willing? Unlikely. Without actually stating it in so many words,
Gillian knew she'd made it quite clear that she was. And where, given that
they actually arrived at that point, would the act take place? Sam said that
he was staying with a friend and never invited her back. Perhaps he was
simply too wrapped up in his scheme to concentrate on anything else.
Something was needed to push the relationship over the top, to sweep
away all the impediments and move them into the next stage. Gillian
was convinced that, once Sam found an investor, things would change.

When she knew that Elizabeth was home again, Gillian went to see
her. To her chagrin, Elizabeth had another visitor. Richard rose to his
feet as she followed her godmother into the sitting room and, despite
her annoyance, Gillian was struck anew by his good looks.

'How nice to see you,' he said, kissing her lightly on the cheek. 'I
think the last time was when I was passing you over to Henry, wasn't
it? No regrets, I hope?'

'No, no.' Gillian subsided into an armchair, laughing at such an ab-
surd idea. 'Everything's fine.'

'How's Henry?' Elizabeth gave Gillian a cup of coffee and returned
to her own chair.

'Very well.' Gillian looked around for sugar, remembered that her godmother never acknowledged its existence and sipped bravely. 'Delighted that his cottages are selling so well.'

'I should think so!' exclaimed Richard. 'He must be the only man in the country selling property at the moment.'

Gillian was silent. This was not quite the reaction she'd hoped for.

'Of course Nethercombe's a bit of a one-off, isn't it?' observed Elizabeth. 'The setting is perfect. Those beautiful grounds and the swimming pool. It was very clever of him to give the residents access to all that. Personally I should hate the intrusion but it must be a very great selling point.'

'We've got our own private gardens,' shrugged Gillian. 'It doesn't bother me particularly. But I think you're right. The setting is very important. Actually—'

'And you're just off the A38 there,' mused Richard. 'Very convenient if you need to get anywhere in a hurry.'

'I'm not sure that matters,' argued Gillian, thinking how very far the site near Dartmouth was from a good, fast road. 'After all—'

'Oh, I think it matters,' said Richard. 'Not many people are buying second homes at the moment, are they? If they're buying them as main residences then they need to get to work. They don't want to be stuck miles from anywhere.'

'I think it depends—'

'It seems to me,' said Elizabeth, 'that people who buy properties in courtyard developments want to live in the country but in an urban environment. You know? Small gardens, neighbours to keep an eye on things if they're out, amenities close at hand and all set in beautiful surroundings. Nethercombe's got all that. Added to which, Henry started just in time. Even he, with all those advantages, would be mad to be thinking of it now.' She bent to place a log on the fire.

Gillian looked at her in dislike. How prim and proper and unbearably stuffy she was! Even her logs looked newly laundered. No chance of a woodlouse running amok or a piece of loose bark dropping into the spotless grate! She caught Richard's eye upon her and hastily re-arranged her expression.

'I think you're right in general,' she said, in what she hoped was a rational voice. 'Although I think there are still a few viable proposi-tions around.'

'Good Lord, Gillian!' Richard raised his eyebrows a little and smiled at her. 'That sounds very professional. Thinking of taking up estate agency?'

'Of course not!' Gillian forced herself to laugh heartily at his in-sufferably patronising remark. Well, he was Elizabeth's accountant, after all! 'It's just that I heard of a project the other day which sounds really good. A wonderful site looking out to sea near Dartmouth. It's only three conversions and the owner's got buyers for all of them. His partner had to back out and he's looking for someone to go in with him.' She grimaced in what she hoped was a casually disinter-ested manner. 'Ought to be a gold mine, I should think.'

Elizabeth had become very still, her eyes fixed on Gillian's face, but Richard gave a snort.

'Minefield, more like. If the chap's got bona fide buyers he should be able to get backing easily enough. If they're really interested they ought to be prepared to sign a contract. No money need be ex-changed until the properties are built but the banks might still back a deal if he's got the contracts and it's a really prime site. If the banks won't lend I should think there's a problem somewhere and I can't imagine anyone else foolish enough to take it on.'

Gillian looked at Elizabeth. A curious smile played around her godmother's lips and she shook her head.

'Don't tell me you've forgotten all those birthday and Christmas presents, Gillian?' she asked softly. 'The answer is categorically "no".'

Gillian attempted to appear puzzled and simply succeeded in look-ing foolish. She flushed brightly and Richard gazed at them both in surprise but was too well-mannered to ask questions. Elizabeth got to her feet.

'More coffee anyone?' she asked but Gillian had risen too with a great show of looking at her watch.

'Must dash, I'm afraid,' she said. 'Just a flying visit to see how you are. Got a lunch date in Exeter. No, no. Don't come out. See you.'

Mortified and disappointed, Gillian covered the road to Exeter in record time but, as she drove, her brain was busy thinking over the things that Richard had said. Even to her infatuated mind it made good sense. If Sam had buyers there shouldn't be a problem and when they were face to face across the lunch table she found herself mentioning it. Sam was far too experienced to show the tiny flicker of anxiety he felt as she put her finger on the weakness he hoped would pass unnoticed. He'd already lined up a couple of chums who, for a fee, were prepared to state to any interested party that they would be buying one of the converted barns but he knew that Gillian would not be easily taken in and realised that the time had come to bind her even more closely to him.

'The banks are very nervous at the moment,' he told her, allowing their hands to touch as though by accident on the tabletop. His fingers stroked the inside of her wrist and she shivered a little. 'At the height of the boom they lent too much with too little collateral and they've been very badly burned. They're all much more cautious than they were even six months ago.' He smiled at her, lifting her hand to his mouth and mumbling kisses into its palm whilst keeping his eyes on hers. 'You know, I simply can't concentrate on work today. Do you have to hurry home?' He watched her breast rise and fall as her breathing quickened and the colour stained her cheeks. 'Jeremy's had to go abroad.' He made it sound as though it had just happened. 'I wonder if you'd care to come and see where I'm living? What do you say?'

Gillian nodded, trying for the insouciance that she usually had at her command in these situations.

'Why not?' she said with a little shrug.

But her voice was husky and her hand trembled in his and Sam smiled to himself as he helped her into her coat and he kept his arm about her as they went out into the cold November afternoon.

Thirteen

NELL WAS ONLY TOO pleased to accept Gussie's invitation to Nethercombe for Christmas and was relieved to find that it needed very little encouragement to persuade John to shut the office for the whole of the holiday. Although the promise of funds tied up in his mother's house had yet to become a reality, the knowledge of it kept him from the despair he had known just before the cottage was sold. Nevertheless, he was withdrawn and preoccupied. There had been no movement now in the market for months and the bills were beginning to mount and the demands starting to trickle in again. By the time the mortgage on the cottage had been paid off, Jack's fees dealt with and his own debts settled there had been precious little left from the sale. It might be possible to raise up to sixty per cent of the value of the house in Bournemouth but the question asked by his bank was: how would the loan be repaid? John suggested that a charge be taken over the property which would be put up for sale but the manager was cautious. Properties had been on estate agents' books by this time for up to two years and prices were still dropping. He might be prepared to take a charge over the house against the loan but how did John propose to pay the interest until the house sold? John had no answer to this interesting question. He put the house up for sale hoping for a miracle but the strain of keeping this from Nell was very great especially as she was given to observing at intervals how much safer she felt now she knew that they had a bolt hole.

Gussie read out Nell's acceptance at breakfast and gave a private sigh of relief. She'd feared that Nell might be too proud to take up the offer and she and Mrs Ridley already had great things planned.

'Perhaps we'll have another little party,' suggested Henry, smiling at Gillian who was fiddling with some toast. She'd been very quiet these last few weeks. When Gussie broke the news of Nell's pregnancy to him he'd wondered, with a great upsurge of joy, whether Gillian might be in that interesting condition. If so she was keeping it very much to herself. 'What do you think? Jack really enjoyed his New Year's party, didn't he? What about Boxing Day? Things can go a bit flat, can't they, when you're young?'

'Absolutely.' Gillian attempted to pull herself together. 'Sounds a great idea. I suppose Mr Ridley's marked out the tree?'

Henry, who always had a Christmas tree from the estate, nodded. 'All organised.' He turned back to Gussie who was deep in Nell's letter. 'How's John doing? He must be pretty desperate.'

'Well, I think his mother's death may have eased that problem a little. Although one shouldn't look at it like that. Apparently there's a big house in Bournemouth which they could sell, I suppose, if things get too bad.'

Gillian, who had returned somewhat listlessly to her toast, frowned and sat up a little.

'House?' she enquired casually.

'Mmm? Yes. That's right. A big family house, Nell says. Not that it would be easy to sell at the moment, I imagine. Still, money could be raised against it, I suppose, if they were in trouble. I hope it won't come to that. I know that Nell regards it as a safe place if things get worse.'

'I can't imagine what they can be living on.' Henry looked worried. 'It must be a nightmare. And yet we've managed to sell another cottage.' He shook his head. 'It doesn't seem quite fair somehow.'

Gillian seemed to have been struck by a deeply engrossing idea and it was Gussie who answered.

'Well, you've kept your prices at a very sensible level, my dear. And the cottages are really so charming.'

'I think it's your knack with the clients.' Henry pursed his lips. 'You've really picked up the jargon. Mr Ellison says that he'll give you a job any time you like.'

'Really, Henry,' said Gussie but she flushed with pleasure. 'We're getting quite a jolly little community, aren't we? The Beresfords are charming and Guy is a very quiet young man. And Mrs Henderson's about to move in at last. I must admit, it took so long for her to sell her previous house, I feared we would never see her here.'

'And what do you think of the new chap?'

'Mr Jackson,' said Gussie thoughtfully. 'He wants it as a *pied-à-terre*. He's been made redundant but he's managed to find a job in Plymouth. He doesn't want to move the family down from Gloucester so they've decided to sink his redundancy money into the cottage. Of course, it's tiny but they can use it as a holiday home and keep it as an investment for when things pick up again. Meanwhile he can live in it from Mondays to Fridays. I thought it was an excellent plan.'

'So does he, I'm delighted to say.' Henry beamed at her. 'Only one to go. We've been incredibly lucky, haven't we?'

He looked at Gillian, inviting her to share with him in their good fortune. It was plain that Gillian hadn't heard a word but Henry was pleased to see that there was a sparkle in her eyes and she looked more like her old self.

'Sorry. I was miles away.' She smiled at them both. 'I was trying to remember where we put the Christmas decorations. Only a week to go. I think I'll pop into Exeter and do a bit of shopping. If the Woodwards are coming I must think about presents for them.'

'Oh yes,' agreed Henry at once. 'Something nice for Jack and something pretty for Nell. Should we get a present for the baby?'

'Not yet.' Gillian pushed back her chair. 'Plenty of time for that when it's born. It'll be Nell who needs cossetting. I'll have a look around for something special.' She went out.

'Seems to have cheered her up.' Henry looked pleased. 'She's been looking a bit peaky. The thought of a party will jolly her up a bit.'

'Mmm.' Gussie looked thoughtful.

For some reason she heard a warning note ringing in her mind. What was it? She shook her head. She was getting old and imagining things, that was all. Henry was watching her and she smiled at him. He grinned back.

'It's going to be a wonderful Christmas,' he said.

IT WAS BOXING DAY, after the party – held in the afternoon because of Jack – before Gillian had a chance to speak with John alone. Gussie hurried Nell away saying that she must rest and Jack went off with Henry into the library to watch a film on the television. John sat on in the drawing room, staring into the fire and wishing that he could stay there for ever. How wonderful to be released from the endless treadmill of worry and fear. He looked back at his naval career now with something like astonishment. Could that lighthearted man who enjoyed life and always had money in his pocket possibly be himself? Since Martin had left, his sense of isolation had increased and he felt terribly alone. He knew that, in these past few months, Nell had been trying hard to stay calm and unworried, to keep the lines of communication open between them, to show him love and support. However, now that he was deceiving her about the house in Bournemouth, he felt a great weight of guilt which in turn made him feel in some strange way almost resentful towards her. He dropped his head back against the cushions and shut his eyes. How unfair life was! Why should he be driven into the ground, beset by problems, whilst Henry lived in this great pile, with two farms, various cottages and a successful courtyard development? John preferred not to think of the responsibilities which tenants and land brought, the careful husbanding and use of resources or the sheer hard physical work which kept Henry busy. He only knew it must be easier for Henry than for himself. He fetched a great sigh of self-pity.

'That sounds like a whisky sort of sigh to me.'

John jumped and opened his eyes. The room was half in darkness; the heavy brocade curtains pulled against the damp raw afternoon and only one lamp lit, casting a pool of light onto the polished mahogany table on which it stood at the far end of the room. By the glow from the fire, John saw Gillian standing at the drinks table. She wore dark leggings that showed off her long straight legs and a loose silky crimson jersey – which continually seemed about to slip from one shoulder but somehow never did – beneath which she was obviously wearing nothing at all. He heard liquid splashing into a glass and presently she stood before him, holding out a heavy cut-glass tumbler two-thirds full of gold. He took it with a surprised but grateful exclamation of pleasure and she curled up at the other end of the sofa, facing him and holding her own glass. She raised it to him.

'So here's to us. We've hardly had time to have a chat, have we? How are things with you?'

John returned her salute and took a sip before he spoke. He'd been very much aware of her during the last few days – private glances, little smiles, a quick kiss under the mistletoe – and he'd enjoyed the sensation. It made him feel like that man he'd remembered earlier; someone who'd known how to enjoy himself and who'd always had an eye for a pretty girl.

'Oh, not too bad.' He would have liked to make a bid for her sympathy by pouring out his troubles but instinct warned him this may not be wise. He didn't want to give the impression that he wasn't on top of things or unable to cope.

'That sigh said that you've got things on your mind. It's a cold old world at the moment, isn't it? And now with a new baby to worry about . . .' Her voice trailed away and the understanding in it wooed him into accepting her point of view – that the baby must be a nuisance rather than a blessing – without question.

'It's come as a bit of a shock.' He turned the glass in his hand, watching it catch and reflect back the flash of the firelight. 'Nell had a few problems after Jack and then it seemed as if she would never have another. We got a bit careless to tell you the truth.' He shook his head and swallowed some more whisky.

'Poor John.'

Her voice was soft and when he turned to look at her she smiled at him with such warmth and intimacy that he was momentarily thrown off balance. After a moment he smiled back and then took another gulp from his glass. He stared into the fire, his heart beginning to tick rather faster than usual and a whole variety of emotions swirling round in his brain.

'How about another drink?'

She kneeled up in her corner and held out her hand for his glass but John held onto it and nothing seemed more natural than that she should subside next to him, her legs tucked beneath her. He felt the warmth of her body and the faint seductive whiff of her scent and, as she bent her head, the short blonde hair brushed against his shoulder.

'It seems almost unfair,' she said, and he had to bend his head closer to hers to catch the words, 'that Henry should be doing so well when other people are having such difficulties.' Since this had been his own thought only moments before he could hardly contradict her. 'It's sheer luck that his is a courtyard development. They're the only sort of properties that are moving. I've got a friend who's got one. He says the market's absolutely dead.'

'It is.' John tried to ignore the proximity of the breast which now, somehow, seemed to be pressing against his arm. 'It's desperate.' He swallowed some more whisky and tried to concentrate. 'Is your friend doing OK?'

'Poor Sam.' Gillian gave a throaty little chuckle. 'His partner walked out on him. Wife trouble or something. Left him in the lurch.'

'That happened to me.' In his readiness to identify with this un- known friend, John made the mistake of turning to look at her. Gillian looked up at him, her golden brown eyes wide with sympathy, her lips parted a little.

'People can be real shits,' she said.

He stared at her and then turned quickly away.

'He's got the site but no money to develop it with,' said Gillian reflectively. 'And three people all waiting to buy the cottages. Tough on him, isn't it?' She shifted a little and the softness of her breasts and the scent in his nostrils made John tremble.

'Bloody for him.' His voice was hoarse.

'Mmm. Sure you won't have that drink?' This time her hand covered his on the glass. 'Whoever goes in with him will make a killing, that's for certain.' She leaned a little to take the glass and her cheek almost brushed his own. 'It's a gold mine. The site has to be seen to be believed. It's really nice here but that one's spectacular. That's why he's got people fighting to buy the cottages when they've been converted.'

Her face was inches from his and as he released the glass into her hand he took her chin in his fingers and kissed her. She seemed to melt into the kiss and the blood hammered in his head, blinding him to everything but the feel of her. She moved in his embrace and he let her go abruptly.

'For heaven's sake don't say you're sorry.' She was smiling at him. 'If you haven't realised that I've been longing to do that all Christmas, you're not the man I think you are.'

Once again she imposed her will on his. It would have taken a different, stronger character to refute the implication that he was a virile, red-blooded male to whom a flirtation with his host's wife was not only acceptable but somehow admirable. She moved away to replenish the glasses and John with an ease born of practice hastened to assuage his guilt by telling himself that, had Nell been more loving, more willing in bed during these past months, this might never have happened. Nevertheless, he cast about for some way of defusing the tension.

'Has your friend approached the banks?'

'Oh, good grief! You know what the banks are like at present.

Everything has to be written in tablets of stone these days, doesn't it? They're too afraid to move. Such a pity. After all, we're only talking of fifty-odd thousand. Whoever raises the money will get it back threefold.'

'Really?' John took his newly filled glass thoughtfully. 'Sounds good.'

'Oh, it is. Everyone who's seen it says so. Look how well Henry's done. The courtyard development is the in thing. All Sam's are cash buyers too. Don't even need mortgages. If he could just get started it would be a matter of weeks before the first one would be ready for occupation.'

John sat up a little and Gillian, curled beside him, watched him over the rim of her glass as she sipped.

'I've had an idea,' he said slowly. He paused and Gillian held her breath.

'Really?' she said lightly when she could bear the silence no longer. 'And what might it be?'

John turned to look at her but the passion had gone from his eyes and it was Gillian's heart this time that started to race.

'It just might be possible that your friend and I could do a deal together.'

Gillian sat back with an incredulous little grimace.

'Really? How on earth . . . ? I mean . . .' She shrugged. 'Sorry. I don't mean to be rude but I didn't think that things were too good for you at the moment.'

'Ah. Well that's where you're wrong.' John's spirits started to rise and he began to feel excited. 'This might be just what I'm looking for. I've got a feeling that this was really meant to be.'

'When you say this . . .' Gillian snuggled closer and raised her face '. . . do you mean . . . ?'

John bent to kiss her and she noticed with relief that all the fire had gone from his touch.

'Well, that would be nice too but I was just wondering . . .'

'Yes?' Gillian sat up and sipped at her whisky. 'Wondering what?'

'Would it be possible for me to meet this friend? Just to have a chat. No strings. A preliminary canter, as it were.' A thought occurred to him. 'Not a word to a soul, of course.'

'Of course. It shall be our little secret.' Gillian managed to keep her tone casual. 'Well, why not? I'm sure he'd love to meet you. We'll make a little plan and slip away, shall we?' She paused. 'When were you thinking of?' she asked almost indifferently.

'Well, we're here all week but it would be nice to do it soon. Would he be available over the holiday? Does he live round here?'

'Exeter. I tell you what,' Gillian uncurled her legs and stood up, 'I'll go and give him a buzz, shall I? There was some talk of his going away for the New Year.'

'Oh, yes please, then.' She had to check her triumphant smile at John's eagerness. 'I'd like to catch him before I go back.'

Gillian stood her glass on the table and slipped out and John resumed his fire-gazing. Now, however, his depression had lifted and ideas chased round inside his head. He lifted his glass and drained the last of the whisky feeling alive and excited. He had a feeling in his bones that things were going to turn out right after all.

fourteen

IT SEEMED AS THOUGH once again the Christmas celebrations at Nethercombe had started the New Year off on a good footing. John, full of plans and hopes, was in better spirits than Nell could ever remember although she had no idea why. In January 1992 the property market reached its lowest point ever and if it hadn't been for the deal which was being forged with Sam, John would have been quite desperate. Nell, unable to see any reason at all for his good humour, was puzzled but the comforting knowledge of the house in Bournemouth prevented her from being too anxious. Surely with that and John's pension — for the thousandth time she wished that he hadn't commuted it — they could cope until he found a job? The recession couldn't last for ever. She turned her thoughts to the baby that she carried and decided that she must relax and look forward to it and try to push her doubts and fears to one side.

Jack went back to school and Nell found the flat quiet and lonely without him. They'd spent happy hours talking about the baby; deciding on names only to change their minds and choose others that became more and more outrageous. Nell bought some wool and began, rather inexpertly, to knit tiny garments whilst Jack wrote a long, painstaking letter to his grandparents and aunt in Toronto telling them about the forthcoming event.

'Why don't they ever come to see us?' He abandoned his task for a moment and came to hang on the back of the sofa. Nell frowned at the knitting pattern, trying to make sense of it and failing miserably.

'It's rather a long way and it's very expensive,' she explained. 'And your cousin is a very sickly child. I told you. Pauline was very ill when he was born and neither of them are able to live normal healthy lives. It's very sad.'

'But Granny and Grandpa could come,' protested Jack. He hung his arms over the chair and drew up his feet, breathing stertorously into the cushions. 'Aunt Pauline could stay in Toronto with Uncle Philip.'

Nell, who had often thought this, considered her reply.

'Pauline's very nervous,' she said at last. 'Sick people often are. She can't bear for them to leave her. You have to remember that they're her mum and dad.'

'They're your mum and dad too,' grumbled Jack, doing complicated things with his legs. 'But they left you when they went out to Canada.'

Nell was silent, remembering the bitterness she'd felt when they told her they were going.

'Pauline needs us, darling,' they'd said, automatically expecting her to understand and accept that her spoiled younger sister must be put first, for thus it had been all her life. 'She simply can't cope with the new baby. She was so ill with him. And Philip drinks. We'll come back and see you, of course, and you must come out. It's so wonderful out there.'

They'd sold everything, giving Nell the small sum of money that had been the deposit on the cottage at Porlock Weir, and set off with promises of visits and money to help with air fares but they'd never been back and Nell had never visited them. It was as if she and the two-year-old Jack were completely unimportant to them and, even when it might have been possible for Nell to scrape up some of the money for a ticket, she was too proud to ask for a contribution.

Jack gave a great kick and tumbled over the back of the chair into her lap where he lay, laughing. Nell dropped her pattern and tried to rescue her knitting but before she could speak, his face changed and grew solemn and he stared up at her round-eyed.

'I can feel it,' he whispered, half alarmed, half excited. 'I can feel the baby moving.'

Nell began to smile a little. 'He's kicking you,' she said. 'Serves you right for falling on top of him. Or her. You'll have to show a little more respect.'

But Jack didn't move or smile back. He continued to lie against her, feeling the fluttering movements, awed by his experience. She lightly brushed the hair from his brow, conscious of so many emotions – joy, gratitude, terror, love – that she felt that she might fly apart, disintegrate into a million particles. Aware of some of these sensations, Jack slipped his arms round her waist and hugged her as tightly as he could whilst trying to be gentle.

'Aloysius,' he said, referring to their earlier conversation. 'Or Persephone if it's a girl.' He watched her smile and felt relieved. 'What if he's twins?'

'Don't even think about it,' said Nell, retrieving her needles. 'And what about that letter?'

Jack sighed and crawled off the sofa on his hands.

'I'll finish it after tea,' he promised. 'I'm starving.'

Now, all alone, Nell longed for his easy natural companionship. Try though she might, she could not keep her fears at bay and John's odd behaviour, cheerful and confident though it was, only served to unsettle her more.

FOR JOHN, THINGS WERE going better than he had dared to hope. He'd taken to Sam at once, was impressed with the site and had no difficulty in believing that there were buyers queuing up. If the courtyard development at Nethercombe could sell the way it had, then so could this. Sam was affable, charming, perfectly ready to give John the telephone numbers of those who wished to buy and showed no sign of his relief when John refused and simply accepted his word for it. When John telephoned to say that his bank was prepared to advance the money against the house in Bournemouth Sam knew he was home and dry. The bank was arranging to take a first charge over the property, agreeing to lend sixty per cent of the value which meant that they must wait until the valuer had made his report to find out the exact sum available.

'Even so,' John told him, 'I've been told that I should be in a position to write a cheque before the end of January. The manager says he'll be reviewing the loan in six months' time. How far d'you think we'll have got by then?'

'Six months?' echoed Sam, hearing the anxious note in John's voice. 'Well, even if we look on the pessimistic side, we should have the first sale contract signed by then. The first unit ought to be ready in seven months. How does that sound?'

It sounded very exciting and the days dragged until, at last, John was able to telephone again to say that money was in his account and he could write out the cheque. Sam arrived at Bristol Temple Meads station the next morning and John met him from the train and took him back to the office.

'Before you write the cheque,' said Sam, as John flourished his cheque book, 'I've got one or two papers here for you to look at. Read them first. If you're happy with them you can write the cheque.' He opened his briefcase and pulled out a file from which he extracted an impressive-looking legal document. 'That's a charge over the property so that no one can sell it without telling you first. It's a second charge, of course. The bank holds the first one. As you can see, I've already signed it and had it witnessed by my solicitor. Even so, you may want your legal man to look over it.'

Impressed, John read through the clauses.

'It seems fine,' he said at last. 'Not that I understand all the jargon. Still. Thanks, Sam. I don't see any point in wasting money to pay another solicitor to do it all over again, do you?'

Sam, who had been praying that John could be deflected from consulting his own solicitor, shrugged, shook his head and clapped him on the shoulder. He knew a desperate man when he saw one and a desperate man who was also a mug was a gift from the gods.

'I've also drawn up a trading agreement,' he said, taking some more papers from the file. 'You mustn't give away large sums without being properly protected. What if I got run over by a bus? Or dropped down dead with a heart attack? Read it carefully and you'll see that I've been as fair as I can be. There are two copies. You keep the one I've signed and I'll take the other when you've signed it. Assuming you approve.'

He watched as John read the document, signed it and wrote the cheque out to 'Whittaker Developments'. He was prepared to take an oath that John didn't understand half of what he'd read.

'So what does your wife think about all this?' he asked as he tucked the cheque into his wallet.

'She doesn't know,' said John at once. 'I think it's best for the moment. She didn't want me to sell the house, you see, so I want everything to be up and running before I tell her. I want it to be a surprise.'

'It'll certainly be that, old boy.' Sam laughed and John laughed with him. 'Come on. This calls for a celebration. Got a good pub round the corner? I'm taking you out for a drink.'

Later, back in Exeter, he telephoned Gillian.

'Who's a clever girl?' he asked. 'When do you want to collect your commission?'

While he waited for her Sam thought long and hard. It had been fun having her around and the idea of being on his own again seemed strangely unattractive. She was amusing company, fun in bed and had proved to be an excellent accomplice. She would lend an air of respectability to meetings with married clients and her availability would solve the tiresome problem of picking up women when he felt the physical need to relax. By the time Gillian had arrived, he'd made up his mind. He made love to her and when it was over, he wrapped her in a rug, sat her on the sofa in front of the fire and brought her a drink.

'So it all went well?' She sipped, cuddling herself into the warm soft wool.

'It went wonderfully well. Now listen, I'm thinking of going over to France for a while. I've got a little business out there as well as my cottage. A bit of development and so on and I help Brits to buy properties without being rooked. You know the sort of thing. How would you like to come?'

Gillian, whose heart had plummeted at the announcement of his departure, stared at him and tried to gauge his meaning.

'For a holiday, d'you mean?'

'No, sweetheart.' Sam chuckled at her expression. 'Not for a holiday. I'm going for longer than that. It means that you'd have to leave Henry and Nethercombe and settle for my little cottage in the sun. What d'you say?'

'Leave Henry . . . ?'

'Don't say you'd never thought of it. You know you should never have married him in the first place. Talk about chalk and cheese. I have a feeling that you'd be a tremendous asset to me – as well as . . .' He stretched out his hand, pushing aside the rug, and touched her breasts with his fingers.

She stared at him, breathing quickly, her eyes growing wide and dark. He leaned forward, took her glass from her, stood it on the floor and began to kiss her. She relaxed in his arms, her eyes closed and he smiled to himself.

'Think,' he whispered, as his lips brushed her cheek, her lips, her eyelids, 'just think of having to waste all that lovely commission paying off your Barclaycard and the bank and your Dingles account. Wouldn't it be a terrible shame?' His lips moved to her breasts and she groaned. 'I need you, Gillian,' he whispered. 'What d'you say?'

'Oh, Sam,' she pressed him closer, 'I don't know. When?'

Sam raised his head. 'Next week,' he said.

'Next *week*!' Gillian's eyes flew open and she stared at him. 'But I couldn't possibly . . . Next week?'

Sam sat up and retrieved their glasses. He passed hers and took a drink from his own.

'Why not? What have you got to do? Pack a few clothes and we're off. Everything's out there waiting for us. You can buy anything you need when you get there. What's there to wait for?'

'Won't John think it odd if you dash off now?' Gillian hugged the rug round her. She was trembling violently.

'Why should he?' Sam stood up and moved away a little. 'I'm not going to build the development myself. Simon can keep an eye on things and I can come over when necessary. He can telephone if there's an emergency. Don't worry about that. It'll all be taken care of but I don't see any point sitting through another cold Devon winter while it's happening. Well.' He shrugged. 'It's up to you. I shall go at the end of the week and I shall be delighted to take you along with me. On the other hand I can see your difficulty. It's easier for me, not being married. Although nobody need know we're not married, of course, and obviously I hope we will be in due course . . .'

'Will we?' Gillian threw the rug aside and crossed with swift feet into his arms. 'Oh, Sam, I couldn't bear to lose you.'

Sam hid his smile at her conventionality in her hair and hugged her close.

'You don't have to lose me if you don't want to,' he whispered. 'It's up to you,' and picking her up he carried her back to the bedroom.

IT WAS GUSSIE WHO made her way down the drive and into the Courtyard to welcome the latest arrival. She tried very hard not to usurp Gillian's position as mistress of Nethercombe but although Gillian had been quieter, less abrasive, of late, she showed no interest in the workings of the estate or in the happenings in the Courtyard. Anyway, Gussie had a personal interest in Mrs Henderson. It was she who had met her on that first occasion and showed her round the cottage and during their subsequent meetings – for Mrs Henderson had been back several times – it had been Gussie who had unlocked the cottage and let her in, suggested that she might like to potter on her own to get the feel of it and invited her up to the house afterwards for a cup of tea. Gussie had taken an instant liking to her, helped on by the fact that Mrs Henderson had an Army background. For a moment, the old mantra reasserted itself and Gussie felt her spine straightening – 'soldier's daughter, soldier's sister' – as they exchanged memories and experiences over tea and Mrs Ridley's excellent scones.

'But my husband's Navy,' said Mrs Henderson, reaching for a second scone and heaping on jam and cream with a liberal hand. 'Quite different in many ways. And now he's left me and shacked up with a Wren.'

Gussie, who had been watching with a tolerant eye, choked on a crumb and had a coughing fit into her handkerchief. Mrs Henderson rolled an amused eye in her direction. She was a natural, outspoken woman who believed in a direct approach and had already decided that it would be foolish to prevaricate with Gussie who was obviously one of the old school. If she bought the cottage in the Courtyard then it would be best all round if everyone knew the truth of her situation and accepted her for the sort of person she was. Gussie, who liked to preserve her privacy, took a hurried sip at her tea.

'Better?' asked Mrs Henderson affably. 'Good. You mustn't mind me. It's living with sailors that does it. Blissful scones.'

Now, as Gussie passed between the tall banks of rhododendrons that sheltered the lawns, she was able to smile at her momentary pang of discomfiture. It was important, she thought, to keep up with the young and keep abreast of the times. Living with Gillian had certainly developed her qualities of tolerance and broad-mindedness and her friendship with Nell had given her an insight into things which she had never experienced. The point was that Gussie liked young people and enjoyed their company and the thought of this little community growing up within the grounds filled her with pleasure and excitement and she wanted to share in it and be part of it. If that meant a loosening of her strait-laced views and developing a more open-minded approach then she was prepared to try.

She paused for a moment under the stone archway which was the entrance to the Courtyard. The stone cottages with their slate roofs took up three sides of the cobbled courtyard; the barns on the fourth side had been made into garages with wooden doors opening out on to the drive. The erstwhile barns, all of different sizes and shapes and washed with a warm cream, had a distinctly Mediterranean appearance. One had a flight of steps leading up sideways to a raised front door: another had two wooden doors, half glazed and big enough to admit a horse and cart: the small one in the far corner had a huge stone trough outside a stable door. Just inside to the left of the archway, Mr Ridley had dug a trench at the foot of the wall which backed on to the garages and had trained a Nelly Moser clematis up its blank side. Even on this chill January day the Courtyard was a charming scene.

Gussie made her way over the cobbles to the far corner and knocked on the stable door which was opened instantly by Mrs Henderson, who had seen her approach.

'How nice of you to come and see me,' she said warmly. 'It makes me feel at home. Come on in. And please don't ask if I've settled in. I'm in complete chaos.'

Glancing round, Gussie could see that the question would, indeed, be quite unnecessary. Cardboard boxes were piled in the tiny hallway and tea chests appeared to fill the sitting room beyond.

'I wondered how you were getting on,' said Gussie, somewhat awed by disorder on such a grand scale, 'and whether you'd like to come back for some lunch. I know that it's so easy to neglect oneself during these occasions.'

'That's extraordinarily kind of you.' Mrs Henderson grimaced comically. 'I haven't found my way to the shops yet and I've been living on black coffee and cigarettes.'

Gussie, who would normally have been shocked at such a statement, found herself beaming back. She realised that she found Mrs
Henderson an enormously attractive woman although, technically,
she was not beautiful or even pretty. Her face was long and thin, her
short brown hair was streaked generously with grey and her figure
was almost as angular as Gussie's own. Her attraction was in the mo-
bility of her expressions, the warmth of her voice and a strange feeling that one had known her for years.

'I should have spoken to the milkman,' said Gussie, feeling that she
had neglected her duties. 'At least you could have had milk and eggs.
I'll leave a note for him.'

'No need,' said Mrs Henderson cheerfully. 'I cornered the young
man in the cottage by the archway. I saw him coming home last night
and I dashed out and accosted him. He's agreed to give the milkman a
message.'

'That's Guy,' said Gussie. 'Guy Webster. There's just the two of
you at the moment. The Beresfords only come down for holidays at
present. Guy strikes me as a rather shy person but he's very pleasant
when you get to know him.'

'I must admit he looked rather nervous,' said Mrs Henderson reflectively, lighting a cigarette, 'when he saw me come leaping at him
out of the dark.'

'I can't blame him,' said Gussie to her own surprise, 'if you were
dressed like that.'

Mrs Henderson opened her eyes wide and stared down at herself.
She wore a pair of ancient cords, a large jersey topped by a ragged
sheepskin waistcoat and her head was wrapped in a multicoloured
turban. Their eyes met and they both began to laugh.

'I simply didn't think,' said Mrs Henderson. 'I haven't got the heating sorted out yet and unpacking is such a filthy job. He soon pulled
himself together. Anyway, he accepted an invitation to come in for a
drink tonight so it couldn't have been too bad.'

'Perhaps he was afraid to refuse,' said Gussie and they both laughed again.

'You know I'm going to take you up on your offer, Miss Merton,' said Mrs Henderson. 'I've just realised that I'm very hungry. I really must do some shopping this afternoon.'

'You'll find everything you need in South Brent,' said Gussie as they went out into the courtyard. 'By the way, my name's Augusta but everyone calls me Gussie. I wish you would too.'

'And I'm Phoebe,' said Mrs Henderson as they passed through the archway and up the drive. 'So now that's over and we can get down to the nitty-gritty. Who's the good-looking chap I've seen you showing round Number Three?'

fifteen

IT WAS THE LONGEST week Gillian had ever known; and the shortest. Thrust between terror and trembling excitement, between guilt and passion, the minutes stretched into infinity and yet the day for her departure from Nethercombe sped towards her. And never had Nethercombe looked more beautiful nor the quiet charm of its daily round been more appealing. The weather which had dripped and wept and howled and raged its way through Christmas and into January suddenly put away its depression and its tantrums and began to smile and sparkle. Several severe frosts hardened the sodden earth and rimed the bare branches with silver. By day the sky was clear, arching serene and cloudless above the frozen land. At night, after a sunset that washed the earth red, the cold white moon rode above tall pine trees etched darker black against the sky and blue smoke rose straight in the chill breathless air from the chimneys of the cottages grouped below. The blunt pale shape of the owl drifted noiselessly across the meadow, his eerie cry haunting the frosty silence.

Gillian, standing at her bedroom window, wondered how she could bring herself to leave at all. She loved Nethercombe more than she knew but, as she turned back into the bedroom, she was confronted by Henry sitting up in bed in his much-loved ancient striped flannel pyjamas, spectacles perched on the end of his nose as he read an article in the *Field*, and her heart yearned away again to Sam; tall, strong, passionate. She gave a tiny gasp of confusion and despair and Henry looked up, concerned.

'Do come and get in,' he begged, throwing back the covers on her side of the bed. 'It's much too cold to stand out there. You're shivering.' He wrapped her up tenderly.

'I was watching the owl.' Gillian's teeth were chattering but not from cold.

'Dear old fellow,' said Henry, returning to his article. 'He's probably starving, poor old boy.'

Gillian huddled beneath the quilt surrounded by hot-water bottles – Henry couldn't bear electric blankets – and closed her eyes, shutting out the bedroom at Nethercombe. Sam would never cover her up, wrap her in things, as though she were an old woman. He would strip off her clothes, throw back the quilt, revelling in every inch of her smooth skin and lissom body. She rolled on to her side away from Henry, arms folded across her breasts, fists clenched. If only he had been given a passionate nature! Gillian screwed her eyes up tight at the unfairness of it all. If only Sam owned Nethercombe! A traitorous voice whispered that, if he had, there wouldn't be much left of it now but it was a faint sickly voice that was easily smothered under a wave of longing for his hard strong body that crushed and took and satisfied. Gillian groaned and Henry, mistaking it for a protest, a desire for sleep, took off his spectacles, dropped the *Field* and turned out his bedside light. He slid beneath the quilt, inserting an arm under Gillian's neck and, wrapping the other closely round her, pulled her into the curve of his body, tucking her cold feet between his calves.

Gillian lay rigid, silent, feeling his breath warm on her neck, the familiarity of his body at her back. If only he might be moved to desire, drag her over, blot out the temptations, satisfy her need, then, even now, her resolve might be weakened. Henry's hands moved, drawing her nearer still.

'You're shivering,' he muttered. 'I don't know why you wear this silly thing.' Gillian's breath was momentarily suspended. 'You ought to buy a good sensible warm one.'

He tucked the quilt more firmly around her, settled himself and slid almost instantly into sleep. Gillian stared resentfully, frustratedly, into the darkness but Henry's body warmth and his regular breathing imperceptibly soothed and relaxed her and presently she slept.

In the morning she went to see Lydia who, fresh from a skirmish with her ex-husband, was delighted to welcome her.

'Whatever possessed me to marry him in the first place,' she cried, clashing coffee mugs and spoons, 'I shall never know. What a fool I was!'

Gillian couldn't have wished for a better opening.

'Oh, Mum, I know just how you feel,' she said plaintively.

Lydia's indignant hands were stilled and she glanced at Gillian warily.

'What do you mean, darling? You can't possibly mean to compare Henry with Angus. Henry's so thoughtful and kind. Angus was always insensitive and selfish.'

'Then why did you marry him?' asked Gillian cunningly.

'Oh, you know what it's like,' said the unthinking Lydia. 'One gets carried away by things when one's young. Girls are so foolish. And of course he wormed his way in with the family. Grannie and Grandpa adored him; he saw to that, of course. I was swept off my feet by all the wrong things.'

'But that's just it,' cried Gillian, seizing her chance. 'So was I! I was bowled over by Nethercombe and all that. Country living. You know? Henry's sweet but he's just so . . . Well.' Gillian shrugged. 'He's boring,' she said flatly, at last.

Lydia put down the jar of coffee that she had been unconsciously crushing to her breast.

'Oh, but darling, what man isn't?'

'Mum! Honestly! Of course they're not all boring.'

Lydia turned back to her coffee-making with a sceptical lift of her brows.

'They're not!' Gillian felt compelled to protest. 'I know lots that aren't boring.'

'Name twenty,' said Lydia provocatively. 'Bet you can't.'

'That's silly.' Gillian, cross at being deflected from the particular to the general, threw caution to the winds. 'Anyway, I'm leaving Henry.'

'Gillian! Oh no, darling. You mustn't! What's brought this on? Look, come and sit down and tell me all about it.' She pushed Gillian into a chair and put her coffee beside her. 'You simply mustn't do anything foolish in a fit of temper.'

'I'm not.' Gillian stared sulkily into her mug. 'It's never worked. Not from the beginning. We're just —' she hesitated, casting about for a phrase, and remembered Sam's words — 'just like chalk and cheese. We have nothing in common. He and Gussie are better suited. It's just so dreary and boring.'

'Oh, darling.' Lydia sat opposite, shocked and distressed. 'I didn't realise. But even so, you must think very carefully. It's such an enormous step. You have to give a relationship every chance. Perhaps if you'd had a baby—'

'Huh!' Gillian snorted derisively, conveniently forgetting the pill. 'Chance would be a fine thing. We make love about twice a year.'

'Oh dear.' Lydia remembered her thoughts at the wedding. So she'd been right after all. 'Yes, I see.'

'And don't tell me that there's more to life than sex. Or that passions fade and it's other qualities that count.'

'I shouldn't dream of saying anything so commonplace,' bridled Lydia, affronted. 'Even so . . . I suppose you've met someone else?'

'Yes. Actually I have. But it's not only that. I'm not just being swept off my feet. Right from the beginning it's been wrong.'

'It's not Simon, is it?' Lydia was following her own train of thought.

'No,' said Gillian impatiently. 'Of course not. His name's Sam Whittaker. You don't know him.' She wondered briefly whether to suggest an introduction and rejected it. Sam wasn't 'meeting mothers' material. 'We're going to France. He's got a house there and a business.'

'France!' Lydia gazed at her aghast. 'Oh, Gillian!'

'Oh come on, Mum. It's not that far. When we get settled in you must come over. You'll like it. It's in Provence.'

'But, Gillian. France! Oh, darling, please don't rush into this. What does Henry say?'

'Nothing,' said Gillian sulkily. 'He doesn't know yet.'

'Well, that's something.' Lydia was relieved. Nothing irrevocable had yet been said. 'You must have time to think.'

'I've had time.' Gillian put her mug on the table. 'We're going on Saturday.'

'Going?'

'To France. Sam and me. On Saturday. It's no good, Mum. It's all arranged.'

'On Saturday? But what about Henry?'

'He thinks I'm going with Lucy.' Gillian flushed. 'It's no good,' she said again defensively, seeing Lydia's expression, 'I just couldn't tell him. I shall write to him when I get there. Oh, Mum! Don't look like that. Honestly. I feel bad enough as it is. I thought at least you'd be on my side.'

'Oh, darling, of course I am. You know that. I'm just so afraid that you might make a mistake. I only want what's best for you, Gilly. I only ever have.'

At the use of the childhood name Gillian quite suddenly broke down. She sat in her chair and bawled like the child she still was and Lydia hurried to her, kneeling beside her, cradling the fair head to her breast.

'I love him, Mum,' sobbed Gillian. 'I know I do. I can't bear to be away from him. He's everything. I never felt like this about Henry.'

Confused and frightened Lydia held her, longing, as she had from the day of her daughter's birth, to wave the magic wand and bring her that ever-shifting, unreachable prize that is known as happiness. Unable to bear the child's disappointment, unhappiness, even boredom, Lydia had hurried to bring her small treats, little pleasures that were calculated to wipe away the tears and sulks and bring smiles and delight; had learned, too, to dread the loss of interest, the casting aside of book or toy, the clouding of the smooth childish brow, the small upturned face with its expression of dissatisfaction which heralded the next request. Even now, Lydia couldn't bear to see the petulantly turned shoulder, the droop of the pretty lips, that greeted refusal or denial. Holding Gillian tight, she tried to decide what was right for her.

'Oh, Mum.' Gillian turned a tear-streaked, quivering face to Lydia. 'Don't be cross. It's awful to be married to a man you don't love. You understand. You've told me how it was with Dad.'

Lydia was silent, knowing that, here, not all the truth had been told. It was, after all, Angus who had gone, exhausted by her demands and desires, hurt at being regarded only as a provider, his own needs and emotions ignored. Had she ever really thought about Angus, wondered about his hopes and fears, considered him as anything but a bottomless purse? Had her own relentless search for that will-o'-the-wisp, call it what you like – happiness, contentment, peace – which clothed its seductive shape in clothes, outings, holidays, finally driven him away? Had it been her own example that had set Gillian's feet on the restless, endless road? Lydia's mind shied away from such frightening ideas and she forced herself to smile down at her daughter.

'We must do what's best for you,' she said. But what was best, really best, for Gillian's well-being? Could denial, selflessness, discipline, really be the answer? If they were Lydia realised that she could never impose them on Gillian. How could she, who had been so careless of such qualities, recommend them to others?

'Oh, Mum. It won't be for long.' Gillian was smiling through her tears. 'We'll have to come back to see to Sam's development. And you must come out. It'll be such fun. All that lovely wine and sun.' Gillian was already miles away from Nethercombe, its beauty and peace forgotten, hands stretched for the new toy. 'Thanks for understanding. You're the best mum anyone could ever have.'

But Lydia, returning her daughter's embrace, had discovered, in that terrible flash of insight, that nothing could be further from the truth.

PHOEBE HENDERSON LOOKED WITH pleasure at her cottage. She went from room to room, all straight at last, and sighed happily. Now she could plan her house-warming party. There were a lot of naval families living in the area and Phoebe knew a great many of them. Despite the final breakdown of her marriage she had kept even her husband's closest friends who generally agreed that Miles Henderson had brought it on himself with his flagrant affairs and indiscretions. Nevertheless, the final separation and divorce had saddened her. Miles was an amusing companion – fun to be with, generous and kind – and he'd always been able to laugh her out of her hurt at his faithlessness. Well, nearly always.

Phoebe sat down at the kitchen table with a pile of invitation cards and lit a cigarette. Sometimes it had hurt too much to laugh. In her heart she believed what he said: that it meant nothing, that it was a physical urge, that it was she whom he loved. She worked hard at believing it and it was true that, all the time she was on hand and available, he never turned to anyone else. In the end, however, she'd been unable to go on laughing. Phoebe shook her head, balanced her cigarette in the ashtray and opened her address book. It had definitely gone beyond being a joke. When she discovered that Miles had been unfaithful with one of her closest friends the shame and jealousy were too much to bear and, frightened by her threats of divorce, he had promised to be faithful, sworn that he'd learned his lesson and his philandering days were over. Why had she believed him? Some months afterwards, he'd come back from sea and several days later, after they'd made love many times, he suggested, shame-faced, that she should have a checkup at a VD clinic. It was the end. After that, she couldn't bear him near her; the humiliation of that visit turned her sick to her stomach and she couldn't forgive him for it. At about the same time AIDS was in the headlines almost daily, and she knew it was time for them to part.

Phoebe inhaled deeply on her cigarette and started to fill in the first card, remembering how he had pleaded with her, sworn that he would never look at another woman ever again and then spoiled it all by adding that, anyway, AIDS was a homosexual disease. Now, nearly three years on, Phoebe smiled sadly. The truth was that she still loved him; for her there could never be anyone else. His whole character was larger than life, everyone loved him. How could she have hoped that she alone could satisfy him? And how terribly she missed him.

Phoebe swallowed hard and threw down her pen. Muttering the rudest words she could think of to herself she stood up and poured herself a large glass of wine. She simply mustn't brood! It was all over, finished. She didn't even have his children with which to console herself. From the very beginning he told her that he didn't want children. Later, she understood why. She was not particularly maternal and, in those early days, had been quite content to look to him for everything, willing to agree that a vasectomy was a sensible – even unselfish – solution.

Phoebe sat down again and shook her head at her naïveté. She'd loved him so much she would have agreed to anything, had been flattered to think that he didn't want to share her even with their own children. What a fool she'd been. And still she loved him. She took a gulp of wine and picked up her pen. The party would do her good, give her something to look forward to, help to make her feel settled. She inhaled another lungful of smoke and settled determinedly to her task.

Sixteen

GUSSIE WALKED ON THE terrace, her breath like smoke in the cold air. There had been a flurry of snow during the night and an east wind shivered amongst the rhododendron leaves. She could hear the water from the stream, rushing noisily along its rocky bed, quite clearly this morning and the high shoulders of the moor were sparkling white against a blue sky, although thick white clouds massed heavily in the west.

'And just think, dear Lord,' said Gussie as she paced, 'I could have been sitting in one room in a back street in Bristol.' How clearly she remembered those days; not enough to eat, afraid to turn the heating on, dreading the plop of the letters on the mat – oh! those frightening bills – and the landlady's discreet tap on the door. Gratitude welled up in her and, being momentarily bereft of words of her own, she cast about for inspiration. ' "The lines are fallen unto me in pleasant places;" ' she quoted quietly; how appropriate that verse was from the Sixteenth Psalm, ' "yea, I have a goodly heritage." '

'Breakfast's in.' Mrs Ridley stood beside her. She was unmoved by Gussie's frequent communications with the Almighty. Mrs Ridley was Chapel but she accepted that Gussie as an Anglican had every right to plug herself in to the spiritual powerhouse and avail herself of its benefits. The fact that she did it out loud on the terrace before breakfast didn't bother Mrs Ridley at all. Her old mum had been the same except that she preferred the graveyard where she could chat to her ancestors at the same time. In Mrs Ridley's girlhood the usual reply to the question 'Where's Mother?' was 'Down with the daiders.'

'What a morning, Mrs Ridley!' Gussie turned back towards the house. 'So beautiful.'

' 'Tis cold.' Mrs Ridley was never openly enthusiastic, it always invited trouble. 'More snow to come I'd say.'

'You're probably right. I'm looking forward to my breakfast.' She smiled at Mrs Ridley and was struck by something unusual; a kind of suppressed excitement in her normally expressionless countenance. 'Is everything all right?'

'Letter from Gillian.' The tone was noncommittal but her eyes held Gussie's meaningly.

'From Gillian?' Gussie was puzzled. 'Are you sure? Gillian never writes. Not so much as a postcard. Anyway, she's due home tomorrow. Henry was driving up to Exeter to meet her.'

Mrs Ridley said nothing and alarmed, although she didn't quite know why, Gussie hurried in through the French windows of the breakfast room just as Henry appeared at the door opposite.

'More snow to come,' he said, unconsciously echoing Mrs Ridley, as he pulled out Gussie's chair. 'Marsh tit on the bird table this morning. Have to try to think of something to keep the squirrels off.'

For once Gussie didn't answer. Her eyes were glued to the blue airmail envelope by Henry's plate. Mrs Ridley fiddled watchfully at the sideboard.

'Good Lord!' exclaimed Henry, examining the sender's name on the back of the envelope, and Gussie's hand shook as she poured his coffee. 'There's a letter here from Gillian. That's odd, isn't it? I've never known her write before.'

'Perhaps you should open it,' said Gussie in desperation when it seemed that Henry might spend the whole morning trying to divine the contents by simply staring at the envelope. 'Could she be ill, d'you think? Perhaps she can't travel.'

Henry slit the envelope open with the butter knife and began to read. The two women held their breath. His expression, at first puzzled, became distressed; he shook his head as if he couldn't understand the words and when he finished his face was grimmer than Gussie had ever seen it. She looked at Mrs Ridley and made an almost imperceptible sideways gesture with her head. As she slipped unobtrusively from the room Gussie put a hand on Henry's wrist.

'Is it bad news?' she asked.

'You could say that.' He didn't look at her. 'She tells me that she's not coming back. She's staying in Provence.'

'But . . .' Gussie hardly dared to probe. 'D'you mean that she's prolonging her holiday?'

'No. No, I don't mean that.' He folded the letter and put it aside. 'It seems that she has no wish to return. She says that she's never been happy here and that she's met someone else. It was this man that she went with, not Lucy. Apparently he has a house in Provence and they intend to make their home there.'

'Oh, Henry.' She stared at him helplessly. 'I'm so sorry, my dear. What a terrible shock.' She was aware of the utter inadequacy of her words.

'It must have been very difficult for her,' he said.

He looked quickly at her and away again and she knew in that moment that Henry loved Gillian; not perhaps with great desire, or even with a romantic passion, but simply and wholeheartedly and irrevocably. Gussie felt a great wave of shock. She'd assumed that, once Henry had seen Gillian's faults and failings, love was out of the question and only his sense of loyalty and duty kept the marriage going. She realised now that she was wrong. Henry did indeed see Gillian for what she was but loved her anyway, in spite of it, perhaps even because of it. Love is a strange and complex emotion and one should never judge of another's ability or capacity. Gussie swallowed. She felt, somehow, small, diminished by the greatness of Henry's affection which could encompass so much and remain generous, and when she next looked at him there were tears in her eyes.

'Does she say who he is?' She simply had to ask the question. Henry shook his head.

'The terrible thing is that I had no idea that she was so unhappy. I know that it took her a while to settle down but I thought that was only natural. She's a town girl really but I thought that she'd come to love it here. I even hoped that she'd come to love me, too.'

'Oh, Henry.' Gussie's cry was anguished.

Henry smiled at her. 'She's a lot younger than I am, you know, and it makes a difference. I should have made more effort. I'm not surprised that she found me dull.'

'Is that what she says in the letter?' Gussie's old resentments struggled with her shame.

'It's a kind letter.' Henry answered the anxiety behind Gussie's question. 'She's let me down lightly. It can't have been easy to write. I wish she could have been able to tell me to my face but that's probably my failing rather than hers.'

'Oh, come now, my dear.' This was going too far. 'How could that possibly be?'

'I've treated her like a child,' he answered. 'I wanted her to be happy, you see, and it's easy to think that letting people off things and giving in to them will achieve it. You don't give them the opportunity to grow. Growing can be a painful process and you try to protect them from it. It's patronising, of course, but you don't really see it like that. I didn't really think about it at all. That's what's so unforgivable. It was such a miracle that someone so young and beautiful and alive should consider marrying me. Just having her here was enough for me. I should have seen that it wasn't nearly enough for her.'

He stood up and placed his chair neatly under the table.

'Won't you have some breakfast?' Gussie watched him anxiously.

'Not at the moment. I want to answer this straightaway. There's a poste restante address.'

After he'd gone Gussie sat quite still, experiencing the real depth of her love for Henry. Should anyone have asked her, she would have said that to make Nethercombe perfect it only needed Gillian to leave it for ever. Now she knew that she would move heaven and earth if she could only bring her back.

JOHN HAD TO RESTRAIN himself physically from telephoning Sam at regular intervals. The knowledge that the new project was getting under way in Devon was the only thing that kept him going. In the end, the valuation on the property in Bournemouth had come out so low that the amount Sam required could only just be met. John had hoped it would be high enough to enable him to keep some back to pay the ever-mounting debts. As it was, his overdraft was paid off but very little else. He was afraid to tell his bank manager about all the other debts, fearing that he might not let him borrow against the house. Sam told him that once things got going there would be a loosening up financially and promised to help out if he got really stuck. John saw in Sam another Martin – calm, assured, easygoing – and once they were in the pub had poured out his troubles to him. Sam had been encouraging and optimistic. More importantly, he'd been lighthearted, laughing at problems that John thought insurmountable, and making John laugh with him, raising his confidence.

For a few days the glow of Sam's charisma carried him up and onwards, helping him to cope with his creditors and to hold off the demands. There were so many of them. The rent was now several months behind on both the flat and the office and the business telephone bill was well overdue. Then there was the long, long list of the usual things: car tax and insurance, Barclaycard, electricity bills, rates. Everywhere he looked he saw a hand outstretched.

At least Nell asked for very little and seemed content to stay in the warmth of the flat during these cold winter days, reading and knitting for the baby. At the mere thought of the baby John felt an upsurge of anxiety and had to remind himself of the new scheme that would save his life. Once again his hand crept towards the telephone and once again he withdrew it. Only two weeks had passed since Sam's visit to

Bristol. He didn't want to look as if he were nagging but he wished that Sam would give him a quick call.

At the end of the third week, John threw away his scruples and telephoned the flat in Exeter. There was no reply. He continued to try throughout the day but there was still no answer. He tried early and late but the telephone rang unheeded and John began to worry. He remembered what Sam had said about being ran over by a bus. Or perhaps he was ill? He thought of phoning Gillian but wondered what he'd say if anyone else answered. Irresolute, anxious, he waited a few more days. Sam had told him that work would begin at once on the site, bringing in the utilities, and he wondered if Sam was out there, perhaps in a caravan, keeping an eye on things.

At last John made up his mind. He filled up the car with petrol – keeping his fingers crossed when he passed over his Barclaycard – prayed that no one would notice that the tax disc was three months out of date and set off for Devon.

GUY WEBSTER LET HIMSELF in, bent to pick up his post and stood looking thoughtfully at the large square envelope for a moment before closing the door behind him. Bertie pottered ahead of him into the kitchen and stood looking into his empty dinner bowl with regret and a certain amount of surprise.

'You ate it all last night, you dumb animal,' muttered Guy. 'It's not the magic porridge pot, you know. Doesn't fill up again as soon as you've emptied it.'

Bertie wagged his tail politely and sat down on his beanbag in the corner. He stared fixedly and hopefully at the cupboard on the wall until Guy, who had been reading Phoebe's invitation, sighed and picked up the bowl.

'I can take a hint.'

He prepared Bertie's dinner and thought about the party. The one problem with the Courtyard was that it would be very difficult to stay aloof whilst remaining on good terms with one's neighbours. It was the risk he had decided to take; there was so much else going for it. Guy put Bertie's bowl on the floor and went into the sitting room to switch on the television. He'd have to accept. He could see no other course unless he said that he was away working, moving a boat perhaps. Guy glanced again at the card. The thing was, he didn't want to have to go out specially on a Saturday afternoon and evening just to keep up the pretence. It would have been different had it been summer. It was worth keeping his little office in the marina open later then and he could potter round to the Royal Castle for a pint and some supper. As it was, it was hardly worth opening at all at the moment. There was simply no money around. Still, he was surviving. With careful management and that very generous gift of money from his father . . .

Guy stirred a little in his armchair. He still felt the prickings of guilt when he remembered how he'd accepted money from the man who had caused his mother so much pain and had been so indifferent to him as a child. He'd never been as frightened of him as his twin, Giles, but there was no doubt that he'd been a very unsympathetic figure who spent most of his time at sea and seemed like a stranger when he came home, creating a feeling of tension, almost fear, in the even, happy tenor of their lives. After the divorce he'd left the Navy and gone to Canada where he still lived. Guy had been over several times now at his father's invitation – and expense – and he knew very well that the presents of money were a way of buying his friendship back and worse, a way of striking obliquely at the wife who had finally left him.

Guy got up abruptly and going to the fridge took out a can of beer. Although she'd never for one moment said so or given any sign of it, he guessed that she must find his disloyalty difficult to deal with. But was it disloyalty? After all, the man was his father and Guy knew with a disconcerting self-honesty that he shared some of his less attractive characteristics. He tipped his head back and drank straight from the can. He loved his mother but that didn't mean that he was obliged to ignore his father. He'd said as much to Giles who simply looked at him until Guy felt uncomfortable. Anyway, he'd needed the money and why shouldn't he take it? They'd had nothing from Mark Webster since their sixteenth birthdays and only the bare necessities since they were ten when their mother had left him.

Guy swore, took another swig and jumped violently as the doorbell rang. Bertie barked excitedly and Guy swore at him too. His face as he opened the door was not particularly welcoming and Phoebe grimaced in alarm.

'Heavens! That sort of day, was it? Then I shan't intrude.'

'Rubbish.' Guy swallowed his irritation and smiled with as good a grace as he could muster. 'Come in. It's too cold to stand about.'

'Just for a moment then.' She followed him inside. 'I've come to ask a favour.' Guy stood silent, waiting until Phoebe cocked a knowing eye at him. 'Just what you were dreading, eh? Boring neighbours bouncing in and out being pains in the neck?'

Guy smiled unwillingly and Phoebe grinned.

'I've just got in . . .' he explained but Phoebe shook her head at him.

'Now that's a sign of weakness I didn't expect from you,' she said reprovingly. 'You know the golden rule. "Never apologise, never explain." Next, you'll be asking me to sit down and then, if you got really carried away and were to offer me a drink, you'd never be able to forgive yourself.'

Guy burst out laughing and she laughed with him.

'All I need is a lift to Dartmouth tomorrow. I want to go to the market and my car's still in the garage. It didn't pass the MOT and it won't be ready tomorrow. I'm meeting a chum for lunch and she's bringing me back but a lift would save my life.'

'I leave early,' warned Guy, unable to quite squash his natural resentment at being cornered.

Phoebe drew down her mouth at the corners and rolled her eyes at Bertie.

'That puts me very properly in my place,' she whispered to him and Bertie wagged obligingly. 'Excellent! Now you've recovered everything you lost when you started to apologise,' she said cheerfully to the exasperated Guy. 'Feel better?'

She headed for the door and Guy, completely wrong-footed, followed her.

'Would you like a drink?' he asked reluctantly and she looked at him, shocked.

'Certainly not,' she said primly. 'I'm going back to have an early night so as to be up in time in the morning. How early is early? Six o'clock?'

Guy's smile was tight-lipped and his eyelids drooped a little.

'Eight fifteen should be fine,' he said as he opened the door for her.

Phoebe guessed that she had very nearly gone too far and her smile was open and friendly and almost disarmed him.

'Thanks,' she said. 'I'm really grateful.' Just outside the door she turned back. 'And don't panic. I shan't expect conversation with my lift. I never talk to anyone before ten o'clock in the morning either!'

Seventeen

HENRY SAT AT HIS desk wrestling with the tax demands for the estate and thinking, as he had nearly four years before, about Gillian. This time he was not marvelling at his good fortune. He knew now that he hadn't worked hard enough at his marriage, that in marrying a girl almost twelve years younger than himself he should have been more aware. Perhaps he'd already been too set in his ways to think of marrying. Gillian said to him once that he was married to Nethercombe and in many ways it was true. The estate had as many calls on him and as strong a hold over his heart as a spouse might and, if he were honest with himself, very little changed when he brought Gillian home as his wife. Yet he loved her. What she'd needed was the ardour of a man of her own age, not the quiet contented warmth of a middle-aged man. Henry knew that in his ways and ideas he was as old for his years as Gillian was immature for hers and he should have made allowances. It was foolish to expect Gillian to love Nethercombe as much as he did and to be prepared to dedicate her life to the same extent. If only there had been a little more money.

Henry took a sip at the coffee that Gussie had brought him earlier, pushed back his chair and wandered over to the window. He dug his hands into his trouser pockets and stared out at the side lawns and the rhododendron bushes, dank and dripping in the February rain. Of course, the Courtyard had taken every penny in those early years. There had been nothing left over for jollies. But it had worked. His dream had been realised and now the cash flow was easier. Money, however, was not the answer. Gillian should have been involved, kept occupied, drawn into things. He remembered her ideas for the conversions — some of which had been used — her enthusiasms, her flair and style. Somehow these talents should have been utilised. But how?

Henry sighed and turned back to his desk. He had written to her; a long letter, describing his deep sadness, his longing for her, his desire for her happiness. He'd said that she would always have a home at Nethercombe, that he would welcome her back absolutely unconditionally if she would only consider it. His single request was that she should do nothing in haste but give herself plenty of time to think. At the very end he told her that he loved her and that he was miserable without her. It was true. Henry's hands balled into fists in his pockets as he thought of that unknown man. To begin with he'd wondered if it were Simon. He knew now that it wasn't but had no intention of making enquiries. Only the household was aware of her departure and he could trust the Ridleys and Gussie. Henry took his hands from his pockets and ran his fingers through his hair. Perhaps he should never have brought Gussie back to Nethercombe; but what else could he have done? It had been naïve to think that they could all live together happily under one roof, no doubt, but it could have worked if Gillian had been more confident in her position, stopped seeing herself as the incomer. He remembered her reaction when he'd suggested that they might redecorate their sitting room. She'd seen the bribe for what it was and he knew he'd been wrong in insulting her with it.

Gussie put her head round the door. 'Alan Tremaine says you're expecting him, my dear.'

Henry glanced at his watch, closed his eyes and swore under his breath. He'd completely forgotten that he'd arranged to see his tenant from Higher Nethercombe Farm.

'Send him in, Gussie,' he said, tidying his papers aside. Gussie smiled at him sympathetically and he nodded as if to reassure her that he could cope. 'Bring us some coffee, would you?' he asked and as she went out, passing Alan Tremaine in the doorway, Henry got to his feet, with his hand outstretched, his marriage and Gillian pushed, for the moment, to the back of his mind.

NELL SAT ON THE sofa with her feet up listening to Vaughan Williams's 'Fantasia on a Theme by Thomas Tallis' while she sewed together a tiny woollen cardigan. Her stock of baby clothes was growing very satisfactorily and, whilst some of the garments didn't look quite like the pictures on the patterns, Nell was very proud of her handiwork. The music soothed and calmed her, which she felt was very important at the moment with John going about as emotionally coiled up as the spring of a newly wound clock. Nell could feel her stomach churning as she looked at his closed inward-looking face. Something was going on but she was almost too afraid to ask. Only days before, the atmosphere had been different. There had been a sense of suppressed excitement, as though he were keeping a wonderful secret that he dared not yet tell. Now it had changed and she felt a terrible foreboding. Part of her was desperate to know, part wanted to go on in this quiet ignorance. With the knowledge that they could pack up and go to the house in Bournemouth had come a great measure of peace. They could scrape by on John's pension until he could find a job – she knew it would be difficult in the present economic climate but surely something would turn up – and they could start again. The house had been left partly furnished and there was a lovely garden for Jack to play in. She almost hoped that the business had collapsed so that they could get this dreadful strain over and go. Jack had been offered a full scholarship to Sherborne and the relief had been so great that Nell had wept. Surely, with all these things coming together, they could manage? If only poor John could swallow his pride, admit the estate agency had been a disaster and get it over with! So many businesses had been wrecked in this dreadful recession that he need not feel ashamed. Knowing his extreme sensitivity in this area, Nell had only been able to approach the subject obliquely and recently, given his mood of the last few days, not at all.

The 'Fantasia' had finished and as Nell prepared to reverse the tape there was a ring at the doorbell. She went to open it and found her neighbour from upstairs on the doorstep. She smiled at Nell and raised her eyebrows at her bump.

'Any day now by the look of you,' she said cheerfully and held out a letter. 'This got put in with ours by mistake.'

'Oh, thank you.' Nell took it and hesitated. 'Would you like——?'

'No thanks, love. I'm just off to the shops, thanks all the same. Can I get you anything? You don't look in a fit state for shopping.'

'I'm fine,' said Nell, grateful that her peace was not to be disturbed by a flow of banalities, 'honestly. But thanks anyway.'

The neighbour went on her way and Nell went back into the flat turning the envelope in her hand. Since John was careful to pick up the post as he went to the office each morning, Nell never saw any letters but her own. She went back into the sitting room and idly opened it. It was from British Telecom. As she read the letter, her heart began to pound and she had to read it twice to make sense of it. The bill had not been paid, it seemed, and since requests for payment had been ignored and no explanation had been forthcoming, the telephone line would be discontinued and the matter put in the hands of their solicitors. Even now, though Nell felt the old sensations of terror creeping round her heart, she could not really panic. She still felt quite certain that – once John could be persuaded to give in – they could move to Bournemouth and, with careful management, survive. Nevertheless, the afternoon seemed endless and it was with a sense of relief, mixed with apprehension, that Nell heard John's key in the lock.

'Hi.' She smiled at him as he came in, staying where she was on the sofa. 'How are you?'

'OK.' His voice was dull and he bent to kiss her without looking at her.

'This came,' she said without preamble and held out the letter. 'I didn't realise that things were so serious. I wish you'd told me.'

He stood looking at the letter, the light throwing an unflattering shadow into his face, and Nell suddenly noticed how old he looked, much older than his forty-two years.

'John.' Her tone was abrupt and John looked at her, frowning a little. 'Why don't we give it all up? Just pack it in?'

'You make it sound easy.' His voice was still flat and lifeless and Nell got up and went to him. She put her arms round him and looked up at him pleadingly.

'It could be easy,' she said gently. 'There's no shame in knowing when to give in. This recession has been too much for so many people.'

'So what then?' He didn't attempt to return her embrace. 'Go on the dole? Live in a DSS bed and breakfast? The landlord certainly wouldn't let us stay on here.'

'But why should we do that? We can go to Bournemouth. I'm sure we'd manage—'

'Oh, for heaven's sake stop going on about Bournemouth!' He pushed her arms away and turned his back. 'You know how I feel about that!'

'Yes but I don't know why.' Nell was puzzled and afraid. 'It's so silly to go on like this. OK, this bill's not a very big one luckily, we hardly ever use this telephone, but what about the other bills and the rent? Are those being paid? Why run up bills needlessly? I know the business isn't working. It can't be. Estate agents are at the lowest they've ever been, I saw it on the news. Why throw more money away? Haven't we lost enough already?' She saw his back go rigid and bit her lip. She must be careful, think about what she was saying. 'Oh, John,' she laid a hand on his unresponsive arm, 'please. We could be so happy. It's a lovely house, more or less furnished for us, with a garden. We could squeeze by on your pension now that Jack's got his scholarship. And with the baby coming—'

'For Christ's sake!' He spun round and she recoiled at the rage and hate in his face. 'Just shut up! OK? Shut up! I don't want to hear about Bournemouth or the bloody baby! OK?'

'John, please!'

He stared into her frightened, pleading face and felt an urge to strike it, to throw her to the floor, to kick the distorted belly. He raised his hand as though he would hit her and, terrified by the hot surge of violent rage that was spiralling out of control, he pushed her backwards on to the sofa and fled from the room. The front door banged. Nell huddled where he had thrown her in the corner of the sofa, harsh sobs tearing themselves up from deep inside her. She drew herself into the smallest ball that was possible in her condition and cried in earnest. After a while, feeling dizzy and sick, she forced herself to relax and sit up. At this rate she'd go into premature labour. Whatever happened she must think of the baby. ' "The bloody baby",' she repeated to herself and wept anew, hugging her bump as though to assure its occupier that it was loved. She dragged herself into the kitchen and went through the familiar motions of making herself some tea. She felt ill and exhausted and made a very real effort to calm herself. It was difficult. She was so frightened. John's volatile temper had often caused her moments of distress but never had he looked at her with such disgust and hatred, as though he would have enjoyed hurting her. At the thought of it, Nell gave a little whimper of terror and misery. Supposing he came back drunk? No longer able to control himself as he had in that last second?

She took her mug back to the sitting room and sat in the corner of the sofa, trembling, sipping at her tea and trying not to cry. What should she do? Should she lock him out? The mere idea of such an act filled her with horror. It seemed so degrading, such a dreadful admission of failure. What could be wrong with him? Why should he hold out so adamantly about giving up and going to Bournemouth? After all, who would know? The family that he had strived to impress were all dead. Did he refuse to go to the Bournemouth house because of memories of his unhappiness there? So then what? Must all their lives be ruined because of his exaggerated sense of insecurity?

Nell shook her head. She simply didn't have the answers. It was as if she were living with a stranger and it was very frightening. With a tremendous effort she composed herself a little and going back to the kitchen she prepared herself some supper which she didn't want and could barely swallow. She knew now that she couldn't lock John out. Somehow it would be the end of everything. She didn't analyse why she felt like that, she just knew it instinctively. Wrapping herself in a rug, she settled on the sofa and waited; but evening passed slowly into night and night into morning and still John did not come.

The telephone rang early. Nell woke, stared round her and crawled stiffly from the sofa. Fear clutched her heart. Maybe it was the police . . . She seized the receiver.

'Nell?' It was John's voice and Nell closed her eyes, weak with relief. 'Nell. I'm just so sorry. Can you ever forgive me?'

'Where are you?' Her brain jumped about, framing and rejecting questions.

'I spent the night at the office. Nell . . .'

'I'm fine. Honestly. I was just so worried when you didn't come home.' Nell strove to keep her voice level.

'I couldn't imagine that you'd want me in the house. Oh Nell . . .'

'It's all right.' She simply couldn't cope with the disintegration process, the change from bully to weakling. 'It's OK, John. But we must talk. We can't go on like this. We've got to make some decisions.'

'I know. I know that. Look. Just give me a few days. I promise I'll discuss anything you like then. But give me a few days, a week, no questions asked and then we'll talk. Please?'

'OK.' Nell was too weary to argue. 'A week. But that's it.'

'Yes. I promise. I'm really sorry, Nell.' She could hear him crying and her spine stiffened in rejection. All she could see was the hate and the upraised hand.

'OK then.' She forced warmth into her voice. 'And I'll see you tonight.'

She put the receiver down, unwilling to prolong his self-recriminations. She was too tired. Pulling the curtains to let in the dull grey morning light, she felt the baby leap and kick and smiled a little to herself. She mustn't give in. Turning away, she went into the bathroom and turned on the taps. She would bathe, dress and make some breakfast. Life must go on.

Eighteen

WHEN LYDIA OPENED THE door and saw Elizabeth standing outside, her first instinct was to slam it smartly in her face. Poor Lydia had been prey to so many emotions during the weeks following Gillian's departure that she felt ill and exhausted. She wanted to see no one, least of all Elizabeth. In her terror that Henry might telephone her she'd unplugged the instrument from the wall and then suddenly, in the middle of the night, she'd imagined Gillian trying to get in touch and unable to make contact. She'd leaped from her bed and plugged it in with a shaking hand, praying her daughter wasn't in trouble and needing to talk to her. Gillian had already written twice which made Lydia suspect things were not quite so wonderful as her daughter had imagined they might be. The telephone remained silent but a few days later Lydia received a letter from Henry. It was a kind, tactful letter that made her cry – again – and wonder how on earth Gillian could be so foolish as to turn her back on him.

'I understand you may be speechless with delight at seeing me so unexpectedly,' observed Elizabeth drily, 'but d'you mind if I come in?'

'Elizabeth. Sorry. Yes, of course. Do come in. It was just a surprise,' said Lydia distractedly, stepping aside to let her pass and then following her into the sitting room. 'Sorry.'

Elizabeth looked at her closely. 'Are you OK, Lydia?' she asked. 'You look terrible. Have you been ill?'

A measure of pride mixed with the old antagonism stiffened Lydia's spine and lifted her chin.

'I'm fine.' She took in Elizabeth's tailored suit with its short skirt showing off the long elegant legs, the sleek dark hair and the discreetly made-up face that looked younger than its fifty years. It was only to be expected that Elizabeth would turn up on the morning she'd dragged on an old sweatshirt and hadn't bothered with her makeup! 'You look wonderful, of course,' she said resentfully.

Elizabeth laughed. 'I've been with some clients who've bought a lovely old Victorian house that needs restoring. I have to look businesslike, you know that. No good getting bitchy about it. I was going to invite you out to lunch.'

She raised her eyebrows interrogatively and Lydia's antagonism vanished and misery took its place.

'Oh, Elizabeth,' she said, visited with an urge to unburden herself. 'Everything's awful. I simply don't know what to do.'

'Heavens,' said Elizabeth, with the calmness we reserve for other people's problems, 'whatever has been going on?' She sat down and crossed her legs, studying Lydia thoughtfully. 'Is it anything to do with Gillian, by any chance?'

'She's left Henry and run off to France with some man or other,' said Lydia flatly and, sitting down beside Elizabeth on the sofa, she burst into tears.

'Good God!' Elizabeth was startled out of her placidity. 'Oh really, Lydia! What on earth came over her?'

'She says she loves him,' sobbed Lydia, attempting to staunch the flow with some kitchen roll she'd ticked up her sleeve against emergencies. 'She says she shouldn't have married Henry. It was all a mistake and she never loved him.'

'Yes, well I can believe that. Who's the man?'

'I don't know.' Lydia sniffed and blew her nose disconsolately. 'I've never met him. His name's Sam Whittaker or something.'

'Honestly, Lydia.' Elizabeth sighed and rolled her eyes heavenwards in exasperation. 'You really are hopeless. No wonder Gillian's such a twit.'

'It's all right for you,' wailed Lydia. 'You've never had a child. You don't know how harrowing it can be.'

'Thank God,' agreed Elizabeth devoutly. 'So where is she?'

'She's in Provence. He's got a house there. She's says it's a little village house, quite nice but, of course, she doesn't speak French and he's away a lot on business.' Lydia's brow wrinkled a little. 'There's something not quite right. You know? I think she thought it would be all sun and wine and romance and I have a feeling it isn't.'

The two women looked at each other.

'You mean she wants to come home?' suggested Elizabeth.

'Oh, I wouldn't go that far,' said Lydia at once. 'It's just that I thought it would be that she'd "lost the world for love" and all that for a while. I was amazed to hear from her so soon.'

'Perhaps they've run out of money,' said Elizabeth cynically and raised her hands apologetically when Lydia cried out hotly against it. 'Sorry, sorry. But you must admit, Lydia, she is the most expensive child.'

'She appreciates good things,' said Lydia defensively.

'Tell me about it,' murmured Elizabeth and smiled at Lydia. 'You spoiled her rotten when she was little. That's the trouble,' she said, but her voice was warm and teasing and Lydia responded, smiling ruefully and looking a little guilty.

'She was such a pretty little thing,' she said wistfully, 'and I'd miscarried with the two before, remember . . .'

'I know.' Elizabeth gave her a friendly pat and hastened to distract her. She didn't want any emotional scenes. 'So what now? You've got an address?'

'Yes. But she's made me promise not to give it to anyone else. Henry writes to a poste restante.'

Elizabeth lifted her brows quizzically. 'Henry writes?'

Lydia shrugged her own amazement. 'Apparently they're keeping in touch.'

'Well, that's a good sign. You're probably right. It's just a mad moment. But would Henry take her back?'

'Oh yes.' Lydia was very positive. 'He wrote me a perfectly charming letter. He feels very responsible it seems. He's such a nice man.'

'Well then.' Elizabeth spoke bracingly. 'Perhaps it will turn out OK.'

'If only she can swallow her pride and come back,' said Lydia worriedly.

'Pride's a very expensive commodity,' said Elizabeth drily. 'Not everyone can afford it. I feel quite certain Gillian will get her priorities right when the time comes.'

She stood up and looked down at Lydia.

'I'll give you five minutes to get changed. Go on. It'll do you good to get out. But get a move on. Richard's meeting us and we're late already.'

JOHN SAT ALONE IN his office. If he'd thought life had looked desperate before, he realised it was nothing to the prospect facing him now. He felt so frightened he could barely speak, eat, think. Why had he been such a fool? He shook his head, burying his face in his hands. It had all sounded so plausible and Sam seemed such an honest sort of guy; showing him the site and the drawings, organising the second charge papers. John nearly cried out in fury and disgust at his own gullibility. Why hadn't he gone to a solicitor or checked with his bank? Why had he taken the word of a man he'd only just met and simply handed over sixty thousand pounds? Sixty thousand! John crashed his fist on to the desk and stood up, thrusting his hands deep in his pockets, his brain churning in his aching head as he tried to think of some way out.

The trip to Exeter, now nearly a month ago, had been quite abortive. He'd driven out to the site, his heart sinking when he saw it standing empty and forlorn, lashed by a gale blowing in from the sea. He'd picked his way through the muddy tracks back to his car and driven away, through the lanes to Totnes and so back to the A38 and

Exeter. With some difficulty he found his way to Sam's flat and, with very little hope, rang the bell. To his surprise the door opened at once and a complete stranger stood regarding him.

'Oh! I . . . Is . . . ?' John stammered uselessly but made an attempt to pull himself together. 'I'm looking for Sam Whittaker.'

Restraining the urge to say, 'Join the club,' Jeremy smiled and shook his head.

'Sorry. He's not here any more.'

'Not here? D'you mean he's moved? Have you got an address?'

'He was caretaking for me while I was abroad. It's my flat,' explained Jeremy, resisting the urge to take John inside and give him a stiff drink. The poor chap looked quite ill. 'I've no idea where he is now except he's abroad.'

'Abroad?'

Sam should be put away, thought Jeremy, guessing he was up to his usual tricks. He wished he'd never lent him the flat but Sam had been desperate and they were old friends.

'Apparently. He left a note. It seems he's not expecting to be back for some time. If ever. He's got a place in France somewhere.' Jeremy shrugged sympathetically. He had no intention of getting involved. 'Sorry, chum.' He shut the door.

John stood staring at it for some minutes before stumbling away. The blood beat in his head with such thick heavy strokes he had to lean against the wall for a time before he could go out into the street. He tried to tell himself that things might still be going ahead and that, because Sam was abroad, it didn't mean that the site wouldn't be built. So why the weeks of silence, why no forwarding address, no telephone number?

Back in the office fear had rendered his brain useless. It paralysed his thinking processes and he sat, cold and still, hour after hour. He felt incapable of thought or action, knowing only that something had to happen, some miracle must occur to put everything right. How else could he go on living?

No magic solution presented itself. All that happened was his row with Nell. His impotent rage with himself and the sheer terror of telling her the truth had – triggered by her insistence that they move to Bournemouth – burst out in a terrifying, unforgivable rage. Afterwards he was sick to his stomach with self-disgust and remorse but at least it had the effect of breaking through the miasmic fog that paralysed him, pushing him into action. He remembered Sam showing him the plans of the conversion and the architect's name in the corner. It was such an odd name that it had stuck in his mind and Sam had used it several times: Simon Spaders. It didn't take John long to track the name down and, when Simon answered the telephone, John felt a surge of relief. He explained who he was and what had happened and there was a long moment of silence.

Simon was thinking very quickly indeed. He'd decided to go ahead with the drawings – work wasn't flowing in and time was heavy on his hands – and out of the blue, he'd had a cheque from Sam thanking him for his work and telling him that time had run out; the bank was foreclosing and he was going back to France, taking Gillian with him. Simon couldn't decide which was most surprising; Sam taking Gillian or that he'd paid him for his work! Simon decided to accept the money and keep a very low profile but this was something else again. Simon knew now how he'd been paid and why. It was, in effect, a bribe. He was shocked.

'Look,' he said at last, 'never mind the rights and wrongs. Let's see what can be done to salvage some of your money. Did you know the bank's foreclosed and the site's going to auction?'

'To auction? But I've got a second charge.'

'Good God!' Simon was still thinking fast. 'Then you might come out with something. I'm surprised nobody notified you, though. Wait a minute! Was it registered with the Lands Registry Office?'

'I don't know. Sam had it drawn up and signed. I assumed he'd done everything necessary.'

Simon sighed. 'Look, give me a minute,' he said. 'I'll come back to you.'

John sat waiting in an agony of suspense but when the telephone rang it was Sam's bank. Everything was made painfully clear. The bank had got possession of the site, had advertised it to auction and — taking into consideration Sam's debts and their own costs — were expecting barely to cover the amount owed.

'But what about my sixty thousand?' John could barely utter the words.

The bank shrugged its shoulders and said they must hope that a good price was forthcoming. A lot of developers were land-banking at present; buying sites cheap and holding on to them until things were better. It was a very good site. Perhaps he might be lucky.

'But can't we hold out for the whole amount?' asked John desperately. 'Put a reserve on it or something?'

The bank smiled to itself a little at such naïveté and told him, firmly but sympathetically, that it was obliged to seek a reasonable market price, nothing more. He must wait and see. Did he wish to attend the auction? No. Well then, it would keep him informed.

So John waited. Nell kept her promise and said no more of moving and, although the atmosphere was heavy with unspoken thoughts, they managed to get along, politely, like strangers. John prayed again for a miracle; that the site should sell for a price that would restore his money to him. If it did there would be no more arguing. He would shut the office, pay off the loan and move to Bournemouth. Nell was right; somehow they would manage and at least there would be no more of these dreadful anxieties. He saw them living economically and quietly together: Nell playing with the baby, himself working in the garden. He would get an ordinary, easy job. He didn't care what it was as long as it carried no responsibilities. They would take the children to the beach and into the New Forest and be simple and happy together. Suddenly it seemed like paradise. Why hadn't he seen it earlier? The miracle must happen. It must! He willed it: pacing the office floor, fists clenched, arms folded. He prayed as he had never prayed before, holding forcibly away from his conscious mind the thought of telling Nell that they'd lost everything.

On the morning after the auction John received several letters at the office. The first was from Barclaycard; he must return his card at once and, meanwhile, they were putting the matter of his debt in the hands of their solicitors. The second was from British Telecom advising him that the office telephone line would be disconnected at the end of the week, unless the amount owing was paid in full by return. The third was a County Court Judgment on behalf of the company who had leased the photocopier. They had come and taken it away long since but they still wanted the money owed to them.

When the telephone rang, John seized the receiver eagerly. It was the landlord asking when the arrears in rent would be paid. He wasn't prepared to wait any longer and if John couldn't find the money by the weekend he would be evicted. John explained that he was waiting to hear that he would be receiving funds from an auction held yesterday. As soon as he had them, he would pay the rent in full. The landlord, unconvinced, said he'd phone again later. John got up and walked about. He couldn't even afford coffee and milk any more. If it hadn't been for the family allowance they received for Jack and the tiny amount of pension – if only he hadn't commuted it! – they would be starving.

The telephone rang again and John leaped to answer it. It was the agent dealing with the house in Bournemouth. Someone had looked over the property and had rather fallen for it. They were prepared to offer seventy thousand.

'Seventy thousand?' repeated John stupidly. 'Seventy thousand! You must be joking. It was valued at a hundred thousand just after Christmas.'

'Come on, Mr Woodward.' The voice sounded weary; no doubt he needed the sale. John felt a momentary stab of sympathy. 'A valuation is just a figure on a piece of paper. You don't need me to tell you that a house is worth just as much as someone wants to pay for it.'

'It's out of the question,' said John. 'It's a ridiculous offer.'

'It's a cash offer.' The voice sounded even wearier. 'My advice would be to bite his hand off. It's the first person we've had to view it in three months. The first cash buyer since last autumn.'

John hesitated. Seventy thousand. It wouldn't even cover his debts. And then what? Where would they go? What could they do? He must get more, much more.

'Tell him I'll drop to ninety-five.'

'Are you serious?' Even the laugh was weary. 'He's got the choice of a dozen good properties, none over seventy-five. He's only offering on yours because his wife likes the garden.'

John's eye fell on the sheaf of letters with their demands and threats. Fear curdled in his belly.

'No,' he said. 'I simply can't. Ninety-five's the bottom line.'

'Right.'

The line went dead. John stood up and walked about again. He was light-headed with hunger and fear. He'd felt too sick to eat any breakfast and had no money to buy any lunch. When the telephone rang in the middle of the afternoon, he took the receiver up with a calm born of desperation. It was the bank.

John closed his eyes and swallowed hard. His heart beat so fast, he thought it would choke him.

'How . . . ?' He cleared his throat. 'How did it go?'

The bank sounded so cheerful that his spirits soared up. The miracle must have happened. Oh, thank God! Thank God!

. . . And so, the bank was telling him, there would probably be as much as three thousand to come to him. Of course, it would take a little time . . .

'Three thousand? Three . . .'

The bank felt everyone had come out quite well, all things considered, and it continued to drone on for some moments in a self-congratulatory vein. In the middle of it, John put the receiver down. He sat quite still and it was some time later that he remembered the offer on the house in Bournemouth. Suddenly he was galvanised into action, opening drawers, searching among his papers for the telephone number.

The weary voice answered.

'It's John Woodward. You phoned this morning about an offer on the house. I've changed my mind. I'll take it.'

'He's offered on another property, I'm afraid. It's been accepted.'

'Phone him,' shouted John. 'Please! Tell him I'll take seventy. Try, please!'

'OK.' The voice sounded resigned. 'If you say so. I'll come back to you.'

John stood taut and still beside the desk. Why the devil hadn't he grabbed the offer? At least most of the debts would have been paid off. Now, starting with nothing looked positively wonderful compared with the vision that stretched before him. The bell had hardly trilled before he'd snatched up the receiver.

'Yes?'

'Sorry, Mr Woodward. He's sticking with it. He's got a very good deal, I'm afraid. The vendor knows how lucky he is and went for it.' The weary voice was reproachful. 'It's too late now. Bad luck.'

John turned away from his desk and went into the lavatory. He stood for some moments wondering what he was doing there. He leaned against the wall, and, after a moment, it seemed easier to slide down the wall and sit, knees drawn up, beside the loo. He sat thus as the time passed, hardly knowing who he was and wishing that somebody would come and tell him. Presently, when no one came and it grew dark, he lowered his forehead onto his knees and began to weep.

Nineteen

PHOEBE'S PARTY WAS A great success. The lights from her window and hall shone out into the Courtyard, guiding her guests across the cobbles to the front door which stood wide open to welcome them. Guy watched the procession of partygoers and listened to the shouts of greetings for some while before he eventually joined them. He hated parties and had never seen the point of drinking too much and generally behaving foolishly amongst a group of people he didn't want to meet and hoped never to see again.

He slipped in unobtrusively and was in the act of putting a bottle of wine on the kitchen table when Phoebe appeared behind him.

'Hi,' she said. 'How nice of you to bring a bottle. I wondered whether you'd turn up. I thought the shrieks might deter you. Don't worry, it won't be that bad. You might even enjoy it!'

Guy wondered if he'd find life easier if smiling came more naturally to him. His countenance was naturally serious, almost forbidding, and he knew that socially it was a great disadvantage. He watched people beaming, grinning, smiling and wondered how they managed it with apparently so little effort. He was extraordinarily irritated by being continually asked if he was OK, advised to cheer up and receiving assurances that it might never happen. Phoebe regarded him thoughtfully and, as usual, he felt that she knew just what he was thinking. It was very disconcerting, not to say annoying.

'Sounds great fun,' he said, hoping to throw her off the scent. 'Wouldn't want to miss it.'

She grinned at him and he knew he hadn't deceived her.

'Gussie's here,' she said. 'Come and help her out. I think she finds my friends a little overwhelming. Henry couldn't come. He's got some parish meeting or something and Gillian's away.'

Gussie certainly didn't look overwhelmed. To Guy's jaundiced eye she seemed to be enjoying herself perfectly well without his assistance, nevertheless he made his way through the throng and greeted her. Before she could answer, a young dark girl stepped in front of him and smiled up at him.

'Hello, Guy. Remember me?'

It was the type of conversational opening that Guy dreaded but when she smiled a memory clicked into place.

'Sophie. How could I possibly forget you?' returned Guy with awkward gallantry. 'Although I must say that there have been changes. No more plaits, I see. And . . . well, we won't go into the other improvements.'

The girl who looked like the young Audrey Hepburn made a little face at him.

'You've hardly changed at all,' she said.

'That's because I'd already grown up when we last met. It must be at least three years ago. At the Wivenhoes' barbecue, wasn't it? What are you doing here?'

'I'm with Mum.' Sophie waved her hand towards the thin dark woman who was talking to Gussie and Guy saw that it was Annabel Hope-Latymer. 'She's an old friend of Phoebe's,' said Sophie as Annabel and Gussie moved across to join them.

Annabel kissed him lightly whilst explaining the connection to Gussie and Sophie studied Guy from beneath her lashes.

'So what's your cottage like?' she asked him.

'Very small,' Guy told her, 'but just right for me. I'm delighted with it.' He hesitated for a moment and she looked up at him with huge grey eyes in her small pointed face. 'You must come over and see it,' he said recklessly and her face lit up.

'What fun!' she said. 'When?'

Annabel burst out laughing. 'Get out of that one,' she said to Guy and he smiled unwillingly.

'When would be a good time?' he asked, his heart sinking, and including Annabel in the invitation.

'Oh, don't look at me,' she said at once. 'You won't want oldies.'

'No, we won't,' agreed Sophie at once, although she grinned at her mother. 'Just me and Gemma. You'd like to see Gemma again, wouldn't you, Guy? She can drive us over. I haven't passed my test yet but she has and her mum lets her drive her car. What about tomorrow?'

'Why not?' asked Guy, his heart sinking even further. Now his Sunday would be ruined by two giggling, chattering girls.

'Great! We'll come about midday. Is that OK? You can take us to the Church House Inn at Rattery for lunch. I love it there.'

'Sophie!' Annabel shook her head and grimaced at Guy. 'As you see, she hasn't changed.'

Sophie made a face and looked at Guy with a mischievous pleading smile.

'I often go to the Church House on Sundays,' he said to reassure Annabel and smiled at Sophie. 'Midday it is.'

He glanced at Gussie wondering if she might be expecting an invitation too but, although her expression was benevolent, her eyes looked as though her thoughts were in some distant place.

'Pity that Henry and Gillian aren't here,' observed Annabel and Gussie started and looked wary.

'Yes,' she began. 'Yes . . . .' She hesitated and looked tremendously relieved as Phoebe poked her head between Sophie and Annabel.

'Anyone for a top up?' she asked.

'Yes,' said Gussie firmly rather to Guy's surprise. He hadn't imagined her to be much of a drinker. 'How nice. Yes please.'

Annabel looked thoughtfully into her half-full glass and Sophie held out her empty one hopefully.

'Heavens!' exclaimed Phoebe. 'Guy isn't looking after you very well, is he?' She grinned at Guy's irritated expression. 'Come on,' she said to him. 'You'd better come and collect a bottle. You'll need it for this lot.

'So what do you think of my surprise?' she asked him when they were in the kitchen and she was sorting through bottles.

'Which particular surprise do you have in mind?' asked Guy grimly. 'Pointing out that I'm a butler and not a guest, after all?'

'No, not that one,' said Phoebe, undismayed by his expression. 'Producing your childhood friend for you. When Abby said that Sophie was home for the weekend, I thought you might enjoy seeing her. Pretty, isn't she?'

'Very.' Guy's tone would have frozen a lesser person but Phoebe laughed.

'OK. No more butlering, no more procuring. I can take a hint.'

'Promise?' asked Guy coldly and taking the bottle he made his way back to Sophie.

HENRY, HOME FROM HIS meeting, debated whether to go down and join the end of Phoebe's party or to stay put by the fire in the library. Knowing that questions may be asked regarding Gillian's whereabouts he decided to stay put. He knew that Gussie would be able to field that sort of thing far better than he could. He poured himself a whisky and went to sit by the fire, thinking about Gillian. He had been delighted – if astounded – to receive another letter from her. Despite its guarded tone and brevity, Henry felt quite certain that he was right to keep in touch. His own letters were written in a chatty, light, easy style; he talked about Nethercombe, the new lambs, the gale that brought down some trees along the avenue, as well as the goings-on in the Courtyard. He wrote as he might to a friend and wisely left himself out of it, concentrating on the small, day-to-day of life.

Gillian, reading these letters in Sam's small stone house and isolated by her inability to speak French, felt homesick for all the things that she had once despised. Perhaps, if Sam had been around more or if she could have made friends, things might have been different for, physically, Sam still held her. The villagers, however, were all elderly and, in her opinion, viewed her with suspicion and although Sam assured her that they all believed that he and Gillian were married, her own knowledge made her feel insecure. She thought longingly of her chats with Lucy and her jollies with Lydia and the days seemed long with Sam away on his mysterious business. When he returned she was able to forget everything once she was in his arms in the saggy double bed but when she begged to go with him on his trips he refused, saying that she'd be bored waiting around for him. He suggested that she spend her time learning French and bought her some books but languages had never come easily to Gillian and she laid the books aside and wandered out into the village. This was situated inland in the arid maze of scrub-covered hills rather than on the heavily populated strip along the coast so that Gillian's dream of basking in a subtropical temperature remained a dream and, when the mistral struck, she wondered why she'd ever complained about Devon's climate.

Reading Henry's letters she realised that she was more English than she had imagined and often caught herself remembering small details of Nethercombe: the great white candle-like flowers of the chestnut trees along the avenue, the tender green of the new beech leaves, the emerald sweep of the lawns and the sound of the river after heavy rain. She recalled frosty nights, echoing with the bark of the vixen and the cry of the owl hunting in the woods, and lazy hot mornings on the sunny terrace with the smell of new-mown grass in her nostrils. When she made the occasional sortie into the little local store – where she struggled to make herself understood by gestures and a few badly pronounced words – she thought of Val and Brian at the mini-market in South Brent with their good-humoured friendliness and remembered her jokes with Patsy at the post office. Even the much-vaunted French bread wasn't as good as Mary's at the bakery near the church.

She was so delighted to see Sam when he returned – always bringing presents of some kind or another – that he didn't guess at her loneliness and his physical power over her was still enough – as yet – to make her think that everything was worth it. The letters, however, from Henry, from Lydia, even a short one from Lucy, reinforced the invisible threads that bound her to her own country and to Devon in particular and, as she waited for Sam to fulfil his promises of a life together, she read and reread them.

Henry could only guess at the effect and continued to work as his instinct guided him. He knew that he loved Gillian and he wanted her back and a regular, though unpressured, communication seemed to be the only means he had of bringing it about.

WHEN THE GIRLS ARRIVED on Sunday – Gemma driving her mother's hatchback – Guy, who had been alert for the sound of an engine, went out through the arch to greet them. A parking place for visitors' cars had been created under the trees at the edge of the drive and at his direction Gemma pulled in and switched off the engine. She jumped out with a quick smooth movement and, before he could react, gave him a big hug.

'Like hugging an ironing board,' she said to Sophie afterwards who was torn between jealousy and admiration at Gemma's daring.

'Goodness!' Guy, unable to respond with such open friendliness, couldn't resist teasing her a little. 'Aren't you too big now to go round hugging strange men?'

'Oh, you're not that strange, Guy,' she said provocatively. 'And I'm not that big.'

'Well . . .' He pretended to let his eye run over her curves and she thumped him on the arm. 'Ouch!'

Sophie came round to their side of the car, not too pleased at this rapid resumption of friendship.

'I'd kill for some coffee,' she said. 'I missed breakfast. Any chance?'

'Everything's ready,' said Guy airily, taken aback at the feeling of warmth that was spreading around his heart. It was, after all, great fun to see them both. 'Come on in.'

They followed him through the arch, exclaiming in pleasure and pointing things out to each other, and then fell on their knees to embrace Bertie who had followed Guy out and was greeting them cautiously.

'Oh, isn't he sweet!' Sophie crouched beside him.

'He's just like Gus.' Gemma looked up from fondling the silky ears. 'D'you remember Gus, Guy? Your mother bred him, didn't she?'

Guy made coffee while the girls explored and admired the cottage which he'd cleaned and tidied earlier and they drank it in his sitting room. One window opened on to the Courtyard, the other looked over the lawns behind the cottage and up to the banks of rhododendron bushes below the swimming pool.

'Swimming pool!' Gemma made big eyes. 'We'll know where to come in the summer, Sophie. Pool parties! What fun!'

'We'll have a wander round after lunch, if you like,' suggested Guy. 'But we ought to be getting off to the pub. Gets a bit crowded on a Sunday.'

'I'll drive if you like,' offered Gemma. 'Then you can have more than half a pint. Or don't you care about the drink and drive regulations?'

'I certainly do,' said Guy at once. 'I can't afford to lose my licence.'

'Well then. We'll take Ma's car. I'm not bothered if I don't drink.' Gemma slipped her arm through Guy's as they walked to the car. 'It's the company I get high on!' She rolled her eyes at him and he laughed back at her, infected by her lighthearted fun.

'What about Bertie?' Sophie was feeling left out again, very much aware of Gemma's year of seniority and experience and not having the close long relationship with the Websters that the Wivenhoes had to fall back on. 'Is he allowed in the pub?'

'Oh yes.' Guy lifted the rear door and Bertie hopped in. 'He's got several friends at the pub. The landlord's got a golden called Shandy and there's a regular with another one called Duke. He always has a good time at the Church House. I'll sit in the front so that I can show you the way.'

Sophie slipped into the back seat wondering whether it had been such a good idea to bring Gemma over. But how could she have come otherwise? She brooded in the back while Guy and Gemma chatted easily in the front, talking of Gemma's brothers, Oliver and Saul, and of Guy's twin, Giles, and of mutual friends. She watched the back of Guy's head and his profile as he turned his face to Gemma.

He's really nice, she thought and her heart thumped.

The ten-year age-gap only helped to make him more desirable. Beside the boys of her own age he was a man and, as such, a challenge. She looked at Gemma – driving easily and well, relaxed, chatting and laughing – and felt another twinge of jealousy. She was so pretty with her long blonde hair and blue eyes; tall and long-legged with a promise of voluptuousness. Nothing could have been more of a contrast to Sophie's dark, gamine, waif-like charm. On the other hand, Sophie knew quite well that Gemma was easygoing, open and friendly with most people of both sexes; also she had a fairly serious relationship with a naval officer of about Guy's age. No, Sophie decided, she wasn't really a threat but it would be nice to attract Guy's attention seriously. Perhaps in the pub . . .

Guy stretched his long legs out and relaxed in his seat. He was enjoying himself. He imagined the raised eyebrows when he went into the Church House with two gorgeous girls and smiled to himself. He often dropped in for a swift half on his way home in the evenings and had quickly become one of the small group of regulars – all male – at the bar. Sometimes he'd stay on for a bite of supper, sitting beside one of the two cheerfully blazing log fires, whilst Bertie watched hopefully for titbits. Sometimes Jill or David – who helped in the bar – teased him about his lack of female company so it would be fun to appear with two girls. And what girls! Guy mentally raised his eyebrows, folded his arms across his chest and stared ahead. Phoebe had done him a good turn after all!

'Where now?' Gemma had reached a junction and Guy sat up.

'Straight over,' he said. 'Not far now.' He turned to look at Sophie, silent in the back. 'Hungry?'

'Starving.' She hoped her look was intimate and, when he gave her a little wink, her heart raced and leaped and she knew without any doubt at all that she was in love and that she wouldn't be able to eat a thing!

Twenty

WHEN JOHN ARRIVED BACK from the office on Friday evening, he looked so tired that Nell knew that their discussion must be postponed at least until the next day. The week she had allowed him was up and they simply couldn't afford to waste any more time. Certain decisions must be taken and there was an end to it. Nell noticed that John carried several plastic bags as well as a bulging briefcase, all of which he took straight into his little study, and she guessed that he was dismantling the office and that one decision at least had already been taken. Her heart went out to him and she held her peace. She dreaded the thought of another scene. The baby was due any day now and her back ached and she felt tired to death. It annoyed her that things had been put off for so long that, should the baby be born over the weekend, all she had to put it in was a secondhand carrycot with one strap missing. She was deeply relieved that Jack had agreed to go on the school skiing trip rather than be at home for the baby's birth. She told him that the baby might not come for another two weeks and so he'd probably be back anyway. As it was she had three weeks' grace to sort things out with John and at Bournemouth before Jack came home for the holidays.

She got wearily to her feet and went to knock at the study door. She could hear scuffling noises, paper being sorted, drawers opening and shutting. When she knocked there was a dead silence.

'John?' she called. 'D'you want some supper?'

After a few moments the door opened and he looked down at her. He was flushed and she looked at him anxiously.

'I'm not hungry,' he said and made to shut the door.

'John,' she said, holding on to the handle, 'are you OK?'

'Fine,' he said. 'Thank you,' he added after a pause.

He stood for a moment as though listening to the echo of his own voice and then, smiling politely at her, he gently but firmly closed the door. Nell stood outside for a while but now there was a complete silence and presently she went back to sit down and ease her aching back. Her suspicions were confirmed on Saturday morning when John didn't go to the office as usual. He'd slept restlessly, muttering in his sleep, while she lay wide awake beside him. When he woke she held her breath. He lay quite still beside her, barely breathing, and presently began to move stealthily out of bed.

'Are you all right, darling?' she asked, trying to make her voice light and normal. 'Can't you sleep?'

'Oh, for God's sake!' she heard him mutter and the suppressed fury in his voice made her heart race. 'Go back to sleep.'

She struggled up on to one elbow, longing for the comfort of normal speech, normal affection.

'Don't be upset,' she begged. 'Please. I'm only worried because you look so tired.'

'Christ!' he shouted. 'Can't you see? It's bad enough not being able to sleep. Now I've got to feel guilty for waking you up as well. Just go back to sleep!'

Nell lay trying not to cry, attempting to relieve the weight and bulk of her body and longing for a cup of tea. She was afraid to get up and go and make herself one and after a while she began to feel resentful. Why should she be stuck here like a prisoner, uncomfortable and thirsty, simply to ease his guilt? John didn't return to bed and when Nell got up late, having fallen into a heavy sleep after a series of fitful dozes, he was already dressed. He made her coffee, wearing a closed unapproachable face, and countered her conversational attempts lightly but with a finality that eventually silenced her. Then he shut himself in the study again and Nell sat at the kitchen table picking at some toast, trying to concentrate on a letter from Gussie, and feeling more and more desperate. At last, when she could bear it no longer, she stood up and hurrying into the corridor banged on the door.

'John!' she called, praying that her courage wouldn't fail. 'Please, John. I want to talk to you.'

This time the door opened at once and the sight of his face made her gasp with terror. She could smell the whisky on his breath.

'What d'you want?' He stared at her as if she were a stranger and an unwelcome one at that.

'Oh, John.' Her fingers twined in an unconscious pleading. 'Please don't be like this. Please come and talk to me.'

With an expression that prayed for patience he came out, closing the door behind him, and followed her into the sitting room.

'Well?' He sounded as if he were humouring an unreasonable request for something that was beyond his comprehension and she wanted to scream and beat at him. Anything to bring him back from behind this unbreachable façade.

'You said that we could talk at the end of the week.' She made an attempt at calm. 'I think the time's come, John. Don't you?'

'If you say so.' He continued to look at her with something like contempt but behind it Nell suddenly became aware of a breath of barely controlled fear that sharpened his voice and flickered in his eyes. She took strength from it.

'I do say so. I want to know what's going to happen to us. Whether you've decided to close the business and if we're going to live in Bournemouth. The baby's due any time now and I need to know.'

'Then you shall know.' He pushed his face into hers so suddenly that she shrank back. A muscle twitched under his eye and his mouth twisted and the words were bitten off between his closed teeth. 'I'm going to become a bankrupt. That's what's going to happen to me. The business is closed down and the bailiffs are there now removing the furniture to be sold. And no,' he was shouting now, 'we're not going to live in Bournemouth. There isn't a house any more. I raised money against it and lost it. All sixty thousand pounds of it. How's that? Does that answer all that you need to know?'

A great dizziness assailed Nell and the room seemed to swing round her. She stretched out a hand and John took it, guided her to the sofa and pushed her down on it. He stepped back and stood watching her, his arms folded across his breast. She pressed her hands against her eyes and then looked at him.

'But why are you angry with me?' she cried. 'It's not my fault. None of it's my fault. If you'd listened to me . . .' She stopped but it was too late.

'Oh, no. No.' He put a hand on each chair arm and the fear and the guilt and the pain burst up in a great flame of rage that seemed to scorch her as she cowered back in the chair. 'Of course it's not your fault. It's never been your fault, has it? You're always so smug! Giving advice, telling me what to do and watching while I get it wrong! Wrong! Wrong!' he screamed at her, his face inches from her own, and letting go of the chair he took her by the shoulders and shook her. 'You're so bloody clever, aren't you? You never get anything wrong, do you? And do you know why? Because you never bloody do anything at all. See?' He threw her back into the chair. 'Well, at least I tried. And I got it wrong. Really wrong. So really bloody wrong nothing can ever be right again!' His breath came in great gasping gulps and as he stared down at her sobbing against the cushions, her eyes wide with terror and her arms crossed protectively across her belly, the rage fled from his face and a look of infinite disgust and self-loathing took its place. 'Oh Christ,' he whispered. He stretched out his hands to her but instinctively she jerked back from him, flattening herself against the back of the chair. He looked wildly at her for a moment then, turning away, he strode from the room and up the passage. The study door slammed.

Nell burst into tears, clutching her belly as pain thrummed through it. She threw back her head to cry out but froze into immobility as she heard a shot ring out. There was silence. Nell sat on, holding her breath, listening, then she leaped to her feet and hurried into the corridor.

'John!' she shouted. 'John!'

She flung open the door and stopped short, clutching the handle for support. John lay in his chair. The back of his head gaped in an appalling mess of bone and brain from which frothy blood bubbled in an effervescent flood. Nell gasped, shivered and began to retch. She stumbled out into the hall and caught her breath. The pains in her belly were coming more regularly now and she dragged herself into the sitting room and fell on her knees beside the telephone. She dialled 999 and cried out in pain as a voice answered.

'I need an ambulance!' she cried, tears beginning to pour down her cheeks. 'Oh, please come quickly. It's my husband. He's shot himself.' She gave another cry of pain, drowning the calm voice asking for her name, address and telephone number. Gulping and shivering, she took a grip on her panic and forced herself to give the information as clearly as she could. 'Come quickly!' she begged and, as she replaced the receiver, felt nausea rising again. It occurred to her, between the pains, that John might not be dead. Supposing he was only injured? With a moan of terror she struggled up but as she reached the door her waters broke, gushing down her legs, and the pain came again, slicing down with a violence that cut her off from consciousness.

SHE SEEMED TO BE swimming up from the bottom of a great pool where she had been struggling and fighting with some black, pain-filled weight. Pushing, gasping, she burst into light and air. She lay listening to the noises that ebbed and flowed; a bell ringing, hammering, voices shouting. There was silence and then a splintering of wood and the sound of hurrying footsteps. Pain clawed her back into the pool and she cried out. As if in a dream she glimpsed shapes, a figure bending over her, its mouth opening and shutting; she saw feet running past and heard voices.

'Oh God! Yes, that's Mrs Woodward. Mrs Woodward? Can you hear me, dear? Oh God.' . . . 'Out the way, madam, please. Come on, love. You're going to be all right. Come on . . .' . . . 'He's dead. We'll have to call the Coroner's officer. Where's the phone?' . . . 'Christ! Is she going to make it?' . . . 'Dunno. We've got to get her into Southmead. Dave's getting the stretcher. Come on, love . . .'

Nell gave a cry and grappled again with the monster, trying to rid her body of its tearing weight. She was lifted, carried, aware of bright sunlight. Now there was movement. Someone was bending over her again and she heard the high insistent whine of a siren. The movement ceased and she saw white coats, anxious faces, lowered voices; felt hands laid upon her, stripping, washing, probing, before the pain wrestled with her again and she gave herself up to it.

SHE OPENED HER EYES drowsily upon a darkened room. Her body was light and free, empty and weightless. Slowly she became aware of her hand being held and, turning her head slowly on the pillow, she saw Gussie. She tried to raise her head but the effort was too great.

'Gussie?' It was barely more than a breath but the grip on her hand tightened.

'Yes. I'm here.'

Nell's brow wrinkled in puzzlement but she was too tired to pursue it. Something was terribly wrong but she simply couldn't remember . . .

WHEN SHE WOKE AGAIN Gussie was still sitting there but now the room was full of sunlight and Nell remembered everything with a dreadful clarity.

'Gussie! My baby, Gussie! And John. Oh God! He . . . Oh, Gussie . . .'

'John's dead, my dear. He shot himself. You must be very brave.'

'Oh God!' Nell saw again the slimy, shiny wound, the drops of blood. She struggled to sit and Gussie stood up, still holding her hand. 'The baby started to come. Is it all right, Gussie? Where is it?'

'The baby died, Nell. They tried to save him but it was too late.'

Nell stared up at her. She shook her head.

'No, Gussie . . .'

'Oh, my dear. I'm so sorry.'

'No!'

The cry echoed in the small room and Gussie put her arms round her. Nell struggled and suddenly went limp. She stared into Gussie's face only inches from her own and shook her head again.

'No, Gussie,' she pleaded.

The tears rose in Gussie's eyes and rolled down her cheeks and Nell watched and her face screwed up in pain.

'My baby!' she screamed. 'I want my baby.'

She fought and cried and the door opened and once again there were people and voices and then the blessed, blessed darkness.

IT SEEMED AS IF the process of the law, once it got under way, would never cease. When she was stronger, Nell agreed to give a statement to the police. They were satisfied by this time that they were dealing with suicide and Henry, who had driven to Bristol with Gussie immediately after the telephone call from Nell's neighbour, stayed in the flat and did what he could to make the process swifter. He was horrified at the state of John's affairs; each day disclosed something new and Nell's future looked bleak indeed.

'She'll have her portion of John's pension and that's it,' he reported to Gussie one evening. 'He owed everybody. He even cashed in his insurance policies. Even if the house in Bournemouth sold tomorrow at a good price, there would be little if anything left. The car will have to go and anything that will bring in a few pennies.'

'Thank God that she'd moved all her precious things to Nethercombe.' Gussie looked quickly at Henry who was a JP. 'You won't tell them about those, will you?' she asked anxiously.

'Of course not,' said Henry indignantly. 'A few sticks of furniture! How is she today?'

'Getting stronger but . . .' Gussie sighed and shook her head. 'What a dreadful, dreadful blow. To lose your husband and baby and then discover that you're about to be evicted and you have no money.'

This had, by now, occurred to Nell. Slowly the loose ends were being tied up and soon she must face the future.

'But have I got a future, Gussie?' she asked one evening at the flat, where Henry had bought her time and a breathing space.

Jack had come home and Nell had told him the truth. He'd stood white-faced and very straight beside her at the funeral of John and the baby boy whom they had planned, during those happy, peaceful days together, to call Henry Augustus. Nell wept for her baby and tried to think of John with some other emotion than anger and Jack put his arm round her and tried to comfort her.

'Of course you have a future.' Gussie's brand of realistic, unemotional sympathy gave her courage but Nell sighed.

'Oh, Gussie. I want to believe it but I don't know what to do or where to go. What shall we live on? Where shall we live? I can't believe that we have no home.' Her voice shook and she swallowed back the tears that these days were always near the surface. She still felt so weak. 'I'm so frightened.'

'My dear Nell.' Gussie raised her eyes from Jack's jersey which she was mending. 'What can you mean? I thought you realised that as soon as you're strong enough and everything's wound up you and Jack will come to us.' She looked at Nell's puzzled face and clicked her tongue impatiently. 'Well really, Nell! What are you thinking of? Where on earth would your home be other than with us at Nethercombe?'

Twenty-one

WHEN SEVERAL WEEKS PASSED and there was no letter from Henry, Gillian began to feel anxious. The days dragged by. Sam had an office in Avignon to which he went most days although he continued to promise her that very soon he would be in a position to delegate most of his responsibilities to someone whom he had taken on and was in the process of training up. When she asked him how things were going at the site in Dartmouth he stared at her blankly for a moment.

'Oh, yes. Sorry. Got a lot on my mind at the moment. Oh, it's going fine. No problems. By the way, I've arranged a meeting with an English couple who want to look at a property we've got on the books. I'd like you to come along.'

'Oh?' Gillian looked at him in surprise. He'd once told her that she was going to be very useful to him but, apart from finding John, there had been no further suggestion that she should interest herself in his affairs. 'Why specially?'

'Oh.' Sam pursed his lips and shrugged. 'I'd just like you to be there. Lend tone and all that. As my wife, of course.'

Fear jumped into her heart.

'But who are they? Suppose they know me . . . ?'

'Oh, come on, darling! They come from the north. He's got a little factory or something and he's made a reasonably respectable packet and he wants to spend it but, having a good, hard, north-country head, he also wants to see it working for him.' He grinned at her. 'And I want to help him. What's the old saying: "A fool and his money are soon parted"? Anyway,' he gave her a tiny wink, 'you'll lend a touch of class to the proceedings.'

'OK. But you'll have to tell me what it's all about.'

'Naturally.' Sam looked more closely at her. She seemed to have lost some of her sparkle. 'What about, something new for the occasion? I want you to look good. Prosperous. Mind you, they'll be so relieved that you speak English that it won't matter too much what you wear. Still, it's time you had a jolly.'

Even the prospects of a jolly couldn't quite lift Gillian's spirits but Sam, on the edge of a rather tricky deal, was too preoccupied to notice. When almost another week had passed and there was still no letter, Gillian swallowed her pride and wrote to Henry. She suddenly felt frightened that her short, guarded, irregular replies may have been so discouraging that he'd given up and a sudden flicker of anxiety which she didn't pause to analyse hurried her across to her little desk. She wrote a more friendly letter than usual, wondering how they all were and if they'd enjoyed Easter.

The week after she'd met Sam's clients, she found a letter waiting for her at the post office and with a surprisingly strong feeling of relief she rushed home with it.

She read it several times, shock and horror mounting in her breast. She simply couldn't take in this dreadful news: John dead, the baby dead, Nell ill and destitute. The pages drifted to her lap as she stared ahead, facts slotting into places, conversations taking on new meanings and the component parts adding up to a horrific whole. Her head reeled as she tried to make sense of it all. Naturally, Henry had no idea that Gillian's lover was the man who had brought about this disaster. He described, simply and straightforwardly, how – having heard of the site through some estate agent acquaintance – John had been taken in by its owner. He told in stark – and therefore effective – terms the depth of the deception practised upon Nell and the effect when John, unable to face life any longer, had left the appalling consequences for her to shoulder alone. Gillian sat, stunned and shocked, prey to a whole host of conflicting emotions, the least admirable of which was terror that her part in the affair may be discovered. And then what?

At this point, Gillian knew without doubt that she wanted to go back to Nethercombe and Henry. But what if he should find out that it was she who had seduced John into the meeting with Sam and then run away with him? With trembling hands she lifted the sheets and read on. Oh God! The police had questioned Simon whose name had been on the drawings in John's desk. Simon, wrote Henry, had done the work at Sam's request and been paid for it but had heard nothing since and, learning through the grapevine that the site had gone to auction, assumed that Sam had gone abroad. John, apparently, had telephoned Simon who'd put him straight on to the bank.

Gillian drew a deep breath. At least Simon hadn't dropped her in it and no one else knew . . . Her hands flew to her lips; Lydia knew! She knew Sam's name and if she should speak to anyone at Nethercombe or to Elizabeth . . . Gillian's heartbeats jumped and raced. She could well imagine Lydia blurting something out in her unthinking way. Gillian looked round desperately. There was no telephone in the little house and the one in the shop-cum-bistro was rather public. Still . . .

LYDIA WAS AMAZED TO have a telephone call from her daughter and only when – having exclaimed and enquired – it was slowly borne in on her that Gillian's voice was full of a kind of muted desperation did Lydia stop chattering and begin to listen. She gathered that Gillian was in a public place and trying not to be overheard.

'I want to come home, Mum,' she was saying and Lydia grasped the receiver more tightly, straining to hear. 'It was all a terrible mistake and I want to come back.'

'Oh, darling. D'you mean . . . ? When you say home . . . ?'

'To Nethercombe.' It was almost a wail. 'Oh Mum, I know Henry will take me back.' She dropped her voice. 'Mum?'

Gillian was almost whispering and Lydia instinctively lowered her voice.

'What? What is it?'

'You haven't told anyone about Sam, have you?'

Lydia thought quickly. Had she? To whom would she have mentioned it?

'No. I'm sure I haven't, darling. I haven't spoken to anyone at Nethercombe although Henry wrote a lovely letter. I told you –'

'Yes. Yes, you said in your letter. Mum, don't say anything to anyone at all. Promise? I'll come to you first.'

'Oh, darling, I'm so glad.' The ready tears were gathering. 'I'm sure it's the right thing to do.'

'I know. I'll be in touch again soon. Only, Mum, just don't mention Sam's name to anyone, OK? Not anyone.'

'Of course not, my darling. I promise. Why should I?'

'I'm out of change, Mum. I'll phone again soon when I've made some plans. 'Bye.'

The line went dead and Lydia sat weeping with relief, the receiver clutched to her chest. She replaced it after a moment, feeling weak with gratitude, and wondering why Gillian had been so insistent that no one should know Sam's name. She went to pour herself a large and restorative drink, trying to remember what Sam's surname was and rather shocked by the fact that she had completely forgotten the name of the man with whom her daughter had run away. Lydia shook her head in self-reproach. She really was a hopeless mother. She took a large heartening swallow of gin and tonic and smiled a little to herself. Someone had said that to her only recently. Who could it have been? Lydia took another sip and nearly choked. Elizabeth! It had been Elizabeth. She had said something of the sort when she, Lydia, had told her how Gillian had left Henry and – Lydia screwed up her face as she performed an almost violent mental exercise – oh God! Yes! Elizabeth had asked, 'Who's the man?' and she had told her. Yes! She was quite certain that she'd told her the name. But would she remember it? And did it matter if she did? After all, it was hardly likely that Elizabeth would go rolling up to Nethercombe and start chatting to Henry about Sam Whittaker. Still . . .

Lydia stood – clutching her glass as she had clutched the telephone receiver – in an agony of indecision. Should she tell Elizabeth, thus rousing all her suspicions, or should she let sleeping dogs lie and hope for the best? As she stood dithering, a saying which her mother had been fond of quoting slid into her mind.

'Oh, what a tangled web we weave when first we practise to deceive.'

TO GILLIAN THE DAY seemed endless. Pictures of John shot dead, Nell in an agony of childbirth, the funeral, rolled and rerolled themselves before her inward-looking eyes. She imagined Nell's desperation as she discovered that she was destitute and Jack's reaction at losing his father. Apparently, Henry and Gussie had taken them back to Nethercombe. There was, as Henry pointed out in his letter, nowhere else for them to go. It was almost as if it were an explanation to her, an apology. Perhaps he thought that she might be less likely to return if Nell were in residence. Gillian, aghast at the results of her double-dealing, lying and cheating, sat quite still. Part of her mind prayed that there might have been a mistake, some sort of misunderstanding that would exonerate Sam and, therefore, herself but in her heart she knew that this relief was unlikely to be granted to her.

When Sam arrived home later that afternoon she was ready for him but not prepared to discover that the revelations contained in Henry's letter had stripped the blindness from her eyes. The magic, the power, all had gone and she felt faint from her own stupidity. He kissed her and she willed herself not to shudder at his embrace.

'How's my beautiful? Jim Mortlake was asking after you today. You made a very good impression on him, I must say. Things are going very well indeed.' He poured himself some wine and raised his glass to her. 'You make an irresistible bait, my darling.'

'You mean like I did with John?'

He looked at her, tilting his head a little, narrowing his eyes, as if sizing up the remark. He nodded. 'If you like.'

'How's it going? With John. Is the site coming on? Do you hear from him at all?'

'Funny you should say that.' He emptied his glass in one long swallow and turned away to refill it. 'I spoke to him today. He telephoned to tell me how things were getting on. No problems, as far as I can see.'

'I can see quite a big problem.'

'Oh?' He turned back to her, eyebrows raised. 'Such as?'

'Such as communicating from beyond the grave. However did he manage it?'

Sam gave a puzzled little laugh. He frowned at her smilingly and shook his head.

'Sorry. Have I missed something? I'm not with it.'

'Neither is he any more. He's dead. He shot himself when the site went to auction and Nell lost her baby and nearly died herself.'

Sam stood stock still, the expression wiped clean away from his face. Gillian knew that behind that unreadable smoothness his brain was working with the speed of lightning.

'So?' she asked him. 'Would you like to rephrase your answer?'

'Where did you hear all this?'

'I had a letter from Simon,' she lied. 'John phoned him when he couldn't find you. The bank foreclosed and put the site up for auction but there was no money left for John. So he killed himself.'

'More fool him.' Sam's handsome face was twisted with contempt. 'What a bloody idiot.'

'Is that all you've got to say?' Gillian hung on grimly to her calm. 'Just that he was a bloody idiot?'

'Only a fool would have been taken in like he was. Christ! He didn't even bother to get his solicitor to check things out. Honestly!'

'And for that he deserved to die?' Gillian's temper was rising. 'You lied to him and swindled him!' She was on her feet now. 'You killed him, Sam! You might as well have pulled the trigger yourself before you left him in the shit!'

'Oh no, I didn't!' He was beside her, his hands on her wrists. She shrank from his touch and he shook her. 'Don't look at me like that. What about you? Who wheedled him into it in the first place? Crawling all over him and leading him on? Oh, I know you! Just remember this! I'd never have met him if it hadn't been for you, wanting money to pay off your endless Barclaycards and bills. You killed him just as much as I did!'

She dragged her hands from his grasp with a moan and, sinking into a chair, buried her face in them. Sam watched her. His mind leaped to and fro; assessing, rejecting, calculating. He went to the table and refilled his glass and poured some wine for her.

'Here.' He held it out to her. 'Have a drink and don't be so stupid. I didn't kill John and neither did you.'

Gillian took her hands away from her tragic face and stared at him. He pushed the glass into her hand and she took it and then sipped automatically. He nodded and took a deep breath as though a dangerous corner had been successfully negotiated and, sitting beside her, took her other hand. It lay limp and lifeless in his as she stared back at him.

'John killed John,' he said gently. 'Not me or you. John killed himself because he was a loser, a non-achiever. He'd never done anything or got anywhere and he couldn't stand the idea of it any longer. Someone like John hasn't got a hope in hell in this economic climate. He didn't have to accept my offer, did he? No sensible bloke would have chucked away all he'd got on a chance like that.'

Gillian looked away from the handsome face, tried not to hear the reasonable, soothing, exonerating words.

'You stole his money. You had no intention of developing the site. You lied to him and took his money and walked out on him.'

Sam sat back and gave a little laugh. ' "We," sweetheart. Get it right. "We." Make no mistake. Your hands are just as bloody as mine.'

'No!' she cried. 'No! I didn't know that you were lying. I thought you were going to do the site and that he'd get his money back. You know that.'

Sam grimaced consideringly. 'But who's going to believe you?' His expression changed a little as he weighed up certain remarks and behaviour patterns and a doubt crept into his mind. 'Certainly someone like your dear old upright Henry wouldn't.' He watched her closely. 'Not thinking of telling him, were you?' He burst out laughing at her silence. 'I think you were. I really think that you were going to rush back to Nethercombe, leaving your horrid murderous lover behind, and unburden your heart to dear faithful old Henry.' He shook his head and his expression was contemptuous. 'What a child you are. Did you really think that you could go back?'

'I am going back!' Gillian raised her chin and stared at him. 'Henry wants me back.'

'How d'you know?'

She looked at him and he nodded slowly.

'I see. You've been keeping him warm just in case. What a cheating bitch you are. First with Simon, then with me. And how many in between? Ah, who cares? Go, then. Go back. But you know that you'll never be able to tell him, don't you? It'll be on your conscience every time you look at him. And that old aunt or whatever she is. But I tell you this, Gillian! If you drop me in it by so much as a whisper, the shit will really hit the fan, I promise you. Every tiny bit of it. Think about it.' He got up. 'I'm going. I'll be back tomorrow evening. If you're leaving, then get on with it. The local taxi will take you to the station. If you're still here when I get back I shan't ever want to hear about John or Nethercombe again and I shall expect your full cooperation in all my deals. OK?'

'You mean with people like the Mortlakes? I suppose it's the same type of swindle all over again and you wanted me there to make it look convincing?'

'That's right.'

He watched her for a moment and she stared back at him, huddled in the chair. Turning away, he emptied some change and some notes onto the table.

'Sure you want to go back?' He was looking at her; the old Sam again now, charming, quizzical, offering her the smooth, easy paths of temptation. 'We make a good team, Gillian. Life's tough and you have to take what's offered, that's all.' He smiled ruefully, implying that she should understand – being a bit of a sinner herself – that survival was all that mattered.

She saw John with a hole in his head and heard Nell crying out in the pain of labour and loss and she turned her face away from him.

His expression changed and he shrugged. 'Have it your own way.'

He went out and shut the door quietly behind him.

Twenty-two

GUY WAS FEELING VERY good indeed. His friendship with Gemma and Sophie added a new dimension to his life which lent a glow to everything he did. He couldn't understand why this should be so. He'd had girlfriends before – one very serious relationship at university – but none had relaxed him in this way or softened his heart to the needs of others. During the Easter holidays the girls were frequent visitors, Gemma driving them both over in her mother's little car. The three of them took Bertie for walks on the moor, went regularly to the pub and explored the grounds at Nethercombe. Guy showed them his office in Dartmouth, took them into the Royal Castle for lunch and afterwards on the river, sailing in his boat. He suspected that Sophie imagined herself in love with him and found himself being gentle with her instead of blighting her hopes and crushing her feelings as had been his way with unwanted admirers in the past. His tall dark good looks attracted attention – girls finding his silent unapproachability a challenge – and he usually had no qualms in squashing their pretensions. With Gemma at hand, Sophie's passion remained undeclared and Guy was able to be generous. Gemma behaved like a younger sister. She was good company, easy to be with and teased him in a way that Guy, very sensitive to being made fun of, found perfectly able to cope with and return in kind.

When the holidays were over and the girls back at school, Guy was surprised at how much he missed them. His life which, hitherto, had been perfectly satisfactory now seemed flat and dull and, although he bore the teasing at the Church House and from Phoebe in good part, he was confused. After all, he wasn't in love with either of the girls and despite the fact that Gemma was very attractive – Sophie was too thin and he preferred blondes – he felt none of that inconvenient lust which had occasionally made his life uncomfortable in the past. So why did he miss them so much?

On the first weekend after they'd gone he took Bertie – who seemed to miss them as much as he did – for a long walk across the footpath that led over Nethercombe's fields to the open moor. The late April air was soft and warm and Guy felt himself responding to the beauty of the world about him. He'd known the moors all his life but today he saw them with new eyes and an unfamiliar piercing joy tinged with melancholy and an unnamed yearning flamed within him.

As he walked into the Courtyard he saw Phoebe standing outside her door staring upwards. Bertie ran to her, tail wagging, and she bent to stroke him, lifting her other hand to Guy.

'The swallows are back,' she said and her voice was almost exultant. 'Look!'

He looked up and saw them wheeling above his head against the blue sky. They watched for a moment and Guy smiled, nodding in acknowledgement of her pleasure.

'The trouble is,' she said, an anxious note creeping into her jubilation, 'I think we've stolen their homes. Isn't it awful? Fancy coming all that way and finding some thoughtless bugger's pinched your house? You can just imagine it, can't you?'

'I expect they'll find somewhere else,' said Guy, who was not so carried away by his sensations as to extend his newfound compassion to a few swallows. 'There are plenty of old buildings around still.'

'They're probably already spoken for.' Phoebe looked at him severely. 'I can see that you're not a conservationist.'

'No, I'm not,' he answered at once. 'I don't give a damn about the whales or the black rhino. Evolution automatically destroys certain species. One day it will destroy us. What difference is it going to make to your life if the giant panda becomes extinct? Do you think that we'd be here now if our ancestors had insisted on trying to preserve the dinosaur or the mammoth?'

'I feel that there's a flaw in that argument . . .' began Phoebe and paused as Gussie appeared in the archway. She waved to her.

'We were watching the swallows,' she called, 'and Guy was just telling me that one swallow doesn't make a summer. I know that I can always rely on him to stop me from becoming sentimental or prevent me from making too much of a fool of myself.' She grinned at Guy's expression. 'How are you, Gussie? Come and have a cup of tea. Both of you.'

'I won't at the moment, thank you all the same, my dear.' Gussie included Guy in her smile. 'I'm glad I've caught you both. The thing is . . .' She paused. 'Oh dear. This is really very difficult.'

Phoebe and Guy looked at her in surprise.

'Spit it out,' said Phoebe encouragingly. 'Has Guy been vandalising the beech walk? Cutting his initials on the trees?'

'Of course not. I shall just have to say it all quite baldly,' said Gussie. 'You can't wrap these things up.'

'Heavens!' exclaimed Phoebe in alarm. 'Whatever can it be?'

So standing there in the warm April sunshine, Gussie told them about Nell and John and the baby and how Nell had come to stay at Nethercombe for as long as she needed.

'I'm warning you so that when you see her you won't . . . well. You know. It's so easy to say the wrong thing without knowing it.'

'Of course,' agreed Phoebe at once, horrified. 'How perfectly dreadful. The poor girl must be quite demented. I haven't met her but have no fear. I shan't talk about anything that might upset her.'

'Obviously not.' Guy was shocked. He remembered Nell's unworldly beauty on the night of the party. 'Don't worry.'

'It's quite unforgivable to tell you these very private things about her life but I knew that you'd understand.' Gussie sounded distressed. 'I just hope that she would. It was a very difficult decision but I know that it won't go any further. It's an intolerable interference on my part but I want to protect her as much as I can. Well, I'll be getting back.' She smiled gratefully at them both and went out through the arch and back up the drive.

'How awful,' said Phoebe sombrely when Gussie had gone. 'And losing the child, too. Poor girl.'

Guy was silent, uneasy in this sort of situation, hating gossip or speculation.

'Come and have a drink, Guy,' said Phoebe suddenly. 'That's really upset me. Please do.'

And Guy, who wanted nothing more than to put his feet up in front of the television with a beer, dimly understood her need and followed her inside and shut the door.

SO IT WAS THAT Nell walked alone and unhindered through the grounds of Nethercombe, searching for some formula that would bring her peace and forgetfulness. When the numbness had worn off all she could feel for John was anger. He had ruined her life and Jack's and, too cowardly to face the results, had opted out and, by doing so, had caused the death of her baby. She felt the empty aching void, remembering with a gush of burning anguished tears the tiny coffin, and her arms would wrap themselves instinctively about her breast as though holding herself together. It seemed impossible even to feel pity for John, let alone grief or love. There had been so many things, some quite small, that seemed unforgivable. She could not yet envisage John himself, desperate in his own small private hell, not knowing which way to turn, his judgement distorted. She only saw that, clearly, he could not have cared for her or Jack or he would never have risked their lives in such a way. He'd even let her fetch Jack from school and take him back again in a car that was not insured. He had taken everything from her and destroyed it. Everything except Jack.

Before Jack went back to school she gathered her courage and told him the truth. She was as generous as she could be, putting as much blame as was possible on the recession and the man who had cheated and swindled John out of his inheritance, reinforcing the fact that John had been temporarily out of his mind having just discovered this deception. The gun was there in his desk drawer and the temptation had been too great. Jack listened, his brows drawn down in a frown, trying to understand.

'But didn't he think about us?' he'd asked, when her voice had trailed away. 'About what would happen to us? If he was so worried about it all that he had to kill himself, how did he think that we would manage?'

'The whole point is,' replied Nell, 'that in those situations you don't think at all. It's as if, just for that moment, you're not yourself, not rational or normal, if you see what I mean? We have to remember that.'

Nell walking in the woods and over the fields tried desperately to remember it and to forgive him. Jack seemed to find it easier; at school several boys had left because of marriage break-ups and an inability to pay fees, all due to the recession, and even suicides were not unknown. Nell had not told him all the truth, however, regarding the baby's death. She told him that the baby had turned in the womb and, having separated from the placenta, had suffocated because the ambulance, due to Saturday morning traffic, had not been able to get her to the hospital in time. She knew instinctively that Jack would find it very difficult to forgive his father if he could be held in any way responsible for the death of the tiny brother whom neither of them now would ever know. It was almost a relief when the term started and she could relax; abandon the pretence that she was recovering quickly and that there was nothing for him to worry about. The school, well prepared, took him back for his final term, and Jack, relieved that Nell was to be at Nethercombe, left her to the care of Gussie and Henry.

She couldn't have been in better hands. Gussie was one of the old school; she believed that nothing aided recovery more than fresh air, plenty of rest and good plain food. She didn't quite approve of the modern methods which involved endless 'talking through' situations and delving into the innermost recesses of the mind. She felt that whatever was said at times of great emotional shock would probably be unreliable and distorted and likely to cause embarrassment later on when a natural balance had been regained. Nell, who would have hated to bare her innermost thoughts to anyone, was grateful for her reticence and slowly the peace and beauty of Nethercombe combined with Gussie's and Henry's love and care began to heal her.

As May was drawing to a close, Henry received a letter from Gillian asking if she could come home. She was with Lydia in Exeter and she would be grateful, she wrote, if she could meet him and talk to him. Henry was so overwhelmed with relief and joy that he wanted to rush into Exeter there and then and bring Gillian back at once. He communicated his plans to Gussie who laid the cold hand of reason on his fevered excitement.

'We can't expect Gillian to arrive back only to find Nell living here,' she explained when it was obvious that Henry could see no reason whatever for delay. 'It wouldn't be fair to either of them. You must see that, my dear.'

Henry wrinkled his brow in an effort to understand.

'But Gillian knows about Nell,' he said. 'I wrote and told her all about it. She was dreadfully upset.'

'I'm sure she was,' said Gussie, 'but it would still be very difficult for both of them.'

'Would it?'

Gussie sent up a short prayer for guidance. She had been prepared for this eventuality ever since she knew that Gillian was back in Exeter. Now it only remained to persuade Henry to agree with her plans for them all.

'You must take my word for it, my dear. I'm a woman and I know how women feel. After all, it's very important that your marriage should be given every opportunity to make a new start.'

'Oh, yes,' agreed Henry. 'But why should——?'

'You and Gillian will need time together alone. And then again, the time is coming when Nell, too, will need a measure of independence.'

Henry looked baffled and Gussie poured his coffee, relieved that this moment had come when Nell was having lunch with Phoebe in the Courtyard.

'You see, it could all work out very well indeed, Henry,' she said, feeling that a positive note was called for here. 'We must just allow ourselves to be flexible.'

Henry nodded obediently and sipped. He was quite prepared to be flexible.

Gussie took a restorative sip of hot coffee to give her courage. 'What I thought was this. Supposing that the Ridleys were to move up from the Lodge and into the house with us? Mrs Ridley would be very glad not to go trailing up and down the avenue several times a day. She's not as young as she was and she hates it in the winter when it's dark . . .' Gussie paused. In her anxiety to sound plausible she'd struck a false note. Mrs Ridley was born and bred a countrywoman and the dark of the avenue held no terrors for her.

'Is Mrs Ridley afraid of the dark?' asked Henry, sidetracked by this rather surprising news.

'No,' said Gussie, rejecting this possibly emotive suggestion despite the fact that it might weigh on her side. She resisted temptation nobly, hoping that the Almighty was listening in. 'No, not the dark. But it's horrid in the winter, going to and fro in the rain and the cold, making sure the fire's still in, looking after two places at once. Now, they could have that very nice little flat at the back. It used to be servants' quarters in your parents' time and it could be done up in no time at all.'

'Well, if that's what they'd like,' said Henry, after consideration. 'From our point of view it would be very convenient. But are you sure that they want to leave the Lodge after all these years?'

'Naturally, Mrs Ridley and I have had one or two little chats on the

subject,' said Gussie, whose discussions and plans with Mrs Ridley
had been exhaustive, 'and they would be very happy now to move
into smaller quarters.'

'We'll look into it. It won't be difficult to get the flat back into a
cosy little home again. But what's that got to do with Nell and Gillian?'

'Well, my dear, it means that Nell can move down to the Lodge
where we can keep an eye on her but meanwhile gives her some independence and freedom. She needs that, especially in the holidays with
Jack home. And,' added Gussie firmly, 'she can pay you rent.'

'Gussie!' Henry sat up straight. He looked shocked. 'If you think
that I could ask Nell for money—'

'Now wait a moment. The Ridleys don't pay rent because having a
roof over their heads is part of their wage. But if Nell moves into the
Lodge she can apply to the Department of Social Security for Housing
Benefit. She's homeless and almost penniless, so she'll get assistance.
It's a start. A way of her becoming a little more independent. Nell
won't stay long under this roof, Henry. And with Gillian coming
home she'll go even sooner and she'd be right to. They both need a
fair start.'

'Yes, I can see that.' Henry looked troubled. 'If only there was a
way . . .'

'There is a way, Henry. I've just told you. The Ridleys want to be
here and if Nell goes to the Lodge she'll be far away enough to be independent and close enough to be kept an eye on. I don't want her to
vanish.'

'Good Lord, no!' Henry looked so alarmed that Gussie would have
smiled if the situation hadn't been so serious.

'No. So you see we've got to do a very quick removal before
Gillian comes. We don't want her to think that she's not welcome
back or that you're in two minds, so it must be quick.'

'Yes, I see that. How long would you say?'

'A week or two to get the flat into good working order. That's all.
Mrs Ridley keeps the Lodge spotless so Nell can move down as soon

as they're in. We might need some help getting the furniture to and fro but between us all we'll manage. Guy will lend a hand. It will be lovely for Nell to be in her own place with her own things round her.'

'And you don't think that she'll feel that we're trying to get rid of her?' Henry was still anxious.

Gussie smiled at him. She was into the home straight.

'I promise you that Nell will be delighted to stay close to Nethercombe without feeling that she's a burden. Trust me, Henry.'

'I'll go and have a look at the flat,' he said pushing back his chair. 'It'll need some tidying up but it shouldn't be too bad.'

Gussie closed her eyes and slumped in her chair. There was nothing more tiring than bending someone to one's will. Positively exhausting! Why couldn't people simply accept that one knew best and leave it at that? All the explaining and going over things . . . Gussie took another sip of coffee.

'Finished?' Mrs Ridley stood in the doorway with a tray.

'Yes, indeed.' Gussie swallowed the last drop and stood up. 'Let me help you clear.'

'Mister 'Enry's out back lookin' at the flat,' observed Mrs Ridley casually, shuffling plates as though they were playing cards.

'Ah.' Their eyes met and exchanged a victorious glance. 'That's good. We don't want to waste time.'

'I've started packin' up, down the Lodge.' Mrs Ridley stacked the tray. 'Shudden take no time at all.'

Gussie opened the door, stood aside for her to pass with the loaded tray and smiled as she followed her along the passage to the kitchen. Now she only had Nell to convince and she would be content.

Twenty-three

ON THE MORNING THAT Henry was to visit Gillian, it would have been impossible to judge who was the more nervous; Gillian or Lydia. Lydia felt two quite separate emotions. The first was a real nervousness of Henry himself. Beside her woolly, undisciplined, easily impressed personality, he seemed a man of upright character; a landowner and a magistrate, running his estate, managing farms, tenants, land. He made her feel inadequate and foolish. The second emotion was a combination of humiliation and embarrassment. Had she been a better mother, Gillian would probably not have behaved so badly and she imagined that Henry might easily despise her. She could see now with the clear unclouded vision that hindsight lends that, when Gillian had turned up en route for France, she should have packed her straight back to Nethercombe with a flea in her ear. Instead, she had almost encouraged her to go. Poor Lydia felt quite ill with remorse.

Gillian's feelings were even more complex. Along with shame and fright, she felt an overwhelming guilt. To know that she had deceived Henry with the man who was responsible for John's death and Nell's desperate situation was something that could never be forgotten. It went to bed with her at night and was waiting for her each morning. Gillian knew that Henry was quite generous enough to put the whole episode – as he understood it – behind him but what if he should ever discover the real truth? Supposing he should find out that it was she who had seduced John into meeting Sam? Gillian felt sick at the thought and wished with all her heart that she could turn back the clock. She lay awake at night, staring into the darkness, knowing that she could never escape from this terrible knowledge. Sometimes she allowed herself to imagine a scene in which she unburdened her soul to Henry and he forgave her freely; more often she visualised an expression of disgust mingling with dislike dawning on his face and knew that she couldn't risk it. Even if Henry could bring himself to forgive and forget, what about Nell? She was the truly injured one; the victim whose life lay in ruins. Gillian's relief had known no bounds when she found that Henry and Gussie had carried Nell back to Nethercombe. Her only dilemma was how to face her; how to look her in the eyes. She wept with shame and self-disgust and Lydia, who didn't know the whole truth, looked upon her daughter's ravaged face with dismay and became even more nervous of confronting Henry.

'You'll stay, won't you, Mum?' asked Gillian as they sat waiting for the doorbell to ring. 'Don't go. Not to begin with.'

Lydia, who had planned an escape into the kitchen under the pretext of making coffee, looked at her in alarm.

'You sound as if you're quite frightened of him, darling,' she suggested and screamed faintly as the doorbell rang loudly.

Both women had leaped to their feet and now they stood, listening, Gillian unconsciously clutching Lydia's arm.

'Oh, how silly.' Lydia attempted a light laugh and patted her chest nervously. 'It quite made me jump. Shall you go . . . ?' Her words trailed away. Gillian looked as though she might pass away in terror. 'I'll go.'

Lydia pushed her daughter back into the corner of the sofa and with trembling knees went out into the hall. She flung open the door with a gesture of bravado and laughed hysterically at her son-in-law.

'Hello, Lydia.' Henry was far too happy to notice if she were behaving oddly. 'How nice to see you. Are you well?' He went into the sitting room and Lydia, following behind him, saw him open his arms to Gillian who stared up at him from her corner. 'Gillian,' he said and his voice was warm and full of love. 'How wonderful to have you back.' And Gillian leapt to her feet, bolted into his arms and burst into tears.

'Oh, darling. Oh dear.' Lydia clucked round both of them and then decided to take the risk of incurring Gillian's wrath and followed her own original plan.

As she filled the kettle and measured the coffee she hovered to and fro, keeping an eye on things through the half-open door. Gillian's sobs had subsided and Henry's deep voice was murmuring tenderly and Lydia gave thanks to all the gods at once that the worst was over. She realised that she was trembling violently and slipping over to the cupboard took a good swig from the whisky bottle. In the act of cramming some biscuit into her mouth, lest the smell should be detected, she was surprised to find Henry close behind her. She clapped a hand over her lips, her eyes round and horrified above it, and nodded brightly at him.

'Gone to mop up,' he explained. 'Shall I carry something?'

He seized the tray whilst Lydia, still nodding encouragingly, swallowed a crumb the wrong way and choked violently. Henry put the tray down so that he could bang her on the back and Gillian, arriving on the scene, poured a glass of water and passed it to her mother. Lydia gulped it back and apologised breathlessly.

'Let's have some coffee.' Gillian looked radiant. 'Henry says he's got all sorts of things to tell us.'

Henry picked up the tray again and, behind his back, mother looked at daughter and they hugged wordlessly before following him into the sitting room.

SOPHIE WROTE FIRST; A shy, almost silly letter, crammed full of the 'most amazing' happenings and goings-on. Guy was rather touched but enjoyed Gemma's letter, which arrived a week after Sophie's, much more. It was quite a casual but interesting letter and brought the writer's easy, happy charm very much to his mind. At the end she wrote that she was hoping to introduce him to Chris Winterton – her submariner boyfriend – during the summer holidays.

Guy found himself feeling worried at the thought of becoming a foursome. He didn't want to give Sophie ideas and, anyway, it had been such fun, just the three of them. He imagined that it had a lot to do with the fact that he'd known them from their cradles until he remembered that he didn't care at all for Gemma's brothers whom he'd known for even longer and, realising that he was in danger of becoming confused again, he whistled to Bertie and wandered up the drive into the beech walk. So immersed in thought was he that it was only when she was nearly upon him did he realise that Nell was walking towards him. How beautiful she was, though much thinner than he remembered her but how well it suited that Pre-Raphaelite unworldliness. She wore a white silk shirt tucked into a heavy cotton skirt that flowed almost to her feet and her dark red hair hung down her back and Guy realised that he was holding his breath. She smiled at him and, after a moment, held out her hand.

'You don't remember me,' she said. 'I'm Nell Woodward. We met at the barbecue last autumn. Is it Guy?'

'Yes, it is.' He grasped her hand readily. 'And I remember you perfectly well.' Several remarks fled through his head, all of which were unsuitable, and he realised that he was still holding her hand and dropped it, flushing darkly. 'Bertie's been stuck in the office with me all day,' he said, at random. 'So I'm taking the long way round to the pub.' He hesitated, watching her crouch to stroke Bertie who looked at her with dark wise eyes and offered his paw. 'Would you like to come?'

He swallowed, amazed at himself, and Nell looked up at him in surprise.

'That sounds . . . really nice. D'you know, I would.' She straightened up. 'I haven't been to a pub for . . .' she shook her head, 'oh, I simply can't remember how long.'

'Well, then.' A strange nervous excitement was surging in his veins. 'It's only the little local one. Nothing too special. But they do a good drop of Bass and an excellent beef sandwich.'

She smiled at him and his heart did strange exciting things in his breast.

'That's an offer I'm quite unable to resist. Thank you.'

'We'll go out by the Lodge,' he said, trying to control himself. 'There's a small wicket gate on to the lane. The big gate's padlocked.'

'I know.' Nell turned to retrace her steps beside him. 'I live there now, you know.'

'In the Lodge?' He stared at her. 'I didn't know that. Have the Ridleys gone?'

'Good heavens, no! They've moved up to the house. It was getting a bit too much for Mrs Ridley, going between the two. So we've swapped. Wonderful luck for me. It's a dear little cottage.'

Guy was silent, unable to think of a single thing to say that wasn't loaded with peril. Nell turned her head and smiled at him and he saw the pain and the fear and the loneliness behind it and felt inadequate and impotent to reach out to comfort her.

'I'm glad you're settled.' How bleak it sounded.

'So am I,' she confided in him. 'I was so afraid of being in a muddle when the summer holidays start. I want to be ready for Jack.' She hesitated and he guessed she was wondering how much he knew.

'I understand,' he said with real feeling and she smiled at him again, gratefully. 'Does he like sailing?'

'Oh! Yes, actually. He loves it. He does a bit at school.'

'I've got a boat at Dartmouth. Perhaps he'd like to go out?'

'Oh, he'd love to! How very kind. Are you sure? He's only twelve and it can be a tiresome age.'

'Rubbish! It's a very good age. That's settled then.' He nodded, smiling back at her. 'What about you? Are you a sailor? Perhaps you'd like to go out? One weekend?'

'I've never sailed.' She looked a little anxious. 'Is it , . . ? Is it quite a big boat?'

He really smiled then, a truly warm, genuinely affectionate smile, and she responded automatically, suspecting that he was about to tease her.

'All I can say to that is,' he said, 'come and find out!'

ONCE AGAIN THE RHODODENDRONS had flowered and, once again, Gussie had watched them turning from bud to bloom as she walked among bushes tall as trees, each covered with the purple and crimson and white blossoms. This spring she felt a special magic. Gillian was back at Nethercombe and Henry was happy again. She and the Ridleys had guarded the secret well. Everyone assumed that Gillian was visiting relations in France and her homecoming had been delayed. When Henry told her that she had nothing to fear from gossip she was grateful and when Gussie greeted her as though she'd just come back from a trip to Exeter, she'd hugged her with the first real affection that she'd ever shown the older woman. Now, on this hot day in early summer, Gussie walked among the rhododendrons remembering that hug and smiling to herself. With that embrace everything between them had been put right and Gussie was being as tactful as she could be in giving Gillian and Henry plenty of time together alone. Even Mrs Ridley, snug and busy as Mrs Tittlemouse in her little house, was prepared to bury old prejudices and extend – albeit cautiously – the olive branch.

Gussie cut off a yellow scented bloom and held it to her nose, sniffing luxuriously. She was surprised at how eager Gillian was to make amends. She behaved like a chastened child who, ashamed of certain exploits, longs to atone. If she'd been asked to guess, Gussie would have said that, in these circumstances, Gillian would have been prone to behave with defiant bravado. Gussie tucked the flower into her cardigan button and strolled on. Even more unexpected was Gillian's reaction to Nell. Here, she had hoped for sympathy on Gillian's part and had been quite taken aback by her sensitivity. She almost seemed to dread meeting Nell and when, finally, it had taken place, Gillian had been almost deprived of speech and it had been Nell who had been obliged to take the situation in hand.

Gussie cut another bloom and added it to the sprays in the basket on her arm. Nell was healing. It was a slow process but all the better for that; slow and sure and thorough. Gussie walked through the little gate that led to the swimming pool. The doors to the summerhouse stood open and she sat down on the Lloyd Loom chair that stood in the sunshine, its cushions warm. The scent of new-mown grass crept to her nostrils, the birds sang riotously about her and, higher up the valley, a goods train rattled over the viaduct. Gussie closed her eyes and turned her face to the sun.

'The thing is, Lord,' she said, feeling that the Almighty would be quite grateful to pause in His labours and rest in the sun awhile, 'it would be impossible not to heal in this wonderful place. We are so lucky, Lord. So very, very lucky. And don't think we don't appreciate it. Of course, the trouble is that we don't realise that Life is just a series of moments and all that is guaranteed to us is now. This moment in time. If we realised that, we'd stop scurrying about, too busy to stop and enjoy the magic moments because our minds are fixed on a future that probably doesn't exist.' She paused politely, giving the Almighty chance to make a contribution. A thought occurred to her which she looked upon as a direct communication and she nodded thoughtfully. 'Well, of course, You're quite right. People are afraid to stop in case they are obliged to confront themselves. Silence is so frightening.'

A figure inserted itself between her and the sun and Gussie opened her eyes. Phoebe stood looking down at her and Gussie smiled serenely.

'Good morning, Phoebe.'

'Hi, there. All alone?' Phoebe glanced around.

'Yes, indeed.' Gussie sighed. 'Quite alone.'

'May I join you?' Phoebe dragged up an adjoining chair without waiting for Gussie's gesture. 'I'm glad to see you. I wanted to ask you how you thought Nell was doing?'

Gussie put her thoughts in order.

'She's coming along very well, under the circumstances. Wouldn't you agree? You see something of her, don't you?'

'Yes, I do.' Phoebe stretched out her long legs in their shabby cords and gazed out over the roofs of the Courtyard. 'She's begun to talk about things a little.'

'Things?' queried Gussie cautiously.

'John,' said Phoebe and grimaced. 'It's terrifying. I'm so afraid of saying too much. Or not enough. The balance is terribly difficult and I'm not one of your tactful women.'

Gussie smiled. 'I'm sure that you're just what she needs. She's very reticent and it's probably easier for her to unburden herself to you, being closer to her age than I am. And, of course, you've been married.'

Phoebe snorted.

'Oh, yes.' Gussie nodded. 'It makes a difference. We all have something different we can give. I'm so glad you've made friends.'

They sat for a while in the sun. Presently Phoebe shifted in her chair.

'Gussie?'

'Yes, my dear?'

'Who were you talking to – when I came up just now? You were saying something about silence being frightening.'

'I was talking to the Lord, dear,' Gussie told her calmly. 'I find it helps to straighten out my thoughts to have a little chat to Him from time to time.'

'Right.' Phoebe nodded, raised her eyebrows, drew down the corners of her mouth, shrugged her shoulders and pursed her lips in quick succession. 'Fine. Good.'

Gussie, her eyes closed against the sun, pictured Phoebe's discomfiture with a certain amount of sympathy. Unlike Mrs Ridley, Phoebe would have difficulty in coming to terms with the idea of chatting to the Almighty, whether it was on the terrace or by the swimming pool.

'After all, my dear,' she said, 'why not? "For in Him we live, and move, and have our being." '

'Absolutely!' said Phoebe, after a moment of profound silence.

'So.' Gussie opened her eyes suddenly and beamed at her. 'Shall we go up? Henry's away today and Gillian likes company.' She looked sombre for a moment. A little bell tolled and was silent. Why did Gillian dislike being alone? It reminded her of that earlier thought, but why?

Phoebe was looking at her anxiously and Gussie shook her head and got to her feet.

'I'm a silly old woman,' she told her. 'Come on. I must get these poor flowers into some water.'

Above them, up on the terrace, they could hear voices and the clink of china. Gussie inhaled the scent of cut grass and nodded her head.

'So lucky, my dear,' she said to the startled Phoebe and led the way through the gate.

Twenty-four

AS THE SHOCK WORE off, Nell became slowly and frighteningly aware of her situation. Apart from the pieces of furniture saved from the cottage at Porlock Weir, she had nothing but the small portion of John's pension and with this and the various benefits allowed for Jack she had barely three thousand a year on which to live. To begin with she revelled in the financial freedom she had gained. It might be a tiny amount but it was all hers to budget with and allocate how she chose and there were no more outstanding bills, no terrifying debts. It had been touch and go as to whether she would have to be declared bankrupt but she could not be made responsible for John's business debts and, unknown to her, Henry settled the arrears on the rent and the telephone bill at the flat. The bank, having a second charge over the Bournemouth property, was prepared to see what the house might bring and agreed to freeze the overdraft on the joint account. Nell opened a separate account which she was not allowed to overdraw. She didn't care. After the horrors of the last four years she vowed that she would never owe anyone anything ever again. Her housing benefit arrived regularly and was passed on to Henry and, at first, she felt quite rich on her small income.

It was as the summer holiday drew nearer that Nell was forced to see that life wasn't quite so simple. Oil was needed to run the Rayburn which, since it supplied all her cooking needs and heated the water and two tiny radiators upstairs, was more economical than buying an electric cooker and using the immersion heater for the water. As

Henry pointed out, the Rayburn also warmed the kitchen and the house in general and Nell agreed that it was the sensible option and arranged to pay for her oil on a monthly basis. She discovered an enormous stock of logs in a shed at the back of the house but the Ridleys refused to take payment for them. They received them free from the estate as part of their wage and they didn't need them now in their cosy little flat. She could have them and welcome. Nell decided to accept thankfully, knowing that there was enough to keep the little woodburner going through several seasons. It was Gussie who dissuaded her from having the telephone disconnected. If an emergency arose she would need to be able to get in touch, she argued. Or Jack might need to contact her. True, messages could be taken at the house but one simply never knew . . . In the end, Nell gave in, saying that she would try it for a quarter and see what sort of bill arrived. Since she had no car to run, the other main cost would be Jack. He had his scholarship but there were so many other expenses. The uniform alone would probably cost a fortune. After much heart-searching, she telephoned the bursar with whom she had a long, frank conversation and who was quite wonderfully helpful.

Nell sat on her little lawn and marvelled at the kindness and generosity that she had been shown. How on earth would she have managed without the help of all these people who had rallied round? She and Jack could, by now, have been living in a DSS bed and breakfast boarding house in some Bristol back street and, instead, she was living in this delightful cottage with its pretty garden which looked across the meadows and up to the moors, blue and hazy in the morning sunshine. Since she had no garden tools Mr Ridley would jolt along the avenue in his old car once a week, take a Flymo from the boot, cut the lawn and do a general tidy round before jolting back again. One morning, Phoebe had arrived with a tray of bedding plants, insisting that she'd bought far more than she needed and would be grateful if Nell could find a hole for them. She returned from her long solitary walks to find new bread or a sponge and some scones left in the porch – results of the big bake at Nethercombe – or a pot of Mrs Ridley's special jam and felt overwhelmed with gratitude.

Nell lay back on the rug, her fingers smoothing and flattening the warm wool. Slowly, very slowly, the loss of her unknown baby was becoming a more bearable pain, probably because he had never become a person to her. She had borne him and lost him but she knew, by the sudden clutch at her heart strings, how very much more terrible it would be if she were to lose Jack. It was not to be thought of! And how would she have managed now with a new baby to look after? Nell rolled over on to her stomach, letting the heat soak into her back, and thought about John. Her anger, too, was subsiding. She could make some effort now to understand all that he'd been through and she could even feel pity for the desperate fear that had driven him to take his own life but, if she were absolutely honest with herself, her most consistent emotion now was relief. Each time a new fear or worry assailed her the anger returned, a stab of fury that he should have reduced them to such a state and then abandoned her, but at least her life was in her own hands. She wondered, as she lay in the sunshine, whether she had ever really loved John at all. It was for Rupert that the spark had been lit and his unattainability had ensured that it had never gone out. Yet she had loved John in a different way. She had loved them both.

'Remember me when I am gone away, Gone far away into the silent land.' Well, they were both gone now into the silent land and the unknown baby with them and she was left alone. Nell let the tears slip from her eyes, soaking the rug beneath her cheek, and Phoebe, standing with her hand on the gatelatch, saw the heaving shoulders and heard the gasping sobs and turned quietly away.

FOR GILLIAN, NELL WAS a permanent reminder of her folly. She woke each morning with a deep thankfulness that she was in her bedroom at Nethercombe with Henry beside her. Their reunion had seen the blossoming of a new sort of love. On Henry's part it was really his old love blessed with a new awareness for Gillian's needs and a confidence to offer a fulfilment of those needs as he saw them. Gillian, nervous, fearful, grateful, clung to him with a passionate offering of herself that even Henry recognised and responded to and, if it hadn't been for the continued proximity of Nell's presence, Gillian's happiness would have known no bounds.

She knew that she deserved no better. Why should she live, surrounded by love and beauty, whilst Nell struggled alone? If, by going to Nell and telling her the truth, there might be some restitution, some relief for Nell, then it would be worth the sacrifice of her pride. As it was, it could do no good and so the knowledge stayed in Gillian's heart, a gnawing canker, eating away at her new love and joy.

Gussie suspected that all was not well but couldn't imagine what could be wrong. Anyone could see that Henry and Gillian were happier than they had ever been but Gussie was not deceived. She noticed that Gillian hated to be alone; preferring the company even of Mrs Ridley rather than solitude, hurrying down the drive to see Phoebe, seeking Gussie out. Rarely now did she go rushing off to Exeter except to see Lydia. Nevertheless, Gillian appeared to have a secret. Gussie pondered thoughtfully.

IT WAS ELIZABETH WHO guessed the truth. When Lydia telephoned to tell her the glad tidings she was relieved and pleased for her old friend. A few weeks later, on her way to Plymouth, she decided to drop in at Nethercombe and turned up unexpectedly to find Gussie on the terrace with a singularly beautiful young woman who made her excuses and hurried off.

'What a remarkable-looking girl,' said Elizabeth, gazing after Nell. 'I seem to have frightened her away.'

'It's a very sad story,' confided Gussie, who considered Elizabeth to be one of the family. 'Her husband was taken in over a property deal. Invested all their money, raised loans against their house, you know the sort of thing. And then found that it was all bogus. He was already desperately in debt and in a mad moment shot himself. Nell heard the shot and the sight of his body sent her into premature labour. They couldn't get her to the hospital in time and there was an abruption of the placenta. They had to perform a Caesarean section but it was too late and she lost the baby.'

'Good God, Gussie!' Elizabeth was staring at her in horror.

'I know.' Gussie shook her head. 'She's lost everything, of course. She's living in the Lodge so I can keep an eye on her. She's a very dear friend.'

'But can't the man be traced?' demanded Elizabeth, her mind still on the practicalities of the case. 'Surely something can be done? Was there no site, after all, or what?'

'Oh, yes. The site was over at Dartmouth. Apparently a very desirable one but the man, whoever he was, was so much in debt that he used John's money to sort himself out. The site went to auction and there was nothing left for John. It seems that the man has gone abroad somewhere.'

'The site was at Dartmouth?' repeated Elizabeth.

'That's right. I expect John heard of it through the estate agents' grapevine unless it was while he was down here for Christmas. It might have been advertised in the local paper. Do sit down. I'll go and call Gillian. She'll be so pleased to see you.'

She left Elizabeth in the library and disappeared. Elizabeth remained deep in thought and when Gillian appeared she studied her carefully. She'd lost weight and all the old gloss had gone. Elizabeth extended her cheek for the usual greeting and took Gillian's hands. Gussie had tactfully left them alone, muttering about tea.

'I'm glad that you had the sense to come home,' she said. She gave the hands a squeeze and let them go. 'I've got hopes that you might have grown up after all.'

'About time, wasn't it?' Gillian's tone was almost bitter. 'It's taken long enough.'

'What went wrong? Did what's-his-name beat you? Sam something, was it?' She broke off abruptly as Gillian gave a gasp of real fear, her eyes on the door.

'Don't! Please don't tell anyone his name, Elizabeth. Please! I can't say why, but please don't!'

She was quite frantic and Elizabeth held up her hands placatingly and shook her head.

'OK, OK. Don't worry.' She paused but decided to test her theory a little further. 'Oh, by the way. What happened about that site in Dartmouth you were trying to sell me? Did you find an investor?'

Gillian was on her feet. 'Oh God, Elizabeth! Please don't mention that! Not to anyone! It was all a mistake. Oh God!'

She looked so anguished, so frightened, that Elizabeth got up and took her by the shoulders.

'Come on, Gillian. Pull yourself together! I shan't say a word to anyone, I promise.'

Gillian stared into her eyes and Elizabeth saw that she was close to tears. She nodded reassuringly, gave her a little shake and pushed her down into a chair just as Gussie arrived with the tea tray. During tea, Elizabeth wondered if her guess could possibly be right and decided that the sooner she spoke to Gillian in private the better. She sipped her tea and made conversation and wondered how long it might be before such a load of guilt might drive someone out of his or her mind.

IT WAS GUY WHO made Nell think seriously about getting a job. Physically, she was much stronger and she'd already come to the decision that she must try to find work of some kind. Although she had a degree in Fine Arts, she'd married before putting her knowledge into practice and now she wondered whether to try for a refresher course, if such a thing were possible. She spent long hours thinking about this and getting books from the library in Totnes when she went in with Phoebe to the Friday market. It was Guy, however, who brought her down to earth and pointed out that, in the present economic climate, she'd be lucky to get any sort of job at all. It didn't take Nell long to find out that he was absolutely right. She had no computer skills and no selling experience and she began to feel frightened again.

'I'll never find a job,' she said to Guy, one evening at the pub. 'I plucked up courage and asked about a sales assistant's job at a shop in Totnes today. The woman told me that I was too old.'

She stared at him in alarm and Guy, who couldn't think of age in connection with Nell, sensed her fear and came to a decision.

'To tell you the truth,' he said, 'I'm glad to hear it. I need someone to help me in the office but I didn't like to ask you. I know it's not the sort of thing you're looking for as a career but, for the time being, it might help both of us.'

Nell was looking at him in surprise. 'But how could I help?' she asked. 'I can only type with one finger and computers terrify me. What sort of help?'

'It's all very simple but time-consuming,' he said, remaining purposely vague. 'And as much as anything I need someone to mind the office. As you know, I often have to move boats to and fro or take clients out and that's always when other customers turn up. I couldn't pay much but it may just give you a chance to pick things up without someone breathing down your neck.' He shrugged and took a swig from his glass. 'Just a thought.'

'Oh, Guy! It sounds exactly what I need. Do you really think I could cope?'

'Of course you can cope! You'll get the knack in no time. And you'll be able to be flexible when the holidays come. Jack can come too if you like. He can help with the boats.'

He looked away from the joy and excitement on Nell's face lest he should forget himself and fling his arms round her and kiss her. He had no idea how he would squeeze enough money to pay her anything. All he knew was that, for her company, he would willingly go without himself if it came to it. The thought of having her with him on the drives to and from Dartmouth or coming and finding her in the office made him want to shout aloud. Instead, he downed his pint and bent to pat Bertie so that his face was hidden until he could control it. He was fastidious enough to imagine that any declaration of love would be quite abhorrent to Nell after her recent experiences. To press his needs upon her would be selfish whilst she was recovering from her loss and coming to terms with her situation. Also, being Guy, he was nervous of the strength of his feelings. Never had he felt so carried away by his emotions, so moved by beauty and distress, and instinctively he listened to the inner voice which urged caution. He didn't know what he wanted. The thought of marriage frightened him to death and it was impossible to imagine having a casual affair with Nell. The sensible thing was to give it time and, meanwhile, the idea of a working relationship seemed ideal.

When he left her at the Lodge, with a promise of picking her up in the morning for a trial run at the office, he felt exactly the same as when he'd been made Captain of the Rugby Fifteen at school. His jubilation was too great to be contained and he began to run, his arms outstretched, his face lifted to the stately beeches towering above him. Bertie ran with him, careering along, barking madly, and the two of them raced down the drive and into the Courtyard. Guy stopped at his front door, gasping for breath, feeling for keys, and quite light-headed with happiness. Little spurts of laughter escaped between the gasps.

'Do share the joke.' Phoebe's voice speaking out of the semi-darkness made him jump. 'What on earth have you and Bertie been up to?'

He saw her now, sitting on the bench in the corner, feet drawn up, the end of her cigarette glowing in the dusk. He gave up the search for his keys and, crossing the courtyard, sat down at the end of the seat.

'You made me jump,' he said. 'What are you doing, sitting on your own in the dark?'

'I've been watching the moon rise,' she answered and, looking up, he saw the thin crescent moon lying on her back in the deep turquoise sky. 'It's nearly midsummer. The longest day. Don't you think we should have a pool party? We can all swim at midnight. It's quite warm enough.'

'I think that's a brilliant idea,' said Guy, who would have agreed to anything in his present mood. 'Wonderful.' He remembered Nell as he had seen her at that last party and his heart beat faster.

'And will all your ladies be there?'

'Ladies?' repeated Guy, his mind still on Nell.

Phoebe shook her head and stubbed out her cigarette. ' "O heaven!",' she quoted sadly, ' "were man but constant, he were perfect." '

'If you mean Gemma and Sophie,' said Guy, feeling a twinge of guilt, 'they aren't my ladies. I've known them both since they were in their prams. Anyway, Gemma's got a boyfriend.'

Phoebe made a face which was wasted on Guy since it was too dark for him to see it.

'Hmm,' she said irritatingly. 'Well, I think everyone should be invited. It will do us all good. Outsiders? Or just Nethercombe and the Courtyard?'

'Oh, not outsiders,' said Guy at once with his usual insularity and natural caution. 'Just us.'

'Not Gemma or Sophie?'

'Well, perhaps them,' said Guy, remembering that they were both due home at any time and would certainly be over to see him. 'They seem to belong somehow.'

'Far too many women,' said Phoebe regretfully. 'I'll have to get to work on Mr Jackson.'

'I hardly ever see him,' said Guy, glancing at the dark windows of the smallest cottage. 'What's he like?'

'OK.' Guy could imagine the shrug. 'Very cosy and very married. Drives down on Monday and back on Fridays and spends most evenings with some friends in South Brent. I expect wifie's arranged it to keep him on the straight and narrow. I met her once when they were moving him in and told her I'd look after him.'

Guy gave a snort of laughter and Phoebe thought how nice he was once he unbent a little and relaxed.

'No wonder he rushes into Brent,' he said. 'He must be frightened out of his wits!'

'And just for that, you rude boy,' remarked Phoebe, uncurling her legs and standing up, 'you can supply the nightcap. And I'm not talking about cocoa!'

Twenty-five

SOMEHOW, THE IDEA OF a Midsummer's Eve party seized the imagination of everyone at Nethercombe and the place began to hum with activity. It was to be, in some way, a celebration; of life, of survival, of love. Each of them could find something to be grateful for and this became, naturally and unconsciously, the spirit of the party.

Joan and Bill Beresford arrived for a fortnight's holiday and were immediately swept up in the excitement. Bill went with Mr Ridley to spruce up the summerhouse and reinstate the lights while Joan, who was a notable cook, offered to help Mrs Ridley with the responsibility of feeding the guests. Gussie and Gillian sorted out all the old plates and glasses that wouldn't be missed if there were breakages and counted knives and forks and Phoebe went round collecting contributions to help towards the wine.

'You can't imagine the relief on Mr Jackson's face,' she told Sophie and Gemma, who had come over early on the afternoon of the party to help, 'when he realised that it was a Saturday and he wouldn't be here. He looked positively frightened at the mere idea.'

'I expect he was imagining Bacchanalian revels,' said Gemma, nudging Sophie. 'What fun!'

'Oh, I do hope so,' said Phoebe promptly. 'I can just imagine Mr Ridley with vine leaves in his hair.'

They burst into fits of giggles and Guy, coming through the archway, eyed them suspiciously.

'I thought that you were taking chairs up to the pool,' he said.

'And so we are,' said Gemma. 'Come on, Sophie. Two for you and two for me.'

They set off up the drive, a folding chair in either hand, grinning at Guy as they went by and he grinned back, feeling the comfortable, warm affection for the pair of them that was something quite apart from his passion for Nell. With a wisdom guided by his natural oyster-like reticence, rather than by any conscious reasoning, Guy had hardly talked about Nell to the girls. He'd given them a brief outline of the tragedy so that there should be no embarrassing blunders and told them casually that she was helping him out a couple of days a week at the office and left it at that. Guy was playing his cards very close to his chest and he had no intention of arousing any suspicions if he could possibly help it.

When they arrived at the pool the girls saw Nell for the first time. Her hair was braided down her back and her feet were bare. She wore a long green cotton dress and was tying balloons to the branches of the rhododendron bushes. It gave the place a party feel and Gemma exclaimed with pleasure.

'What a clever idea! They'll look so pretty when the fairy lights are on.'

Nell turned and smiled at them. 'Hi. You must be Guy's friends. He told me that you were coming. I'm Nell Woodward from the Lodge.'

They introduced themselves and Gemma offered to help with the balloons while Sophie set out the chairs. Gillian arrived with a hamper full of plates and glasses, Mr Ridley began to set up the barbecue and Guy and Henry appeared, carrying between them a trestle table for the food. For a while the place was a scene of intense and good-humoured activity and then slowly it began to empty. The girls went down to Phoebe's to change, Gussie swept the Beresfords up to the house for a cup of tea and Henry and Gillian strolled off into the beech walk, arm in arm. Mr Ridley picked up his tools and bits of wire and, with a smiling nod to Guy and Nell, disappeared through

the gate. Guy glanced at Nell and was quite suddenly and unreason-
ably overcome by shyness. She never looked quite real to him, not of
this earth. He thought of her as a girl in a fairy story who might vanish at a touch. She was standing staring out over the pool and the roofs
beyond and her thoughts were far away.

'Nell?' he said at last and she turned a look of such brooding despair on him that he recoiled from it.

'I'm sorry.' She shook her head as if to dispel the memories of that
other party when she'd arrived from Porlock Weir, pregnant and
alone. 'What did you say? I was miles away.'

'It was nothing.' The look had unnerved him. 'I'm going to take
Bertie for a walk.'

He left the invitation unspoken and she made no attempt to acknowledge it.

'That's a good idea. It'll be cooler for him now. See you later
then.' She slipped her feet into espadrilles and, smiling vaguely at
him, drifted through the gate and away into the shadows. Guy
watched her go with confused feelings of longing and fear. He pushed
his hands into the pockets of his shorts and stared down into the blue
water of the pool.

'Hi.' Gemma stood beside him, young and pretty in her blue
denim miniskirt and her thin flowered shirt.

'Hi.' He tried to sound sociable. 'I thought you were at Phoebe's
getting changed.'

'Sophie's taken first bath and I wondered whether I might have a
quick swim.'

'Good idea.' The words were an effort but somehow her presence
had a soothing effect.

'Don't think I will.' She seemed to think about it and shook her
head. 'No. Hey!' She looked up at him. 'What about giving Bertie a
walk? You've had him shut in all day in case he tripped someone up or
got in the way. Shall we give him a run in the woods?'

'That's just what I was going to do, actually. You've very welcome to come along. I thought you'd want to be getting all done up or whatever.'

She grinned sideways at him, the old provocative grin.

'Plenty of time. It doesn't take that long, you know, to make myself presentable.'

He knew she was teasing him and suddenly his spirits lifted. 'I don't know,' he said, pretending to consider her as they went out through the gate. 'All those lines and wrinkles . . .'

She punched him on the arm, dodged as he feinted a blow at her and set off at a jog trot down the drive.

NELL WANDERED ALONG THE avenue, gazing up at the great chestnut trees and the ancient oaks whose leaves made a canopy through which the sunlight could barely penetrate. It was unnerving how swiftly these reminders of the past could engulf her, toppling her from the delicate balance of acceptance and determination, rendering her both breathless with terror at the prospect of loneliness and poverty and despairing at the knowledge of all that she had lost. Scents, music, tastes, a chance remark, all these things had the power to swing her back in time, robbing her of her contentment and destroying her hard-won peace. She'd remembered herself at that other party, sitting in the summerhouse and looking at the moon, battling with the misery of losing her precious cottage at Porlock Weir and terrified at the knowledge of the new life under her heart.

Nell crossed her arms over her breast as though she would crush the intolerable ache. Would she ever be free of it all? She willed her mantra to the forefront of her mind: Jack, her friends, the cottage, Nethercombe. Somehow, it seemed almost wicked to be ungrateful when she still had such blessings. Many, many others in this terrible time had lost so much more.

But I am not being ungrateful, she thought suddenly, staring up into the great noble arches of wood and leaf. I am mourning. I am mourning John and the baby and my home. I have lost all of them and surely I am allowed to mourn without feeling guilty?

The great dim spaces had a cathedral-like quality and Nell felt a measure of a quietening calm stealing back into her mind and heart. She dreaded this party as she had dreaded the other but she knew that she must go. That much at least she owed to these kind friends who cared so deeply about her.

SOPHIE LAY IN THE bath and thought about Guy. She had built up such a romantic picture through the term that the reality was bound to be a little disappointing. Even so . . . Sophie languidly soaped her leg and remembered what Gemma had said at the beginning; something about falling in love at least once a week until she'd started to mature a bit. Sophie, convinced that her love would last for ever, felt certain that she was different. But now she was beginning to wonder if Gemma might not have had a point. Several young men had swum into her ken during this last term and she was beginning to see that it would be foolish to tie oneself down too soon.

She'd enjoyed the Easter holidays, 'making Guy human' as Gemma had put it, and, no doubt, there would be lots more fun this holiday. Still . . . Sophie lay back in the hot scented water. Perhaps Gemma was right. What was she always saying? 'If there's anything better, than one man, it's two men. *Ad infinitum.*' She giggled and, reaching for her towel, stood up and started to dry herself. She was looking forward to the party.

GILLIAN PARTED FROM HENRY at the study door and stood for a moment, listening to the rise and fall of Gussie's voice joined with the Beresfords' over the teacups in the library, before slipping away upstairs. In her bedroom she sat on the broad window seat and stared out over the countryside. How strange it was to be split so much in two. To be restored to this place which she had grown, almost without realising, to love so deeply and to have Henry's love, given unconditionally and wholeheartedly, brought such happiness. Yet beside the happiness, intertwined with it, lay the guilt. When Gillian thought back over her marriage she felt hot with shame, mortified by self-disgust. She thought of the cheating and lying and felt that she would suffocate with humiliation. It was as if the shock of hearing of John's death had woken her up, opened her eyes upon the stupidity of her way of life and made her see the waste and senselessness of her behaviour. Practically overnight she had changed from a selfish spoiled child to a woman who, whatever she did, or however hard she tried to make amends, would have blood on her hands.

The fields seemed to shimmer in the heat of the late afternoon sun and, as she watched, Mr Ridley appeared in the meadow below, a gun on his arm and his elderly spaniel, nose to ground, running in front. He crossed the field and disappeared among the trees by the stream and Gillian knew that he'd gone to pot at rabbits or a pigeon in the woods that edged the swampy area under the viaduct. It was a no-man's-land on the perimeter of the Nethercombe estate where no one but Mr Ridley went; a dank wet gloomy place where even the locals never ventured, though the stream was easy enough to cross in summer, their children warned away by stories of the swamp that would swallow them whole. These stories went back beyond Henry's childhood until they had reached the proportions of legend and Gillian reminded herself to warn Jack when he came home that it was one area that he mustn't explore.

It would be good for Nell to have Jack home again. At the thought of it, Gillian shook with a spasm of horror. The enormity of what she had done was almost too much to live with. She started as the telephone rang and waited to see if Henry would answer it in the study. The bell was silenced and Gillian resumed her reverie which was interrupted by Henry's voice bellowing up the stairs.

'Gillian! Are you there, darling? It's Elizabeth. Gillian!'

'OK!' she shouted back. She went over and, perching on the bed, lifted the receiver. 'Hello, Elizabeth.'

Elizabeth and Henry spoke together and then there was a clunk as Henry replaced the receiver in the study.

'Hello, Gillian.' Elizabeth's voice was cool and clear as always. 'How are you?'

Gillian was suddenly overwhelmed with a desire to tell her the truth: to unburden her hot, shamed heart and blurt out the whole crippling weight of horror. She swallowed several times.

'OK,' she said at last. 'Fine. You?'

'I'm very well. I wondered if you could come to lunch the week after next? I haven't seen you properly since you got back. What about Wednesday?'

'Oh.' Gillian bit her lip, wondering if she could face Elizabeth without breaking down completely. Obviously Lydia had told her Sam's name and she must be wondering why she, Gillian, had reacted so wildly when she mentioned it.

'If Wednesday's no good, we could try another day. Monday?'

'Wednesday's fine' Gillian spoke quickly. She could hardly avoid her godmother for the rest of her life. 'That'll be lovely. Sorry to sound so dozy. We've got a party here this evening and it's all a bit hectic. It's a Midsummer Eve pool party.'

'Sounds fun.'

'Well,' Gillian hesitated, 'you'd be terribly welcome if you think it's worth the drive. We'd love to see you.'

Elizabeth laughed. 'Sweet of you. But I don't think it's quite my scene, lovey.'

'No.' Gillian laughed too. She couldn't imagine the fastidious Elizabeth perched on the side of a pool eating a barbecued sausage and plunging into the water for a midnight swim. 'Neither do I. Wednesday week, then.'

'Look forward to it.'

The line went dead and Gillian wandered back to the window. The sun was edging behind the trees to the west and long shadows crept across the meadow. The pool with its paved surround lay peacefully below in its circle of green turf. Nell's balloons barely stirred in the tall branches and the chairs looked inviting, waiting for occupants. Gillian took a deep breath and turned back into the room. It was time to bathe and change and make herself ready for the party.

IT WAS GUSSIE WHO, realising that a party consisting only of the Nethercombe inhabitants might be a little restricted, had suggested that each person should invite a friend or two. It was a sensible decision and brought a different, more festive, atmosphere to the gathering than had it consisted of the usual group. Only Nell had no friend to invite but there was no chance to sit gazing at the reflection of the lights twinkling in the water or watching the moon – just on the wane – sailing in the clear evening sky. This time she was not allowed to sit quietly, her privacy respected and protected; she was drawn in, involved, and she was happy to let the evening flow over her and envelop her in its friendly gaiety.

It was quite warm enough to swim and no one needed to hurry up to the house for coffee to warm them afterwards. Henry moved amongst his guests wondering what on earth he had done to be blessed with such joy. He was aware that there was still some reservation deep in Gillian's heart but, instinctively, he knew that it was nothing to do with his own actions. In nearly all people's lives is the knowledge of some past deed, the shame of which has to be borne, and Henry hoped that, in Gillian's case, time would give it proportion and allow her to realise that it is only the lucky few – or the wilfully self-deceiving – who have no dark corner. He hoped that she would be gentle with herself. After all, he reasoned, it is the dark corners in our own lives that allow us to be generous with others' weaknesses and, as such, our failures have their positive side.

Gussie smiled at him as he topped up her glass and her heart expanded at the knowledge of his joy. In her opinion he deserved it all and more and she only prayed that Gillian might learn to forgive herself for running away and Nell might be healed so that her bliss might be complete.

'Going in for a swim, Gussie?'

Phoebe was at her elbow. Gussie smiled serenely at her, knowing very well that she was being teased and loving every minute of it.

'Very possibly, my dear. In a moment. I have my swimsuit on underneath my dress.'

Phoebe's expression of amazement was all that Gussie had hoped for and she burst out laughing.

'Gussie!' Phoebe shook her head at her. 'I thought you were serious. Serves me right! It's a lovely party, isn't it?'

'A splendid idea of yours. We're all such a big happy family here now.'

'Except for Mr Jackson,' sighed Phoebe. 'He spurns and rejects me at every turn and rushes home to wifie.'

'So I should think,' said Gussie reprovingly.

'Oh well,' said Phoebe, resigned. 'I'll just have to make do with Guy.'

They both turned to look at him, his dark head bent to Gemma's blonde one, his eyes fixed on Nell who was talking to the Beresfords.

'Ah,' said Gussie thoughtfully.

'Quite,' said Phoebe. 'Story of my life. It looks as if I'm just going to have to make do with Mr Ridley after all.'

Twenty-six

IT WAS TO GUY, rather than to Gussie, that Nell began to voice her fears. Possibly this was because she found herself more in his company and possibly because, unlike Gussie, he was an unemotional listener. Nell sensed an anxiety in Phoebe that tended to thrust her back into her natural privacy and make it difficult to talk to her on the subjects that worried her most deeply. Guy considered her fears with a judicious calm which was much more soothing to Nell than excited horrified sympathy could possibly be. One of her greatest terrors was security. She lay awake at nights staring into a black terrifying future that held no job, no home, no peace, until she got up to make herself a drink or fell into an exhausted unrefreshing sleep.

After one particularly harrowing night she went with Guy to the office where she was beginning to get the hang of his very simple computer programme. She was slightly hampered in her dealing with clients in her complete lack of knowledge regarding boats but Guy gave her very comprehensive details about his stock which, usually, answered the questions of the most indefatigable sailor. On this particular day, after a busy morning, they strolled over to the Royal Castle for a lunchtime snack. Guy raised his hand to Nigel, the landlord — resplendent as always in his bow tie — and went to the bar whilst Nell found a table.

'Hello!' Mary, beaming and bubbly as ever, smiled at Guy across the counter. 'And how are you? Haven't seen you for a bit. Been neglecting us, you have! The usual, is it?'

'Yes please, Mary. And a glass of house white. Dry.' Guy was always at ease with this pretty blonde Devonian woman whose sunny charm and easy friendliness made her, in Guy's opinion, one of Nigel's greatest assets at the Castle. He decided, as she poured his beer and pulled his leg about having yet another girl with him, that she reminded him of Gemma; different ages, different background but both possessing that generous warmth that eased and relaxed. As he approached the table, he noticed that Nell looked strained and tired, her usual pallor accentuated by the shadows beneath her eyes.

'Thanks.' She smiled at him as he passed her the glass of wine. 'I love it here. Is it always so busy?'

'Height of the season,' said Guy, squeezing in beside her. 'But it's always crowded in here at lunch time, even in the winter. It's a popular place.' He took a drink and glanced around, wondering how to encourage her to share her problems. 'How's Jack?'

'He's fine.' Nell's face relaxed a little. 'I had a letter yesterday.' She sighed and the anxious look returned. 'I worry about him. About how I shall manage. I can't bear the thought of Jack having to go without things. I don't mean luxuries, I mean the things that will guarantee him a future. If only John had never left the Navy, he'd still be alive and Jack's future would be secure.'

She shook her head and bit her lip. She'd made it sound as if the only purpose in John's life had been as a provider but she was too tired to explain. Guy seemed to be brooding over her words.

'People make the mistake of believing that security in this life is possible,' he said after a moment. 'Or that it should be. It very rarely is. What, after all, is security? If you're talking about material security, very few of us have it. Very few people now have such secure jobs that they don't live under the shadow of cutbacks or early retirement. And the self-employed man lives in a perpetual state of anxiety. Even if you're one of the lucky few who own their own home outright, how many of them can absolutely guarantee an income to heat it and repair it for the rest of their lives? Or know they'll be able to provide for their children or their grandchildren? Where do you stop? But it's always been so. It's no different for us than it was for our ancestors trying to defend their caves and praying that there would be enough mammoth to go round. And what about drought or famine or war? How can you legislate for everything? And even assuming that we've taken care of our material well-being, what about our health? Nothing can guarantee that. Nothing is certain in life except death.' He smiled at her. 'I think that's a quote. The knocks only harden us up and make us better prepared for the next one. Am I depressing you?'

'Oddly enough, no.' Nell spoke truthfully. 'You've cleared my mind and made me see things in proportion. And you're also saying that if Jack has to put up with hardship now it will serve him in good stead later.'

'I'm certainly saying that you can't, indefinitely, protect him from life. It's always tough when the blows hit the young but are any of us really ready for them when they strike? At least he's got you, a stable point of love, which is a lot more than a lot of people have at their moment of crisis. The young are terribly resilient. Probably because they're selfish.' His face wore an inward-looking expression. 'I know I was when the blow struck us. I didn't think at all about my mother's well-being or happiness, I was only concerned with mine. I'm ashamed of that now.'

'I'm sorry.' Nell looked distressed. She realised that her absorption with her own difficulties might easily make her insensitive. 'I've been droning on about myself for far too long. It's not only the young who are selfish. And I'm sure your mother understood.'

'So am I.' Guy smiled at her. 'Unfortunately that doesn't stop me feeling guilty. Luckily she had Giles, my twin brother. We're very different.'

At this moment, to Nell's relief, the food arrived and she was able to change the subject. Nevertheless, Guy's calm good sense encouraged her and the thought of Jack's imminent return from school obliged her to live, in the present and put her worries to one side for the time being.

GILLIAN ARRIVED AT HER godmother's house feeling unusually nervous. She'd spent hours going over various scenarios which might excuse her fear at the use of Sam's name at Nethercombe but none of them seemed the least bit plausible. She prayed that this would be simply a friendly visit and that she would not be called upon to explain anything. Elizabeth came out to greet her, looking tall and elegant in a navy blue cotton jersey dress, and took her into the drawing room for a pre-lunch drink. The long windows were wide open and the scent of the roses on Elizabeth's desk drifted delicately on the soft summer air. A mahogany-framed tapestry hid the empty grate and sunlight filled the room with a glowing warmth.

'It's a very weak one,' explained Elizabeth giving Gillian a gin, 'because of all this drinking and driving but I thought you'd need it.' She sat opposite and crossed her long legs. 'Now. What's all this about Sam Whittaker?'

Gillian gasped and the glass shook in her hand. 'Oh, Elizabeth . . .'

'It's no good, Gillian.' Elizabeth got up and fetched a tissue. 'Here you are. You've spilled a few drops on your skirt. Drink some and pull yourself together. I want to know the whole story. It's all to do with the site at Dartmouth you told me about and John's death, isn't it?'

Gillian sat so still that it appeared as if she had even stopped breathing. 'How did you guess?' she asked at last

'It wasn't difficult,' said Elizabeth. 'Lydia told me his name and Gussie told me that John had killed himself having invested in a site at Dartmouth where the man had absconded with his money. Your reaction to the name of Sam Whittaker made me put two and two together and come up with a rather distressing total.'

Gillian sat staring at her glass. Now that it had come she felt surprisingly calm. Or perhaps she was simply numb.

'Yes,' she said at last. 'Sam was looking for an investor to put up the money to develop the site. And then John and Nell came for Christmas and he seemed an obvious candidate. He hoped to make a good profit out of it.'

'I take it that you didn't know that Sam intended to take his money and run?'

'No!' exclaimed Gillian. 'Of course I didn't. He said that he was going back to France for a bit while the building was going on. Honestly, Elizabeth!'

'OK, I believe you. Then what?'

'Every time I asked him about the site he said it was doing fine. And then one day I had a letter from Henry telling me that John had killed himself.' Gillian paused and took a hasty gulp at her gin. 'Henry didn't know who I went off with. He still doesn't and Nell doesn't know that it was me who told John about the site.' She swallowed and her face crumpled, the sensation of calm deserting her. 'Oh God, Elizabeth! I killed him and the baby and ruined Nell's life. Oh!' Sobs burst from her and the tears streamed down her face as she bowed over her hands clasped round the glass stem. 'Oh, God. It's so awful. Whatever shall I do?'

'Wait a minute.' Elizabeth was kneeling beside her with a handful of tissues. 'Let's keep a sense of proportion, shall we? All you did was to tell someone about a perfectly legitimate business opportunity. You didn't know how it was going to turn out.'

'But I did it for the money. Sam offered me a commission if I found him a lender.'

'A perfectly normal business arrangement.'

'Oh, Elizabeth,' Gillian looked at her godmother, 'I wanted the money because, as usual, I was in debt. If I hadn't been in debt I wouldn't have needed the money and John would still be alive.'

'Not necessarily.' Elizabeth sat back on her heels while Gillian gazed at her, puzzled.

'What d'you mean?'

'Look, Gillian, we all know that you're a spoiled selfish little baggage and I really believe that all this has taught you a much-needed lesson but don't take too much to yourself. If you hadn't told John about this deal, he'd have probably found another that was just as risky and the result would probably have been the same. The trouble with the Johns of this world is that, when their backs are really against the wall, they just haven't got what it takes.'

'Sam said something like that,' said Gillian slowly. 'When I told him that he'd killed John, he said that John had killed himself because he was a loser.'

'Much though I dislike agreeing with the sort of person that Sam Whittaker appears to be,' said Elizabeth drily, 'he has a point. However, in his case, he has no right to evade responsibility. He is morally responsible for John's death and Nell's desperate situation. He stole John's money. It was probably the last straw in a long series of disasters and Sam has no right to close his eyes to his part in it. But you were completely innocent, in this respect. You genuinely believed that it was a good deal and that John would get his money back.' She smiled a little at Gillian's amazed stare and nodded. 'I mean it, Gillian. You're not guilty. It's a salutary lesson which, in my days, was summed up in the excellent phrase "Satan finds . . ." but you must keep things in proportion. Having affairs, getting in debt, leaving Henry, those things you can feel guilty about.' She smiled at her, patted her knee and stood up. 'More than enough to be going on with, I should think.'

But Gillian was too dazed to smile back. She could hardly take in the fact that she was not to blame for the whole tragedy yet, if Elizabeth believed it, she knew that she could, too. She took a deep breath and a huge wave of relief surged through her.

'It's been awful,' she said shakily. 'Oh, Elizabeth . . .'

'I can imagine. Drink up. How are things with you and Henry?'

'Wonderful.' Gillian sipped and shook her head with a kind of disbelief. 'He's taken me back as if nothing has happened. And there's no . . . you know . . . well, martyrdom or anything. No making me feel guilty. He's . . . he's just fantastic.' She shook her head again. 'I must have been mad.'

Elizabeth pursed her lips and nodded. 'Very likely,' she agreed. 'So now you can put it all behind you and start again. Lucky girl! Many people would give their right arms to be able to do just that.'

'Oh, I know. I really do know how lucky I am. But . . .' She sighed and frowned a little.

'But what?'

'Well. Even with what you've just said and the relief, I know that when I see Nell I shall still feel that terrible guilt. I've got so much and she's got so little. I'd really love to have a baby now but can you imagine how I'd feel ballooning out and knowing that she lost her baby because of me? OK, OK, I accept what you say but even so. There I'll be with Henry and Nethercombe and a baby and there she'll be with nothing.'

'She has a child, I believe?'

'Yes she has. A little boy of twelve or so.'

'And if you'd been left homeless and penniless and your husband dead, d'you think you'd want a newborn baby to worry about on top of it all?'

'Come on, Elizabeth! That's a bit much, isn't it?'

Elizabeth held up a finger. 'D'you know, I think you should make friends with Nell. You'd probably be surprised at how she's feeling.' She paused for a moment and Gillian finished her drink feeling quite light-headed with shock and relief. 'What's she doing with herself?'

'She's looking for a job. She's helping Guy in his yacht brokerage at the moment but I think it's just to break her into the workplace as gently as possible. He can't afford to employ anyone full time. You can imagine how difficult it will be for her.'

'Yes,' said Elizabeth thoughtfully. 'Yes I can. Oddly, one of the reasons I asked you over today was to offer you a job.'

'A job? Me?'

'Well, you know what I said about Satan finds? I think a lot of your . . . well, indiscretions were due to not having enough to do. I wondered if you'd like to join me in my business? Don't look so nonplussed. I'm not getting any younger and you've got excellent taste and judgement which is really what it's all about. Naturally you'd have to come about with me to begin with. Generally, though, I work for people who haven't a clue how to start to decorate or furnish their new house but have a good idea of what they want the finished product to look like. They spend hours looking through my catalogues and colour swatches and I recommend decorators and so on until we arrive at the desired effect. A client may want the entire house done with everything in the same period, others want a drawing room done over, or a study. Something special. They'll give me a budget and I go round the salerooms and auctions looking for the right pieces, or rugs and even paintings. It's great fun and enormously satisfying. I thought you might enjoy it. And the money.'

'Oh, Elizabeth . . .'

'I know, I know. That was a blow below the belt. But what d'you think?'

'It sounds . . . It sounds fun and . . . Well, I don't know what to say. You've rather taken my breath away. I'd love it. But I do want to have a baby, you know. I shall go on trying.'

'I understand that. And I've been thinking. Supposing you asked Nell if she'd like to work for me, too. D'you think she'd be any good at my sort of business? Is she trainable?'

'Gosh!' Gillian sat up, her eyes shining. 'What a brilliant idea. She'd be great, I'm sure she would. Gussie told me that she took a degree in Fine Arts and it's just the sort of thing she'd be interested in.'

'Good. Supposing you sound her out? There's no rush. Give her time to think. You could work together, perhaps.'

'We'd have to. Nell hasn't got a car.'

'Of course, you'd get less money if I took her on.' Elizabeth watched Gillian thoughtfully. 'I couldn't afford two good salaries.'

'I don't want the money, Elizabeth. No, don't look like that!

Things are easier now and I . . . Well, I don't dash about so much and Nell really needs everything she can lay her hands on. Oh, Elizabeth, it would be fantastic!'

Elizabeth smiled at her goddaughter and stood up.

'Excellent! I shall leave it in your hands to arrange. Why don't you bring Nell over one day?'

Gillian stood up too. 'I don't know what to say, Elizabeth,' she said unsteadily. 'I know you've been getting me out of the shit all my life. But this time—'

'This time,' interrupted Elizabeth, 'it's given me enormous pleasure. So forget it. Come on! Finish that drink. It's time for lunch!'

Twenty-seven

JACK, HOME FOR THE holidays, did more than anyone else could to restore Nell to hope and happiness. He loved being at Nethercombe. He had decided to follow his Uncle Rupert into the Army and spent most of his time exploring, making camps and helping Mr Ridley on the estate. He adored this elderly countryman who entered into all his games with a great seriousness and began to teach him how to use a gun. Had Nell known how far from perfect Mr Ridley's eyesight was, she would probably have been a great deal less happy at Jack's forays with his unlikely companion at arms. Fortunately, ignorance is bliss and Nell was relieved and delighted that Jack seemed able to put all the tragedy behind him and enter into life with such great zest.

With Jack's arrival Mr Ridley, too, seemed to be having a second lease of life.

'Daft ole fewel,' remarked his wife when he told her about each day's exploits but secretly she was pleased.

'Got 'is 'ead screwed on right,' said Mr Ridley, eating his tea with relish. ''E'll mek a good sojer.'

'Since when've yew bin in the recruitment officer's confidence, then?' asked Mrs Ridley, heavily sarcastic, pushing a plate of ham nearer to his hand.

'Ah. Doan'ee fergit, I was in the desert, maid. A desert rat, I was,' said Mr Ridley, who had celebrated his twenty-first birthday in North Africa. 'I c'n tell 'im a thing or two!'

Mrs Ridley raised eyes and shoulders heavenwards and snorted.

'I thought that ole desert'd come into it some'ow. Get that 'am down. Yewer gonna need all yewer strength if yewer gonna be playin' games at yewer age.'

'I'll 'ave a bit o' that cake, maid. Cut a slice for the boy. We're doin' a bit of target practice direckly.'

'Yew be careful.' Mrs Ridley cut cake with a generous hand and wrapped it in a napkin.

'No call to worry, maid. I won't let no 'arm come to 'im. 'Twas I taught Mr 'Enry remember, when 'e was a tacker.'

Mr Ridley ate his cake while his wife looked on, arms folded across her aproned bosom. Their only daughter had married a Welsh farmer and they rarely saw her or their two granddaughters. Jack, with his rosy face and cheerful smile, took them back to their younger days and filled an empty niche in their lives. In their different ways they both loved having him around.

'Told 'im 'bout that time yew met Monty, then?' asked Mrs Ridley casually. 'Told 'im what 'e said to yew?'

Mr Ridley washed his cake down with a gulp of tea, pocketed Jack's slice and made for the door. He beamed shyly at her – lips pressed together – nodded, gave her a quick wink and disappeared.

'Daft ole fewel,' muttered his spouse, tears in her eyes as she collected up plates. 'Still a tacker at 'eart fer all 'e's more'n seventy.' And she mopped fiercely at her eyes with her apron, clicking her tongue in disdain at her own weakness.

GUY, TOO, WAS MORE than happy to take Jack under his wing. He took him out sailing and let him row his little dinghy on the Dart, so long as he kept within view of the office in the Marina. Jack went with him when he had to move craft from one mooring to another and during the long weeks of the summer holiday he learned to handle boats with great confidence. Guy took him into the Royal Castle where he was charmed by Mary who asked if he'd like a pint and pretended to be amazed when he told her that he was only thirteen.

Nell was filled with a heartfelt gladness that his life was so full and happy. When he recounted the day's doings to her she could have wept. She couldn't decide, however, whether she was relieved or worried that he seemed to have almost wiped John out of his mind altogether. It seemed to her that, being unable to identify or understand his father's last awful action, he had let him go. They talked of him sometimes but rather as a dear — if distant — old friend who had gone away on a long holiday, than as a father or husband. Nell understood her own feelings, knowing that her love for John had always held reservations, but she felt sad for Jack. Of course, John had been away at sea so much in those first eight or nine years of his life that it probably wasn't terribly surprising and, when John came ashore, Jack was already settled at boarding school. Nevertheless, he was his father . . .

Nell sighed and put it away from her. She had enough worries without inviting more by wishing that Jack was grieving for his father and missing him. As for the baby, it was only natural that Jack should rarely think of him at all. That was all in the past and real life was here and now; going out with Mr Ridley to pot at rabbits, sailing with Guy or exploring Dartmoor — or as much of it as they could reach on foot.

No one was aware how terribly Nell missed her little car or how she hated being dependent on others but she knew that until there was a prospect of a proper job with a decent wage there was no chance of one. At least she was surrounded by people who were very ready to help out. She enjoyed her days in the office and had gained a great deal of confidence but she knew that it couldn't last for ever. She realised by now that Guy was going short himself to finance her and she wasn't prepared to accept his kindness for much longer. She saw that on the days he had to be out of the office she was useful to him and, when the holidays started, she cut back her time to those days only. Thinking that Guy had been helping her out of the kindness of his heart, she imagined that he would be relieved to have his expenses reduced, not suspecting that he would have given even more to have her with him. However, the holidays were a natural break and Guy was intelligent enough to accept that his relationship with Nell must take a back seat until they were over.

It was during these weeks, as the summer lengthened and autumn approached, that the friendship between Gillian and Nell began to flower. It started cautiously. Nell had never taken much to Gillian while John was alive and Gillian, despite her talk with Elizabeth, still felt terribly guilty. Slowly, however, barriers were pushed back and common ground explored. Jack was a great help. He still liked Gillian enormously and her partiality to him softened Nell's heart as nothing else could. Even the most balanced, sensible parent is not immune to praise of his or her offspring; the most cynical and hard-headed is easily able to swallow the most gratuitous flattery. Nell was no exception and at least Gillian's praise and affection for Jack was sincere. Gussie, of course, was another route to Nell's heart and her obvious pleasure at the two girls' burgeoning friendship encouraged it even more.

So it was that, by the time Jack went off to school, Nell was glad of Gillian's companionship. She was very anxious at the thought of him at public school. She knew that the transition from a small school, where he had been one of the biggest and most important, to a school four times the size, where the oldest boys were men of eighteen and Jack would be amongst the smallest and least important, was a very big step indeed. Fortunately, Jack had no idea that he was in such an ignominious and humble position and plunged into his new life with his usual enthusiasm and confidence. Nell received his first letter with trepidation and read it with mounting joy, rushing up to the house to share her delight in its contents with all Jack's friends. Henry heard with private relief that he'd made some new friends as well as there being several old ones from his prep school, Gussie heard with pleasure that he had come top in a history test and the Ridleys learned with various degrees of emotion that the food was nowhere as good as Nethercombe's, that he'd joined the CCF and, having made a good showing on the rifle range, was being considered for the team. When this last was reported, Mr Ridley – his eyes suspiciously bright – was obliged to get up and take a few turns round the kitchen so great was his pride. Mrs Ridley beamed privately into the Aga oven and planned great things for the first exeat.

Gillian knew that the time had come to moot the possibility of the job with Elizabeth and lay awake for most of the night writing scripts for herself and Nell until she was exhausted. She walked along the avenue on a misty morning in early October, telling herself not to be so silly, and knocked lightly on the door of the Lodge.

'Gillian!' Nell's pleasure certainly looked and sounded genuine and Gillian breathed out thankfully. Even now, she stood rather in awe of Nell's beauty and reserve and, coupled with her guilt, it was always a tricky first few minutes. 'Come in and have some coffee. I was just reading the paper and looking for a job.'

Gillian's spirits soared up and she immediately jettisoned all her carefully thought out scripts. There simply could not have been a better opening.

'Anything in particular?' She followed Nell into the kitchen and perched at the old oak refectory table.

'Oh, I don't know. I don't think I'm going to be in a position to pick and choose.' Nell shook her head despondently. 'It'll have to be something pretty lowly. Guy's been preparing me for that. I can cope with the telephone and customers and very slowly with his computer. The trouble is that I'm in competition with bright school-leavers who have advanced computer skills.'

'It's funny you should talk about a job.' Gillian's heart beat fast and she took a calming breath, choosing her words carefully while Nell made coffee. 'My godmother's looking for someone to help her out. I think you've met her briefly. Tall, elegant, dark woman. Looks about thirty although she must be fifty.'

'I think so. On the terrace with Gussie once.' Nell put mugs and a sugar bowl on the table. 'What does she do?'

'Well, the quick answer is interior design. She advises people on how to decorate and furnish their houses. Sometimes she does the whole thing from scratch. Sometimes just a room. Not the actual physical decoration, of course. But she goes to sales and auctions for them and generally sorts them out. It's fascinating, actually.'

'It sounds it.' Nell was staring at Gillian as though she could hardly believe what might be coming. 'Does she want an assistant?'

'That's it!' Gillian spooned in some sugar. 'Says she's getting old for all the dashing about. I think she's thinking of handing it over in the not-too-distant future. She's worked at it all her life and it would be tragic to just let it go when she retires. She's got a first-class reputation.'

'But d'you think she'd consider me? I got a First in Fine Arts but never did anything with it. I got married instead.' Nell shook her head and sat down opposite. 'It sounds too good to be true. She'll want someone with experience, surely?'

'She doesn't actually,' said Gillian casually, clasping both hands round her mug to keep them from trembling. It was so important to get it right. 'In fact she's asked me to have a go for the time being. I don't want to make it a full-time career because I hope to have a baby . . .'

She flushed scarlet and bowed her head in horrified shame. How could she have been so tactless? This was just what she had dreaded and feared. Nell, too excited by the thought of such a wonderful chance to think of her own tragedy, watched her in surprise. She hadn't thought that Gillian was so easily embarrassed. What was wrong with wanting a baby?

'Of course you do,' she said. 'That's only natural. Gillian, would you ask her if she'd consider me? I'm sure I could do it if she's prepared to train me. I'd be so grateful.'

'Absolutely.' Gillian had recovered herself. 'Personally, I think you'd be just right for her.' She looked around at the Welsh dresser with its display of lovely china and at the old heavy oak chairs. 'I can see by all your lovely things that you've got good taste. Perhaps . . .' She shrugged a little, casually. 'Perhaps we might start off together. You know? Give each other confidence? Then later, when I drop out . . .' She stopped again and glanced at Nell.

'It sounds far too miraculous to be possible,' breathed Nell. 'It would be lovely to start off together if your godmother would allow it. I'm quite terrified of going out there alone. Anyway,' her face fell, 'I haven't got a car.'

'Well, there you are,' said Gillian quickly. 'That's no problem. We can use mine and, if all goes well, you'd probably be able to afford a little one quite quickly.'

'I can't bear it,' said Nell, her cheeks flushed with excitement. 'It's too exciting. This could be so perfect. Just exactly what I would have asked for if I'd thought there was the least chance of it happening. Oh, Gillian. When will you see your godmother next?'

'I'll phone her up,' said Gillian promptly. 'The minute I get back to the house. Tell you what!' She sounded suddenly inspired. 'Supposing you come over with me to meet her? I'm supposed to be going over to lunch very soon. How about it?'

'Well, I can hardly invite myself to lunch,' said Nell doubtfully.

'Rubbish!' said Gillian cheerfully. 'Anyway, I'm inviting you. She'll like to meet you properly and I know she'll be delighted if we can come to some arrangement workwise. She'd hate to take a stranger into the business.'

'But I am a stranger,' objected Nell.

'What nonsense!' said Gillian lightly. 'Good heavens, you're one of the family. We all think so.'

'Oh!' Nell looked absurdly touched. 'How nice . . .' She looked suddenly shy, swallowed and took a sip of coffee.

'And we're all quite passionate about Jack,' continued Gillian, surprised in turn at Nell's loss of poise and concerned about her ability to guide them both round this tricky corner. 'I know I am. Mrs Ridley's already planning Christmas with all his favourite food on the menu.'

She looked anxiously at Nell wondering if she'd gone too far in this potentially dangerous emotional minefield. Dear God, she prayed, please let it be all right. Please! It was all right! Nell was smiling, albeit shakily, and Gillian smiled back.

'D'you think . . . ? Would it sound very rude . . . ?' Nell took a deep breath.

'I know just what you're trying to say,' said Gillian. 'Why don't I finish my coffee and get back to make that phone call!'

'Oh dear,' said Nell remorsefully. 'Put like that it sounds terribly rude. And you could use my phone.'

'It doesn't sound rude at all.' Gillian finished her coffee with a gulp and stood up. She didn't want to make this particular call with Nell listening in. 'I can't do it here. Elizabeth's ex-directory and I can never remember her number. She's on holiday for a few days so her business number will be on answerphone. At least, that's what usually happens when she takes time off. I'll go back and see if she's there and I'll phone you the minute I've got news. OK?'

'Wonderful. I don't know what to say.' Nell smiled at her. 'Thanks. I shall live in terror that she's changed her mind.'

'No fear of that.' Gillian shook her head confidently. 'I'll be in touch. Thanks for the coffee.'

Nell waved her off, went back into the kitchen and, ignoring her now cold coffee, sat staring at the wall, her hands tightly clasped. Could such a miracle possibly happen? It was too much to ask! After a moment she got up and walked about, too excited to sit still. Her imagination flew ahead on wings of hope although, at the base of her stomach, terror churned. How could she expect to step into such a position? Surely such a woman as Elizabeth would not want a raw beginner? But Gillian had said that she wouldn't want to take a stranger into her business, so if she and Gillian started off together . . . She remembered what Gillian had said about being one of the family and she sat down again and put her head in her hands. She was continually surprised at how emotional she had become since the disasters of the last few years had made such a muddle of her life and how easily the tears started in her eyes.

Nell gave herself a mental shake. It was no use sitting in a state of overcharged excitement and anxiety, waiting for the telephone to ring. She took a book from the shelf and, sitting down in the rocking chair, began to read.

Gillian hurried back down the avenue in much the same mood that Guy had passed along it a few months before. Like Guy, her happiness was too great to contain and, like Guy, she suddenly took to her heels, arms outflung, face turned up to the stately trees, and fled back to the house, her heart full of gratitude and joy.

Twenty-eight

THAT AUTUMN, IT RAINED with the unremitting vigour that the West Country knows so well. Front followed front and, when it wasn't raining, the sky loured – a dirty, gloomy, leaden colour that promised more rain soon. Overhead, everything dripped dankly: underfoot, everything squelched muddily. There were no more pool parties and no more happy hours for Mr Ridley on the mowing machine. Phoebe watched the stream become a full-scale river and shuddered at the thought of the long winter months. Bertie was not allowed to sit outside Guy's office door on the quay but was forced to stay inside, peering mournfully through the glass door, whilst Guy cursed because people no longer wanted to look at boats.

'The only sort of boat I could sell at the moment would be a bloody ark!' he muttered. Bertie sighed deeply and with great sympathy.

Guy thrust his hands into his pockets and wandered back to his desk. He longed to see Nell, to feast his eyes upon her beauty and to talk to her. She'd been very busy just lately and he'd finally caught up with her yesterday by telephone as she was dashing out, so they'd made a quick plan for a pub supper that evening. Guy stretched his long legs beneath his desk and wondered if he dared risk telling her how he felt about her. The mere idea of it filled him with the usual misgivings. After all, what did he feel about her? Was it love that he felt: this desire to see her beauty, to experience the glow of pride when he took her out? She obsessed his thoughts and haunted his dreams; always elusive, just beyond his grasp. But was this love? Was

it worth getting married for, having children and all the attendant responsibilities? And did the fact that she was a few years his senior really make any difference? A stab of fear gripped his entrails and he
drew his legs in abruptly and stood up. A drink at the Castle with
Mary's cheerful nonsense to amuse him suddenly seemed very attractive. Bertie glanced round enquiringly.

'Come on, old chap,' said Guy. 'I need a pint,' and taking his wa-
terproofs from a peg behind the door they stepped out into the rain.

Back at Nethercombe Henry, too, was braving the elements. He
came out and, staring around him for a moment, set off down the drive
humming gently to himself, quite undeterred by the gloomy morning.

' "Sing, 'hey! to you – good day! to you.' Sing, 'Bah! to you, ha!
ha! to you,' " ' he sang. He wore an ancient Barbour, gumboots and a
rather disgraceful old tweed cap. ' "Sing, 'Pooh! to you. Pooh! pooh!
to you.' And that's what I shall say!" ' The words died on his lips as he
reached the bend in the drive and Nell appeared from the avenue.
She, too, was wearing gumboots and an all-enveloping weatherproof
garment. She waved to him.

'Hello. Good morning!' Henry called, removing his cap. 'Going
for a walk?'

'Only to the Courtyard.' Nell fell into step beside him. 'I want to
leave a message for Guy. Where are you off to?'

'Just going to check Number Five. Air it through, make sure
there's no damp. You know what a place is like if it's left empty.' He
was struggling to get something out of his pocket and now produced
a key. 'Here we are.'

They passed under the arch together and Nell paused to push a note
through Guy's letterbox. She straightened up and looked around.

'How lovely it is,' she said. 'Even on this dreary morning it has a
certain charm.'

Henry looked gratified.

'Come and have a look at Number Five,' he suggested. 'Like to?
Or has Gussie shown it to you already?'

'I'd love to,' said Nell with alacrity, following him across the Courtyard to the door opposite Guy's. 'I've never seen it properly. Phoebe and I peered through the windows once but I've never been inside.'

Henry unlocked the door and stood back to let her enter. She kicked off her boots, leaving them under the roof canopy over the front door and went into the hall.

'Help yourself,' said Henry. He gestured at each door in turn. 'Kitchen, leading to utility room. Small study. Sitting room.' She poked about in the kitchen and the study – whilst Henry stamped about upstairs opening windows – came back into the hall and, pushing open the third door, stood amazed. The sitting room was large; much bigger than Phoebe's, or Guy's. On the far wall was a stone fireplace and to its left was a window facing east. French windows, opening on to the lawn, looked south. The room was washed a warm cream and a huge and ancient beam divided the ceiling in half.

'Nice, isn't it?' Henry had arrived behind her. 'This is the only one that was ever originally used for habitation. The head groom lived here so it's got much more atmosphere than the others. I think so, anyway. The garage block takes up half of this north wall which helps to keep it warm, although the only evening sun you get is through the front door and the little window into the hall. But you get all the sun in here and the kitchen, of course, even in the winter when the sun is low, because all the leaves are off the trees.' He beamed at Nell who, never having heard Henry make so long a speech, was gazing at him in amazement. 'It's my spiel,' he told her with simple pride. 'Rather good, eh? Gussie taught it me. She's much better at it than I am. It's all true but I would never have thought of telling anyone. What d'you think?'

'I think it's terrific,' said Nell, beginning to laugh. 'And I think the cottage is, too. I'd buy it like a shot if I had any money. It's certainly got a wonderful atmosphere and even on a gloomy day like this it's so bright. It must be wonderful when the fire's going.'

'Get a good bed of ash in there and it'll stay in a treat,' said Henry.

'Old Mick used to keep it in right through the winter. Of course, this was two rooms but we opened it out. Want to see upstairs?'

Nell followed him up the stairs which turned sharp left halfway up. At the top, the landing ran the full length of the cottage with four doors opening off. First came the bathroom which was very modern, and bright, next a good-size bedroom with built-in oak cupboards and then a small boxroom. Henry pushed open the last door with a flourish and Nell caught her breath. Like the sitting room it faced east and south but, though the ceiling was heavily beamed, the whole feeling was of space and light and Nell went over to the window to look down to the stream and beyond to the woods.

'It's really lovely, Henry,' she said. 'It's so beautifully done. Nice and simple and no cheap tat.'

'Glad you like it.' Henry looked round, pleased. 'Gillian had quite a say in it, you know. And we had a first-class architect.'

Nell felt a little dart of envy accompanied by a sense of loss. How wonderful it would be to have a home of one's own again. She thought of her cottage at Porlock Weir and clenched her fists.

'I shall hate whoever buys this one,' she said, but she kept her tone light lest Henry should feel that he had been tactless in showing her round. 'I'm surprised it wasn't the first to go.'

'Well, it's bigger than the others and it's got the garden which Guy and the Beresfords didn't want. Or Mr Jackson. Phoebe's got the little bit on the end which she felt was more than enough and none of them wanted a big open fire.' He frowned a little. 'Perhaps we got this one wrong.'

'Oh no,' said Nell at once. 'It's lovely. It's waiting for someone special.'

Henry smiled at her and all at once remembered her own situation. She saw his expression change and hastened into speech.

'Thank you for showing me. I find any sort of development and conversion work absolutely fascinating. It's amazing how differently people approach it. I like the way you've put good-quality basics in but left plenty of room for the people who buy it to stamp their own personality on it.'

Still talking she led the way downstairs and outside where she stepped back into her boots. A voice hailed them and they turned to see Phoebe at her door.

'For God's sake!' she cried. 'Take pity on me! Come and talk to me. Have some coffee. Stay to lunch. I haven't seen anyone for days. Will it ever stop raining ever again, d'you think?'

Nell laughed and nodded acceptance but Henry shook his head, waved his thanks and set off back through the arch. As he went, he thought of Nell; reproaching himself for his insensitivity in showing her a cottage she couldn't afford when she'd lost her own home and her husband as well. He shook his head at himself. Thank goodness she and Gillian were getting on so well and how wonderful that Nell had been given a job with Elizabeth! Gillian had really thrown herself into this project; driving Nell about, going with her to give her confidence until she felt able to cope alone. Recently he'd felt that the reservation which seemed to prevent Gillian from experiencing complete contentment was slowly melting away, or perhaps she was coming to terms with it. Either way, it meant more happiness for them both and their relationship was becoming all that Henry had ever dared to hope for; the companionship, the sharing, the love, they were all growing.

And perhaps, thought Henry, when everything's right perhaps we'll have a baby!

He drew in his breath sharply at the exquisite pleasure the thought brought him. A child of their own! An heir for Nethercombe! Henry couldn't prevent a beam spreading over his face. His joy expanded into his chest and he burst into song.

' "Sing, 'Hey! to you!' " ' he sang to a surprised cow in the adjoining meadow. ' " 'Good day! to you!' And that's what I shall say!" '

BY THE TIME NELL set off back to the Lodge, the rain had stopped. She had been prevailed upon by Phoebe to stay to lunch and the dull grey November afternoon was drawing in. Although it was still and mild, Nell shivered as she hurried up the drive and along the avenue. She was looking forward to the warmth of her kitchen and knew why, now, country people invested in Agas or Rayburns or Esses. The gentle constant warmth seemed like a glowing heart in the house; welcoming one back from a raw, damp day or giving cheerful comfort in the middle of a cold night when sleep eluded one and there was nothing for it but to get up and go downstairs. Many early hours Nell had spent huddled in her rocking chair by the Rayburn, drinking cocoa whilst her brain reeled and scurried in and out of her problems.

Of late, ever since Gillian's suggestion and Nell's subsequent meeting with Elizabeth, those wakeful hours of fear and loneliness had become fewer. Now, she had hope for a future of her own. She'd been offered a chance and had seized it with both trembling hands. Now, her anxieties were more concerned with whether she could cope with what she'd taken in; whether she could justify the faith that Elizabeth was putting in her.

She'd liked the tall, composed woman at once. She admired her elegance, her house, her innate, understated good taste and sensed that here was someone who would dislike anything messy; whether it was a drawing room or other people's emotions. She could imagine her recoiling from anything dramatic or untidy and knew, instinctively, that she could trust her absolutely. This was a tremendous relief. She suspected that, although Gillian would have told Elizabeth about her situation, no matter how she might feel she wouldn't have passengers in her business. Nor would she embarrass Nell by sympathetic outbursts.

Nell liked this clean unfussy approach. It was a chance to put mess and muddle behind her and give herself a new start and she intended to avail herself of it. She'd been amazed at Gillian's encouragement. Her previous encounters had never led her to believe that Gillian would be prepared to put herself out for anyone, yet she was doing everything she could to get Nell started although she obviously had no intention of making it a career for herself. So far it had been tremendous fun. Elizabeth was giving them plenty of time to find their feet and Gillian, with her witty tongue and quick brain, could be very amusing, so it was only when she was alone again that Nell remembered that this wasn't just fun but her future. It was terribly important that she should succeed so as to make a good life for herself and Jack; after all, there was no longer anyone else to take the weight. It was all up to her. At this point, the old nightmares and terrors would return for she knew that she would never get another chance like this one.

Nell let herself into the Lodge, kicked her boots off in the porch and went into the warm kitchen, hanging up her mac behind the door. Her sole comfort was Elizabeth herself. She had succeeded on her own, built the business up from nothing, lived alone in quiet contentment. If she could achieve it, reasoned Nell, so could others. A wave of confidence flooded over her. There was absolutely no reason to think that she couldn't learn the business or train herself as Elizabeth had. As often as not it was a matter of confidence and she watched and listened closely as Elizabeth advised her clients, told them her own ideas, discussed fixtures and fittings and the way to bring harmony to a room; to make this room one which encouraged activity and ideas and that room a place of peace and relaxation. Nell was determined to learn as much as she could from her employer. Suddenly she felt light and free and happy. Unlike Henry, however, she didn't burst into a snatch from Gilbert and Sullivan but took a book from the pile that Elizabeth had lent her and sat down in her rocking chair to read about antique furniture.

GUY FELT A TREMOR of anxiety as he picked up Nell's note and saw her distinctive handwriting. Surely she wasn't crying off! Luckily it was simply to confirm the time. She'd been in such a rush, she wrote, that she wanted to be certain that she'd got it right. Guy sighed with relief. Mary had cheered and encouraged him at lunch time, as he had guessed she might, and he felt as ready as he would ever be to take the plunge and tell Nell how he felt about her. He was practically ill with terror at the prospect but he was determined to risk it. After all, she could only turn him down. Only! He groaned with frustrated impatience and Bertie looked at him anxiously. Guy caught the look and attempted a smile.

'Don't worry,' he said, somewhat bitterly. 'I'm not so far gone that I'm about to forget your dinner.'

Bertie wagged a tentative tail and looked more hopeful at the mention of this magic word. Guy took out the tin-opener and reached for the can of food, feeling glad that he'd stayed later at the office so that he might be able to go out again almost immediately to meet Nell. He knew that if he'd had to sit waiting he might well lose his nerve. It was raining again so Guy shut Bertie in the back of the car and drove along the lane to the Lodge. He tooted loudly and got out but Nell was already letting herself through the little wicket gate. He caught his breath as he glimpsed her face, radiant and glowing, and opened the door for her. As they drove the short distance he was aware of her buoyant air of happiness and his own spirits rose accordingly.

'So how's it going?' he asked when they'd got their drinks and ordered some supper. 'Is it as good as you hoped?'

Not for worlds would he have let her see the disappointment he'd felt when she told him about her opportunity with Elizabeth. There was nothing he could do about it. He couldn't afford to pay her a decent salary and the new job sounded absolutely right for her. He couldn't stand in her way just because he liked to have her around.

'It's wonderful! I'm really loving it! There's so much to learn . . .'

He watched her glowing eyes, her lips, the shining hair and suddenly took her hand. 'Nell!'

She stopped mid-sentence and looked at him in surprise. 'What's the matter?'

'Nothing's the matter.' In the face of her beauty and detachment, he felt his confidence slipping away and made a desperate grab at it. 'It's just . . .' He looked at her despairingly and she looked back puzzled.

'Just . . . ?' she prompted and squeezed his hand encouragingly. 'Just what?'

'I think I love you,' he said flatly. 'I can't stop thinking about you. It gets between me and everything else. I think I'd like to marry you.'

Nell couldn't prevent a smile, despite her shock.

'You don't sound terribly sure,' she suggested.

Guy released her hand and glanced round as if surprised to find himself still in the pub. 'You've completely wrong-footed me,' he explained. 'I had decided that I would never marry. I haven't got the temperament for it. I'm like my old man and he wasn't made for it either. We're too selfish. But when I met you . . . Well, all that went out of the window.'

Nell watched him with anxious sympathy. This was the last complication she needed now, when everything seemed to be levelling out. She wondered what she could say that was not unkind. He'd been so good to her and very generous, despite his claims to selfishness. She decided to cheat.

'Oh, Guy,' she said. 'I feel very touched. I'm terribly fond of you, too, you know that. But the thing is . . . it's very soon after . . .' She let the words trail away, praying that the inference would be enough. It was.

'I know that' Guy flushed and she felt ashamed. 'I didn't mean to be insensitive—'

'You're not,' she said quickly, taking his hand. She couldn't let him take that to himself. 'Absolutely not. I'm probably being morbidly oversensitive but there were so many things.' She shook her head. 'I need much more time.'

'Of course.' He shrank instinctively from the thought of confidences or explanations. 'I understand that. It's just that things had reached a point where I felt that it was only right to explain how I feel.'

'You were quite right. Is it terribly selfish of me to want things to go on as they are for a bit longer? I've got so much to deal with at the moment that I'm simply not up to becoming more involved.' This, at least, was certainly true. The thought appalled her but she didn't want to hurt him.

'It's not a bit selfish. At least I've got it off my chest.' He felt strangely relieved and lighthearted and able to smile at her without embarrassment. 'Let's have another drink.'

Nell watched him go up to the bar and felt a strange desire to burst into hysterical laughter. How blind she must have been! She watched his tall lean shape as he waited to be served and smiled at him as he turned to give her a quick grin. Her happiness had deserted her and she suddenly felt tired. Life was so complicated, so exhausting. She didn't want to laugh any more, she wanted to burst into tears and push all her burdens on to someone else. But whom? There was no one else; not without complications of the sort that she had just witnessed. Nell felt utterly and entirely alone. The penalty of freedom is loneliness. Who'd said that? She sat up straight and arranged a bright look on her face as Guy turned back to her, bringing the drinks. She mustn't let him suspect her thoughts.

'So,' she said, as he gave her the glass and slid into his seat. 'How many boats did you sell today?'

Twenty-nine

LYDIA, STANDING SIDEWAYS AND breathing in, stared at herself disconsolately in the long looking glass. No matter what she did, those few – rather more than a few – extra pounds simply refused to be disguised. She sighed, undressed and added another garment to the discarded pile on the bed, wondering whether more exercise or a strict diet would be the answer. She ignored the tiny voice of truth which advised that neither would prove helpful since she was far too self-indulgent to pursue either course for the length of time necessary to achieve the desired results. For Lydia, life was a series of tests each of which might, this time, prove a triumph of hope over experience. It had come as rather a shock to see the needle swinging up when, for the first time for months, she'd climbed in the scales that morning. The telephone call from Nethercombe had been the cause of the experiment.

'We're having a Christmas party,' Gillian told her. 'It's going to be great fun. No, no. Not the family one. We're having that on Boxing Day. This is for all our friends. You'll come, won't you, Mum? And Henry says, is there anyone you'd like to invite? A friend you'd like to bring? Anyway, think about it. I'll be in later this week and we'll have lunch.'

After they'd finished their little chat, Lydia hurried into the bedroom and looked through her smarter outfits. When nothing seemed to fit she went into the bathroom and stood on the scales. She peered shortsightedly at the needle. Surely the scales must be wrong! She stepped off, twiddled the little knob so as to adjust them correctly, and tried again. Presently, after a restorative cup of coffee – in which she'd felt obliged to use a sweetener instead of sugar although she hated the taste – she tried the clothes on again, this time over a rather more disciplining undergarment.

She was struggling out of this quite agonising concoction of rubber and satin when the doorbell pealed. With a gasp Lydia plunged about trying to find whatever gloriously comfortable clothes she'd put on first thing that morning and finally got to the door at the third peal. She flung it open and looked out, hair on end, eyes wild with effort, cheeks red with exertion. It was Elizabeth. Spotless as ever she looked at her old friend with what – to Lydia at least – could only be described as insufferable condescension.

'Whatever have you been doing?' she asked, going in and turning an amused stare on the dishevelled and annoyed Lydia.

'I was trying things on,' said Lydia, looking as dignified as she was able with her buttons done up wrong and her skirt on back to front. 'And I do wish that you'd phone, Elizabeth. Surely it's not too much to ask! I know I'm not a busy working woman . . .'

Elizabeth smiled at the exhumation of this very old bone of contention and gave her a rare – and very brief – hug.

'I know I'm tiresome,' she admitted, 'but when I come to Exeter I do like to see you if I can. The trouble is that I never know quite how long appointments will take.'

Lydia, disarmed at once by the hug and the apology, shrugged further explanations aside. 'It's always lovely to see you,' she said. 'Let's have some coffee. The thing is that Gillian phoned to invite me to this party at Nethercombe and I was wondering what to wear. You caught me experimenting.'

Elizabeth leaned against the door jamb and looked at Lydia affectionately.

'She seems very settled now, doesn't she?'

'Oh, she does! I'm so relieved I can't tell you. There seems to have been a complete change. It was good of you to take her on, Elizabeth.'

'Not really.' Elizabeth strolled back into the sitting room so as to avoid any effusive thanks. 'I need help. Gillian's only doing it until she starts a family as I expect you know.'

'Yes, she told me that.' Lydia raised her voice above the noise of the kettle. 'I was enormously relieved to know that she was even considering having a baby, to tell you the truth. She seems so altered that I can't help thinking that running away was quite a good thing. She came in last week with her friend. Nell something. She's working for you too, I gather.'

'That's right.' Elizabeth sat down as Lydia appeared with the tray. 'She wants a full-time job. I think she'll train up quite well.'

'What an attractive girl. She reminded me of those old paintings. You know? Burne-Jones, is it?'

'She's very striking,' agreed Elizabeth, accepting a cup of coffee, 'which will go down well with the clients. I was delighted with Gillian for introducing her to me. She lives in one of Henry's cottages, apparently.'

'That's right.' Lydia picked up the sugar bowl, put it back, shrugged and picked it up again. 'She lost her husband, so Gillian told me. And she's got a small boy, so she must be glad to have a job.'

'She is,' said Elizabeth, who now knew how much Gillian had told her mother about Nell. 'So are you going to the party?'

'Oh, yes!' Lydia stirred vigorously and sipped gratefully. Much nicer than those horrid sweeteners! 'Have you been invited?'

'I have.' Elizabeth took a mouthful of unsweetened coffee, a cynical eye on Lydia's antics with the sugar bowl. 'Gillian has kindly suggested that I invite a friend.'

'Oh?' Lydia's eyes were bright with interest. 'Shall you invite Richard?'

Elizabeth raised her eyebrows. 'I do have other friends,' she murmured. 'And who are you going to invite?'

'Well.' Lydia hesitated. It was extraordinarily irritating how

Elizabeth never seemed to divulge information whilst at the same time managing to winkle other people's secrets out in moments. She bridled a little and Elizabeth hid a smile.

'Did you want to borrow Richard?'

'Certainly not!' cried Lydia indignantly, rising to the bait immediately. 'As it happens, I've met someone.'

She didn't exactly add, 'So there!' but it was implicit in her tone and Elizabeth opened her eyes at her.

'Goodness! Are you going to tell me about him? Or have I got to wait for the party?'

Lydia set down her cup and prepared to be indiscreet. 'I met him in the Refectory a few weeks ago. Oh, I know you despise it but it's very pleasant there and very good value for money. Anyway. I was looking about for somewhere to sit and trying to manage my tray and my umbrella – you know how it's just rained and rained? Well . . .' Lydia lost the thread for a moment and then started off again. 'I was wondering where to sit and this gentleman stood up, so politely, and took my tray from me and put it down on his table. "Allow me," he said. I could see at once that he'd had some sort of military training. So upright. And the hair so short! And I was quite right. He's a major. Well, retired now. In the Devon and Dorsets. They're based here in Exeter, you know. He was so charming . . .' Lydia paused for breath.

'And you've invited him to the party?' suggested Elizabeth, hoping to stem the flow.

'Not yet.' Lydia looked rather shocked. 'After all, Gillian only told me about it this morning. But I might. We met for tea last week and he's invited me to a concert at the Cathedral. He's a widower. Been on his own for five years. We have much in common,' said Lydia, looking long-suffering and brave, and Elizabeth nodded.

'He sounds like one of the old school,' she said. 'Must be a nice old-fashioned sort of chap if he was having coffee in the Refectory. I think you should invite him.'

'Mmm.' Lydia thought pleasurably about how impressed he'd be with Nethercombe and how nice it would be to go with a man of her own. 'I think I might.'

'Excellent.' Elizabeth stood up. 'Must dash, I'm afraid. Lovely to see you and thanks for the coffee. Let's lunch soon.'

Lydia, suffering from a sensation of anticlimax, followed her into the hall and received a quick peck at the door.

'See you at the party then,' she said, rather wistfully.

'Absolutely. Oh, and Lydia?'

'What?'

'Try turning your skirt round the right way. That's the trouble with elastic-waisted skirts. You have to be so careful! 'Bye!'

'Oh, really!'

Lydia didn't quite slam the door but she would have liked to vent her frustration on some inanimate object. She hadn't nearly finished telling Elizabeth about the Major and she still didn't know whether Elizabeth intended to invite Richard to the party. She wandered into the bedroom and stared at the mound of clothes. As she hauled her skirt into place, the telephone rang and she went to answer it.

'Oh, Charles. How nice . . .' Her cheeks flushed a little and unconsciously she straightened her shoulders and pulled in her stomach muscles. 'I should love to. Thank you . . . It sounds lovely . . . I will indeed . . . Six thirty, then.'

She replaced the receiver, patted her hair and looked at the pile of clothes. It was quite obvious now she came to think of it; in fact she couldn't imagine why she hadn't thought of it at once instead of bothering with all that nonsense about sweeteners. She simply needed some new clothes. Lydia smiled and glanced at her watch. Plenty of time for a trip to the shops and her hairdresser. Charles was the sort of man who liked to see a lady looking her best and she felt it only right to make every effort to comply.

'AND AM I TO be invited to the party?' asked Richard, having listened with amusement to Elizabeth's version of her earlier meeting with Lydia. 'I feel it only fair now that I should be allowed to meet the Major.'

Elizabeth smiled but shook her head. 'You know the rules,' she said.

'Yes,' sighed Richard. 'I know the rules.' He pushed his plate aside and nodded to the waiter. 'I just don't know any other man who would have been stupid enough to stick to them as long as I have. Coffee?'

Elizabeth was silent as he ordered coffee and brandy. She hoped that he wasn't about to become difficult; it would be such a pity after all the years they'd shared.

'We did agree,' she said gently, after the waiter had gone, 'that it was best for all concerned.'

'So we did.' He looked at her with his direct thoughtful gaze. 'And now, twenty-five years on, do you still think it is?'

'Do I gather that you don't?'

'Oh, Elizabeth.' He shook his head. 'No answering a question with another question. I'm too old a hand for that.'

'Well.' She sat considering the question, aware that her answer might precipitate the emotional showdown that had been hitherto avoided. Presently she straightened and looked at him. 'Yes. Yes, I have to say I do. Considering all the facts and your particular situation. Yes, I do.'

'How cool you are,' he marvelled. 'Did you ever love me, I wonder?'

They both sat back in their chairs as the waiter deposited coffee and glasses of brandy but, when he'd gone, this new atmosphere – tense, painful, brittle – closed round them once again.

'I think that's a little unfair. It wasn't me who was married.' Elizabeth poured their coffee with a steady hand, determined to keep the situation under control. 'And you couldn't leave Anne. Or so you said at the time, as I remember.' This reminder, intended to put the responsibility where it belonged, was the only evidence of the pain she felt at his bitterly unjustified question and she let it hang for a second in the air before she added, 'and I agreed that you couldn't. I still do.'

Richard took the cup and saucer.

'If only I knew that I was right!' His voice held an impatient note. 'Would it have made so much difference after all?'

'Oh yes, it would,' said Elizabeth at once. 'I'm sure it would! Can you imagine how she would have felt? Rejected and abandoned, crippled and unwanted? And how would we have felt? Grabbing at our happiness at her expense. No, Richard. I'm sure we were right.'

'I wish I had your confidence,' he muttered. 'I think that we were too honourable. We could have had some happiness. Surely we were entitled to something.'

'Haven't we known happiness?' countered Elizabeth. 'Aren't you actually talking about sex? We've had an amazing friendship, Richard. Don't deny it simply because we haven't sweated and gasped and writhed about in bed together.'

'What a charming picture you paint.' A smile touched his lips but not his eyes. 'I don't think that I can see it quite as you do. You keep me so firmly on the edges of your life.'

'For your sake as much as mine. Be fair,' she pleaded. 'We agreed that no breath of gossip should touch Anne. We meet as business friends and often more than that. You know several of my oldest friends, although I admit that even they don't know the real situation. Don't get distorted vision now, Richard. It's a danger as one gets older to muddle the past. To feel cheated and hard done by. We must try to remember how things really were.'

'How sensible you are.' He smiled at her but there was an edge to his voice and an unspoken criticism in the words.

'You're trying to put the blame on me.' She attempted to make him look at it squarely. 'Because I have been able to accept the situation, live with it, even twist it to make it work for me, you imply that I didn't care. And so it must have been easy for me. Can you really believe that?'

He wouldn't meet her eyes but fiddled instead with the spoon in his saucer, his head bent. Elizabeth waited for him to face the facts. What he thought he wanted was to have remained in his marriage without guilt whilst Elizabeth proved her love for him by becoming his mistress. Could it be that he still believed it might be possible? Still she waited.

'Of course not,' he mumbled at last.

'It wouldn't have worked,' she insisted. 'Once we'd become lovers we'd have wanted more and more. Stolen meetings, hole-in-the-corner love would never have been enough for us. At least I remember the agony of those early years well enough for that! Good God, Richard! Can you not honestly be thankful that all that pain is past and just be grateful for what we have now?'

At the passion in her low voice, he looked up at her at last. She saw both gratification at having resurrected her pain and guilt from the knowledge that he was almost certainly responsible for her single state mirrored on his face and she gave a short laugh. He had succeeded in piercing her armour and she had to steel herself from the temptation to feel contempt at his satisfaction.

'I'm sorry. That was very unfair of me.' He swallowed his coffee and set the cup back in the saucer. 'I just need, sometimes, to break down that coolness and see that you do really care. Not just as an old friend.'

'I'm still single you notice.' She held his eyes and he looked ashamed.

'Forgive me. You can't imagine how I long to take my place at your side openly. To meet your friends. To go to this damned party at Nethercombe!'

'I know.' Knowing that she should try to reconcile him, she covered her hand with his own and he returned the pressure.

'I'm behaving like a boor. You're quite right. I want it all ways round as usual.'

'Who doesn't?' Elizabeth filled the cups again. The atmosphere had lightened and the brooding look had left his face and he smiled properly at her as she passed his cup. 'We all want everything. It's just that sometimes it simply isn't possible. Sometimes it's a case of second best.' She smiled back at him, a warm, intimate smile that moved his heart and made him feel a bastard. 'We've had a pretty good second best, Richard. Better than most people's best.'

It would have been churlish not to agree, not to make an effort but he couldn't resist one more question.

'If Anne . . . If anything happened now – you know they've never promised her a long life – would you marry me?'

The silence was just fractionally too long.

'My dear Richard, you know I would.'

But he felt his heart plummet and was too immersed in his own feelings of betrayal to be aware of her resentment that he should force the issue, handle their fragile relationship – so treasured, so carefully preserved and worked at – with such clumsy insensitive fingers.

Elizabeth began to collect up her belongings, quietly angry at being pushed into making admissions and bolstering his ego, yet still being the one to go home alone to an empty house. She'd abided by the rules – made to accommodate his situation, not hers – and saw no reason why she should be made a whipping boy for his regrets. She was relieved that his car was parked at some distance from the restaurant while hers was just outside the door. He, still feeling a little sorry for himself, made no attempt to comment on her brittle farewell but, as he walked to his car with the memory of her light delicate scent still in his nostrils, he felt an overwhelming reaction of regret and a frightening awareness of loss.

Thirty

GUSSIE CAME OUT OF the kitchen, paused in the hall to do homage to Gillian's transformation of the Christmas tree and climbed the stairs to her bedroom. She shut the door behind her and went to pull the curtains. The full moon poured its cold white radiance on fields and woods, bleaching them of colour but bathing them in so bright a light that she could pick out certain landmarks as though it were daytime. A curtain in either hand, Gussie paused, arms outstretched, glorying in the beauty of the scene and filled with gratitude.

'And the thing is, Lord,' she said, closing the curtains reluctantly and going to rummage in her wardrobe, 'things seem to be turning out right for everyone. Henry so happy, bless him. And Gillian much more settled. And Mr and Mrs Ridley, so cosy in their new quarters . . .' Her hands passed over the navy blue paisley dress and she stopped abruptly, remembering the day that she had bought it more than four years before and how she had met Nell in the café. 'It's perfectly true, Lord,' she said, wandering away from the wardrobe, 'how You work in a mysterious way Your wonders to perform. If I hadn't gone in for a cup of tea at that moment I should never have met Nell and I almost certainly would not be here now.' She had to stop at the sheer horror of the thought that her future at Nethercombe had hung by so frail a thread. Where might she be instead? She shook her head and sat down in an armchair. 'And where would Nell be?' she wondered. 'At least we have been able to give her some comfort during this terrible time. And now she has a job. Of course, some people would say that

You tend to give with one hand and take away with the other, Lord, but I don't think it's that simple, is it?' She laid her head back and shut her eyes. 'I think that people were more content,' she observed, after some silent communication, 'when they didn't feel they had Rights. Human Rights. Animal Rights. Perhaps it would be better if we looked upon good things as a kind of bonus . . .'

There was a knock at the door and Henry put his head round.

'Thought I heard voices,' he said, not looking in the least surprised that Gussie was alone in the room. 'All well?'

'Perfectly splendid, Henry dear.' Gussie beamed upon him. 'And looking forward to the party.'

'As long as you haven't been overdoing yourself helping Mrs Ridley.'

'Not at all. Joan Beresford's made nearly all the puddings. You know how wonderful she is at that? Perfectly delicious concoctions! I've hardly done a thing.'

'Good. Splendid. See you later then.'

He shut the door gently. Alone again, Gussie tried to recapture her previous train of thought but it eluded her. She closed her eyes so as to concentrate better and presently she was fast asleep.

GUY GLANCED AT HIS watch, decided he had another half an hour before he needed to shower and change, and continued to slump before the television. When he had first been invited to the party he'd immediately seen himself going with Nell. Despite their trips to the pub and her days with him in the office, he was aware that no one saw them as a couple. He was not certain that he did himself. Even when they were together there was an invisible barrier. Part of this was due, he told himself, to the fact that they were both reserved people. They were not, by nature, outwardly emotional or physical people. She never clutched him or threw her arms round him as Gemma did. Of course, he'd known Gemma all her life and she was like a little sister . . . And that was another thing that had to be taken

into consideration. Nell was quite a lot older than he was. Here Guy
usually tended to let his thinking become less clear: Nell had an age-
less beauty, so the age-gap really didn't show, he looked old for his
age, and so on . . . When it came down to it, however, there was no
getting away from the fact that she had a boy of nearly thirteen. If he
did his sums, he knew he should take into account the fact that Nell
had graduated before she married and even by being as generous as he
could – sending her to university at seventeen, marrying her off immediately on graduating, supposing Jack's conception to have taken
place on her honeymoon – he still couldn't make Nell's age less than
thirty-four. And he was just twenty-seven.

Seven years was nothing. So argued Guy, when his cautious alter
ego whispered wisely about older widows with adolescent sons, and
at least he and Jack got on tremendously well. 'You're not his stepfather,' muttered the tiresome voice. Guy tried to visualise being a father to Jack and failed miserably. Taking him sailing was one thing:
laying down the law and trying to discipline him without upsetting
Nell quite another. He remembered his own resentment when, at
about Jack's age, he'd realised that he and Giles might be presented
with a stepfather. He remembered, too, his reaction and the way he
and Giles had broken up the relationship. Guy shuddered. How ruthless the young could be!

He stood up and went into the kitchen to pour himself a beer. After all, Jack was away at school for most of the time and when he
came home for the holidays . . . Guy tried to imagine the three of
them in his little cottage. For the life of him he simply couldn't do it.
One of the difficulties here was Nell's otherworldliness. He simply
couldn't see her in the role of wife: cooking, cleaning – Guy was
fairly old-fashioned in his ideas – and generally behaving like other
women. He knew this was stupid. She had been a wife and, since the
Lodge was always clean and tidy, she was obviously quite capable of
running a home. He tried, instead, to picture them living all together
at the Lodge but that was no use either. Something always seemed to

block his vision of married bliss. Perhaps everyone felt like this before the final step was taken.

Guy sat on the sofa again and fiddled with the television remote control. He wished he had the courage to phone her, to ask if he could go and meet her so that they could go to the party together. Why not? The walk along the avenue would be dark . . . 'Not with this moon,' whispered the little inner voice. 'Anyway, she's got Jack.' And that was true. Jack was home from school and was coming to the party. Sophie and Gemma were being driven over with Sophie's parents, the Hope-Latymers – who, it seemed, were friends of Henry as well as Phoebe – and bringing Sophie's two younger brothers as company for Jack. Guy sighed and switched off the television. There always seemed to be some good reason why he and Nell couldn't simply behave like any other couple. She'd asked him to wait, which was perfectly reasonable, but he'd hardly seen her of late with this new job of hers and it was time that he made another effort. He brought the image of her into his mind and his heart beat faster. It would be lovely to see her. He finished his beer feeling more cheerful. Perhaps an opportunity might arise this evening . . .

IN THE END HE walked up with Phoebe – who was always delighted at the prospect of a party and was always ready to enjoy herself – and the Beresfords. Nell, looking breathtaking in sea green with her hair piled high, was already there and talking to a tall dark woman whom she presently introduced as her boss: Elizabeth Merrick. They were joined by Lydia who introduced Major Charles Hart and Guy went to find a drink. He was waylaid by Gemma and felt the familiar sense of ease and lightheartedness steal over him.

'What have you done to your hair?' he demanded.

'Don't you like it?' She gave him the old provocative smile. 'Chris thinks it's very sexy!'

'Oh well,' Guy shrugged, 'if you're going to listen to a submariner . . . When am I going to meet him, by the way? Keeping him a bit dark, aren't you? What's wrong with him?'

'Nothing.' Gemma tilted her chin at him and made a face. 'Simply that, unlike most people I could mention, Chris actually works. Away at sea, suffering privations for Queen and Country.'

'Oh yeah?' Guy gave a derisive hoot. 'Didn't you say he was on a bomber? Sitting on his arse for six weeks at a time, watching the latest movies more like!'

'Oooh! You're a pig!' Gemma pinched his bottom hard and Guy gave a cry of pain which caused Gussie, passing by, to raise her eyebrows at him in alarm.

'Are you all right, Guy dear?'

'Fine, thanks. Fine. Twinge of arthritis.'

'Good heavens!' Gussie looked distressed. 'It must be all that water. Boats are such damp things, aren't they?'

She moved away and Gemma burst into fits of giggles. Guy looked at her disapprovingly.

'I don't know about sexy! Pigtails would be more appropriate. And that jolly well hurt!'

'Sorry! Shall I kiss it better?' She grinned up at him and slipped away into the crowd before he could retaliate.

He watched her go and went to find a drink. By the time he got back, Elizabeth was deep in conversation with Lydia and Charles whilst Nell looked as if she were about to slide off. Guy smiled at her and manoeuvred her a little away from the others.

'How are you? You're being very elusive lately.'

'Oh, Guy.' She shook her head and sighed. 'It's simply that I'm so busy! There's so much to learn that it'll take me years and years to get the hang of it. And it's all so exhausting. I've never worked full time, as you know. But it's lovely to see you. I realise now how very kind and patient you were with me in the office.' Her smile made his heart soar. 'How are things with you?'

'Not too bad.' He didn't want to talk about business. 'I'm hoping we can have an evening out together. A Christmas dinner or something. Would you like to? Just the two of us,' he added quickly lest she suppose that the invitation included Jack.

'Oh!' She looked flustered for a moment and then pulled herself together. 'What a nice idea. I'd love to. When?'

He could have shouted with joy.

'Monday? I'll book a table at the Church House Inn. I expect they'll find a quiet corner for us.'

'Lovely. I'll have a word with Phoebe about Jack. He'll probably insist that he's OK on his own but I'll be happier if I know she can be on the end of the phone.'

'Good. I'll pick you up about seven thirty then.' He was so happy that he didn't object too much when other people joined their group and he could no longer speak with her alone. He had Monday to look forward to now. He excused himself, collected another drink and went to talk to Abby and William Hope-Latymer.

LYDIA WAS HAVING A wonderful time. Charles was a charming companion: chivalrous, kindly, interesting. She was terribly proud to show him off at Nethercombe and flushed with pleasure when Elizabeth sent her a definite signal of approval behind Charles's unsuspecting head. Even Gillian was impressed.

'Gosh, Mum!' she'd whispered whilst Henry shook Charles's hand and welcomed him warmly. 'He's really nice. Very distinguished.'

Lydia glowed and, when he was introduced to William Hope-Latymer and they discovered they had mutual friends and had been at Sandhurst at about the same time, her cup was full to overflowing.

Elizabeth, watching her from a quiet corner, smiled to herself. She noticed the new outfit in generously forgiving cotton jersey and the haircut that made her old friend look more youthful and was quite suddenly pierced with a terrible sadness. She remembered being a bridesmaid at Lydia's wedding – Angus, dashing in his top hat – and how happy a day it had been for them all. How wonderful life could be. And how terrible! Lydia had been such a scatty girl; falling in and out of love with monotonous regularity and each time it was the great love of her life. Why had Angus been so different that she'd married him? It was impossible to remember now. She'd warned her that marriage was a serious step and Lydia had teased her for being cold, indifferent, unnatural. And then she'd met Richard.

'You're looking very thoughtful.' Elizabeth looked up to see the tall thin odd-looking woman who lived in the Courtyard surveying her. 'Phoebe,' said the woman obligingly. 'And you're Elizabeth Something. Gillian's godmother.'

'That's right.' Elizabeth made room beside her. 'Come and sit down. I'd rather switched off, I'm afraid.'

'Why not?' said Phoebe, sitting beside her. 'Parties can have very strange effects. Sometimes good, sometimes bad. Not bad in your case, I hope?'

'Good heavens!' said Elizabeth lightly. 'Was my expression that forbidding? Do you have a husband here? I know we've met before but I don't remember . . . ?' She paused enquiringly.

'Divorced,' said Phoebe succinctly.

'Ah.' Elizabeth's voice was non-committal. One never knew whether to commiserate or congratulate.

' "Ah" 's about right,' said Phoebe cheerfully. 'Sums it up quite adequately. So you and Gillian's mum are old friends. That's nice. Old friends are so comfortable. The older I get the more I realise that. The people who mean most are the ones who've been through all the traumas with you, don't you think?'

'I certainly do,' agreed Elizabeth readily. 'Although new ones can shake you out of the old ruts, make you rethink things.' Her glance strayed to Nell.

'Sounds uncomfortable,' complained Phoebe. 'I like my old ruts and I hate rethinking things.'

'But surely you've made new friends here,' protested Elizabeth.

'After all, you can't have been here very long. Haven't you enjoyed that? You certainly seem to be well bedded in – as the locals say.'

'Well, I am, really,' admitted Phoebe. 'You're right, of course. I hadn't thought of these being new friends. I feel as if I've known them for years. Odd, isn't it?'

'Sometimes that can happen,' agreed Elizabeth, her eyes still on Nell. 'Occasionally one meets a kindred spirit. Lucky for you to meet six or seven in one go.'

'I love them all,' admitted Phoebe. 'All except Mr Jackson.'

'Mr Jackson?' Elizabeth frowned a little. 'Is he here? I don't re- member him.'

'No, no,' said Phoebe, shocked. 'Goodness, no! He's gone rushing home to wifie for Christmas. He simply doesn't belong in the Court- yard. But never mind. I'm working on it. I don't think he'll stay long.'

'I think, if I were Mr Jackson, I'd feel a little nervous.'

'Mr Jackson always feels nervous,' said Phoebe cheerfully. 'That's why I don't think he'll stay. I'm wearing him down. It's very impor- tant in a courtyard development that the residents get on together. We've told Henry that we're going to interview anyone who offers on Number Five.'

'Poor Henry.' Elizabeth laughed.

'Oh, Henry agrees with us. We're like a great big family now. It'll have to be someone very special who buys Number Five!'

IN THE KITCHEN MR RIDLEY was carefully stacking the dish- washing machine: one of Gillian's innovations. At first, Mrs Ridley had felt it incumbent upon her to despise it and continued to wash up by hand but, slowly, secretly, after several private experiments, she'd grudgingly agreed that it had its uses. The unspoken feud between them was over. Gillian was making great efforts and Mrs Ridley was prepared to meet her halfway much to Mr Ridley's relief.

'Goin' all right then, maid?' he enquired as his wife came in with a loaded tray.

Mrs Ridley, flushed with exertion, lips tightly compressed, nodded. 'Got they kettles on?'

'Boilin' away!' he announced. ' 'Ow's the boy be'avin' 'isself, then?
'Avin' a good time, is 'e?'

' 'Course 'e is.' Mrs Ridley unloaded the plates and started to collect the coffee cups. 'I 'eared 'im tellin' Mr William's boys about all
they antics 'e gets up to. You 'n 'im. Reckon you'll 'ave 'em all over,
the way 'e's goin' on.'

Mr Ridley chuckled. 'The more the merrier,' he said.

Mrs Ridley tossed her head and clucked derisively. 'See yerself
with yer own platoon or whatever, I s'pose,' she said. 'Givin' 'im that
great knife for Chrissmus! Dunno what 'is mum'll say to that!'

'Sensible woman, 'is mum,' said Mr Ridley reflectively. 'Showed
'er it, I 'ave. 'Er ses 'e's gotta learn if 'e's goin' in the Army.' Mrs Ridley snorted as she manhandled the kettles and the coffee pots with an
experienced hand. Mr Ridley watched her, smiling to himself. 'Real
looker, she is,' he said appreciatively.

Mrs Ridley snorted again, louder this time.

'No fewel like an ole fewel,' she observed.

'Still got the use o' me eyes.' He slipped his arms round her from
behind and she gave a loud squawk. 'Mind! 'Er can't 'old a candle to
yew. Give us a kiss.'

Mrs Ridley, loud with protests, suddenly remembered how her
sister's husband had dropped down dead with a heart attack, threw
her arms round him and kissed him heartily. Encouraged, he kissed
her again and they clung together closely.

Gussie, coming suddenly upon them, backed out quietly and stood
for a moment in the passage, moved almost to tears by the unexpected
tenderness in the elderly couple's embrace. After a moment, she
coughed and made rather a to-do with the door handle. By the time she
entered, Mr and Mrs Ridley stood well apart. Mrs Ridley, her cheeks
flushed, was making coffee; her husband, his face peaceful and happy,
was piling cups and saucers on to the trays. Gussie felt strangely shy.

'I just wondered if you needed some help with carrying things,' she said.

They both looked at her and smiled and she felt as though they encompassed her, too, in their love for each other and their affection for Henry and Nethercombe and she beamed back at them, gratefully, joyfully, her heart too full for words, knowing that they understood and accepted her love in return.

Thirty-one

HENRY, SITTING AT HIS desk and struggling half-heartedly with some insurance forms, was finding concentration impossible. He folded his arms across his chest and gave himself up to happiness. Yesterday afternoon Gillian had told him that she was expecting a baby, due in September. A baby! Henry shook his head, ran his fingers through his hair and unable to sit still for a moment longer, pushed back his chair and wandered over to the window. Pools and drifts of daffodils, bending and blowing in the southwesterly gale, grew in the long grass which wouldn't be mown until their glory was over. Henry thrust his hands into his pockets and listened to the March wind roaring round the house. A baby!

He clenched his hands into fists as his heart winged and soared with joy. It was the final drop in his cup of happiness which now was overflowing. He remembered Gillian's face, full of excitement and pride, and had to swallow hard to prevent himself from weeping, so great was his emotion. He had begun to believe that he would never be a father but, since Gillian's return, there had been so much love between them that he had started to hope again. Surely, with Gillian so much more contented, it was possible that he might be granted this extreme joy.

Nethercombe was made for children. Henry allowed his imagination to run riot. He saw his son growing up, as he himself had, at Nethercombe. Perhaps there might be several children! His mind's eye peopled Nethercombe with his offspring; playing cricket on the lawn, acting at mothers and fathers in the summerhouse, paddling in the pool, roaming the grounds. He saw celebrations at birthdays and Christmases, heard their voices ringing through the house, imagined accompanying pretty daughters, who looked like Gillian, up the aisle as brides and thought of training up a son to take over where he left off at Nethercombe.

Henry turned back into the room and bent to place a log amongst the hot ashy remains of his fire. Perhaps, in thirty years or so, his son would be working here, sitting at his desk . . . He straightened as he heard a light tapping. Gussie put her head round the door.

'Lunch in five minutes, Henry. Gillian's gone into Exeter to see her mother so it's just the two of us.'

Henry nodded. He knew that Gillian had gone to break the glad news to Lydia. She'd suggested that he might like to tell Gussie himself and he'd blessed her insight. He swallowed once or twice and beamed at this tall angular woman who was his closest relative.

'Don't go for a moment,' he said, as she prepared to withdraw. She hated to interrupt him whilst he was working. 'Got a bit of news.'

'Oh?' Gussie came right in. 'Someone to view Number Five?'

'No.' Henry shook his head. 'Not that.' Words and sentences formed and reformed in his head. It was surprising how difficult it was to actually say it. 'We're going to have a baby.' There! Quite simple after all. 'Gillian went to see the doctor yesterday to confirm it.'

Gussie stared at him, her hands clasped at her breast.

'Oh, Henry . . .'

'I know.' He nodded, accepting her unspoken delight, and had to press his lips tightly together to contain a sudden uprush of emotion.

'Oh, Henry,' Gussie started again and then burst into speech. 'Oh, my dear, how wonderful. I'm so happy for you. And for Gillian. This is so exciting!'

They plunged together, neither used to displays of emotion, and hugged rather inexpertly but with a great deal of feeling.

'Lunch is in.'

Mrs Ridley stood in the doorway watching them with a mixture of anxiety, amazement and hastily assumed indifference as Gussie and Henry broke apart, half-laughing half-crying.

'Mrs Ridley . . .' began Gussie and hesitated. This, after all, was Henry's moment, not hers. She looked at him, raised her eyebrows meaningly and gave him an encouraging nod. He looked suddenly rather shy but he spoke out bravely enough.

'We've had some rather exciting news, Mrs Ridley.' He smiled at her. 'My wife's expecting a baby. Due in September.'

'Well, then!' Mrs Ridley took the news in slowly. She looked from one to the other and her eyes began to shine. 'Well! Congratulations, Mr 'Enry!' She shook her head as though deprived of further speech and then nodded furiously at him.

'A toast!' cried Henry. 'I think we should all have a little celebration, don't you? Just a little one. Champagne tonight when Gillian gets back but I think we could have a little one now, don't you? Is Mr Ridley about? Good! Good! Go and fetch him and I'll find something to toast ourselves with.'

They swept out of the study and across the hall and Mrs Ridley clattered down the passage to the kitchen, her voice upraised.

'Just a glass of sherry now, perhaps,' Henry said, seizing the decanter whilst Gussie assembled glasses.

He poured with an unsteady hand and Gussie gave a little snort of joy.

'Oh, Henry,' she said. 'An heir for Nethercombe.'

And they stood for a long moment, gazing speechlessly at each other, while the Ridleys' voices, raised in excited question and answer, drew nearer and nearer.

NELL SAT IN THE rocking chair by the Rayburn, a pile of Elizabeth's books on the table beside her. She felt peaceful and at one with herself. Her grief and anger, as well as her fear and bitterness, seemed at long last to have faded away leaving her with this sense of well-being. She knew that she had much for which to thank both Gillian and

Elizabeth. Without her engrossing and satisfying work, she might still be floundering in the darker waters of despair. Instead, she woke to a sense of purpose and commitment; an excitement at what the day might bring. Gradually, Elizabeth was giving her more and more responsibility and professing herself delighted with Nell's ability.

Nell put her book aside and, drawing her heels up on to the edge of the seat, hugged her knees as she had hugged to herself the latest piece of unbelievable good fortune. Elizabeth had suggested that it was time she had her own car. It would be a company car; not too small because of transporting pieces of furniture but not too large and difficult to park. Nell had been too thrilled to be able to utter a single word but Elizabeth explained that the business could afford it and had made it sound – in her cool voice – as though it were quite natural in the circumstances, thus relieving Nell from the crushing emotion of gratitude for favours generously granted. Instead, Nell felt – as Elizabeth intended that she should – more confident and determined to do even better. It would be so much easier with her own transport. Although it had been fun to have Gillian with her in the early days, it soon became evident that Gillian's heart was not in it. Recently she was little more than a chauffeur, often dropping Nell off with Elizabeth or at an appointment with a client and disappearing until later. She seemed more than happy to fetch and carry but Nell felt relieved at the thought of being independent again.

She put her feet to the ground and went to push the kettle on to the hotplate. Whilst she waited for it to boil she crossed her arms across her breast and hugged herself in excitement. One of the most difficult things to get used to had been her dependence on others. In a town, perhaps, it wouldn't have been so bad but out in the country it was very hard. She grimaced with joy at the thought of being able to drive upcountry to fetch Jack at the end of term. It had been very pleasant to go to and fro with Henry but it was not quite the same as being alone with Jack, listening to his excited chatter.

She made coffee and her joy subsided a little as she wondered what

on earth she was going to do about Guy. Just after Christ
he took her out to dinner at the Church House Inn at Rat
proposed to her again. And again, unable to hurt him, she'
cated, using the same excuse as she'd used before and rein
by pleading pressure relating to her new job. He'd accepted
tantly and she was so relieved that she'd dropped her gua
than she intended, allowed him to kiss her and felt obliged to
as much as she was able. Luckily, Jack had come rushing out
come them home and the moment had passed but Nell had felt
able and confused. She wished that she'd been completely
with Guy from the beginning but she'd suspected that – unde
his forbidding exterior – Guy wasn't nearly as confident as he lo
And he'd been so kind to her. Luckily for her, Guy had gone to
a boat back from somewhere in France soon after the evening at
tery and she'd been given a breathing space.

Nell sighed and sat down again in the rocker but before she co
pick up her book the doorbell rang. She stood up, felt about for
shoes and hurried to the door. Gillian stood outside with a most p
culiar expression on her face; joy and pride mingled with exciteme
and something else that Nell couldn't quite place.

'Come in,' she said. 'I'm glad you've come. I've got some excitin
news.'

'Really?' Gillian preceded her into the kitchen and stood by the
Rayburn, warming herself. 'So have I.'

'Spit it out!' Nell started making a second cup of coffee.

'No. You go first.'

'Elizabeth's giving me a car.' Nell shook her head, still hardly able
to believe her luck. 'Well, not giving, obviously. It's owned by the
business but I can have the use of it. Oh, Gillian, you can't imagine
what that means to me. And you'll probably be pleased, too. You
won't have to keep carting me about.'

'It's wonderful news,' said Gillian warmly. 'You had to have your
own transport. Especially now . . .'

She hesitated and Nell looked at her enquiringly.

'Why especially now? I know that you didn't want a full-time ob . . . Oh!'

Gillian met her eyes and nodded. 'I'm expecting a baby,' she said and looked at Nell almost fearfully. 'It's due in September.'

'That's wonderful! I'm so pleased for you. Henry must be off his head with joy.'

Gillian smiled but there was still a reservation which Nell couldn't understand.

'He's terribly excited. He and Gussie have been rushing about dragging cradles and rocking horses out of the attics . . .' She stopped and bit her lip.

'And why not?' Nell watched her, puzzled. 'I think it's terrific. Are you . . . ? Is there . . . ?' She hesitated. 'Is there something wrong, Gillian?'

Gillian gripped the mug Nell passed to her tightly. 'Wrong?'

'You seem to have something on your mind. Apart from the baby. Are you OK?'

'Of course I am. It's just rather difficult coming to tell you about the baby when you . . . when . . . Oh hell!'

'Oh, I see!' Nell's brow cleared. 'Honestly, Gillian! Please don't get upset about that. I'm truly thrilled for you. Really! Don't get the idea that I shall be sitting here with morbid fancies after you've gone. It will probably horrify you if I say that, as things worked out, it was probably a blessing in disguise. Don't look so shocked! I know it sounds dreadful and at the time I was devastated but how I would have coped with a new baby as well as everything else I really can't imagine. And what would I be doing now? I could hardly be working with Elizabeth, could I?'

'You mean that you don't really mind?' Gillian could barely believe her ears. Could Elizabeth have been right, after all?

'About what? Losing the baby? It wasn't as though we'd planned it, you see. And I've still got Jack. I'm not really hard-hearted, although it must sound like it, but quite honestly it was probably the best thing in

the circumstances. If he had lived I should have loved him as I love Jack
and no doubt we should have survived somehow. But he didn't. You
simply can't keep looking over your shoulder otherwise you just carry
all the bitterness and grief with you. Thanks to you I've got a home
and a job and, to be truthful, I'm happier than I've been for years.'

'For years?' Gillian looked as though she'd been given present.
'Really?'

'Really!' said Nell firmly, surprised at Gillian's intensity. For some
reason Gillian needed some sort of reassurance on this point and
Nell, with a little effort, put aside her natural reticence so as to be
able to give it to her. 'John and I weren't particularly happy during
those last years.' She hesitated a little and decided to hold nothing
back. 'To be honest I should never have married him. I was in love
with his elder brother. He just saw me as a little sister, rather like
Guy and Gemma, and in the end I married John as second best. And
that's how he stayed. I cheated him although I hope he never realised
it. Rupert was killed during the assault on Mount Tumbledown. He
was a platoon commander with the Scots Guards. John's death has released me from living a lie, if you like, and although I wouldn't have
wanted him to die, any more than the baby, he did. It's all over. My
life is here with all of you now. And if I'm absolutely honest, it's
wonderful to be free, in charge of my own future and a new career.'

There was a long silence. Nell felt exhausted, as though she'd just
been given a blood transfusion. She wondered if Gillian was shocked
or contemptuous but was too tired to care. She finished her coffee
and looked at Gillian. She appeared strangely happy, although there
were tears in her eyes.

'Thank you for telling me that,' she said. 'It's meant a lot. I'm glad
you're happy here.'

'I'm very happy. And truly grateful. So. Let's forget about me.
What about this baby? What with Henry and Gussie and the Ridleys,
not to mention the Courtyard, I suppose you realise that you'll never
see it?'

They both laughed and Nell felt a measure of relief. The crisis, whatever it had been, had passed.

'It's a daunting thought,' admitted Gillian. She hesitated for a moment and then plunged on. 'Henry and I had an idea and I said I'd ask you. D'you think that Jack would like to be one of the godfathers?'

'Jack!' Nell stared at her and then burst out laughing. 'What a wonderful idea. He'd love it, of course. My word! He'll burst with the importance of it. But isn't he a bit young?'

'Well, we thought about that but Henry thought it would be nice for the baby, as it grew up. You know? He'd be more a friend for it, wouldn't he?'

'What if it's a girl?'

Gillian shrugged. 'Jack can still be friend to a girl.'

'It's a fantastic idea and Jack will be over the moon. But you must write and tell him yourselves and invite him formally. He'll love that.'

'We will.' Gillian put her mug on the table. 'I'll be off then. It's blowing a Hooghly out there. I hope it doesn't bring any of the trees down.'

On the doorstep she hugged Nell rather shyly and Nell responded warmly.

'Tell Henry I'm thrilled,' she said. 'I shall expect some champagne next time I'm up at the house.'

Gillian slipped away up the avenue and Nell closed the door thoughtfully. She still didn't quite understand Gillian's need for reassurance or her reluctance to talk about the baby, unless she feared that Nell was envious of her good fortune. Nell decided that this must be the case. Gillian had so much by comparison. Perhaps that was it. Nevertheless, Nell still felt there was something more and wondered, now, at herself for baring her soul quite so readily. In retrospect it was difficult to remember that instinctive impulse which had told her that it was necessary. Well, it was done. She sat down in the rocking chair, pulled her book on to her knees and, moments later, was lost to the world.

Thirty-two

THERE WAS MILD REJOICING in the Courtyard when Mr Jackson's cottage went up for sale. The Beresfords, down for Easter, wondered who might buy it.

'Let's just hope,' said Guy, who was in a rather black mood having discovered that Nell was going to Italy with Elizabeth on a working holiday whilst Jack was in Scotland with friends, 'that it's nobody worse. Mr Jackson was quite harmless, after all, even if he wasn't as friendly as some of us might have liked.'

Phoebe laughed outright at this oblique attack.

'Dear Guy,' she said. 'Always so optimistic. Anyway, it was nothing to do with me. He said that the cottage wasn't big enough for wifie and all the little Jacksons to have their hols in, after all. He's looking for something a bit bigger in South Brent.'

Guy gave a disbelieving snort which sent Phoebe into further fits of mirth and he stalked off, whistling to Bertie who was having a wonderful game with Bill Beresford and who followed rather reluctantly. Joan and Bill raised their eyebrows and Phoebe grimaced.

'Crossed in love,' she said succinctly. 'Never mind. Now. What about a little party to celebrate?'

At the top of the drive Guy was detained by Gussie and Gillian, who were deciding whether it was warm enough to sit out on the terrace, and only agreed to stay when he realised that Nell would be along presently. When she arrived both Jack and Elizabeth were with her and Guy found himself recounting the story of Mr Jackson's rout.

'So she's done it,' Elizabeth chuckled. 'It hasn't taken too long.'

'Well.' Guy shrugged. He felt a little happier now and was prepared to admit to himself that he might have been a little churlish with Phoebe. 'I know he never fitted in but we could do worse. That's the problem with a small courtyard development. So much depends on one's neighbours.'

'Poor Henry's quite terrified of selling Number Five to the wrong people,' said Gillian. 'He thinks that the Courtyard will rise in a body and come up to lynch him.'

'I wouldn't put it past Phoebe,' muttered Guy and smiled at Nell.

'The problem is,' said Nell, 'that you can't possibly know what people are like from one or two viewings.'

'Phoebe says that a questionnaire should be sent out with the details and prospective viewers should be selected accordingly,' said Gillian and everyone burst out laughing.

Even Guy smiled unwillingly and Nell was relieved when Elizabeth suggested that they should be on their way to Plymouth. She felt increasingly shy and uncomfortable with him now and knew that the time was approaching when she would be able to prevaricate no longer. When they got up to go, Guy decided to continue his walk with Bertie, Jack disappeared in search of Mr Ridley and Gillian and Gussie sat on together, speculating on the fate of Mr Jackson's cottage. However, it was several weeks before they heard through Mr Ellison that the house had been bought by someone upcountry and was to be let for the time being.

Phoebe watched anxiously as people, sometimes alone, sometimes in twos and threes, crossed the Courtyard with Mr Ellison to view the cottage. Poor Mr Ellison grew to dread the sight of her, leaping out like a trap-door spider to waylay and question him. The owner, apparently, was very particular indeed and had made several rules; no children, no pets, no smoking, no DSS. Mr Ellison could have let it ten times over, so great was the need now for rented accommodation, but no one yet had been able to comply with all the restrictions. Phoebe was rather impressed with this comprehensive list of prejudices – 'Nearly as long as your own!' Guy said somewhat acidly when she told him – and was beginning to wonder if she knew anyone who might fit the bill when fate stepped in and took a hand.

ON A HOT DAY in late May, Nell parked her shiny new car at the end of the avenue, paused to admire it for the hundredth time and let herself through the little wicket gate. Her own gate was slightly ajar and she wondered if the postman had been with a letter from Jack. Nell, who received very little post, felt a thrill of anticipation. When she saw that the back door stood open, it occurred to her that Gussie – who had a spare key – might have come along with some newly baked offering. As she paused to drop her bag and kick off her shoes, she called out, feeling rather surprised that Gussie, who rarely let herself in, had ventured further than the kitchen. There was a sound of running feet on the stairs and a figure loomed in the doorway. Nell opened her mouth to scream, saw the raised arm and felt an agonising blow to the head before she fell, unconscious, against the Rayburn.

It was Mr Ridley who found her. He'd jolted slowly along the avenue in his old car with the Flymo in the back and, seeing the doors open, had put his head in to announce his presence. He found Nell bruised and bleeding, huddled against the Rayburn. She'd been very sick and blood was still trickling from the ugly gash on her head. Pausing only to cover her gently with a rug from the rocking chair, he telephoned for an ambulance first and Gussie second and then kneeled down beside her.

' 'Tis all right, maid,' he said, tucking the rug round her and using the kitchen towel to try to clean away the vomit and blood without moving or hurting her. 'They be on their way.'

Nell opened her eyes with difficulty. 'Don't leave . . .' The words trailed away and her eyes closed again.

'I bain't goin' nowhere,' he assured her and looked up with relief as Gussie and Gillian came rushing in.

'Oh, Mr Ridley!' Gussie caught sight of Nell and gave a gasp. 'Oh, dear God!'

She kneeled down beside Mr Ridley and took Nell's hand whilst Gillian stood with horrified eyes, her palms pressed to her lips.

''Twas an intruder,' Mr Ridley was saying. 'Winder's bin took out. See? 'E panicked an' 'it 'er.'

'We called the police,' said Gussie, her eyes on Nell's face. 'Her breathing seems quite regular. D'you think . . . ? Ah! Nell dear, it's Gussie. You're going to be quite all right. The ambulance is on its way.'

'Gussie.' Nell's voice was very faint. 'Don't leave it.'

'I shall come with you. Of course I will. Gillian dear?' Gussie's eyes remained fixed on Nell's face but she turned her head a little. 'Could you bring a glass of water?'

'No, no.' Nell sounded distressed. 'Not me. He might come back . . .'

She sank back and Gussie stroked the hair tenderly away from her white face.

'Don't worry, my dear. You won't be here. No need to be afraid.' Gussie took the glass from Gillian and held it to Nell's lips.

Nell raised her head to sip and gave a wince of pain.

'My things,' she whispered. 'Please . . .'

'I think,' said Gillian, watching from behind Gussie, 'that she's afraid that the man might come back with a van and take her furniture. Now he's seen what's here. She doesn't want the house left empty.'

Nell sent Gillian a look of pure gratitude and closed her eyes again.

'Of course,' said Gussie remorsefully. 'It's all she has. But how—'

'I'll stay,' said Mr Ridley. 'I'll get Doris to bring me gun down.'

Gussie looked quickly into his eyes, inches from her own, and felt a twinge of anxiety. She felt that there would be nothing he'd like better than to have a go at Nell's assailant. She opened her mouth and shut it again as an ambulance siren could be heard wailing its way closer and closer.

Nell, reassured by Mr Ridley's promise not to leave the Lodge empty for a single moment, gave herself up to pain. As she listened to the voices and the footsteps and felt herself lifted and jolted to the ambulance, she thought for one dizzy, dreadful moment that she was back in the flat and losing the baby and she cried out in despair. Her hand was seized and held and she opened her eyes to see Gussie beside her and remembered and was comforted.

DURING NELL'S STAY IN hospital the whole of Nethercombe rallied round. Guy and Mr Ridley took it in turns to stay at the Lodge whilst Gillian and Gussie did their best to decide what might have been stolen. Certainly nothing obvious was gone and they all hoped that the thief had been disturbed before he'd had chance to find anything of value.

Nell, recovering from concussion and severe bruising, tried to help and it was finally agreed that, apart from several pieces of jewellery, everything else was intact. Nell, weak from shock and pain, was terrified that the man might return and wondered how she could have lived in such an isolated place for so long without worrying about it before. She knew that she would never be able to let herself in to the Lodge again without the fear of that huge shadowy figure with its arm upraised looming at her, and wondered how she would be able to be alone at night there without finishing up mad with fright. She communicated her terrors to Gussie who in her turn reported them to Gillian and Henry whose reactions were immediate and identical: Nell must move back to Nethercombe.

Nell shook her head when Gussie suggested this as an alternative to going back to the Lodge. It might serve as a short-term answer but it couldn't possibly work as a final solution. Big though Nethercombe was, now that Henry and Gillian were starting a family there would be no room for outsiders. Gussie was different; she was one of the family. As for herself, she must make other plans. But where should she go? How could she possibly bear to leave the people who had become like a family to her? Guy's suggestion, faithfully transmitted by Gussie, was that she should have a dog. A good guard dog would frighten away a would-be intruder and would be company for Nell. She smiled a little at this. She guessed that what he really wanted to suggest was that she accept his offer of marriage and move in with him. Unfortunately for Guy, the time never seemed to be right to make this suggestion and he felt, in some obscure way, that he would be badgering her whilst she was at a disadvantage. After all, she was aware of his feelings for her. She only had to accept for her problems to be over. 'Or just beginning!' muttered his cynical inner voice.

It was Phoebe who provided the answer. Newly returned from a holiday with her family, she had been met with the dreadful news and the problem of Nell's terrors. She sat on the terrace having an early evening drink with the Morleys and Gussie and the solution was so obvious to her that she was amazed that nobody else had thought of it.

'Mr Jackson's cottage,' she said. 'Nell must rent Mr Jackson's cottage.'

The others stared at her in awed silence for so long that she was irresistibly reminded of Keats with Henry, naturally, cast as stout Cortez.

'Honestly!' said Gillian at last 'What idiots we are! It's so obvious.'

'It's very clever of you, Phoebe dear,' said Gussie and Phoebe smirked a little. 'She'll feel quite safe with you all down there. I really can't imagine why we never thought of it.'

'It's not let, then?' asked Henry and immediately doubt and anxiety crept in amongst their sensations of relief like foxes in a chicken run.

'Not as far as I know . . .'

'Supposing the owner won't let Nell have it? He sounds terribly fussy . . .'

'Henry dear, telephone Mr Ellison at once . . .'

They all spoke at once, anxious lest their brilliant idea should come to nothing. Henry hurried into the house with Gillian and Phoebe finished her drink and smiled encouragingly at Gussie.

'Surely nobody could object to Nell!' she said bracingly. 'Professional woman, non-smoker, no pets.'

'She has a child,' objected Gussie.

'Jack's hardly a child. What is he? Thirteen? That's not a child. And he's away at school nearly all the time.'

'I wonder if she can afford the rent,' mused Gussie. 'We've no idea what it is, have we? The Lodge is very reasonable . . .'

'Oh hell!' Phoebe stared at Gussie in dismay. 'I never thought of that. He's probably asking an extortionate amount.'

Henry and Gillian reappeared looking excited.

'Mr Ellison's getting on to the owner's representative,' he said, pulling out Gillian's chair for her and sitting down beside her. 'Apparently he has his private number. It's not let yet so we'll keep our fingers crossed.'

'And you did point out Nell's suitability?' questioned Gussie anxiously.

'You'd have thought it was the archangel Gabriel applying,' grinned Gillian.

'How did you get over the "no children" rule?' asked Phoebe.

'We glossed over Jack a bit,' admitted Henry. 'Said he was nearly finished at school and was away for most of the year.' He looked rather defensively at Gussie who beamed at him approvingly.

'Quite right, my dear,' she said. 'It is, after all, a matter of degree. How quickly can we hope to hear?'

'Maybe tomorrow. John thinks that the fact that she lives on the estate and that we can personally recommend her might be in her favour.' Henry paused. 'I asked about the rent.'

'Aah!' Three pairs of eyes were riveted on his face.

'It's very reasonable. Almost exactly the same as she pays for the Lodge. Shouldn't be a problem.'

'I think,' said Gillian, eyeing Phoebe's glass, 'that we need another drink.'

'Hear, hear,' said Phoebe cheerfully and when her glass was full, she raised it. 'Here's to us! And now there's only one problem left.' They stared at her. 'I suppose we ought to take into consideration the fact that Nell might not want to live in the Courtyard. Perhaps we should have asked her first!'

NELL COULD HARDLY BELIEVE her good fortune. The suggestion wasn't made until Henry heard through Mr Ellison that the owner was prepared to grant Nell a lease and then Gussie told her everything. Nell imagined herself in the delightful little cottage with all her precious things round her, safe in the Courtyard, amongst all her friends and, when Gussie had gone, she wept. The only drawback would be her proximity to Guy but, in her heart, she knew that the time had come to put an end to the whole business. Guy might be hurt but it was unfair to keep stringing him along. She prayed that it wouldn't spoil their relationship or make things difficult and spent many hours wondering how to put it to him as tactfully as possible. Although part of her was preoccupied by this problem, she was full of excitement and longing to get back to Nethercombe and take up her life again. Elizabeth had been to visit her and assured her that she mustn't worry about anything except getting well and told Nell that she'd been wondering if it was the sudden appearance of the nice new car that had given the thief ideas. The car was now safe in the Courtyard's car park and Elizabeth appeared to be deeply relieved at the news that Nell was to live in Mr Jackson's cottage.

'Phoebe had the right idea after all,' she said. 'Let me know when you're in and I'll be over.'

Gussie and Gillian helped Nell to pack and, between them, Guy, Henry and Mr Ridley with a hired van moved her belongings down to the Courtyard. Very quickly she made herself as comfortable and homely as she had been at the Lodge.

'You can't imagine what a relief it is to have you here,' said Phoebe, who had popped in to make sure that all was well. 'Like it?'

'I love it,' said Nell at once. 'I have the morning sun in the kitchen and my bedroom, and the afternoon and evening sun in the sitting room. The Lodge was a bit dark and gloomy with all those great trees around. And I've got French windows on to my little paved bit and no garden to worry about. It's wonderful.'

'Well worth getting hit on the head for then,' said Phoebe cheerfully. 'You know what Gussie's always saying! "Out of evil cometh good." Now we've only got Number Five to worry about!'

Thirty-three

NELL'S RECOVERY AND REMOVAL to the Courtyard seemed to give an extra edge to the Midsummer Eve party round the pool. It was obviously all set to become a Nethercombe institution like the Christmas party. The lights were put up and the summer-house swept and refurbished and extra chairs and china were hunted out. Gemma came over early to lend a hand but Sophie – her infatuation for Guy over and with a boyfriend now in the sixth form – was coming later with her parents. Gemma, just home for the holidays from Hungerford where she was at the Norland Nursery Training College, was surprised and rather disconcerted to find Nell living in the Courtyard and horrified by the story of her attack. She seemed unusually subdued and when Guy teased her about it she said that she was missing Chris. Guy was somewhat taken aback. He'd never really taken the idea of Chris very seriously and he felt rather resentful that this unknown man should change Gemma in any way.

He had, as yet, made no attempt to approach Nell again. She still looked so battered and bruised that he hadn't the heart to harass her, although they'd had a few quiet evenings at the pub. He'd been looking forward to seeing Gemma, expecting her to jolly him along and make him laugh, and he felt somehow cheated. At the back of his mind he'd accepted that she had a bit of a crush on him and it was only now, when he seemed in danger of being supplanted by this Chris, that he realised how much he'd counted on it to boost his ego and how much he'd taken it for granted. It seemed something quite apart from his passion for Nell but he didn't stop to analyse it or wonder whether it was fair to encourage Gemma, knowing that his heart belonged to Nell. Since Nell was still taking life gently, Guy decided to draw Gemma out of her preoccupation. After all, she was far too young to be serious about anyone yet. When he told her so she merely looked thoughtful but he soon had her laughing and by the end of the evening she was more like her old self. Guy was inordinately pleased with himself and, when Nell refused – very gently and politely – an invitation to the Church House Inn for one of their delicious Sunday lunches the next morning, Guy had no compunction in seeking Gemma out and asking her instead. She accepted and he was surprised at the relief and pleasure he felt.

AFTER THE PARTY NETHERCOMBE settled back into its calm ordered routines. Gillian, now in her seventh month, was quite glad that the excitement was over and she could relax and, one morning in early July, she wandered out on to the terrace and settled in a shady corner with a book. Gussie was in Totnes and Henry was going up to Higher Nethercombe Farm.

'I've had nothing but people phoning with wrong numbers all morning,' he said, bending to kiss her. 'I should ignore it if it rings, if I were you. See you later.'

When the bell pealed half an hour later, however, Gillian got up and went into the study to answer it, half expecting a call from Lydia. She said the number clearly and a muffled voice asked who was speaking.

'It's Gillian Morley here. Can I help you?'

'I sincerely hope so,' said Sam Whittaker. 'Thank God your old man didn't answer again. I thought I'd never get you!'

Gillian lowered herself into Henry's chair. The blood pounded in her head and her hands shook.

'What do you want?' she whispered. 'I told you I never wanted to see you again.'

'So you did.' He gave the old easy laugh. 'But I want to see you.'

'Why?' asked Gillian desperately. 'It's all over. Finished.'

'No, no. Nothing's that easy. You should know that by now. The echoes go on for ever. Haven't you learned that yet? I need some money, Gillian.'

'I don't care!' she said fiercely. 'I haven't got any money. And if I had I wouldn't give it to you. Can't you find any other poor fools like John to swindle and cheat?'

'I came over to get some money from someone who owed me.' His voice was more urgent now, as though he were running out of time or money. 'Only he's let me down. I've got to get back to France quickly. It's not particularly healthy for me over here as you may have guessed. Don't worry. I shan't keep coming back for more but I must have some to get home. I've tried everyone else. You don't want me to come and knock on the front door, do you? Introduce myself to Henry?'

'He'd pass you straight over to the police,' cried Gillian. 'Make no mistake about that!'

'But not before we'd had a nice long chat.' Sam laughed again. 'Can you imagine it, my darling? Think of the things I could tell him about you. Did he ever know about you and Simon, for instance? And all the money you borrowed? And all the things you told me about him? Remember? About how useless he was in bed . . . ? And of course you've confessed to seducing John?'

'Shut up! Shut up!' Shame swept over her in a scalding tide and sweat made the receiver slippery in her hand. 'Don't you dare come here!'

'So you never had the courage to tell him!' Sam's voice was fat with satisfaction. 'I guessed as much. Well, it's up to you. I need two hundred quid, that's all. And don't tell me you haven't got it. I've seen the spread you've got there. You can find two hundred.'

'You've seen Nethercombe?'

'That worries you, doesn't it? Oh, yes. I've seen it. I'm right here in the thriving metropolis of South Brent. So what are you going to do about it? And be quick. I'm running out of money.'

'OK.' Gillian felt weak with terror at the thought of Sam so close. 'I can find that amount, just about.' She thought quickly. 'Now listen carefully and I'll tell you where we can meet . . .'

She replaced the receiver and sat for some moments, her hands pressed between her knees, her eyes closed. His voice had brought the memories of that dreadful episode sweeping back and she felt sick with shame and humiliation. How could she have behaved so? She'd betrayed Henry and Nell and it struck her that, if any of the people whom she now loved knew about any of the things that she had done, they would turn from her in disgust. The child leaped in her belly as if it, too, repudiated her and would be free of her and she laid her head on the desk and wept bitterly. She'd imagined herself free of it all; that by giving Henry all her love, by trying to make restitution to Nell, the past could be wiped out. What a fool she'd been! Sam was right. Our actions go on echoing and rebounding all through our lives and we can never escape from them. She imagined Sam confronting Henry, the easy laugh, the pleasant voice telling him awful unspeakable things! Gillian writhed in self-disgust and wept until she was exhausted. At last, the sound of Gussie's voice pulled her together and she slipped out of the study and hurried upstairs.

SAM MADE HIS WAY through the network of lanes round Nethercombe and into the woods beyond its boundaries. The river was low in its bed, running sluggishly after the long dry spell, and he worked his way upstream until he came to the stepping stones that Gillian had described. He glanced round him. There was nobody about; even the birdsong seemed muted in the still heat of the afternoon. He looked up quickly as an echoing hooting filled the air and shattered the peace. A train was crossing the viaduct higher up the valley and he watched it for a moment before crossing the stream by the stepping stones. He walked cautiously now, the marshy ground sucking at his shoes as he skirted it, following the path that Gillian had described. It was very overgrown but just discernible and he gradually climbed up through the trees until the path swung round to the right. The ground was clearer here and he found himself at the edge of a little cliff, looking down on the swampy damp ground. He glanced at his watch. He was early but that was just as well. At least he wouldn't be taken by surprise. A woodpigeon clattered out of a nearby tree, startling him, and the sun beating into the clearing was hot. He felt suddenly very tired, as though the nervous energy that had kept him going up to this point had suddenly deserted him.

He sat down on the edge of the little cliff, his legs dangling, pulled his holdall onto his lap and took out the pasty that he'd bought earlier in the village. At the first bite of juicy meat and gravy, he salivated copiously and realised just how hungry he was. He ate with great enjoyment, wishing that he'd bought two pasties, and thought about seeing Gillian again. He'd missed her for a while but he was too busy wheeling and dealing to have time for too many regrets and, after all, there were always women to be had. Sam scrunched up the paper bag and dropped it back in his bag. He knew that he'd completely misjudged Gillian. He'd imagined her to be as ruthless and tough as himself and it had come as a shock to find how wide of the truth his picture had been.

He swore softly under his breath when he thought about John. Bloody fool! As if anything was so bad that you'd need to kill yourself! Even now, with the chips down and his own back to the wall, there was a certain excitement, a buzz, in finding a way out, even if you did have to kick a few people in the teeth to achieve it. And, let's face it, these gullible idiots were simply begging to be stitched up and if lives and relationships were damaged in the process – well, it was too bad. The trouble was that people were getting wise. The word 'scam' had been invented and even the most naïve were beginning to be cautious. There were reports in the newspapers, too, that put the unwary on their guard. He'd got out just in time, no doubt about it, and he'd been crazy to come back. If he hadn't thought that he'd be able to bring it off just one more time, so getting himself out of the shit, he wouldn't have risked it. And then the stupid bastard had dithered and delayed and finally backed off. He'd taken the chance for nothing! Still, nobody knew he was here. He'd travelled by public transport and only Gillian knew where he was. He thought about John again and gave a derisive snort. It was a miracle that he'd managed to kill himself. He was the sort to bungle it and spend the rest of his life as a cabbage, totally dependent and a bloody nuisance to everybody. His wife was well rid of him and Gillian's attack of conscience had been completely over the top. Well, she wouldn't suffer. She'd hardly miss a few hundred quid. Sam shook his head. Having prowled about a bit and seen it for himself, he felt quite flattered to think that she'd been prepared to give Nethercombe up for him. He wondered briefly whether the old charm might work a second time but dismissed the idea almost at once. He didn't want to be lumbered with a woman now, especially one who'd shown herself to have such extraordinarily inconvenient scruples.

Sam stretched his back a little and longed for a cigarette. It had been a choice between a packet of fags or the pasty and he'd decided to be sensible. As soon as Gillian passed over the cash, he'd go back to the village and get a few things before heading back upcountry. He glanced at his watch. She should be here by now. Even as he had the thought, he heard movement in the woods behind him. He sat perfectly still, hardly breathing as he listened, trying to block out the noise of another approaching train. The searing, agonising pain in his back struck him before he could move; the gunshot and his anguished cry both drowned by the rumble of the goods train now rattling noisily and slowly over the viaduct. Sam's instinctive jerk forward sent him over the cliff edge and into the swamp below. The evil-smelling mud filled his nostrils and his screaming desperate open mouth and sucked him greedily, eagerly down and, by the time the train had disappeared, there was silence.

BELLA, THE SPANIEL, QUARTERED the ground above the swamp, her tail wagging enthusiastically. To and fro she went, nose to ground, intent on the scents around her. Mr Ridley followed more slowly, enjoying the sun on his back. He felt sure that he'd hit the rabbit that darted across but he knew that his eyes weren't all that they might be and the thick foliage and the deep shadows made it impossible to judge. He reached the clearing and looked about. Bella still ran questing to and fro but there was no sign of his prey. He moved to the edge of the little cliff and stared down into the viscous turgid mud. There was evidence that the surface had been recently disturbed and he gave a disgruntled sigh.

'Come away, girl,' he said to the still excited Bella. ' 'Twas only an ole rabbit. Knocked 'im in the swamp, I reckon.'

He turned away following the overgrown track that led downstream. Bella remained behind, confused by conflicting scents, but finally gave up and raced breathlessly after him. When he was nearly out of the woods and he could see the sunlit stretches of the meadow ahead, Mr Ridley fired at a wood pigeon on its dipping flight between the trees. The bird soared on, untouched, and, calling to Bella, he climbed the stile into the meadow and turned for home.

GILLIAN SLIPPED OUT THROUGH the orchard and into the woods that clung to the side of the valley. The money was in a pocket of her loose shirt and she kept one hand clutched over it. Years before, steps had been cut in the side of the hill; broad, shallow steps, that led eventually to the floor of the valley where a deep, dark, secret lake lay whose edges ran out into the soggy damp marshy swampland. Gillian descended slowly. She had no intention of falling or doing anything that might damage the life she carried within her. She was about halfway down when she saw movement below her. Her heart beat faster as she peered through the foliage. A horn blared as a goods train rumbled on to the viaduct and, suddenly, between the branches of a great beech, Gillian glimpsed Mr Ridley below her.

She drew back startled. It had never occurred to her that he might be having one of his rare rabbit-potting afternoons down here. Her heart beat strong and fast. Supposing he came across Sam! Gillian locked her hands together and rested her chin upon them, thinking hard. Should she shout out, giving Sam fair warning? Or should she just pray that Sam would be alert and hear him coming? The latter choice seemed the wisest and she stood, straining her ears above the rattle of the train that echoed round the valley. It was impossible to hear anything above the racket and Mr Ridley was out of sight but Gillian stood quite still. The noise of the train, at long last, faded into silence and Mr Ridley could be heard quite clearly now, pushing his way through the underbrush. Slowly, cautiously, Gillian began to descend again. She slid behind a tangle of sallow and listened. If Mr Ridley had come across the meadow and up the stream then he would return by way of the steps. If he did, Gillian knew that there was no way she could avoid him. Even if he didn't see her then Bella, his spaniel, would smell her out. Gillian held her breath, praying that Mr Ridley had come down by the steps and would then return by the meadow. The minutes passed. The noise of his footsteps receded slowly and she started violently when a shot rang out. Birds crashed and clattered out of the undergrowth, complaining vociferously, and Mr Ridley's voice, encouraging Bella, was distant now. Gillian gasped with relief. She guessed that he must be far downstream, almost at the meadow.

She moved out into the open and approached the meeting place. There was no sign of Sam. She stood quite still, waiting, watching, listening; allowing plenty of time for him to see her and approach. There was only silence. At length, Gillian sat down on a nearby fallen tree trunk. Mr Ridley must have frightened him away but surely there had been time, now, for him to creep back? She sat on whilst the minutes ticked by and the sun slipped away behind the trees. Presently she stirred; soon she would be missed. She looked at her watch and shook her head, mystified. He'd sounded so desperate for the money. Gillian stood up and made her way back to the steps. As she ascended, pausing at each one to listen and look around, a new and terrible thought slipped into her mind and terror gripped her entrails. Suppose, after all, he'd changed his mind and had decided to come to the house, to confront Henry and tell him about John? She felt sick with apprehension. If only he'd come and she'd given him the money she'd have felt free of him but now . . . Gillian stood quite still. She'd never be free of him. At any time he could return and deliberately destroy the fabric of her life. As long as she lived, she'd fear the telephone bell, the knock at the door. For the first time, Gillian faced the fact that happiness which is built on falsehood is bound to be ephemeral and terrifyingly fragile. She stared into the bleak future, gripped with misery and despair. There was nothing she could do . . . Or was there?

Folding her arms about her belly, she went slowly up, made her way through the orchard and into the house. She crossed the hall and looked into the study. Henry smiled at her from behind his desk.

'Time for tea?' he asked.

'Not yet.' She swallowed the lump in her throat and smiled back at him, realising at that moment how very dear he was to her. 'I have something to tell you, Henry,' she said and she went inside and closed the door gently behind her.

Thirty-four

LYDIA PUSHED OPEN THE restaurant door and paused to look about her. Elizabeth waved to her from a corner and Lydia threaded her way towards her. As she reached the table and greeted her old friend it struck her, quite suddenly, that Elizabeth was looking her age. It wasn't anything particular, like her hair turning grey or new lines upon her face, but it was there just the same. She looked thinner, more gaunt than elegant. Slightly thrown off balance, Lydia sat down.

'So.' Elizabeth made room for Lydia's shopping bag and her jacket on the third chair. 'How's the grandmother then? I must say you're looking remarkably well on it.'

Confused by her impressions of Elizabeth's own appearance, Lydia smiled, gestured with her hands, shook her head deprecatingly and said nothing at all. Elizabeth raised her eyebrows at her and Lydia pulled herself together.

'I'm loving every minute of it,' she confessed. 'Oh, he is a lovely boy! You know, I've often wondered if I'd feel different, being a grandmother. You know? Whether I'd feel suddenly rather staid or more responsible? And I have to say I don't feel a bit different.'

She opened surprised eyes at Elizabeth who burst out laughing.

'I'm sure that it would take more than a grandchild to change you, Lydia,' she said, but her voice and smile were affectionate and Lydia smiled too.

'I'm so happy,' she said simply.

'So you should be,' said Elizabeth. 'And what is this other thing you have to tell me?' She filled Lydia's glass from a wine bottle already open on the table. 'Let's have a drink first. We'll order in a minute.'

'Well.' Lydia took her glass. Her eyes shone and her cheeks were bright and Elizabeth was struck by how young she appeared. Far from looking like a grandmother, she was more like the girl that Elizabeth had known at school all those many years ago. 'You won't believe this . . .' She paused, took a deep breath and started again. 'You'll probably think I'm a complete idiot . . .' She stopped and took a sip of wine.

'Just say it straight out quickly.' Elizabeth was regarding her with amusement. 'If Gillian wants me to be godmother to the next generation, the answer's no!'

'Oh, it's nothing like that,' Lydia assured her hastily. 'No, no. It's . . . Well, the simple fact is that Charles has asked me to marry him.'

It came out in a sudden rush and Elizabeth gazed at her in surprise.

'Goodness!' she said.

'And I've accepted!' added Lydia defiantly and stared at Elizabeth, her chin raised almost aggressively.

'So I should imagine,' said Elizabeth mildly. 'Why not? I think he's a really nice man.'

'Oh.' Lydia was taken aback.

'I'm delighted,' said Elizabeth sincerely. 'I hope you'll be very happy, Lydia. Shall we drink to it?'

'Oh, yes,' said the disconcerted Lydia, who had expected all sorts of arguments and advice. She picked up her glass again.

'Much happiness, Lydia.' Elizabeth touched Lydia's glass with her own. For once her cool demeanour deserted her and the alarmed Lydia saw a suspicion of tears in her eyes. 'You're very lucky. And so is he.'

She drank and Lydia followed suit, moved by Elizabeth's generosity and obvious emotion.

'Thank you,' she said.

'So when's the great day?' Elizabeth was businesslike once more and Lydia was almost relieved to see that her emotional moment had passed and she was her old self.

'We thought Christmas,' said Lydia, excitement welling up in her again. 'Gillian says they'll be having another Christmas party this year, so we thought just before it would be rather fun. What d'you think?'

'I think it's an excellent plan. And then we can all drink your health at the party.'

'That would be lovely.' Lydia smiled happily. 'And you'll come to the wedding, won't you, Elizabeth? It'll be a very small affair. Just one or two of our closest friends and Gillian and Henry, of course. But I shall want you there.'

'Nothing would keep me from it.'

There was rather an odd expression on her face and Lydia asked the next question more timidly.

'And Richard? Would you like to ask Richard? He'd be most welcome, especially after he stepped in so kindly to give Gillian away.'

There was such a long pause that Lydia wondered if Elizabeth had actually heard the question and fiddled awkwardly with her wine glass. Of course, Elizabeth had always been so touchy about Richard and perhaps, under the circumstances, it wasn't terribly tactful . . .

'No. No, I don't think so.' Elizabeth was smiling at her and Lydia felt relieved. 'Let's keep it to family and close friends. I think that's best. Well, it's wonderful news, Lydia. It's made me feel quite hungry. Let's order, shall we, and then you can tell me all the details.'

GUSSIE WALKED ON THE terrace at Nethercombe in the late October sunshine and praised God for all the blessings of the last few months. Below her, Mr Ridley was giving the lawns a last cut before winter set in and she smiled at the sight of him astride the mower; cap set jauntily, shirtsleeves rolled up in the warm autumn sun. The woods glowed and burned, orange and gold and russet, and the sky was a soft tender blue. The scent of woodsmoke from one of the chimneys in the Courtyard below crept in her nostrils and she felt a deep blessed peace as she stared out, her hands smoothing and stroking the old stone of the balustrade at the edge of the terrace.

How many generations of Morleys, she wondered, had stood here, looking out over their woods and fields and giving thanks for their existence? And now, at least one more generation would do so.

'And such a beautiful child, Lord,' she said, unable to keep her thoughts to herself any longer and wondering if He might like an update. 'And Gillian's taken to motherhood as though she's been doing it for years. And what's more, that reservation in her, Lord, or whatever it was, seems to have completely vanished away. Perhaps it was the baby. But it was more than that, I think. She's had that smoothed-out look, as if some burden has been taken from her. It reminds me of something . . .' Gussie's brow wrinkled and then she smiled. 'You're quite right, Lord,' she said. 'It's the same look that people have when they've been given Absolution. How wonderful it must have been to be alive when Jesus walked this earth. Imagine hearing him say, "Your sins are forgiven you . . . "' She paused as, in turning from her contemplation of the countryside, she came face to face with Mrs Ridley. 'Is it teatime already, Mrs Ridley?'

Mrs Ridley, unperturbed by having her sins forgiven so freely and in public, nodded.

'Gillian thought yew'd like it outside, seein' it's so warm. She's bringin' the baby down.'

'Splendid!'

As Mrs Ridley bustled away, Gussie wondered if it mattered that the formality of her own generation was unlikely to survive the next. It had clung on with Henry but she could see that it was passing away. The important thing was that people continued to love and respect each other; that was what really mattered.

'And if only we could, Lord,' murmured Gussie, 'how happy we could be. "Beloved, let us love one another, for love is of God." If only it were as easy as it sounds.' And she hurried forward to help Mrs Ridley with the tray.

GILLIAN, STANDING AT HER bedroom window, watched Gussie on the terrace below. How long it seemed now since those early days when she'd looked upon Gussie and Mrs Ridley as virtual enemies, to be outwitted and despised. But even the remembrance of her childish stupidity could no longer destroy this new peace which had come upon her once she'd told Henry the whole story of her involvement in John's tragedy.

He'd been quite shocked, there was no doubt about that; sitting first at his desk and then getting up to walk about the room, pausing to stare out of the window over the side lawns which were smelling sweetly of new-mown grass. Gillian knew now that all her life the loveliest of summer smells would always transport her back in time to Henry's study and she would feel again the gut-wrenching sickness of her own terror as she put the weapons of her own destruction, one by one, into Henry's hands. She had told him nothing that would hurt him more than absolutely necessary. She'd decided this on the long walk up from the woods and through the orchard. She would tell him nothing about her affair with Simon who had been Henry's friend or about her shocking betrayals of their most private life together. Trying desperately to be honest with herself, she could see no benefit to Henry in telling him those things. And, if Sam should turn up and accuse her to Henry, then he might well put them down to spite and jealousy. She did, however, tell him the whole extent of her extravagance and the truth about John.

She didn't spare herself. Nor did she fall into the error of being so moved by her own honesty, or so carried away by the simple fact that she'd been brave enough to confess, that she expected forgiveness and even admiration to be automatically conferred upon her. She knew well enough that she was confessing because she would rather Henry heard it from her than anyone else and also in the hope that she could save her marriage. And it had worked. Being Henry, once the shock was past, he forgave simply and wholeheartedly any injury to himself although no one could wholly relieve her of the moral implications of her actions regarding John's death or Nell's losses.

Gillian knew that already. All she could cling to was the fact that Elizabeth had once pointed out to her. She had believed that Sam was genuine and that he intended to use John's money to build the site. John may well have made money from it. She realised that the guilt didn't lie in telling John about the site – anyone might have done that – but in that she'd told him because of her infatuation for Sam and because she needed money. This she would have to live with for the rest of her life; the might-have-beens and the if-onlys that dog our steps and cause us to lie wide-eyed at night, imagining how differently things could have turned out but for those tiny actions.

Henry had seen no point in Gillian confessing to Nell. After all, what benefit could it bring? And might it not add insult to injury to think that John had been talked into it by an attractive woman? All they could do was to continue to look after Nell as far as they were able. At last he'd taken Gillian in his arms and she'd wept without restraint and, anxious lest she damage herself or the baby, he'd hushed her and quietened her, sitting her down in his armchair and pouring her a glass of brandy.

'Why d'you think he didn't come?' She huddled in his chair, sipping at the brandy, trembling with exhaustion and relief.

Henry pursed his lips and shook his head.

'Who can say? Probably lost his nerve. He must feel very uneasy, knowing that he could be picked up, especially in this area. We don't know the extent of all his double-crossings, do we? Perhaps he saw someone who recognised him.' He smiled at her. 'Try not to worry about it. There's nothing he can do to harm us now.'

'Oh, Henry.' Her lips trembled and her eyes filled with tears. 'I'm so sorry.'

'Now, no more tears.' Henry came to crouch beside her. He pulled out an extremely grubby handkerchief and mopped inexpertly at her cheeks. 'It's all over. I'm so glad that you were able to tell me.'

'So am I. I love you, Henry.'

'And I love you. And now you should rest. You've had a terrible day and we can't afford for anything to happen to either of you. Come along.' He helped her to her feet. 'Up to bed with you. If he turns up here I'll deal with him. You've removed his sting and rendered him harmless. You know, I doubt if he ever meant to come here. The risk was far too great. He was counting on your sense of guilt.'

'Yes, I see that now.' She smiled up at him rather tremulously. 'I was so afraid. I've got so much to lose now, Henry. I simply couldn't take that chance.'

'Bless you for that.' He kissed her and went upstairs with her and helped her into bed.

She lay awake for a while, watching the shadows lengthening, tensing each time a door shut or voices were raised, but at length weariness overtook her and she slept.

Now, three months later, her heart was full of love and gratitude. She turned from the window as she saw Mrs Ridley going out to Gussie and went along the passage and into the nursery.

Thomas Henry Augustus Morley lay on his back. His eyes were wide open and his tiny fists waved spasmodically. Gillian watched him for a moment and then picked him from his cot and held him in her arms. She cuddled him closely, studying his minute features whilst his eyes gradually focused on her face.

'It's teatime,' she told him and could see him listening to her now-familiar voice. 'Which is an old British tradition and one which I shall expect you to continue to uphold.'

He mewed and struck out at her face.

'Don't argue with me,' she told him and laughed at herself.

Kissing him tenderly, she laid him in his carrycot and took him down to the terrace. Gussie had placed two chairs side by side and

Gillian laid the cot across them. Gussie bent over him and Gillian marvelled anew at her restraint where Thomas was concerned. She knew very well that Gussie sometimes longed to snatch him up and cuddle him but she never attempted to usurp Gillian's position or trade on her own. She always asked permission before she performed any task for him and never gave advice.

'Pick him up,' said Gillian off-handedly. 'Go on. I expect he'd like a little look round. I changed him just now so he should be respectable.'

She wandered over to the tray and started to pour the tea, keeping her back to Gussie so that she might be as emotional as she liked without witnesses. She instinctively knew that Gussie's overwhelming love for the child often took the elderly reserved woman by surprise and that the baby was a whole new shattering experience to her. The way she held him – awkwardly, tenderly, full of awe – was quite different from Lydia's experienced relaxed hugs and cuddles and Gillian had often caught Gussie watching Thomas and his grandmother with an expression of heart-rending envy on her face. Gillian was determined that Gussie should feel as involved and as necessary as Lydia and, whenever she could, she encouraged Gussie to pick Thomas up and talk to him.

'I think he's beginning to know your voice,' she said, strolling back with her cup.

'D'you really think so?' Gussie stared into the baby's face, opened her mouth to say that he was all Morley and shut it again. 'He does seem to be looking at me.'

'Of course he is. You are his favourite aunt, after all.'

'Oh, well . . .' Gussie's mouth worked a little and she turned away, pretending to show Thomas the view from the terrace.

'With me and Henry being only children, he's lucky to have a ready-made aunt already in situ.'

Mrs Ridley, on the pretext of forgetting the cake, appeared in the doorway. 'Cake,' she said unnecessarily, her eyes straying to Gussie.

'And lucky to have Mrs Ridley,' added Gillian, sitting down and cutting herself a piece of cake. 'I'm such a rotten cook that he'd probably starve to death.'

'Poor little tacker,' said Mrs Ridley, as though this had already happened.

She sidled a little closer and looked at Thomas over Gussie's bony shoulder. Gussie moved slightly so that they could share this wonderful moment and Thomas mewed and squeaked and gave a loud sudden yawn. Gillian watched the two heads together and smiled to herself. How simple and natural it seemed to be, now, to bring pleasure and happiness to those around her. She thought of how easily she might have missed all this and felt quite cold with horror. She wondered where Sam had got to on that July day and where he was now. She suspected that Henry's guess had been right; that Sam had seen someone he knew and had been obliged to run for it. She no longer feared the knock at the door or the peal of the telephone bell and was glad that she'd been spared the meeting with him.

She knew deep inside that it was all over and in her great happiness could even hope that Sam was safe somewhere. She'd loved him once, he'd been part of her and that, too, would go on with her through her life. She thought of the happy moments; of Sam, relaxed, loving her, and felt a strange sharp sadness and hoped that nothing had happened to him on his flight back to France.

She pushed aside her forebodings as she heard Henry's baritone echoing in the hall and turned to smile at him as he came out through the door and into the sunshine.

Thirty-five

JUST AS NELL'S REMOVAL to the Courtyard and her recovery from the attack gave an edge to the Midsummer's Eve party at Nethercombe, so Lydia's wedding lifted the Christmas party on to a higher level of excitement.

The only tiny cloud on Nell's horizon was her unresolved relationship with Guy and, although each time she saw him she meant to make it quite clear that she could never marry him, somehow it never quite got said. They had slipped into a rather strange relationship which seemed to be waiting for something to happen before the next phase could be embarked upon. Guy was sometimes away for weeks at a time. In the winter he supplemented his income by moving boats for people and these extended absences helped to keep the friendship in a rather static situation.

Nell, too, was very busy. Elizabeth had no compunction in putting more and more on to her plate – 'throwing you in at the deep end,' as she called it – and Nell, far from finding this daunting, seemed to thrive on it and rise to greater and greater heights with each new challenge. She was loving every minute of it and was overwhelmed with gratitude that – through Gillian – Elizabeth had given her this chance. With so many friends surrounding them she was able to continue working even when Jack was at home. He'd come home for Christmas positively glowing with the importance of being a godfather. He'd already been introduced to his godson at half-term and had been busy at school making him a wooden horse in his wood-work class. It was surprisingly good and Gillian was deeply touched. So was Gussie when he went to her to discuss the religious duties implicit in being a godfather. He had been confirmed at school that term and was taking the whole thing very seriously. Gussie promised that she would look into it and, in his absence, keep an eye on Thomas. They solemnly agreed that he was a little young at present for any formal instruction and Jack had to content himself with studying the Publick Baptism of Infants in Gussie's Book of Common Prayer in preparation for the great day at the end of the Christmas holidays.

Phoebe came upon him circling the swimming pool and reciting quietly to himself.

'You sound like Gussie,' she said, falling in beside him. 'Having a quiet word with Him Upstairs?'

'I'm learning my responses,' he told her seriously. 'Everyone else will have done it before, I expect, and I don't want to look a twit. Gillian says that I can hold Thomas when we're at the font and I shall need to concentrate on him and I may not be able to manage a book at the same time. So I'm reading it up. It all began with Noah, you know. I didn't realize that.'

'Neither did I,' said Phoebe, mystified. 'Mind you! I've always had a lot of time for Noah. Must've been a pretty big boat to get that lot in and he built it all on his own. Or so I understand. I must remind. Guy of that next time he starts whingeing about moving a forty-foot boat without assistance. At least he hasn't got a zoo breathing down his neck at the same time.'

'And then there was Moses and John the Baptist, said Jack, refusing to be sidetracked by Phoebe's meanderings down this interesting byway. 'I have to renounce the devil and all his works and the vain pomp and glory of the world, as well as the carnal desires of the flesh. I have to say, "I renounce them all."'

'Golly!' said Phoebe, deeply impressed. 'That's a bit stiff, isn't it? Doesn't really leave you much scope, does it? Life'll be a bit flat, I should have thought.'

'It's only till Thomas is old enough to renounce them for himself,' Jack assured her. 'That'll be when he gets confirmed.'

'That's a comfort,' said Phoebe, relieved.

'It doesn't really matter much,' said Jack. 'I've just been confirmed so I've had to take the vows anyway.'

'Sounds a bit tough to me,' admitted Phoebe. 'Which d'you think you'll find the hardest? The pomp and glory of the world? Or the carnal desires of the flesh? What was the other one?'

'The devil and all his works.' Jack sighed. 'I don't quite know. It'll probably get more difficult as I get older.'

Phoebe nodded thoughtfully and sucked air through her teeth. Jack looked at her a little anxiously.

'D'you find it very difficult? Or are you too old to really worry any more?' he asked.

Phoebe expelled her breath, shook her head consideringly, and shrugged. 'Sometimes yes. Sometimes no,' she said.

'There's a lot to be said for stocking up beforehand. You know? Getting it out of the system young. At least you've got something to look back on when you're twenty or so. Got an idea! I don't know that I can do much about the carnal desires of the flesh but why don't we go into Brent and get a few videos and a fourpack from Val and Ian and make an evening of it?'

'A *fourpack!*'

'You're right. Two fourpacks.'

'Really? Gosh! Can we?'

'We certainly can. Come on. You've got an awful lot to fit in before the end of December. We may as well get started.'

'Gosh!' said Jack again. He tried to decide whether fourpacks and videos came under the heading of the devil and all his works or the vain pomp and glory of the world and gave it all up with a certain amount of relief. 'Thanks.'

He grinned up at her expectantly and they hurried through the little gate and set off down the drive together.

GUY, BACK FROM A few weeks away, was surprised at how happy he was to return to the Courtyard. It was a pleasant scene at dusk; lights twinkling from the windows and smoke rising gently into the frosty air. The moon sailed serenely behind the black outlines of the bare trees and the owl drifted from the woods, his call plaintive and strangely eerie.

It was such an evening – or late afternoon – when, returning from a stroll along the beech walk, he saw Gemma hurrying across the bottom of the drive. It looked as if she had been to his cottage and, finding it empty, was going away. His feeling of disappointment that he should miss her was unbelievably sharp and he let out a loud shout which made Bertie jump. Gemma either didn't hear or ignored the call and hurried over to where her car was parked. Guy raced down the last few yards, his feet slipping and sliding on the gravel whilst Bertie skittered from side to side, ears flattened, trying to keep out of his way. As he came level with the entrance to the Courtyard, Gemma's little car was just backing out of the space allocated to Guy's visitors and he ran towards her, waving his arms. Still she didn't seem to see him but pulled away and vanished down the drive and out into the lane.

Guy stood perfectly still, a prey to several different emotions. He was confused by his disappointment and the other quite unreasonable feeling of rejection and hurt, as if she had deliberately ignored him and had been trying to avoid him. Why on earth should she come into the Courtyard if she didn't wish to see him? He wondered if she'd put a note through his door and dashed over to his cottage, feeling in his pocket for his key. There was a note, lying on the mat; a folded piece of paper. He snatched it up and his eyes flew over it.

Dear Guy,

Just to say that I shan't be over this holiday. I suspect that I'm
a bit of a nuisance to you and you've been very sweet about it but
I won't bother you any more. Chris will be home for Christmas
and I've decided that it might be more sensible to concentrate on
him. We'll still be friends, won't we? It's been fun.

Love, Gemma.

Guy was back out of the door in a flash, stuffing the note into his
pocket, urging Bertie into the back of the car, leaping in, turning and
racing down the drive with spurts of gravel flying from beneath the
wheels. He knew just which way she would go and he turned the car
on to the Ivybridge road and headed for Cornwood. As he drove
across the moor, his brain reeled as it grappled with his thoughts. It
was as though a curtain had been ripped away in his mind and he saw
what an unutterable idiot he'd been. He realised that his determined
adulation for Nell had blinded him to the glaringly obvious truth. He
thought of the pleasure he felt when he saw Gemma, the comfort and
confidence she gave him, the ease and happiness he experienced in her
company. It was Gemma, the real flesh and blood girl with her teasing loving ways, that he loved; not the dream that he'd built round the
ethereal Nell and which he'd persisted in keeping fixed before his
eyes. Oh, yes! Nell was beautiful, vulnerable, alone. And that had
woken his chivalrous tendencies and made him believe that he was in
love with her. He'd been like a sixteen-year-old, infatuated by a film
star; there was no reality in it. He knew, now, why he'd been unable
to imagine Nell in the role of mistress and wife. As he drove, he put
Gemma into the role with no difficulty at all. His heart started to
pound furiously and he hit the steering wheel several times with his
clenched fist.

'Fool!' He cursed himself aloud and Bertie cowered in the back,
scrabbling to keep his balance as the car fled round corners and up
hills.

He was out beyond Wotter before he saw her taillights and he drew close up behind the little hatchback and flashed his lights at her. Still she drove on without slackening her speed and finally, in desperation, he overtook her on the long stretch before Cadover Bridge. He glimpsed her startled face as he flashed past, his two offside wheels bumping over the moorland, and then he pulled in front of her car and gradually slowed down until she was obliged to stop. He was out of the car and opening her door before she had even grasped that it was him and she gave a cry of relief as he hauled her out of the car.

'Guy! I didn't realise it was you. I wondered whatever was going on!'

'Why did you go away?' he demanded, holding her shoulders and giving her a little shake. 'Didn't you hear me shouting to you?'

'I left you a note,' she said evasively, looking up at him rather shyly. She pushed the hair out of her eyes. 'I put it through the door.'

'I saw it,' said Guy contemptuously. 'Never saw such rubbish in my life.'

'Was it rubbish?' she asked and he bent suddenly and kissed her. His blood raced and he felt dizzy and weak and clutched her to him, her face crushed into his shoulder.

'Absolute bloody rubbish,' he mumbled against her hair. 'But it was my fault. I've been a grade-A monumental fool.' He swallowed hard, pushed away his instinctive urge for self-preservation and caution and spoke the simple truth. 'I love you.'

She strained away from him, peering at him in the fast-fading light.

'Oh, Guy. Really and truly? I love you, too. I have for ages. Years.'

He laughed and held her close. 'Since you were in your pram? I'm delighted to hear it. No more rubbish about Chris then.' And he bent and kissed her again.

Presently she realised that she was shivering.

'What shall we do?' she asked, her eyes enormous with love. 'We're halfway between the Courtyard and the Rectory. D'you want to come back with me? The boys are home for Christmas.'

'No,' said Guy at once, who had no desire to face the Wivenhoes *en masse* whilst he was feeling so unlike himself. He needed to get used to these feelings and to be alone with Gemma. 'Could you bear to come back with me now? I'll drive you home later on and I'll come and fetch you tomorrow so that you can get the car.'

'Or,' said Gemma, with her familiar provocative grin. 'I could stay the night with you. I'm sure Ma and Pa would understand. Us all being such old friends.'

'You'll do nothing of the sort,' said Guy, his old puritanical instincts coming to the fore. 'It would be all over Nethercombe in minutes. We'll wait.'

'Heavens!' said Gemma in mock dismay. 'I'm not sure I can. How long do you suggest?'

'I've been thinking.' He grinned at her. 'I'm going down to pick up a boat from Fowey just after Christmas. Like to come along?'

'Love to. As long as you don't order me about too much!'

They kissed again and Guy hesitated as they prepared to climb back into their respective cars.

'Gemma?' She paused, one foot inside. 'You know that I'm asking you to marry me, don't you?'

She grinned and shook her head at him.

'And about bloody time, too!' she said.

BY THE TIME THE party actually took place, everyone was on a high. Guy had gone to Nell and told her the truth, praying that she wouldn't be hurt and upset. Part of him knew that she'd never been in love with him and that it was only because she hated to hurt his feelings that she had tried to keep him at arm's length. Nevertheless he felt very nervous and foolish. She embraced him warmly, wished him luck and told him that she was delighted.

'Apart from anything else,' she told him, 'I'm far too old for you. And, anyway, I've discovered this latent urge to become a career woman.'

They parted with a good deal of warmth and enormous relief on both sides and settled down to enjoy Christmas.

Lydia's wedding took place three days before the party and the celebrations seemed to continue right up to the night of the party and well into it. Everyone was happy for her and Charles fitted into the Nethercombe scene with no trouble at all. He'd assumed his role as step-grandfather with amazing aplomb and had enjoyed a long conversation with Jack about the Army.

'Some women get all the luck, that's all I can say,' said Phoebe, sitting down beside Elizabeth as the evening of the party wore on. 'He's rather a sweetie. After all, what's she got that we haven't got?' She looked at Elizabeth and was shocked to see the pain in her eyes.

'A great deal more in the way of curves,' answered Elizabeth lightly and they both laughed.

'I can't believe that it's a year since we sat here,' mused Phoebe. 'And what a year! Babies, weddings, engagements! And I can't get over Guy. Love has done him no good at all. I simply can't get a rise out of him. He smiles and agrees with everything I say. It's positively sickening!'

'Some of us simply can't deal with it,' agreed Elizabeth and Phoebe was struck once again by the sad expression on her face.

She studied her covertly and noticed that she'd lost a lot of weight since she'd seen her last. The lines on her face were more pronounced and she looked much older.

Man trouble! thought Phoebe and began to clap with everyone else as Charles could be seen climbing on to a chair, preparatory to making a speech. They'd already had some speeches, toasting the new heir to Nethercombe – Jack, very flushed and proud – and Gemma and Guy's engagement – Guy, also very flushed and proud – and everyone was in the mood for more.

'You've all been very patient,' Charles began, amidst cheers, 'and I shan't keep you long' – boos of disbelief – 'but we have just one more announcement to make.' Cries of 'Get on with it!' 'It's simply that Lydia and I have bought a small house in Exeter and we invite you all to our house-warming party. But not until Elizabeth has wrought a transformation on the house which is in need of a great deal of care and attention. You will all be notified in due course. Please watch this space.'

Phoebe, cheering with the rest, was surprised to see tears on Elizabeth's cheeks as she turned to smile at her.

'Dear Lydia,' said Elizabeth and shook her head. 'Forgive me. I'm just so happy for her. For you all.'

Phoebe smiled uncertainly but, before she could reply, she was being hauled to her feet by William Hope-Latymer who wanted her to meet someone and she could only glance back apologetically over her shoulder before she was borne off into the crowd.

Thirty-six

ONCE THE BAPTISM OF Thomas was over – and Jack had played his part with tremendous aplomb – the inhabitants of Nethercombe found themselves looking forward to the housewarming party at the newly renovated house in Exeter. After some consideration, Lydia and Charles decided to wait until the Easter holidays arrived before the celebration took place. The Beresfords would be down, Jack and Gemma home from their respective seats of learning and everyone could be assembled once again under one roof for another party.

The only person with misgivings at this time was Nell. Everyone seemed so happy, so settled, and Nell found herself envying their security. She reminded herself of what Guy had said on this subject, finding comfort in the fact that she at least had a job with a good income. Nevertheless she would often lie awake at night wondering what on earth she would do if the owner of her cottage decided to move in himself and asked her to leave. Of course, she could always go back to the Lodge. As yet, Henry had made no attempt to relet it but he wouldn't leave it empty for ever. She still had nightmares about her attack, seeing that burly shadowy figure with its arm raised menacingly, wondering if, even in the ultimate crisis, she could ever live there alone again. Moving into Nethercombe simply wasn't an option and there was no way, yet, that she could even begin to think about buying her own home, however humble. Most of the time she was able to push these fears to one side but very often, when she was in one or other of the Courtyard cottages, she envied the owner's ability to decorate as he or she pleased and to change or alter things without permission. Having learned so much from Elizabeth, she longed to try out her own ideas without restraint but she knew that she must wait patiently and be grateful for what she had.

Elizabeth was putting more and more responsibility into her hands now and Nell was beginning to wonder whether she was, at last, seriously thinking of retirement. After all, that was why she had offered Nell the job in the first place and over a year had passed since she'd started to work with her. Nell felt surprisingly confident at the thought of running the business – Elizabeth would still be there in the background – but she knew that she would miss her dreadfully in the day-to-day meetings and consultations and during their trips together. She had found a real friend and she gratefully treasured their moments together. The holiday she'd spent with Elizabeth in Italy was one of the happiest times of her life and this new relationship was doing so much to reconcile her to her grief and loss.

As Easter approached, Elizabeth talked of going to Italy again but this time she didn't invite Nell to go with her. Nell began to wonder if she might be going with someone else and suspected that it might be Richard. She'd met him several times and had been much struck by his distinguished looks and good-mannered charm. She discovered that he was Elizabeth's accountant, which explained certain things but not others. She began to feel quite sure that theirs was more than just a business relationship and longed to know what kept them apart. It would never have occurred to her to broach the subject, any more than she expected Elizabeth to discuss it with her. They were both reticent women who respected the other's privacy but Nell noticed enough small incidents to make her feel that change was imminent.

A few days before Elizabeth was due to leave for Italy, Nell arrived to see her at home to receive some last-minute instructions. She was rather earlier than she expected and parked behind a Rover which she was fairly certain belonged to Richard. She had hardly left her own car when the front door opened and Richard came out. He seemed in a great hurry and barely paused to greet her. His face was strangely twisted, almost, thought Nell, as though he were trying to hold back tears. He certainly appeared to be in the grip of some strong emotion and Nell looked after him quite anxiously as he drove somewhat erratically down the drive.

'Nell.' Elizabeth was standing on the step above her. 'You're early. That's good. We've lots to get through.'

'Right.' Nell followed her inside, wondering whether to draw attention to Richard's distress but as usual, when confronted by Elizabeth's cool facade, she found that she was unable to mention anything so personal.

They were soon immersed in the lists of things which Nell would be required to deal with during Elizabeth's absence and the various clients she would be expected to see and Richard was forgotten. Nell noticed, however, that Elizabeth was less poised than usual and her face held traces of strain. She wondered if they'd quarrelled or whether Elizabeth was going to Italy with someone else and Richard was jealous. Whatever it was, there was no doubt that Elizabeth was not looking her best.

'This holiday will do you good,' said Nell impulsively. 'You must relax in the sun and eat lots of lovely Italian food.'

'Do I understand by this that I look haggard and thin?' wondered Elizabeth and smiled at Nell's quick flush of embarrassment. 'Don't worry! I know I do. Lydia told me quite plainly last week that I look ninety. I had the tiniest suspicion that she was rather pleased about it!'

They both laughed and Nell shook her head.

'That's nonsense, of course. She must be sad that you'll miss her house-warming party, especially after all the advice you've given her. It looks wonderful now. I love their new house.'

'Better than your own?' asked Elizabeth, passing the folders of work across to Nell and sitting back in her chair.

'Oh, no.' Nell put the folders on the floor beside her and relaxed too. 'Now that I've settled in, I really love my little place. They're all so different, you know, that it's difficult to choose between them but I think mine's in the best position. It gets the most sun and my little terrace at the back is quite private. No.' She sighed deeply. 'My one terror is that the owner will want to move into it himself. I'm praying that he's bought it as an investment and that I'll be able to stay there for ever.'

'For ever's a long time,' remarked Elizabeth lightly. She leaned to place a log on the fire. The evenings were drawing out but it was remarkably cold. 'You don't find it difficult, living in such close proximity to other people?'

'No,' said Nell thoughtfully, 'it surprises me to say it, but I don't. They're all so sweet and they seem to understand that, simply because we do live at such close quarters, privacy has to be respected.'

'That's good.' Elizabeth sat back again in her chair, her face in shadow. 'No regrets then?'

'What, about moving down to the Courtyard? Oh, no.' Nell shook her head decisively. 'And after my attack, I would have been terrified to stay at the Lodge alone.'

'And what about coming in with me?'

Nell stared at her for a moment and then laughed. 'Regrets?' She shook her head. 'You must be joking. It's the best thing that's ever happened to me. I shall never be able to thank you enough.'

'Splendid.'

There was a moment of silence and Nell wondered if she should now mention Richard. She'd never had quite such an intimate talk with her before and she wondered if Elizabeth had been upset by whatever had happened earlier and would have liked to speak about it.

'Are you . . . ?' She cast about for ways of furthering this precious moment without sounding inquisitive. 'Shall you be staying with friends? You seem to know so many people in Italy. And, of course, you speak the language. I was very impressed.'

Elizabeth was silent and Nell was frightened that she'd gone too

far. She sat quite still, her face still shadowed, and Nell seized desperately on the first thing that came into her head.

'Perhaps we'll go together again one day? I should like that so
much. Perhaps next spring? It was so beautiful in the spring. But I
should need you to help me along. I'd be useless on my own.' She
stopped, hearing her foolish words ringing on in the peace of the gracious room, now filled with the last golden light of the day.

'I'm afraid not, my dear.' Elizabeth spoke at last and her voice was
sad. 'I'm dying. I have only a few weeks left to live and I intend to
spend them in Italy. I've good friends there who will help me painlessly
out of the life I have left to me. I shan't see you again after today.'

The terrible words, so calmly spoken, quite paralysed Nell, who
sat staring into the shadows that were thickening about Elizabeth's
chair. Presently she shook her head, as a child might, dumbly rejecting something which it simply cannot or will not believe. She swallowed once or twice and her throat was restricted and dry. She heard
Elizabeth sigh.

'Poor Nell. Perhaps I shouldn't have told you. It's been a very difficult decision but I felt the shock would be even greater if it had come
from Richard afterwards. He knows, of course.'

'I thought there was something . . .' Nell's voice was husky but
she had gained some measure of control and had no intention of con-
tributing to Elizabeth's burden by adding her own outburst of grief to
it. 'He will miss you dreadfully.' She felt, even more now, the desire
to give Elizabeth the opportunity to speak if she so wished.

'We've missed each other all our lives.' Nell heard rather than saw
the sad smile in Elizabeth's voice. 'Naturally enough he regrets all the
lost and wasted moments. There have been many of those in this last
year, I'm sad to say. It's always thus. It's too much to expect a poor
human being to be able to live every moment as though it were his
last. That's the only way that there can be no regrets.'

She was silent for a moment and when she spoke again her voice
was brisk and cool. 'The business is yours, of course, with enough

money to keep it going until you're fully confident. Richard will go into it all quite carefully with you. Don't worry! He'll keep you on the straight and narrow. You can trust him absolutely.'

Nell realised that the rare and all too brief moment of intimacy was over and that Elizabeth was expecting her to behave as though everything was back to normal. Nell accepted the challenge proudly. It was the least she could do for Elizabeth now.

'I hope that I can live up to your trust in me,' she said and was relieved to hear that her voice shook only very slightly. 'I hope that you realise that you've given me a future, a career? Because of you I'm independent. And terribly happy.'

Her voice broke on that last word and Elizabeth rose swiftly to her feet. Nell got up, too, grateful that the room was in virtual darkness, lit only by the flames of the fire.

'I shan't ask you to stay to tea, my dear. It would be too much to ask of either of us. One of my great sadnesses is that I shall never know you better. But being able to pass into your hands everything I've worked for gives me a tremendous satisfaction. Goodbye, Nell.' Elizabeth took both her hands and kissed her lightly on the cheek. 'Be happy, my dear. And good luck. Please go quickly.'

Nell went quickly; picking up the folders, hurrying out through the hall, stumbling down the steps, climbing into the car. She fought to hold back her tears as she drove through the darkening lanes; dry sobs escaping from her closed throat, exclamations of pain bursting from her pent-up heart. All those who had died from her seemed now to be travelling with her in this lonely little capsule, hurtling along the familiar roads; she heard Rupert's teasing voice in her ears, saw John's pleading face before her eyes and felt again the intolerable ache for her dead baby. And now Elizabeth would soon join them. 'Remember me when I am gone away, Gone far away into the silent land.'

She turned in between the stone pillars at the bottom of the drive, fled past the Courtyard, up the drive and pulled up outside Nethercombe. She left the car and went into the hall where she paused. The voices of Gillian and Henry could be heard beyond the library door and, after a moment, Nell passed on swift feet up the staircase and came to a halt at Gussie's door. She heard a low murmuring within and turned the handle.

'Nell, my dear! What a lovely surprise.' Gussie peered at her over the top of her spectacles and got quickly to her feet. 'Whatever is the matter, my dear? It's not Jack?'

'No. Oh, no.' The sobs were beginning to tear themselves from her chest. 'Oh, Gussie . . .'

Gussie sat down in her chair with a bump, her hand pressed to her heart. 'Thank goodness. Then what is it? Oh, my dear . . .'

Nell ran the last few steps and fell on her knees at Gussie's side. The tears were pouring unchecked now and Gussie gathered her to her breast, concealing her own terror, stroking. Nell's hair as though she were a child.

'Hush, my dear. Hush, now. Tell me what's happened?'

'Elizabeth's dying, Gussie. She's going to Italy to die.' Sobs burst from her afresh as Gussie sat quite still, staring over her head. 'Oh, whatever shall I do? Everyone I love dies. How shall I manage without her? I'd just begun to love her . . .'

Gussie sat on, holding Nell to her heart while she poured out her grief, and their tears mingled as they mourned together.

ELIZABETH WENT BACK INSIDE and shut the door behind her. She felt drained and limp. Richard's desperate outburst, cut mercifully short by Nell's arrival, had exhausted her. She'd watched his shock, listened to his pleadings that he should come with her to Italy, comforted him when he wept, as if she were distanced from his pain. The knowledge of the terrible, ineluctable advance of her own death had put a barrier between her and those who were closest to her.

She stood in the hall, listening to the silence of the house which was disturbed only by the weighty ticking of the grandfather clock, and wondered who would come after her. Who would cherish her

beautiful things which had been so lovingly cared for during her life-
time? Who would sit in her quiet drawing room, work in her kitchen,
wander through the garden? Gillian would inherit it all and, although
Nethercombe would easily swallow the lovely pieces of furniture, the
house must either be sold or rented.

Elizabeth went back to the drawing room and put some more logs
on the fire. She always felt cold now. Her thoughts ran on. Perhaps
Gillian and Henry would keep it as a dower house, to retire into
when Thomas took over at Nethercombe. She sat down, pulling her
chair closer to the fire. She would never know and it really couldn't
matter less. The line from the Burial Service crept into her mind.
'We brought nothing into this world, and it is certain that we can
carry nothing out.' Elizabeth stretched her thin hands to the leaping
flames. Her belongings had given her comfort; more comfort perhaps
than other people had ever brought her. She knew in her heart that
the blessings of human relationships had never been for her. It would
be easy to look back now and imagine that she had missed out on the
most important things, had sacrificed passion in order to maintain
and protect her peace and privacy. Elizabeth knew, however, that the
warm, messy muddle of human love could never have made up for the
peace that comes with solitude or the satisfaction given by achievement wrought solely by one's own efforts and talent.

How well Gillian had developed over the last year and how determined that her own inheritance should be diminished in order to
make reparation to Nell! Elizabeth had been only too pleased to be
persuaded to arrange certain things to Nell's advantage and had been
touched to see both Gillian's relief and her indifference to her own
subsequent loss, although she had no idea that the result of her generous pleadings would take effect so quickly. And how amazing that
Gillian's own muddles had brought her Nell! Elizabeth shook her
head in relieved gratitude. Her business had been her child, lover,
friend; into it she had poured all the very essence of herself. To have
known that it would simply vanish or pass into the hands of strangers

would have hurt far more than the thought of her house inhabited by others and her belongings dispersed or sold. The business was herself; her ideas, her creations, her original concepts would all be going on now, in Nell's caring, sensitive hands. In this she would be thought about, remembered, missed. It was enough.

How brave Nell had been, how determined to keep her emotion to herself, to spare Elizabeth the extra pain and the draining of energy which would have been required to comfort her. Elizabeth took the soft light shawl that hung on the back of the chair and wrapped herself in it. Richard had shown no such consideration, had no thought of saving her at the expense of his own grief. His remorse for the coolness which he had allowed to develop between them in the last year had been overwhelmingly distressing. He would probably never be able to forgive her for not making the final, ultimate sacrifice. Elizabeth sighed and lay back in the chair. She knew it would never have been enough and would only have served to destroy the precious friendship they'd shared.

Had she been right to hold out against him? She would never know that either. It was too late. Too late . . . The words, echoing in her head, struck a chill to her heart and she had to fight back weak tears. She huddled the shawl more closely around her, trying to ignore her ever-present companion of pain, and presently she slept.

Thirty-seven

GILLIAN, WHEELING THOMAS ALONG the beech walk, was beginning to learn that true happiness was rarely unalloyed. Her delight in her son was accompanied by an ever-present tiny fear; supposing something should happen to him, some accident or illness blot out his small breath of life? When she stroked his soft skin, smoothed his feather-like hair, caressed his perfect limbs, dreadful visions possessed her. She saw him crushed, ill, dead, and was able to enter even more fully into Nell's anguish at the loss of her child. Gillian cradled Thomas in her arms and imagined Nell's sufferings. She knew that she would never be able to forget her part in the tragedy and that her life would always be inexplicably wound up in Nell's.

Gillian walked slowly, looking up at the new tender soft green of the unfurling beech leaves. She realised that it was terribly important to keep things in proportion, knowing, now, how close madness lay beneath the surfaces of the human mind. When she watched television or read the newspapers she imagined Thomas behind the faces of children ravaged by war, disease or evil and her heart was wrenched with agony and rage and fear. How fragile human life was, how transitory: a single stroke and it was gone for ever. Even her own life was more precious now. She found herself afraid to take risks lest she be rendered incapable of caring for him or watching over him or, by dying, be deprived of sharing in his life.

She took a deep breath and concentrated on the calm warm beauty of the day, on the clear blue of the sky and the billowy white clouds that floated gently above the budding branches of the great trees. What a comfort Gussie had been to her! That pragmatic acceptance of life as it was, and her ability to take each moment as a gift and live in it absolutely, gave Gillian confidence and hope. She was learning to concentrate on the positive and the good, knowing that at this moment it was right for her and for her family. Passive acceptance does not right wrongs but there are times when its healing calm is necessary for the mind and soul.

A loud hail disturbed her thoughts and she saw Phoebe coming towards her. Gillian's spirits rose. Phoebe was another person whose presence dispersed gloomy thoughts. She waved.

'What a day!' Phoebe blew out her lips appreciatively. 'Even I was compelled to come out and walk in it. I must say, Gillian, that it's very generous of you and Henry to allow us all to come tramping through your grounds. Don't you ever regret giving us permission? Did you think, "Oh hell! There's that old bat coming. I'll have to be sociable!"? You can be honest with me, you know.'

Gillian was laughing. 'Not a bit of it. Quite the reverse actually. We've got our own part if we want to be private and it's nice to see you. I can be a bit broody at the moment, if I'm not careful.'

'Goodness!' Phoebe stared at her in alarm. 'You're not thinking of having another one just yet, I hope?'

'We-ell.' Gillian looked rather wistful. 'I wouldn't mind, actually.'

'Hear that, Tonks!' Phoebe peered into the pram. 'Make the most of it, my boy! Your days of adulation and worship will soon be over, such is the fickle way of the world.'

'Oh, I shall give him a bit longer but I know Henry would love a little girl.'

They began to stroll back together.

'It would probably be sensible,' said Phoebe. 'After all, with all these worshippers, he might well get spoiled if we're not careful. It's a miracle that no one falls out over him.'

'It's wonderful,' said Gillian fervently. 'I must say that I've had one or two anxious moments but it's all worked out wonderfully. Mum's great with him. Terribly loving but not the least bit possessive.'

'Well, of course she's got the Major to concentrate on, hasn't she? Rather a feat, becoming a wife and a grandmother all in one fell swoop. She's handling it all splendidly.'

Thomas woke up and began to croon to himself. Gillian moved to sit him up, propped about by pillows. He gazed at them both and smiled benevolently. Phoebe grinned.

'What a love he is,' she said, 'and how glad I am that I'm not the maternal sort. It must be agony.'

'It can be,' said Gillian, surprised by her perspicacity. 'You can get a bit obsessed.'

They set off again, Thomas waving his arms and crowing loudly with pleasure.

'I can well imagine. Still, he'll grow up with lots of friends. Very wise of you to give him a young godparent as well as the two older ones. They'll be good chums. The age gap will be nothing when they're older. By the way. How's Elizabeth? Is she still in Italy?'

'As far as I know. She's been gone a month but she really needed a break.'

'She was looking a bit seedy at Christmas,' agreed Phoebe as they came out on to the drive. 'Aha! Activity, I see.'

On the terrace, Mrs Ridley and Gussie were moving chairs. Gussie waved whilst Mrs Ridley mopped the moisture from the wrought-iron furniture. The little cavalcade went to meet them and Gillian decided that, for her, the ability to be able to remain in the light, rather than to be sucked into the shadows, was very much in her own hands.

LYDIA WAS INDEED MANAGING splendidly. She'd almost forgotten what it was like to have a man in the same house with her and she was enjoying it enormously. His years in the Army had made Charles self-sufficient and he was quite capable of turning his hand to almost anything. He was very good at making life more comfortable for her: moving shelves, mending things, cherishing her in a practical way that she found very pleasant. He was also very good company. He wasn't in the least put out by her scattiness, her inability to concentrate on one subject for very long, her requirement for little jollies and outings to keep life on tiptoe with anticipation. Being a conventional man, he looked upon it as quite properly feminine and charming and was happy to indulge her. Having sold both flats, and with Charles's pension, life was very comfortable materially and they were very openhanded to their friends whom they loved to entertain.

On most Sunday mornings, however, they were usually to be found at Nethercombe where various members of the Courtyard also tended to gather for a lunchtime drink.

Guy allowed Lydia to mother him a little and talked to her about Gemma and their plans for a future, although he preferred to yarn with Charles about the Falklands or the Gulf War, and Nell always found it easy to relax in this atmosphere of friendly give and take. Phoebe gossiped with Lydia, teased Guy and pulled Charles's leg on the old eternal rivalry between the Army and the Navy.

'You mustn't mind, Charles,' she'd say soothingly. 'Somebody has to go into the Army. You simply mustn't mind about it being second best!'

Charles was very happy. He'd been rescued from what looked like a solitary and lonely old age and plunged into this gregarious group, with a warm, generous, loving wife as a constant companion. He was fascinated by the running of the estate and Henry, discovering this, was only too pleased to discuss things with him. Charles had grown up on such an estate in North Devon and Henry found him both knowledgeable and wise. Mr Ridley, too, was pleased to find that Charles, who missed the physical activity of army life, was only too ready to roll up his shirtsleeves and get down to a bit of hard labour whilst the womenfolk fussed over Thomas. He knew he'd really been accepted, however, when Mr Ridley showed him the mysteries of the lawn mower and allowed him to have a trial run on the wide sweep of grass that stretched from the Courtyard to the wall beneath the terrace, Charles was gratified and performed more than adequately.

' 'E didden do bad,' Mr Ridley admitted later to Mrs Ridley, 'fer a beginner. Yew can tell 'e's Army. 'Course, 'e was a Regular, not Hostilities Only like me.' He'd been delighted to find that Charles had been in his old regiment.

'Oh well,' said Mrs Ridley with weighty irony, 'that's bound to 'elp 'im drive a mowin' machine.'

' 'E's gonna lend me some books,' said Mr Ridley, oblivious to sarcasm after fifty years with his wife. 'All about the war in the desert. Got photos an' everythin', 'e ses. P'raps I might be in 'em.'

Mrs Ridley rolled her eyes expressively and began to put away the ironing board, successfully concealing her pride at the way her husband and the Major got on together.

'Bound to be!' she said. 'Monty'd never've done it without yew.'

'Young Jack'll be int'rested.' Mr Ridley continued to follow his own train of thought. ' 'E's 'ome fer 'alf-term soon. The Major's gonna give 'im a trainin' programme. Prepare 'im fer Sandhurst.'

'Poor l'il tacker.' Mrs Ridley pushed the kettle on to the hotplate. 'Yew'll 'ave Thomas at it next.'

Mr Ridley's face glowed at the idea and she snorted.

'Daft ole fewel. Get on out of it! I got the tea to get.' She relented as he got up obediently. 'Go an' pick some vegetables fer dinner an' I'll 'ave a piece of cake ready when yew get back.'

NELL, FINDING IT ALMOST impossible to recover from her latest shock, felt as though she were merely marking time until the news of Elizabeth's death should arrive. She realised that neither Gillian nor Lydia had been told the truth about Elizabeth's holiday in Italy and kept silent. So did Gussie. At her age death seemed a much more commonplace event than it did to Nell, despite all her personal losses. Apart from which, Gussie had her faith to sustain her. Nell, plunged by the terrible news into old memories and fears, found it hard to find any comfort during the ensuing days but went on grimly with her work, comforted at least by the knowledge that she was carrying out Elizabeth's wishes.

Her confidence that she could continue the business alone had deserted her. It was one thing to try out her wings with Elizabeth standing by as a safety net and quite another to be left to manage totally alone. She didn't quite know how to proceed and merely carried out Elizabeth's instructions to the letter, praying that nothing would come up that she couldn't handle.

She was also waiting to hear from Richard. She imagined that he would contact her to give her advice and instruction on the running of the business and it suddenly came to her that he was waiting for Elizabeth to die. Then, no doubt, her final wishes would be made clear.

He arrived in the Courtyard one afternoon at the end of May. The rhododendrons were in full flower and the sun was hot. The deserted Courtyard drowsed peacefully in the afternoon sun and the ring of Nell's doorbell seemed louder than usual. When she opened the door and saw Richard, her heart leaped in her breast and she felt a cold weight in the pit of her stomach. She led him through to her little paved terrace at the back which looked across the meadow and up the valley to the viaduct.

'I expect you know what I've come to say.' He looked pale and tired and much older.

Nell nodded, not trusting herself to speak, and wrapped her arms about herself. He looked around and indicated the little table with its chairs placed in a patch of shade.

'May we . . . ?'

'Yes, of course.' Nell pulled herself together. 'I'm sorry. Would you like a cup of tea? Or something cold?'

'Not yet.' He smiled at her but it was a smile which held nothing but politeness. 'Won't you sit down?'

Nell skirted the table and sat opposite, her hands clenched between her knees.

'I'm glad you've come,' she said. 'The waiting has been terrible. I'm almost relieved it's over. Forgive me for saying that.'

He shook his head and raised a hand as though accepting her sentiment and even agreeing with it.

'We shall have a lot to go through,' he said, looking over the sunlit meadow where Henry's Devon Reds grazed peacefully, 'but I haven't come for that. I suggest you come into my office and we'll go through everything properly. You'll find it all in order and I shall be very happy to help you in any way I can. I know much more about the business than just an ordinary accountant would. I was there at the beginning and Elizabeth . . .' he stumbled over the name and Nell looked away from him lest she should be unmanned by any sign of emotion. 'Elizabeth discussed nearly everything with me. I should be delighted and honoured if you felt you could continue along those lines.'

Nell bowed her head in acceptance and waited and Richard took a deep breath and began to open a folder that he'd placed on the table.

'She asked me to come to you as soon as it was all over,' he continued, after a short pause. 'She wanted me to give you this.' He passed her a document and Nell put out a trembling hand to receive it.

'What is it?' she asked, gazing blindly at the stiff paper with its legal binding. 'Is it to do with the business?' She frowned at it.

'No,' said Richard gently and this time his smile held more warmth. 'It's the Deeds to this cottage. Elizabeth's last gift to you.'

Nell stared down at the document, trying to assimilate what Richard had just told her.

'I don't understand,' she whispered at last. 'How can it be . . . ? Do you mean . . . ? I don't understand!' she cried almost angrily and her lips trembled.

'Elizabeth bought the cottage from Mr Jackson,' explained Richard, still gently, understanding her conflict of emotions. 'She knew how much the Courtyard feared the wrong people moving in, so she decided to protect them as far as she could and meanwhile intended to leave it to you. Although she had no idea, then, that it would be so soon. I acted for her. She was delighted when you decided to move in. Her one fear was that it would be too claustrophobic for you, after the Lodge.'

'But why?' Nell's brain was reeling as she tried to understand. 'Why should she leave it to me?'

Richard looked away from her. He'd been rather surprised himself at the measure of Elizabeth's generosity to this woman whom she'd met so recently. The sum she'd left for the running of the business was almost ludicrously large . . . He realised that he was feeling jealous and controlled himself.

'She had become very fond of you,' he said, 'and she was so happy to know that you would continue with the business. That meant an enormous amount to her. She wanted to feel that you were as secure as you could be so that you could forge ahead without too many distractions. You've got an awful lot on your plate.'

'But to leave me a whole house . . .' Nell was stunned.

'Absolutely and entirely yours to do with as you please,' said Richard as cheerfully as he could. 'She had no family, you know. No relatives. The residue of her estate goes to Gillian so she's not going to complain.' He raised his eyebrows at her. 'You had no idea she owned this cottage?'

'None!' cried Nell. 'We all thought it was someone from upcountry and, for some reason, we all imagined it was a man. We were surprised at how many rules and regulations he made, though. I felt tremendously lucky to get in.'

'That was her way of keeping it empty for as long as possible. She rather looked on your attack as a blessing in disguise. Once she knew you had recovered, that is.' He remembered her anxiety and felt again the worm of jealousy gnawing at his entrails. 'As I said, she was very fond of you,' he said again, with an effort.

Nell looked at him. 'I loved Elizabeth,' she said firmly. 'I really loved her. And not just because she'd given me nearly everything I have that I most cherish. She was strong and . . . and truthful. With herself as well as others. I shall never forget her. Or what I owe her and I shall try to repay it by making the business succeed.'

Richard stared back at her and his eyes filled with tears. He remembered how he had accused and reproached Elizabeth during this last year and his mouth twisted. Nell saw his emotion and sprang to her feet.

'Thank you for coming,' she said in a high clear voice. 'I'd like to be alone if you don't mind, to take it all in. We'll meet soon, won't we?'

He nodded, not trusting himself to speak, recognising in her Elizabeth's dislike of public displays of emotion and feeling a last bitter twist of resentment.

'Very soon,' he said. 'I'll let myself out.'

Nell stood perfectly still until she heard the front door slam. Her eyes fell on the Deeds to the cottage and, sitting down at the table, she laid her head upon her arms and broke into a violent storm of tears.

Thirty-eight

THE NEWS OF ELIZABETH'S death touched everyone at Nethercombe. Each of them had known her to a greater or lesser degree and they all felt the loss. Gillian, who alone knew how very, very much she owed to her godmother, especially since her return from France, was quite simply stunned with shock. She wasn't hurt that Elizabeth hadn't warned her, she knew her too well to expect that, but she felt an almost unbearable regret when she thought of all the things she longed to say to her which, now, would never be said. She remembered how she had taken her generosity and repaid it with contempt and how she had wondered, avariciously, whether Elizabeth would leave her the house in her will, and her tears were bitter. Well, she had left her the house, as well as everything in it, and money, too, and they were as heaped coals on Gillian's repentant head.

Amongst the papers and documents was a letter. It was addressed to her in Elizabeth's elegant hand and Gillian opened it, her eyes eagerly scanning the lines. ' . . . and I can imagine exactly how you're feeling.' Gillian could almost hear Elizabeth's cool amused voice. 'Please don't tear yourself apart with useless remorse. I've always been extremely fond of you, my dear Gillian, despite – occasionally – apparent evidence to the contrary and I was always very pleased to be able to help you out of your difficulties.' Gillian's eyes filled with tears.

I want to say how impressed I've been with your behaviour since your return from France, both as a wife and mother and

also as a friend to Nell, and you will see that I've carried out
your instructions and Nell now owns the cottage in the Courtyard, although only you and I know that this suggestion came
from you when I took you into my confidence and admitted that
I was the owner. It hasn't been easy for you, I know that. You'll
carry the guilt with you always but that need not necessarily be
a negative thing. It's usually the bad experiences which happen
to us that – used wisely – can strengthen us and help us to grow.
You're doing just that and I'm very proud of you . . .

Gillian dropped the sheet, covered her face with her hands and wept
in earnest.

Lydia, on the other hand, was very hurt indeed that Elizabeth
hadn't forewarned her of her death.

'I was her oldest friend,' she sobbed to the distressed Charles.
'I've known her since we were at school together. How could she let
me hear it like that from Richard? She told him! And he was only her
accountant!'

'It can't be an easy thing,' said the reasonable Charles. 'Maybe she
loved you too much to be able to bear your grief.'

At this, Lydia's sobs burst out afresh and he held her close and
passed her his handkerchief.

'She couldn't bear scenes,' she admitted tearfully. 'But I would
have liked to say goodbye to her . . .' The mere thought of the emotional luxury that had been denied her set her off again until the real-
isation that never again would she see that elegant figure standing at
her door made her really weep with such sincere grief that Charles
began to be seriously worried and she tried, for his sake, to pull herself together. 'Gillian will be here soon,' she began, struggling to her
feet but, even as she spoke, there was a tap at the door and Gillian
came in.

They took one look at each other and flew into the other's arms and Charles, retreating thankfully into the kitchen, put the kettle on for some coffee and gazed out into the garden, whistling through his teeth and waiting for the storm to pass.

In the end it was decided that the truth should be told about Nell's cottage. She couldn't go on pretending to be renting it from some mythical landlord and she and Gillian agreed that it should be explained that it was a part of the business. Everyone was far too delighted at Nell's good fortune to be particularly interested in the details and Nell, for the first time, felt that she could take her place in the Courtyard on equal terms with the other residents. Richard had put his bitterness to one side and was giving her all the support he could and she was beginning, once again, to have the confidence to believe that she could make the business work.

By midsummer everyone's emotions were still raw but much more under control and it was agreed that the Midsummer's Eve party should go forward as usual, and, slowly, grief was put aside and they began to look forward to it.

GUY, WHO WAS PROBABLY the one least affected by Elizabeth's death, was looking forward, even more, to having Gemma home again. He had thrown all his native caution to the winds and could see no reason why he and Gemma should not get married as soon as possible. If there were to be parental opposition because of Gemma's tender years, he was prepared to overcome it. After all, both their mothers had been married practically from school and it wasn't as though he intended to prevent Gemma from pursuing a career. Now that she had qualified, he could see no point in their continuing to be apart. He had no fears that there would be any other grounds for anxiety. Their mothers had been close friends all their lives and he knew that they were delighted at the idea of the union between the two families. He longed to have Gemma with him in the Courtyard and, between them, they were tentatively planning a Christmas wedding.

Everyone at Nethercombe was prepared to egg them on and when the summer term was over and Gemma came over, driving as usual in her little car, they were almost as pleased to see her as Guy was and he had to drag her away for a walk in the woods so as to have her to himself.

THE BERESFORDS HAD ALREADY arrived and the usual preparations started to go forward. It was really a very special year; Nell settled and Thomas approaching his first birthday. Mrs Ridley and Joan were closeted as usual in the kitchen and Mr Ridley and Bill were organising the coloured lights. Gillian gave the summerhouse a good cleaning whilst Thomas, sitting safely in a playpen at the side of the pool, chuckled good-naturedly at their antics.

'It's such a pity that Jack can't be here,' said Nell, tying her balloons to the rhododendron branches.

'Oh, it is,' sympathised Gemma, who was setting out the chairs. 'Couldn't he get time off or something? He's the only one missing.'

'No, no,' said Nell. 'They're terribly strict. Never mind. He comes to the Christmas party and that's probably more his style. He can't wait to see Thomas again. He grows so fast.'

Gillian glanced anxiously at her, on the lookout for any signs of grief, but Nell looked contented and at peace and Gillian sighed with relief.

They drifted away on their various paths and the swimming pool lay placidly beneath the clear skies, waiting to come into its own when the dusk deepened.

GUSSIE, STARING OUT OF her window, was looking forward to dusk falling, the first faint stars twinkling in a darker sky and Mr Ridley pulling the switch that would make the fairy lights around the pool glow like fireflies in the bushes.

'. . . and we are so very, very blessed, Lord,' she continued aloud for, increasingly these days, she spent her time in communication with the Almighty, 'that it is almost too much to bear. Even while

I talk to You and look out on all this beauty, someone is being mur-
dered and people are killing each other and others are dying of terrible diseases. Yet how are we to know, Lord, what might be in store
for us? We must accept the good things that are given to us gladly and
without fear and go forward in hope and faith . . .'

There was a knock at the door and Henry put his head round.

'Thought I heard voices,' he said. 'All well?'

'Perfectly well, Henry dear,' she said serenely, successfully hiding
her reaction to the sight of the shorts which he'd donned with his ancient Aertex shirt. 'And I haven't forgotten that I'm showing some
people round Number Five at seven o'clock. I do hope they're nice.
Mr Ellison was very optimistic that they'd fit in with our little group.
Is it time I was going?'

'I think so.' He thought that she looked rather tired suddenly, almost distressed, and he held out his arm to her in a courtly, old-
fashioned gesture. 'Shall we do this one together?'

GRADUALLY THE AREA ROUND the pool filled up with guests, all
talking and laughing whilst some of them swam in the soft warm water. Gemma waved across the pool to Sophie as she arrived and Lydia
and Charles moved forward to welcome Abby and William. Joan was
asking Nell's advice on some redecoration to their cottage whilst Bill
assisted Henry at the barbecue.

'So's how's life with you?' asked Guy, fetching up beside Phoebe as
Gemma ran off to talk to Sophie.

'My dear, now I've seen Henry's shorts I know that I can cope with
anything that life might chance to throw in my path,' said Phoebe
solemnly.

Guy gave a brief explosive snort. 'Empire-builders,' he said.

'His great-grandfather wore them when he was with General Gor-
don at Khartoum,' explained Phoebe. 'To be honest, I can't decide
whether they're long shorts or short longs.'

'I hope you're not mocking my dear old Henry's shorts,' said

Gillian, strolling up. 'It was such a relief to get him out of his mole-
skins I was only too delighted to see him putting them on, though I'm
not certain where he found them. He'd wear the same thing every
day of his life, winter and summer alike, if I let him. Wouldn't you,
darling?'

She raised her voice a little and he beamed at her. Unknown to
Gillian, Elizabeth had written a letter to Henry, too, telling him in
absolute confidence of Gillian's extraordinarily generous gesture
with her inheritance, and his love for her and pride in her were very
great. He glanced down at his shorts rather proudly.

'I thought they were more partyish,' he said simply and Guy
smiled to himself.

The two women exchanged glances.

'And so they are. Phoebe likes them. Don't you, Phoebe?' said
Gillian encouragingly.

'I'm quite overwhelmed by them,' admitted Phoebe and Guy snorted
again and moved away. 'Have you got the pith helmet to match?'

'It's in the attic somewhere,' said Henry casually, doing clever
things with some sausages, and Phoebe was silenced.

The evening advanced and a sickle moon swung clear above the
trees. Bats swooped above their heads and the owl was calling down
in the woods. Nell found herself beside Gussie and they smiled at
each other.

'Oh, Gussie.' Nell shook her head. 'It seems such a long time ago
since that tea shop in Bristol. Who would have believed that all this
could come out of you buying a dress for Henry's wedding?'

'Oh, my dear. And you offered to lend me your hat. Such a kind
gesture.'

'It was very odd.' Nell frowned a little. 'It was so unlike me. Talking to a complete stranger and offering hats. I don't know what came
over me.'

'Do you sometimes wonder where we'd be now if you hadn't?'
asked Gussie.

'Sometimes,' said Nell reflectively.

'And?' probed Gussie.

'And,' said Nell after a long pause, 'I'm ashamed to say that I wouldn't change a single thing. Not now.' She looked at Gussie anxiously. 'Is that very sinful of me?'

'Why sinful, Nell dear?' Gussie looked surprised.

'Well . . .' Nell paused. 'Honestly, Gussie. What I'm saying is that I don't mind John dying or losing the baby or, on a different level, the cottage at Porlock Weir. It sounds so callous and selfish. But, to be perfectly truthful, I'm happier now than I've ever been. Apart from Elizabeth, of course. Oh dear!' She shook her head. 'I feel very ashamed.'

'But you weren't responsible for any of those things,' said Gussie. 'It wasn't your choice who should live or who should die. Those things happened to you and they are in the past and they have helped to make you what you are. One cannot live in the past. We must do the best with what we have. I think it's far more sinful to live your life with your chin on your shoulder, staring back. It's now we must live for.'

'What a comfort you are, Gussie,' murmured Nell. 'Whatever should I have done without you?'

'Or I without you?' countered Gussie.

They smiled at each other, conscious of the deep love between them, and instinctively and simultaneously backed away from further displays of emotion.

'What d'you think of Henry's shorts?' asked Gussie surprisingly.

Nell, who had already noticed them, glanced at him and smiled affectionately.

'I think they're very Henry,' she replied. 'Not everyone could carry them off but I think he looks perfectly splendid.'

'They belonged to his father,' said Gussie and her eyes were full of memories. 'I remember them very well indeed. He was wearing them the day he proposed to me in the rose garden.'

'Gussie!' gasped Nell. 'Did he . . . ? Did you . . . ? But why . . . ?'

'I havered. I was afraid to commit myself,' said Gussie. 'I loved him very much and, to my shame, I loved Nethercombe even more, but I was afraid of such a great emotional commitment. And then war broke out and he joined his regiment and I went away, too. When I came back he was engaged to my cousin Louisa. When I look at Henry, and now Thomas, I sometimes wonder how it would have been if I hadn't been so cautious and I had been the mistress of Nethercombe.'

'And?' asked Nell at last.

Gussie shook her head a little and smiled at her serenely.

'Like you,' she said, 'I wouldn't change a single thing.'

Introducing two new friends
to fall in love with...

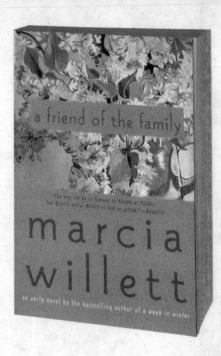

In these two heartwarming stories,
Marcia Willett once again gives us vibrant characters to
connect with and a beautiful backdrop to daydream against.

AVAILABLE WHEREVER BOOKS ARE SOLD

 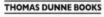